THE BLACK WIDOW

WEBSTERLAND
BOOKS

The Birch Widow

"I recommend this story to people who like science fiction, dystopian novels."

--S.J. Main

"If you are a fan of Hunger Games or Divergent, you're probably gonna love this story!"

--Larissa Lopes, Best-selling author of the Alec Brock Series

Praise for

THE RAYNE PROJECT

"Lyna Lopez has created a fantasy world in The Rayne Project inhabited by fascinating characters on a breathtaking adventure."

--Dr. Trish Hopkins, Author of The Crowfoot Society Series

"Dark and riveting!"

--Anya Pavelle, Author of The Moon Hunters

The Black Widow

WEBSTERLAND
BOOKS

The Black Widow
Copyright © 2021 by Lyna Lopez
ISBN: 9781734364521
www.lynalopez.com

Library of Congress Control Number: 2021907713

Book Cover Design by CReya-tive
Edited by MK Editing Services LLC

To My Ladies.

After writing The Rayne Project, your encouragement to make sure I brought out book two, helped me accomplish just that.

You are essential to my life. Thank you so much for making sure I didn't give up. This book is for you badass super women!

LYNA LOPEZ

THE BLACK WIDOW

PROJECT HERCULES SERIES · BOOK TWO

Project Hercules Data Notebook 2

05/23/21	
	The children got in trouble again today.
	Most of them have learned to stay clear of General Braggart,
	but the others tend to rile the man up.
	They've been showing more signs of abnormalities and abilities that
	aren't normal at all. I decided to keep it from Braggart.
	The abilities they've shown me will end the world in
	Braggart's command.
05/25/21	General Braggart continues to stare at Rayne with such severity
	the girl has voiced her concerns with me. My baby girl
	Rayne is such a quiet child. She cries often, but
	the general ignores it because she does as she's told
	every time—unlike the rest of her siblings. I told her to
	ignore him and continue being the good girl she already is.
	He won't do anything to her. He can't.
05/30/21	I can't believe I hadn't been able to jot down any notes for a few
	days. Chaos had broken out in the bunker because the boys
	decided to start a riot. They're only 6! I've definitely come to
	the conclusion that he has no patience for Batch 001.
	I heard recently that he has a son about a few years
	older than the batch. I've never met the boy, but I can only wish

	him the best. Braggart doesn't seem the type of winning
	Father of the Year. That's why I hate it that my little Rayne
	shares the same DNA as that man. I wish I knew what he was
	thinking when he decided to do this.
	No matter how much I refused, he didn't budge and clearly told
	me that if I didn't do as I was told he'd kill me and give
	my project to Robert Plumboy.
06/03/21	Thunder keeps creating static friction between himself and the
	other nurses. No one's caught on that it is an ability he can
	conjure, so thank goodness for that. I've had several talks with
	him already. He's older than the others and the rest
	look up to him. Hail got in trouble again with Braggart. The boy
	has noticed that the general pays way too much attention to
	Rayne. He's clung to her like glue. Silk doesn't like the
	attention he's showing her either. The girl has been distant from
	the males in the group lately. Her distance is alarming me.
	It is as if she has built a wall between herself and others. She's
	my greatest achievement. What is happening to her?
	I caught Braggart twirling that confounded mustache of his while
	watching Rayne get ready to sleep. If I only knew to what
	purpose he wanted her to share the same blood as him. He
	already has a child, although there's been no word of a woman
	standing by his side. Braggart only cares about his duty,
	not anything familial. Why Rayne? It just doesn't make sense to
	me. I can't fathom why.

CHAPTER ONE

Sector Charlie
Edge of Academic District in Trēbeta

THE STARS HAD always been my favorite part of the evening.

The bothersome night sky had made it its mission to hide the stars away behind thick, cumbersome clouds. No matter how far the eye could see, no stars were visible on this night—nor any night I could remember. Gavin's voice reached my sensitive hearing as I sat perched on the windowsill in the far corner of his vibrantly colored living room. There were window drapes and couch cushions in a variety of colors and patterns.

Gavin had spent each night in the fully equipped

kitchen, separated from the living room by the bar and hovering stools, creating one deliciously aromatic meal after another, his shoes squeaking against the pale gold ceramic tiles. Each time, I refused. Eating a meal with him meant we were on friendlier terms— the action seemed too personal. Other than a few pieces of fruit here and there, I hadn't sat down to a meal in a few days.

There was no use in giving the guy any false impressions. From my perch I heard him push his glasses back up his nose for the sixth time since taking his father's phone call. Gavin and his father had a love-hate relationship where they both felt strong enough to get on each other's nerves.

Their bickering reminded me of my family.

Feeling somewhat depressed that I could not find a single star in the sky, I removed my legs from underneath me to stretch them out. Trēbeta's lights shone from below. I could make out the university grounds a few blocks from Gavin's apartment. From this height, the people walking below were tiny ants I could squash with my feet. The apartment was on the building's highest floor, but it wasn't too difficult for me to identify the colors of their outfits or the hues of their skin.

Looking away from the people below, I played with the silver band on my wrist. Underneath the band was a thinner bracelet I pet as a reminder of Pops. The lightweight plastic could've been ripped off ages ago, but the weight of it kept me centered and stable. Its weight reminded me someone loved me once, and no matter what abilities I possessed, his love for me had been true. The identification printed read, *Silk – PH062.001*. It wasn't a time in my life I should cherish, but the crazy spider-woman inside of me couldn't part with it.

Gavin's voice filtered in from his bedroom. I had stayed in his house for far too long. Three days was my limit. During my time here, I had followed Gavin to his university or shops—preferring to stay out of sight. Gavin had this idea my being here would get us chatting—make us friends, but he was wrong. There was nothing I needed to say to him. His father was a significant contributor to my messed-up life. After finding out back in Safe Haven that Gregory Foxhand was a wealthy patron who regularly funded government projects, like Project Hercules, I'd made it a personal mission to keep his son at a distance.

Every man I came across was interested in me, and Gavin was no exception. It was a curse. Any male near me fell for my black widow charm. Some women reveled in that kind of power. But not me. All men made me sick—both mentally and physically. The sole one I tolerated was Thunder, my elder brother, but since finding out he had lied about Rayne's whereabouts for years, my trust in him wavered.

For years, I felt guilty I'd caused our sister Rayne's death. For years, I blamed myself for not being strong enough during the Foxtrot escape. For years, I watched my brother Hail mourn for Rayne, unable to let go—rushing off any chance he could to find her, in the hopes she wasn't dead after being taken captive by those responsible for the human experimentation.

My lost, little Rayne.

Although not entirely religious or spiritual, I closed my eyes and prayed Rayne was alright. I couldn't bear to lose a sister because I had already so little to my name. Putting on a brave face was harder every single time something awful happened.

Gavin threw the phone across the bedroom. I opened my senses further, picking up his rash breathing and quickened steps toward the phone he had thrown. I couldn't see him, but I knew what he did and where he was at every moment.

His scent was pretty straightforward to pick up. The guy showered with rose oil that fused into his skin's pores and mixed with a natural old-book smell he carried on him all the time. Stretching my muscles from prolonged sitting, I waited until Gavin left his room to call out I was ready to leave his home. I polished off a few cookies I had confiscated from Gavin's cookie jar. They were good but not as good as I remembered when I lived in Foxtrot. I wiped a crumb from my lip with my thumb as my mind flitted to the baker lady who'd filled us with treats.

The sound of heavy footsteps brought me back to Gavin's apartment. Gavin Foxhand had an adorable air about him—a quality few men had. I understood why Rayne cared about him so much—not like I'd ever let him know. I'd noticed how several females effortlessly tried to make eye contact with the young man, but he was blissfully ignorant. Gavin either had his nose buried inside a book or absorbed on his altered KeViewer, which doubled as some supercomputer, more advanced than even normal KeViewers. If he took down the "fuck off" sign on his forehead, he'd see how many girls wanted to get to know him.

He'd be better off than pining over me.

Not like I should talk. The same sign Gavin had on his forehead, I posted on every available surface on my body. The two of us were more alike than I wanted to admit. He came barreling around the corner. Gavin's hair flowed around his head in disarray, his glasses left behind in the bedroom. When he wore them, he was safe and adorable. But, when Gavin took off the glasses and looked at me with an air of innocence, it made him inexplicably provocative.

"Why are you leaving? Why now?" He turned to stare at the open window and at the night sky I had been staring at earlier. "It's dark out there."

If he should need to learn anything about me, it was that I thrived in the darkness. While the rest of the world slept, it was my time to explore. I didn't bother to reply. Gavin had not heard much come out of my mouth since having been given this mission from Thunder. The last thing I told him as we had made our way into his apartment building was that I was not a friend coming to stay. I advised him to think of me as a fixture. Gavin's floor bodyguards didn't bat an eyelash when I slunk my way into the apartment in my blonde disguise, and wouldn't give a damn when I left—so long as Gavin was alive and well.

I did my job.

No one followed him.

No one set out to kill him.

"Damn, Silk. For three days, you either followed me from God knows where on the outside, or you'd sit on the windowsill refusing to eat or sleep." He slid his fingers once more through his dirty-blond hair while the deep air he inhaled made his bony shoulders rise and fall. "What the hell do I have to do to be your friend?"

Gavin didn't want to be my friend.

No man wanted my friendship.

For one, I was a poisonous bitch who said or did anything I wanted without regard to someone's feelings, and two, they all asked for my friendship as a pretense to get into my pants. Nausea rose from deep within my belly as it usually did when confronted with this situation. My mind slipped into the past as Gavin ranted.

The assistant doctors and male technicians at Foxtrot would take more than my vitals while performing their medical rounds. Their greedy hands would touch me in places they had no business touching. For so long, I thought Unit 13 allowed it—that it was okay even though I hated every minute. Until the day Pops walked in on a lecherous male nurse trying to place his hands into my waistband. I remembered the fury on my old man's face and learned then about molestation.

The male nurse had lost the ability ever to use his hand again.

I made a promise to myself that day that no man would ever get to touch me. For a while, I made things harder for Pops, who couldn't get a woman to stand to be near me long enough to perform medical tests, and because I was not too fond of all things male, Dr. Lester had to run all the checks himself. I loved the old man very much and missed him every day since he passed. He gave his life to save us and happened to have been one of the only men in my life I didn't consider a male.

I watched Gavin inhale again as if giving up on trying to get me to say something.

"Not all men are asses, you know."

They were for me.

Men swarmed to me like bees to pollinated flowers. It was a side effect of the experimentation—powerful pheromones that drew them in. Because of it, I couldn't walk around like an average human female. Unless I used my cloaking ability, men and women would notice my every move as if drawn to me like a moth to a flame. I was lucky my cloaking ability didn't come with an expiration date, because I had it on all the time.

Gavin stomped into the kitchen. He threw open one of the four doors on the stainless steel refrigerator to peruse the items inside. "I don't care what you say. If you're leaving, then you will eat something."

I felt the tiny threads of my sanity snap. One of my pet peeves was men telling me what to do. My leg muscles twitched, and my feet propelled me underneath the archway separating the foyer from the kitchen.

Startled, Gavin dropped the fixings of a sandwich in his hand. The blood in my veins boiled to aching degrees. "You are nothing but a plague. A disgusting, pus-filled human being I'm forced to watch because you prove to be more of a hindrance than an asset."

I watched as those sharp blue-green eyes dimmed at the onslaught of my words, but I had no control left. "I was here to do a job, and I did it. You have no say over anything I do. Men—all men are the bug under my shoe, so unless you want to be my next meal, I suggest you fuck off."

Gavin's shoulders dropped, and his eyes averted contact with mine. His fingers jerked, and his chest deflated. I knew it was the wrong thing to say to him, but I couldn't bring myself to apologize. Gavin didn't mean me any harm. I projected my feelings about disgusting, perverse men onto him. The silence in the room felt heavy. The weight of it almost crushing. Gavin shrugged those shoulders once more, depleted. Suddenly, I didn't know if I wanted to slink away or keep my ground.

Strange, unidentified sounds approaching took the decision away from me.

Seconds into the silence, footsteps in the hallway beyond Gavin's front door reached my ears. The bodyguard posted in front of the door opened his mouth to speak, but the unexpected visitors shot both floor guards with a silenced gun. I had enough time to process—these were not welcome guests. I leaped into the kitchen. My body slammed into Gavin's. His breath shot out when we clashed and again when we landed on the floor on the other side of the kitchen, though I took the brunt of the impact.

The door had exploded behind me. Gavin's eyes shot wide open as he tried to comprehend what had happened. Debris flew throughout the once alluring interior. Lit, splintered pieces of wood fell around us.

"Get up, Gavin."

I pulled Gavin off the floor as two men in masks came barreling through the front door with their weapons drawn.

Stuck in the small kitchen, I picked Gavin up by his pants and shirt to throw him over the bar. I didn't have time for niceties or alternative actions. Once he was over, I flew forward. A bullet whizzed to my right, smashing right into the cookie jar, and another to the left. I blinked, baring my fangs at the first man. Ripping the gun from his hand, I aimed it at his partner and shot. The man gasped when his partner dropped to the floor and again when I pushed him across the room. His body slammed into the wall, raining plaster all around us, and through to the other side.

Movement from the door caught my attention. I noted three more men dressed head to toe in black gear with weapons strapped to every available pocket. They saw me at the same time I saw them. They aimed and fired as I turned to get Gavin. Bullets whizzed past me—one came dangerously close to my arm. Human weapons couldn't bring us down, but it didn't mean it hurt any less.

Gavin lay unconscious on the floor by the wall. I lifted him over my shoulder and ran toward the window. For days I had studied the outside of the apartment. Every brick, awning, and decorative sculpture would serve us as a means of escape.

Leaping from the top floor, I held in my desire to scream as cuspate glass embedded in my shoulder. The sharp pain hit me like a wave. Ignoring the problem, I shot my arm out and clutched the curved window sill of a different apartment. Gavin shifted on my shoulder, sliding down my left arm. But I held on.

My right arm screamed with the strain—the blood around the glass in my shoulder trickled down my side. My fingers pressed harder into the cement as the weight pulled me toward the ground. We had at least another fifty stories down. I didn't care what anyone else thought about mutated humans. Not I nor any of my brethren could survive this kind of fall.

One stranger hung out of Gavin's window and shot a bullet my way. I pulled the arm holding Gavin closer to myself. I could withstand the hit of a human weapon. Gavin would not.

"She's holding the boy, you idiot!" one man yelled at another.

Are they after Gavin?

"Get to the bottom."

I didn't have much time left. My hand was slipping, and the kidnappers would be here soon. I slammed my foot into the window as I hung off the pediment above it. When my boot connected to the glass, Gavin woke up and shifted in my sore arms. He shouted a few choice cuss words. My hand slipped farther.

"Gavin, shut up and stay still, or we'll both get killed."

Gavin went unnaturally motionless. I kicked once more. The sound of breaking glass rang through the whipping wind of the freezing night. Blood dripped from the fingers holding us and down my arm to meet the blood from my aching shoulder. Sweat covered my forehead, causing the borrowed blonde strands to stick to my skin. Gavin whimpered.

"Hold on, Gavin."

He didn't say a word. I pulled my arm back and pushed with my forearm, letting go of Gavin as he got near the window. He dragged out a cuss word when he dropped into the open window. It was too bad I couldn't shoot webs like the comic book hero. If I could, this would be a hell of a lot easier.

The momentum made me lose the grip I had on the window. I couldn't get a foot on the ledge below me. I dropped. A dense, sinking feeling accosted me. My foot hit the cement ledge and sent me backward, farther away from the building.

I groped around to grab hold of something—anything. With nothing within reach, I knew this time I was in genuine danger. I felt something squeezing my ankle, and then I slammed into the wall. A grunt escaped my lips. I looked up to see half of Gavin's body hanging out the window and both his hands on my ankle. He gritted his teeth. I saw the muscles in his arms quiver with the strain.

Not willing to risk how much longer he could hold on, I bent upward at the waist and grabbed his wrists with my hands. He dropped my ankle and locked his hands around my wrists—both of us unwilling to let go of the other. He pulled up, and I assisted by using my boots on the building as leverage.

Next time, I needed to use the setules in my fingers to get us down a building, because jumping out the window would not happen again. My muscles throbbed and quivered. With more than half my body through the window, Gavin released his hold on me, and I dropped on top of him.

"Let's. Not. Do that. Again." Gavin punctuated between taking gulps of air.

One of those rare smirks pulled at my lips. I pushed myself off him, satisfied to hear a burst of air shoot from his lips.

"Which part?" I asked as I studied the dark bedroom we were in. "The part where we almost blew up, got shot at, jumped out the window to our deaths, burst through more broken glass, or when I landed on top of you?"

I no longer paid attention to Gavin as I walked toward the door, but I heard him when he said, "All of the above, except for *E*." The sound of his footsteps told me he was following behind. "Yes, *E* can definitely be done again."

I stopped so abruptly that Gavin skidded to a halt right behind me. In the few minutes since our kitchen argument, I realized two things. Gavin *was* and then *wasn't* like the men out there. He perplexed the hell out of me.

Not willing to comment, I took down my disguise. By manipulating the cells within my body and thus the genes within them, my borrowed blonde hair darkened to its usual shiny, black curls. I blinked and allowed my eyes to shift from their green disguise to their black coffee color. The roots of my hair tingled as I conjored my usual deep black color, and the hot pink froufrou outfit that sat on my skin turned back into black pants and tunic. I still didn't know how it was possible to alter clothing that touched touched my skin. But perhaps Pops' notebooks held the key to my genetic makeup. Unfortuantely, there were so many and none easily understood.

Gavin stood there and watched. "Have I ever told you that this beauty mark" —he reached toward the tiny birthmark below my right eye— "is my favorite part about you."

Before his finger could graze my skin, my hand shot out and grabbed it. "Do not touch me," I uttered through clenched teeth.

The familiar pangs in my stomach told me his touch wasn't welcome, but a new sensation fluttered to life behind my ribcage, and I couldn't place the emotion.

A feeling similar to the one I had felt several, several years ago.

CHAPTER TWO

THE EXPLOSION IN Gavin's apartment had caused the electricity in the entire building to go out. Sporadic emergency lights flickered with a high-pitched buzzing sound echoing in the homes and empty hallways. Many of the building's residents had already made their way outside. I noticed a half-eaten meal sitting on the dining room table. The residents of this apartment must have run out right before we crashed through the window. Gavin was close behind me. I reached out my hearing to listen for strange footsteps. The emergency stairwell door slammed open, and two sets of steps fell onto the plush carpet.

Adrenaline coursed through my veins. The welcome tingle amplified my strength and healing. The cuts on my arm healed, stitching themselves together and leaving behind an itchy sensation. I reached back and pushed Gavin behind me.

"Do you hear something?" Gavin whispered into the darkness. His breath fanned the side of my neck. The same flutter I'd felt when he touched me earlier enveloped me from within, bringing goosebumps to my flesh.

I hushed him and shook off the weird feeling.

There were two apartments on every floor. One unwelcome guest kicked in the door on the opposite end, and the other approached the apartment door before us. I grabbed Gavin by the shoulders to haul him against a wall between a glass and metal buffet table and a faux, tall bamboo tree in a decorative planter. "Stay here. Stay down."

He knew better than to argue with me. Gavin nodded and sat stock-still. I placed my body flat against the wall by the corner opposite the ornamental buffet table. Someone kicked the door of the apartment open. I heard the intruder's rapid breathing. The smell of sweat coming off his body. I sensed the rifle aimed in front of him and the limp in his right foot.

The blood reached my nose, and I knew where to place my target. I flew from my hiding spot with unnatural swiftness. The man shot his weapon. He missed. Staying low to the ground, I made it to his right leg and side-kicked him in the tendon right above his knee. A shout filled the room as he went down. I grabbed the gun and aimed it back at him.

"Who sent you?"

He gritted his teeth in pain. "That's none of your business, bitch."

I placed my foot on top of the open wound I knew was on his thigh. He bit back another scream. The sound of his partner's footsteps joined the fray. I squeezed down harder on the man's quad and aimed at the man entering the room. I shot the weapon but missed my target. The partner moved out of the way when the one on the floor reached up to grab the rifle.

"Big mistake," I whispered.

Bullets rang around the room as the new guy shot his gun at no one in particular. I lifted the other one off the floor to use as a shield. Remorse didn't even cross my mind as the man hung limp from my hands. They were the first ones to come in here with their guns. I threw his body across the room toward the other, slamming them both against a wall. The man's eyes grew wide when I used my incredible speed to reach him.

"W-what are you?"

I leaned down to meet him face to face and grabbed the gun that had slid away from him in the chaos. I removed the slide and dropped the clip, clearing the chamber.

"I'm the one you should watch out for." I leaned in closer. "Why do you want the boy?"

The man went to push himself off the wall, but I was there with one hand to pin him right back on it. He strained to fight me. His efforts were useless.

"Why the hell do you care?"

I manipulated the eumelanin in my hair again, going blonde. The kidnapper's eyes shot wide open. I could smell the fear pulsing through his pores as realization dawned.

"Y-you're the blonde who jumped out the window."

I didn't confirm nor deny his words as my hair went back to black. "What do you want with Foxhand?"

The static from his walkie-talkie rang throughout the dark room. "Cape and Harper report."

Indecision crossed his features for a split second before he reached for his walkie with one hand and my hand with the other. He pushed up on my hand to remove it from his chest. For a moment, I lost my balance and rocked to the side. He pressed the walkie to his mouth and called out for help, but he didn't have time to finish. I had landed and used my leg to kick him in the face—knocking him unconscious.

"Harper. Repeat. Harper..."

I grabbed the device and placed it to my lips. "Harper and Cape are indisposed at the moment."

The rough voice came back on the line. "Identify yourself."

With a wicked smirk on my lips, I replied, "I'm Foxhand's bodyguard. To get to him, you'll have to defeat me."

There was a brief silence before the man came back on the line. "This has nothing to do with you. Give us the boy, and we won't hurt you."

I heard more footsteps and guns cocking coming from the stairwell. As I placed the walkie-talkie back to my lips, I grabbed the two make-shift hand grenades hanging from the man's waist belt. The rings stayed behind while I held both firmly in my hand.

"Time to go, Gavin."

He rounded the corner. Gavin's glasses were gone, and his hair shimmered in the light from the window.

For a moment, I lost my breath.

"Are they dead?"

I stared back at the men without answering him. On the walkie-talkie I replied, "I warned you."

The hall door shot open. Alert, I grabbed Gavin's hand and threw the slim grenades at the group pushing through the door. Within seconds, an explosion blasted behind me while I ran with Gavin in the opposite direction. We flew through the other stairwell door. Shots rang out. I pushed Gavin against the wall to avoid the bullets and jumped on the metal rail, swinging to the flight above ours. Before the intruder could get off another hit, I slammed into him. He hit the wall and slid down three steps. Within seconds, I grabbed his gun and jumped back down to the floor, where I'd left Gavin.

I took his hand as he watched the unconscious man on the stairwell in shock. "W-why are they after me? Are they military?"

I stopped and stared at Gavin. "Gavin, these men are thugs. If the military wanted you, they would have gotten you."

He turned to me. "You sure know how to make a man feel good."

Within minutes, Gavin had made me smile twice. "The sarcasm isn't lost on me."

"Sarcasm?" He dared to look affronted. "What sarcasm?"

I laughed as I pulled him down the stairs. The sound of my own laugh surprised me. With these guys coming at us so quickly, I needed my mind off the mundane and into the fight. Another man bolted from the door of another level. 1 shot him with the borrowed gun before entering the same door he had come through. We weren't down far enough to jump out a window, and the stairwells would be too dangerous for Gavin.

So, 1 stopped in front of the gridlocked Gidget. 1 dropped the gun and used both hands to pull open the metal doors. A rush of air pushed through the opening. My fingers quivered under strain, the adrenaline in my body almost depleted. There was no Gidget above us when 1 peered inside. The Gidget platform was about ten floors below us.

Unlike the unused elevator shafts in our bunker, Gidget shafts were encased in metal from top to bottom with no cables or stairs to get us to each floor—only shiny, untouched metal all the way up and all the way down. The darkness in the shaft would have deterred the average human. But 1 wasn't easily scared off. 1 could see better than average in the dark, and 1 could also make ten floors on a jump. The next step was to convince Gavin. He saw what 1 was about to say before 1 even said it.

"Oh, hell no. 1 like my bones where they are, thank you."

The doors behind us burst open. 1 held Gavin to my chest and fell back through the Gidget opening before the intruders could react. He couldn't help but scream as he buried his face within my breast. The air rushed past us. 1 locked my legs around his and braced for impact. The Gidget platform met my back in a collision, which rocked my muscles and jarred my bones. Sudden pain coursed through my entire body.

I couldn't breathe. Couldn't move.

"Silk. Damnit, Silk!"

I heard Gavin's voice but couldn't get my body to move or my lungs to take in air. Gavin's body shielded mine as gunshots rang inside the Gidget. A voice above us yelled at the person shooting.

"I need him alive, you idiots."

Gavin removed his lithe body from mine.

"Get down there," I heard again from the same voice.

"Damnit, Silk. Please get up."

I wanted to but couldn't get my body to respond. Later, I felt Gavin giving me chest compressions. My mind warred with my lungs, begging for air. He stopped and pressed his lips to mine, breathing his lifeforce into me. My traitorous body eagerly sucked it up. He started compressions again. Right before his lips met mine, I felt my entire body spark with life. My lungs sucked in air, and the muscles loosened enough to allow me to move my joints.

"Oh, thank goodness."

My eyes met the man ten floors above us. His grayish-yellow eyes met my dark ones. I saw the moment he realized Gavin wouldn't be the only capture that would benefit him. The man dropped the mouth shield from his face with a gloved hand. A large scar ran from his top lip down his chin to hide behind the hair on his Balbo beard. He had a turned-up nose complementing his down-turned eyes.

"You are one ballsy chick," he called out.

I let Gavin help me up from the floor, stretching my muscles. The leader of the group seemed off to me somehow. Something about him kept me on my toes. I knew I had two minutes before his men would join us on this floor. I turned to eyeball the leader of the group as I dusted myself off. Without a word, I saluted him and grinned.

The leader grinned back a set of white, straight teeth, except for two pairs of sharp canines. "I'll find you," he called out behind us as we exited the Gidget.

I had a bad feeling he would. He wasn't human, but he didn't seem entirely altered either. He didn't look like someone I could outrun forever.

I ran down the hall and into another stairwell, refusing to shed light on it at the moment. The men came after us from above, so I led Gavin down the stairs. We sprinted without stopping. I pushed open the door and saw military and Ground Force vehicle lights filtering through the windows on the bottom floor. Personnel placed themselves in groups to enter the building. The soldiers had weapons that could put a damper on our efforts to escape. I couldn't afford to risk going through the front, so I ran to the back of the empty building as another explosion went off above us.

My heart hammered wildly. I strained my hearing to make out whatever I could. My senses picked up stragglers shutting off gas burners in the kitchen before rushing out some doors. The kitchen was to my left, so I pulled Gavin in its direction. The walls in the hallway had white and gray tiles. Fake plants greeted us every few steps. I passed employee-only doors until I reached one with a round porthole window. Inside the kitchen interior, the walls had paint—no longer tiles. Every surface glistened in shiny steel. Stations had unfinished meal preparations. The pilots were off. The room was eerily quiet.

"We need to run, Gavin."

Gavin panted, bending at the waist with a hand on his knee, trying to catch his breath. "Haven't. We. Been. Running?"

I noticed for the first time his fatigue. A tiny amount of guilt wormed its way to my heart. "Gavin, those guys are right on my heels. Their leader smelled odd—unnatural."

Gavin turned to me. "Unnatural? Is he from Project Hercules?"

I shook my head and listened for sounds of impending danger. "No, he didn't smell like any from the first or second batch. And if he were from Project Hercules, he'd have caught up already. He was just off. I also saw canines."

My words must've sparked something in Gavin because he got up from his position and pulled me toward the other end of the kitchen. "I'm not waiting around to find out. Let's go."

I allowed him to pull me, reveling in the feel of someone trying to protect me even though I knew he wasn't capable of saving a flea from a poodle. We made it down another hallway with a cooling unit on one side and a row of sinks on the other. At the end of the corridor was a tall metal door with a push-bar in the middle. Gavin pushed on the bar, but it was locked. Movement that rustled the leaves of the potted plants we passed in the hallway earlier reached my ears. Fearing we would get ambushed by a whole lot of guns, I moved past Gavin and kicked the door open. He watched, shaking his head from side to side.

"Emasculated? Check."

I ignored his little jab and pulled him through the door and outside. The cold air hit us both at the same time. I closed the door and did a quick search of the area. There was one dumpster and nothing more. The cumbersome dumpster would be plenty sufficient to keep the kidnappers back long enough for us to escape.

The building had been destroyed on the side that housed Gavin's apartment. Fire licked from the windows to the side of the building. Emergency workers did what they could to contain the spreading flames while the residents and bystanders watched with ever-growing concern.

I took a deep breath and closed my eyes. Gavin's dwelling didn't concern me as much as the man's well-being. My promise to Thunder had been to protect him, and it was what I'd been doing. I might have been cold, hungry, and my body in excruciating pain, but my job to keep him safe wasn't over. We ran farther away from the chaos. I felt it deep in my bones; the group trying to kidnap Gavin tonight wasn't going to let us go. Their leader had qualities a superhuman would have, even though they weren't like mine.

We ran as far as we could without rest until Gavin collapsed on the ground. I turned to pick him up, but my arms trembled with the strain. I had nothing left in me. The night swallowed the world around us, oblivious to the two struggling runaways trying to catch their breath. With what little I had left, I pulled Gavin inside a warehouse building abandoned in the throes of its youth—barely enough time to change the world with its product.

I felt the bitter cold sink into my bones. I wrapped a shaking, unresponsive Gavin within my arms, hoping to share my warmth with him. As much as I was ready to sleep off the stupor, I couldn't afford to get caught unaware.

My job was to protect Gavin. I stared into his gentle face. Long, dirty-blond lashes rested on the top of high cheekbones. His golden hair scattered about his forehead made me want to move the strands with my fingertips. But I didn't. I wouldn't touch him more than necessary. He'd sleep off his fatigue, and we'd get back to running back to Safe Haven or...

My entire body shut down.

CHAPTER THREE

Sector Charlie
Edge of Academic District in Trēbeta
Seaa – ID: PHO49.OOI

I WATCHED FROM my perch as the building Silk and her charge had been in crumbled from explosions. Emergency and Ground Force personnel flittered in and out of the building. Glass exploded. Ground Force officers pushed spectators back. There was no way we could get in there undetected. Although Silk and I were from the same batch of genetic experimentation, Silk cloaked her scent from people. It made others incapable of finding her if she didn't want to be seen. My fear wasn't how far Silk had run to get away from the danger, but if they had hurt her in the uproar.

"Silk is alive. So is Gavin," Rome said.

Roman Braggart, the son of General Brockton Braggart, knelt beside me with his ancient-Roman-god good looks and immeasurable strength. Rome had been my enemy until my baby sister Rayne showed us that he held no allegiance to his father, the leader of Project Hercules. Rayne loved Rome, but then she was taken, the way I had been taken. Only, Zane, Rome's best friend, hadn't been able to save Rayne the way he had saved me. It would risk him being caught, and we needed a man on the inside until we could save Rayne.

I watched how Rome's eyes had lost their vibrant luster. Or how his posture seemed to fold within itself. He didn't look like the man who had once pursued us. Watching him grieve for Rayne, though we still believed her alive, was more painful than grieving my own Pops, and he was well and truly dead. Roman Braggart seemed to lose more and more of himself every day.

"How do you know?" I asked as Rome watched the people filing in and out of the crumbling building. "I can't sense either one of them. Silk masks her scent, and I haven't met Gavin."

My hands glistened—my scales were alive in an ombré of deep purples into turquoise blues. The device around my neck, designed by Pops specifically for my mutation, kept me plenty hydrated, unlike a fish out of water. My fingers found the choker, stroking the little gem-like bulbs. "I bet you could sniff out Gavin Foxhand, but Silk is another matter altogether."

Rome turned to stare at me. "I can *sense* Silk too. Our batch has the unique ability to connect scents to our memory banks. We don't have to smell them out anymore to know if they are around."

"You can sense them," I parroted.

Rome nodded.

I huffed out a laugh. "Silk must hate it."

Roman Braggart got up from the ground beside me, dusting off his jeans at the knees. "Yeah, she wasn't too keyed about the ability, but I don't think she minded it much because her pheromones didn't work on me."

"Is sensing her a Batch 002 thing?"

Rome shrugged. "Nah, I think it was more a *me* thing."

I got up to stand beside him. Roman was tall like the rest of my brothers, especially compared to me. My long legs weren't enough to catch up to these men. "I'm sorry about Rayne, Rome."

He seemed concerned and puzzled by my apology. "It wasn't your fault, Seaa."

That's where he was wrong. Rayne's capture and involvement in this whole thing was my fault as much as I hated to admit it out loud to anyone. I had to at least admit it to him. "Rayne got involved because of me. You said it yourself the day in the alley. I got an innocent mixed up in this whole thing. She had a life before meeting us."

The handsome man placed a hand on my shoulder, squeezing it. "No, Seaa. Rayne has a mind of her own. She followed you out to the alley. Her life taking a turn for the worse was my fault. I tracked her to her home. Her adoptive parents killed themselves to keep from getting arrested or tortured for answers. So, this is more my fault than any of it is yours."

I hadn't known her parents had killed themselves when Rome's men grabbed her. Rayne had gone through so much and stayed as resilient as she did during their endless rounds of abuse. "I'm still sorry, Rome."

He pulled me in for a hug, and God, it felt nice. Weird, but welcome. Rome saved me from the operatives taking me to the base located in sector Alpha and again in Dr. Ferdinand's clinic when he realized I was suffocating and shoved me in the steam bath. Those two times made all the fights with one another seem trivial. The night's breeze chilled my bones, so I wrapped my hooded robe tighter around me.

"Come on," he said as he pushed me away from himself with his hands on my shoulders. "Let's get out of here. At least we know they are still alive."

Sector Charlie
Somewhere in The Waste

THE UPPER HALF of my body shot up. A huge breath of air rushed from within me. The area around me was empty, but for the years of filth gathering by the walls holding the building up. I reached out my hearing. Gavin stood a few feet away from me behind a cracked wall. He came around the corner.

"You're awake."

I didn't remember falling asleep in the first place. "How long have I been out?"

He shrugged. "I don't know myself. When I woke up, the sun was out, and you were pretty much unconscious."

I stretched my muscles and got off the floor. I seem to be doing that a lot lately. Gavin stared at his watch.

"It's a quarter to three."

Why did people do that? What was so difficult about saying 2:45 in the afternoon? I cleared my throat and closed my eyes. I pushed through all the sore, stiff joints and got my senses to expel from me like invisible vines growing from my body. Drifters walked around The Waste in search of food or trinkets to sell. The Waste was the remnants of the old world that were in such disrepair the government had labeled it "off limits" to humans. It didn't stop anyone from coming in here and collecting antiques to sell in the underground markets.

I pushed farther and could hear the citizens of Trēbeta moving about without a care in the world. There was a group of thugs gathered by the border of Trēbeta and The Waste. They cleaned their weapons and laughed around a roaring fire.

"They are close and more than likely waiting 'til nightfall."

Gavin ran a hand through his fussed hair. The strands stuck around his head in disarray. I felt my heart skip, and the next minute I couldn't control the anger coursing through my blood.

"Stop doing that!" I yelled. "I'm so sick and tired of you running your hand in your hair like some scared animal. It's a stupid nervous gesture that will ultimately get you killed."

I stomped around the interior. There was a piece of old timber on the ground, so I kicked it. The wood flew across the open space with so much ferocity it burst through the old wall to the other side. Long seconds later, we heard it slam against debris.

Gavin stared at me with his hand laid flat on his head. I had no reason to be upset at him. He hadn't done anything wrong, but I couldn't seem to get my emotions under control.

"Uh, I'm sorry?"

I didn't want to look like an idiot, so I turned on him. My legs got us practically toe to toe. He slowly dropped his hands, eyes wide. Gavin stared into mine, unwilling to break contact. Inside, I was seething. My fingers curled into fists. The muscles in my body coiled like a snake preparing to attack. The next minute, Gavin lifted his hand, reaching out for a black curl winding itself around the broken threads of my tunic. I stopped breathing. My entire being told me to flee— to run away, get angry, stomp around. But something else, something I've never felt before kept me in place.

He gingerly lifted the curl and unwound it from the ripped sleeve. The double-crossing spiral wrapped itself around his fingers, unwilling to part with him. There was an intriguing contrast between my hair's dark color and the warm tones of his palm. Gavin moved his hand to place the curl back with the rest, and when he did, I felt the warmth of his fingers brush against my sensitive skin. Dozens, hundreds—no, thousands of flares burst at one time. The inside of my body felt like one giant wave of turmoil. The sea of flames coalesced in my belly. The sensation burned everywhere and nowhere at once.

It was too unpleasant.

I couldn't hold in my desire to hit something.

"Don't touch me again, Gavin."

I turned my back on him before I could register all of the thoughts in those baby blues. His thoughts were way too transparent. Knowing we didn't have much time, I stared at The Waste while I figured out which way to go from here. The thugs would be on us very soon, and wherever we went, it wouldn't be back to Safe Haven. I couldn't afford to lead the new genetic back to the compound. Even though he wasn't exactly like the first or second batch, the criminal had some congenital anomaly, and tracking with his nose had to be one of them.

Gavin leaned against a wall. He didn't say anything to me, only stared. He faced the dirty ground and avoided eye contact with me. I wanted to say something insightful, but I think I preferred the silence.

"We need to go."

He looked up at me and nodded. Gavin didn't try to talk to me again. We stepped out of the building and moved in between years of decay. The concrete jungle had once been home to citizens and now was home to rodents and the occasional wanderer. The government called this area "forbidden" because they couldn't stand the reminder of their actions. The new "Americans" preferred it that way too. No one wanted to be a part of the past. Everyone looked toward the future—or what little was left of it.

But they forgot how wonderful old things could be.

I swept over steel beams and concrete blocks. Gavin followed close behind. The men couldn't track *me*, but they were trailing him. If I could get him through The Waste and into Sector Delta, I could probably make it underground where it would mask our scents. The smells underground made it almost impossible to track anyone. And right now, I needed to keep him alive, at least long enough to figure out a different plan.

With my stomach in knots, I took a quick and smooth pace for Gavin to keep up with. I had lost quite a lot of blood the night before and hadn't slept or eaten well for days before, too stubborn to let the young man into my life. I balled my right fist, trying to control all of the nerves running rampant in my body. Inside my thoughts were hordes of men coming toward me like mindless creatures unable to contain themselves. I didn't create me. Pops created me. And no matter how much I hated what I'd become, I didn't fault Pops one bit.

Holding on to the cloaking ability full-time got exhausting, although I could use it consistently for months if I had to. Being on all the time meant a lack of proper sleep though. I didn't have to use it when I was back in Safe Haven—at least not often. The power to draw men to me, to be entranced, didn't have much of an effect on the guys of Batch 001 so long as I didn't let it completely out. I shook my head, thinking of Guy, my hormone-crazed brother. He would be the only idiot to get tormented by my spell.

Before Batch 001's escape from Braggart, I used it

to keep the male nurses and doctors, the soldiers, or technicians away. Women were affected too when it was "on," but the female mind had more control over their sexual desires than the male species. Keeping my ability reined in kept it from creating lust-minded zombies and made me background noise. I did anything I could to feel normal—even fall to the background of Batch 001. Trying to be normal, I fancied myself a pretty girl with enhanced strength. I even stupidly thought I was in love with Cameron, one of my batch brothers and the one boy who had not once complimented me.

It was the stupid, whimsical mistake of a teenage girl.

Now, I depend on no one but myself.

Gavin slipped when he placed his foot on the slope of an iron cylinder. I reached back in time to grab him. Being a genetically enhanced human had its pros and cons. Being able to help someone without wasting time walking beside them to keep them upright proved beneficial. Gavin thanked me, but I said nothing in return. I hadn't done it because I was a nice person. I had done it because it was my mission. Thunder knew better than to give me a job, and yet, here I was, babysitting a twenty-year-old man.

"Keep up the pace, Gavin."

He increased his steps.

We climbed over large concrete blocks, remnants of a recent collapse. Buildings crumbled within The Waste on an almost daily basis, it was very common. I stepped on the largest of the blocks and stared at the expanse in front of me. The night was quickly approaching us. I could see no end in sight for this nightmare. Walking at this pace was detrimental to my health and using my speed would deplete my reserves.

"I'm not trying to complain or anything, but we've been walking for hours. I'm tired and hungry, Silk. You may not need to eat all the time, but I do."

My entire body froze. The blood in my veins coursed through me like a geyser. "I may not need to eat all the time? Why is that, Gavin?" I asked him in a tone that left no room for misinterpretation.

His eyes went wide. "Silk, it's—"

I cut him off.

"You mean because I'm not human like you?" I jumped off the block and landed right in front of him. "Why? Because I can do tricks like this?" I leaned down and grabbed a massive concrete stone. Using a good chunk of my strength, I tossed it almost fifty feet behind him.

Gavin shook his head, squeezing his eyes shut tightly. He ran that damn hand through his hair again, and it infuriated me further.

"Dammit!" My hands in fists, I slammed them down on top of a metal beam. The explosion of debris and dust made Gavin cover his face. He hacked and coughed while I worked vigorously to control the fire in my veins. "In case you're not aware, but us *mutants* need almost three times more calories than you do because of all the energy we use."

Gavin didn't stop coughing, his head hidden between his folded arms. I turned, flipping my curls away from my face. We increased our pace down a slope—all the while in deafening silence. The voices in my head told me to apologize. My body kept fighting with my head to make this uncomfortable situation better. When we moved away from the dust cloud I had caused in my outrage, I absorbed the worst kind of smell.

It was Gavin's blood.

CHAPTER FOUR

THE AMOUNT OF blood wasn't enough to kill a person, but it was more than enough to make me feel sick to my stomach—wracked with guilt. I stopped moving to take in what my eyes refused to see. Blood dripped from a cut somewhere on his face. He didn't whimper or complain but dabbed at it to cut off the bleeding. There was a war raging in my head. I tried to focus on the steps in front of me. He dabbed. I took a step. He patted again. I took another step. My legs got into a rhythm of their own. Butterflies invaded my insides. There was a deep, gut-wrenching feeling percolating, moving up and down my throat in a game of cat and mouse.

I could no longer pretend.

"Let me see it."

Gavin flinched when I about-faced right before him. He almost tripped on some ground debris in his haste to pull away from me. The sickness within me grew. *Is he scared of me now?* It was better if he was. He was better off not feeling anything for me other than unease and caution. My legs froze with my hand about a foot away from his face. I dropped the arm and focused on The Waste ruins behind him to avoid staring into his face, or worse, the damn gash.

I scratched my head. "Uh, we're going to have to clean it up, or it might lead the thugs straight for us."

He blinked a couple of times. "Silk?"

I ignored him, preferring to keep my wits about me by not paying him any attention.

"Silk?"

I closed my eyes, mentally preparing myself for the guilt.

"Silk, would you stop ignoring me and look at me?"

With a deep sigh, I opened my eyes and stared into his. My insides felt like jelly the moment I took one glance at him, and he showed no fear or regret in those baby blues. Gavin stared at me like Pops used to do whenever I did something wrong, but he wasn't mad about it. I felt a weird quiver and weight press down behind my chest. Unable to pinpoint it, I did what I always did in these types of situations.

I bluffed my way through it.

"I'm fine, Silk. See? The blood is practically coagulated."

With a brief nod, I went to turn around. Gavin stopped me by grabbing my hand. The urge to vomit, scream, and cuss overpowered me, but before I got to open my mouth to tell him to let go, Gavin wrapped me in his arms.

I went cold from head to toe.

"I'm not holding you because of some weird need I have or whatever you may be thinking, Silk."

He started as I tensed even further.

"I'm holding you because *you* need it—not me."

My tongue marinated with a few choice words. Gavin didn't have a right to hold me or touch me, for that matter. There was nothing he could do to make me believe I needed any of his embraces. I didn't need a damn person to pretend with me. I'd lived a rough-enough life, and no sheltered, spoiled, little rich boy was going to come around and pretend he knew what I needed.

I didn't need it.

I didn't need him.

I didn't need anyone.

I...

Fresh tears ran down my face and onto Gavin's shirt. My eyes went wide as I blinked back the salty water. The weight in my chest flooded over. I went to push away from him, but he squeezed me tighter. I slammed my fist on his shoulder, but he held me so close we melded into one. I sobbed over and over again in the middle of The Waste in front of a guy I wasn't sure I could trust. The strength I possessed would have made it easy to get away, but my mind kept me in place—my feet rooted to the ground as if cemented there. He didn't talk or make any weird cooing sounds. Gavin held me close to him, comforting me with a hand to my hair and the steady beat of his heart.

When I finally felt better, I pushed away from him. "If you tell anyone about this moment, I'll rip your balls out through your throat."

Gavin swallowed with a brief nod of acknowledgment. We said nothing else to one another and walked through The Waste. The sun had set, painting the sky in fiery reds and oranges. The sounds died down. I'd occasionally hear a rat but nothing else. The guys trying to kidnap Gavin would be on us in about two hours at average speed, but if any of them were genetically enhanced, I gave myself one hour, tops.

"Gavin, we're not going to be able to outrun them. I'm going to sleep."

Gavin blinked a few times, confused. "Uh?"

I closed my eyes when I found a comfortable enough spot on the dusty ground between a large concrete boulder and a metal beam. Gavin's presence floated in front of me. I didn't need to open my eyes to know he paced and worried.

"Gavin, I haven't eaten in days."

"Your choice," he cut in.

One eye opened to glare at him. "I need a real rest. Not the kind I had last night."

I closed my eyes again, but the man didn't stop pacing or gnawing on his full bottom lip. He ran a hand through his hair, and I about jumped to my feet to kill him. Instead, I yanked on his wrist to pull him down beside me. It was a tight squeeze, but he managed to work his slim build between mine and the steel beam. His chest pressed against my arm. The side of my body warmed as he molded himself along my hip and down my thigh.

"You should rest too. Trust me. I'll be up before these guys think to get the jump on us."

He agreed by making a sound deep in his throat, and I almost jumped out of my skin. His voice sounded more vibrant than it usually did at this proximity. Inhaling, I relaxed my entire being and let out a long, deep breath. My job was to keep him safe, and I'd do so, even with my eyes closed.

MY EYES SHOT open. If someone glimpsed them, they'd see darkness and nothing more. I heard the strangers before they came around the corner of a building. About twelve of them had guns and some other fun gear hanging off their belts and vests. I stretched the muscles on my neck and shoulders. Gavin slept soundly beside me. I peeled my body away from his as slow as I possibly could to not wake him. He didn't need to be up for this part of the games. Feeling ten times better than I did before, I grabbed a long slab and pulled it over Gavin and on top of the steel beam. I braced it so it wouldn't fall off regardless of what happened.

I made my way away from him, getting closer to where the men approached. Kneeling on top of a large fixture, I watched as they came closer. A large man with a bandana around his mouth led the group. He didn't carry any weapons in his hand, but a hunting knife and a pistol hung on his lean hips. The leader had two men beside him and in the back with rifles. The rest had handguns in their hands, facing the ground they walked. My cloaking ability allowed me to move off the fixture and down to the earth beside them.

The men looked left and right, walking right past me without a second glance. All of them were human, except for the one at the very forefront of the group. He was human but not quite. Something was off with him, and it piqued my curiosity. I walked behind them, completely undetected. Both of the thugs with rifles collapsed to the ground when I slammed their heads together. The rest of the group turned around, but I was already gone.

"Damnit! Keep an eye out, men. She's not human," I heard the leader call out.

I felt slightly offended. The man should take another look at himself in the mirror.

Already behind another mercenary, I slammed him back against a large rock. He fell unconscious. The rest of them panicked. I soundlessly made my way around to the other side, slinking between broken debris and large fixtures. A man in a khaki-colored vest pointed his gun everywhere but where he should have. I stood a foot behind him, unnoticed. One guy turned around and shouted.

"Baker, move!"

The guy named Baker didn't have enough time to move because I wrapped my arm around his neck, pinning him against my body. He dropped his gun. The rest of the group aimed their weapons in my direction.

"Now then, I guess the question we are wondering about now is, will you shoot Baker, here, to get to me?"

The leader came forward. "I won't kill my guy, so save yourself the inquisition."

The comment made me laugh. "Ah, so you care about your men, then?

Said men didn't bother to look at his expression or gauge his response. Years in a facility where soldiers lived and breathed taught me what compliance and respect meant. None of us had it for Project Hercules' creators, but we did have it for Thunder. These men had it for him.

"If my men die, it is for a cause, but they know I wouldn't needlessly use them for my own gain."

I pulled my arm back tighter. Baker gasped. His arms flailed around, trying to dislodge mine from around his neck. All the guys took a step closer with their guns aimed at my head, but none bothered to shoot.

"So, will you watch him die, then?"

"I will not," the man said and took two steps back.

His men followed suit and promptly dropped their weapons.

The group leader put his hands up, but not before dropping the mask over his mouth. "You're obviously a military super-soldier. Did Foxhand hire you to babysit his son?"

I loosened the arm around Baker's throat. Baker sucked in air like a fish deprived of water. "That's none of your concern. Just know I will watch over Foxhand's heir and will kill your men if I have to."

"I need the boy, super-soldier."

Another simper graced my face, but this one not as pleasant. "I see or hear you coming anywhere near Gavin Foxhand, and I'll rip your throat out with my bare hands. Understood?"

The man grinned too, the light from their flashlights glistening off his teeth. "Then I suggest you watch him closely, super-soldier. Because the moment you get your eye off the target is when we'll pounce."

"I'm not kidding when I say I will find you and destroy every person standing in my way."

"Noted," the man replied. "Now, will you let Baker go so we can be on our way?"

I pushed Baker back into the arms of his teammates and disappeared to a location with an excellent vantage point. I watched quietly from my spot as they gathered their men and weapons. The man sniffed the air in the direction I had hidden Gavin, confirming my suspicions before. He could sniff him out.

"Viktor, what are we going to do now?"

Viktor stared at all the broken bits around him. "For now, we fall back. We'll regroup. Now, let's go, because I'm pretty sure the woman has excellent hearing."

He grinned while walking behind his men. He took one last look around him. His eyes settled on the spot where I knelt. Viktor smiled again, saluting me.

So, it seems the man can do more than sniff people out.

THE PLANNING ROOM was full of members of Safe Haven, our headquarters, trying to get in a word after Rome and I dropped the bomb about Gavin's apartment. I watched when Suzanne came into the room, followed by Cameron—a proprietary hand on her right shoulder. With everyone now in attendance, Rome and I took the point at the head of the large conference room table.

"I know this is a shock to everyone, but we'll try to clue you in on what we know," I began.

Rome placed his hands on the rickety table. "Although Silk's blood was at the scene. It wasn't enough blood to be a fatal wound. Gavin is unharmed. I couldn't pick up any blood from him."

I flinched when Cameron slammed the same table. "Why the hell would you send her to guard some pubescent boy?"

Everyone stared at Thunder, our leader. Silk had not been able to get over her part in Rayne's disappearance during the escape. Coupled with her inability to be around people or men for long periods made sending Silk a mistake.

"Cam, Silk is not a child anymore. She was the perfect person to send because the 'boy,' as you call him, is in fact, a great asset to this team. Silk is also a soldier and warrior and should not be taken lightly."

"She's not ready to handle those kinds of missions."

Thunder placed his hands on the table as well. The

wood groaned but stayed put. "And who are you to say so? You're hardly ever here, Cameron, and when you are, you avoid her like the plague."

Cameron flinched, his eyes darting beneath his lashes to lock on Suzanne's face. Not like she could tell if he outright looked at her or not. Suzanne was blind. She was also Cameron's on and off again female companion. They had a very complicated relationship, and my best bet was it was solely a physical one. I wouldn't know. No man had ever looked at me like someone they wanted, let alone even touched me without feeling repulsed by my mutations.

Once upon a time, Silk had deep feelings for Cameron that weren't brotherly. He knew about it, although she hid it from anyone she could. Unfortunately for her, we weren't built emotionless, and her feelings came out in every mean thing she said or did to us. The meaner she was to us, the more we knew she felt. Cameron had been on the receiving end of way too many arguments and fights. We also knew the extent of her troubles and the mental scars left behind by the jerks at Project Hercules. She wasn't ready to be in a relationship, so he had treated her like a pariah. He avoided her so much he eventually moved in with Suzanne and had occasionally come home to check-in.

Snow leaned back in one of the chairs. "Ha, the black widow spider is fine. The woman is indestructible," he joked.

Snow wasn't wrong. I've always wondered why Rayne was an obsession to Braggart, even in our youth. Silk had an ability that caused zombie-like compliance in everyone who surrounded her.

Cameron lurched upward as if he were going to dive over the table at Snow, but Guy restrained him with an arm. He took a deep breath instead.

"The point is, Thunder, she could be really hurt. They both could be. We need to find them before the people who caused the explosions at Gavin's apartment reach them first."

Thunder stared at Rome and me. "In which direction did they go?"

Rome studied Cameron. "She's alive, Cam. They both exited the back doors of the apartment kitchens. I caught their essence headed toward The Waste. She'd more than likely try to head to the subterranean system in Charlie."

Cam nodded. "Thunder, let me go find her. I have a better chance of not being spotted."

Appeased, Thunder gave him the go. Cam left to find Silk and Gavin, but not before placing a hand on Suzanne's shoulder and whispering to her, "I'll be back soon."

Thunder released the rest of the group from the Planning Room. I stayed behind to talk to Rome, who stared at the floor in deep thought.

"A penny for your thoughts, Mr. Roman Braggart."

His head popped up to stare at me. "Just Rome, Seaa."

I came around the table, sliding my rear on top of the worn surface. "Are you worried about Rayne?"

He stared at me but said nothing. Instead, he grabbed a seat by the table and sat down. His shoulders dropped as if unable to hold the weight of his worries anymore.

"I miss her."

I could relate. "Me too, Rome."

He took a deep breath and exhaled loudly as if shaking away all of those troubling thoughts in his head. Rome looked up at me from my perch on the table and grinned fiendishly. "So, since when had Cameron been pining over the black widow spider?"

I laughed. "You noticed, did ya?"

"Kind of hard not to. The boy has it bad. Does she know it?"

I let out a sigh like Rome had and stared at the metal walls. "No, Rome. The woman doesn't know anything about real relationships, let alone the ones right in front of her. I'm hoping one day she'll know what it feels like to care. What it feels like to love someone and be loved by them in return."

"Do you know what that's like, Seaa?"

I dropped my head. "Nope. I guess it makes me defective too."

CHAPTER FIVE

Sector Echo
Traces
Operative Rayne — ID: PHO64.001

THE STREET PUNK quivered on the ground, his back against the wall of a brick building. He put his bloody hands up to place distance between himself and me. His teeth chattered. I watched as blood trickled down his jaw from the corner of his mouth. There was a horrid smell coming off him—coming off almost every resident in this poverty-stricken neighborhood. The man urinated on himself, his fear of me evident.

"Leave him. He obviously has no answers."

My partner lifted the disgusting human by the

shoulder, pushing him away from me. It wasn't the first time Trevor had interfered with my tactics. He may not care much about not capturing the rogue soldiers from Batch 001, but not pleasing General Braggart was akin to a death sentence. I promised not to make that mistake again.

There was the sound of music and lively banter coming from within the brick building. Ignoring Trevor Dallas, I walked toward the front of the structure and through the front door. Standing beside another entry of the establishment was a giant man with dark skin and equally dark hair. His hand alone could probably cover my face.

I studied him from my spot by the first door. He didn't move, only stared back at me. He gave a quick nod and opened the second door of the establishment. One side of my mouth lifted. He'd either fooled himself into thinking I was not a threat, or he enjoyed looking at the pretty females.

"Shit, Rayne. Where the hell are you going?"

I turned to Trevor before entering the bar. "I'm going to do some recon, Operative Dallas. I suggest you do the same." I added before walking in, "Somewhere else."

He glared at me like he had every day since I woke up in Unit 13. It didn't bother me one bit. My allegiance was to the Project and to General Braggart. Ignoring the greenish-brown-haired cowboy, I walked into the bar and to the sounds of laughter and gossip. People sat around the tables, drinking a prohibited beverage and chatting with their neighbors. Others danced on a worn floor. Some even canoodled in the dark corners in embraces I hadn't witnessed before.

"Holy cow, Marie! Where the hell have you gone?"

The man at the bar stared straight at me as he asked the question, calling me by a name I couldn't identify. It took me a couple of steps to get to the bar. "Who's Marie?"

The guy grinned. He was attractive and well-groomed. The veins in his arm flexed as he dried a tin canister with a clean rag. He had what headquarters called a "man-bun" with dark brown hair so much like mine. His eyes were light brown, and he had at least a week's worth of facial hair.

"Long time no see, cutie." He leaned on the bar. "When are you going to make me the happiest man alive?"

The guy was obviously delusional. "Does that line usually work on women?"

He grinned a set of straight, white teeth as opposed to the other men in this deprived area. "I'm serious, Marie. We've missed you around here."

There's that name again. "Who's this Marie?"

He shook his head and put a finger up as he ran over to a patron calling out for more alcohol. He served the man more amber liquid from a tap underneath the bar, cleaned his hands on a rag hanging from his tapered waist, and walked back to me. I found nothing off with his actions. He didn't act suspicious or disturbed. He honestly thought I was this woman he claimed was Marie.

The bartender leaned in closer. I inhaled the scent of hops and mint as he said, "Rayne, what's wrong with you?"

Ah, so he does know me.

"Nothing is wrong," I replied.

He shook his head with the lines of concern written all over his face. "The last time you were in here, you followed some woman out and didn't come back." He took a deep breath and called out for another guy to watch the bar. He stepped to the side and opened a latch on the counter to step out.

He approached me, and I noted his worn jeans and faded boots. The bartender had about four inches in height more than I did. His cold hand reached out for mine, so I let him drag me to a lonely spot in the loud interior.

"I heard about your parents, Rayne. I'm so sorry."

The weight behind my chest dropped to the pit of my stomach. My head throbbed and muscles tensed. I yanked my hand from his. "What the hell are you talking about?"

The man searched my eyes, and I noticed the exact moment he realized he had made a mistake. But it wasn't the façade of a man mistaking a woman for another. No, this man looked like he was talking with a ghost—as if Marie were dead and I'd stolen her body. The bartender shifted his body to go around me. My arm cut off his access while the other took hold of his neck. I slammed him against the wall. He garbled, his hands clawing at mine to let go.

The patrons around the bar stopped talking. Some ran out the front door, while others thought they were brave enough to stop me. One older man put his hand on my wrist, so I grabbed it with my free hand and snapped it. The bartender tried to shout. Chaos had erupted inside of the bar. The big man who had let me in before stomped inside and took one good look at me.

"Boss?"

The guy turned a few different shades before our eyes. The big guy realized I wasn't playing a game with the bartender and finally came over to do his job. If it were me, I would have fired him a long time ago. By the time he reacted, his boss here could have died. As it was, I needed answers. I came in here to find information on Batch 001's whereabouts, but instead have found something about myself that didn't quite add up. Who was Marie? Where or when was she last seen? And why is it that he's confused me with her?

Killing him wouldn't benefit me right now. The big guy stomped closer. I shot my hand out to push him away, but he barely moved back a couple of steps. The man had a little more girth in him than I thought. He ran full speed, so I stepped back away from the wall.

The bartender dropped to the floor haphazardly while the big guy slammed into a table and some chairs. "Calm down, big guy. If I wanted to kill your boss, I would have."

"R-Rayne, who changed you?" the man asked from his spot on the floor.

"I need answers. Send your guy away and close up shop. Do it quickly while I'm asking nicely."

He stared, wide-eyed at the bouncer. "It's fine. Go."

The big man hesitated but obeyed. I watched as he walked back out. The space empty of patrons, the bartender tentatively got up from the floor, eyeing me for any sudden movements. He dusted off his jeans.

"You're Rayne, but then you're not Rayne," he muttered.

I tried to analyze his words. What could he mean by implying I am but I'm not? "How do you *think* you know me?"

The tall man walked over to a chair, pulling it around to straddle it. "We've been friends for about five years, Rayne." He ran a hand down his face. "You lived in a building not far from here with your parents before they died."

"I know for a fact my father does not live here. He's also very much alive."

He shook his head before I even finished speaking. "No, we buried them. We..." The words got caught in his throat. "I thought you were dead too."

Hearing the sincerity in his voice, gave me pause. *Why doesn't any of this make sense to me?* "Why do you call me Marie?"

"You asked me to. Your parents told you it would keep you safe from bad people finding you."

Bad people? What did that mean?

"The military's been poking their nose around here a lot lately. Loads of incidents have happened since you disappeared."

A pounding headache formed behind my eyelids. I placed my thumb and forefinger on my eyes, applying pressure to ease my discomfort. The KeViewer in my back pocket went off. The man looked up.

"What is it," I called out once I'd accepted the call.

"There's reports that a super from the first batch is in the tunnels. We need to go."

I didn't reply, hanging up the phone instead. "Don't

go anywhere handsome. If you do, I'll find you and not give you a chance to explain. Got it?"

He visibly swallowed. "Yeah, I got it."

Sector Charlie
Old Subway Tunnels

THE DIFFERENT DISGUSTING smells in the tunnels beneath Charlie made me dizzy. I feared one day Ground Force would wise up and light up the tubes. The amount of methane circulating in some of these passageways would explode and cause a ripple effect under Trēbeta and the academic district's surface.

Gavin didn't say much to me, upset with me over leaving him trapped underneath a giant boulder, to fight a group of mercenaries alone.

Before we found a safe spot to jump into, I had found us some stale bread and water to eat for sustenance. The extra sleep I had gotten and the hard food made me feel ten times better than I had before. Being created in a science lab didn't make me indestructible. If I went any longer without eating or drinking something, I'd be no help to Gavin, especially if I was dead.

I hated to admit it, but Thunder sending me out of Safe Haven was the right thing to do. Not because I had the ability to stay hidden, but because I needed to do more than I had been doing. There were a lot of things I'd done wrong in the past five years. It was about time I rectified some of it. Now, if I could get Gavin to safety and get on with the real issues, I'd be satisfied.

Gavin dug into the pocket of his jeans. I watched from my spot behind him. He pulled out his KeViewer to fidget with the buttons once more. The phone doubled as a set of computers he used for his hacking. The entire time I watched over him at his home, he was on the damn things doing one job or another. He yelled at the screens quite often, but not once did he stop using them. Because of our immediate run from danger, his KeViewer had cracked, and without any tools on us, he couldn't get the technology to work.

Project Hercules had nothing on our whereabouts. I knew a lot of us worried Rayne or Hail had given up the information. The brainwashing on Hail had created new memories for him and temporarily erased the old ones. With Rayne, we didn't know. Seaa... I didn't even want to think about it.

Gavin stepped over a crate filled with crushed tile. I wondered what he thought of our situation. The unfortunate man didn't show it, but I sensed his fear every time he ran his fingers through his hair or gnawed on his lower lip.

A smile spread across my face. I promptly erased it.

I took great pleasure seeing Gavin make the nervous gestures I hated when he thought I wasn't looking. He'd pretend to scratch his eyebrow and look back at me from under his lashes. I'd stare at the wall or pretend to look behind me, all so he could get the nervous-tick out of the way.

"Silk?"

I grunted.

He stopped as he shoved the phone into his pocket again. "Can you hear The Market?"

The Market was the underground system for goods and services not sold in the sectors anymore to any New States citizen. The government wanted to conform the society we had left for new technology versus the old. To appease him, I reached out my hearing. Nothing sounded like The Market.

"I hear nothing right now."

He nodded, taking a deep breath of air. "If you hear it, please let me know. I need some things to fix the KeViewer."

"Gavin, we have all you need at Safe Haven."

He nodded again but didn't look entirely convinced. We walked for about another hour. I yawned, starting to feel the fatigue in my body. In the distance, a flurry of subway dwellers screamed and ran for cover. My hand shot out, clamping onto Gavin's shoulder.

"Stop, Gavin."

He turned to look at me. Gavin must've seen something on my face because his features shifted, and he slunk his way back to me.

"What do you hear, Silk?"

I listened carefully to a fight and people running for cover. One man and one woman fought in close-quarter combat. I couldn't decipher who fought from the tunnels' smells, but the sounds of their blows meant genetic enhancement.

"Gavin, stay hidden." I moved forward.

Gavin grabbed my hand to stop me but managed instead to almost fall flat on his face. I grabbed hold of him before he hit the fetid, tiled floor. "Gavin, stay here," I repeated.

He shook his head. "Why are you always pushing me behind you? I'll fight with you."

I yanked his fingers from my wrist with more force than necessary. Gavin grabbed his hand to his chest. I hurt him so he could see for himself the reason why he couldn't fight alongside me. He was a human man. I was a freak.

"Stay here."

He didn't say anything as he nursed the pain in his hand. I could've broken it, but I wasn't going to do so to him. I injured it enough he'd get the picture. Being around genetically enhanced humans was foolish. The guy was way too smart for all this.

The noises increased. Blood reached my nose. Simultaneously, I felt my own simmer as the smell registered in my brain. The blood belonged to Cameron. There was no denying it. I ran down the interior, opposite of the direction the others ran. The innocents who slammed into me bounced off like pennies on a sumo. I jumped over debris on the floor and maneuvered away from the people cowering on the ground.

I stopped, almost plowing over people in the way.

There was more blood.

And this scent belonged to Rayne.

CHAPTER SIX

BY THE TIME I got to the scene, blood had painted the interior walls of the tunnels in a deep, burgundy red. Squatters ran for cover. The stench of the subway smacked me in the face. With eyes wide open, I watched Rayne repeatedly punch Cameron in the face as his body twitched on the ground underneath her. She seemed disconnected from reality, her eyes slightly glazed over. I ran to them, using my stealth to be as silent as possible. Rayne's head turned to see, but I had already jumped high enough to make it to the opposite side of her. I yanked her back by her hair. Rayne flew off Cameron and into stacked crates in the far corner. She got off the crates and dusted herself off.

"Shit, Rayne. Please break free from Braggart's hold."

Her actions told me she wasn't in her right mind. Having dealt with Hail not too long before this, we knew when Braggart had interfered. We could smell the alteration.

I stood in front of Cameron, hopefully giving him enough time to get to safety. I couldn't avert my eyes to see him. Rayne would relish the opportunity and take both of us down. Cameron's breathing was choppy. He didn't move. The overwhelming iron hints of blood made me sick. She cracked her neck, staring at me with cold, almost lifeless eyes. Whatever Unit 13 had done to her, it was on a grander scale than Hail. She had no recognition of who we were anymore.

"Rayne, please. I'm your older sister, Silk."

Her eyebrows narrowed. "First, I had parents, and now I have a sister?"

She took one step. I mentally worked on a plan to get us both out of this safely. Rayne would not be coerced out of the hypnotism as easily as Hail—I didn't think any of us had the heart to beat it out of her. With Rayne, we'd have to capture her and get her looked at by Dr. Ferdinand. Unfortunately, I didn't think I had enough strength in me to make it happen on my own.

"It's true, Rayne. I'm your sister."

She ran forward. I dropped to the floor, watching in slow motion as she swerved back and forth to try to confuse me. I may not be faster than my brethren, but I could see their moves better than they could see mine. Once she was close enough, I shot up with one hand. Rayne flew once more to the other side of the cavern, slamming against the stone and tile. I heard Gavin's approach and quickly stopped him with one look.

Taking my eyes off Rayne for a millisecond proved foolish. She reached me before 1 could stop her. 1 swung. Although 1 missed, she didn't. Instead, 1 flew into the wall beside Cameron, the plaster exploding around me. The pain traveled my entire body from head to toe. 1 had a difficult time concentrating, but 1 shook it off in time to see Rayne pick Cameron up and toss him on top of me. His weight landed right on my chest. The air in my lungs escaped.

"Hey!"

1 felt the world around me sink when 1 looked up to see Gavin hollering from the other side of the tunnel. The guy had a death wish. Rayne stalked over to him and had him in the air before he could squeak. 1 pushed Cameron off me and bolted to my feet. 1 raced over to Rayne in time to steal Gavin away mid-toss, and then sped back to Cameron, leaving Gavin with him.

"Watch over Cam for me."

He nodded. Gavin had genuine fear in his eyes for the first time since this mess started. For some reason, it broke me to see him that way. 1 turned to face my sister, who smirked from her spot by the other tunnel entrance. Rayne ran toward me. My vision took in everything. Gavin's reaction. Her distance. Cameron's guns.

1 grabbed the guns from the holster, aimed, and shot. Rayne flew back as my heart broke. Salty tears flowed down my face in long streams. 1 watched as Gavin used his body to cover Cameron. Rayne hit a wall, sliding down and leaving a blood trail on the sur-

face, because Cameron carried bullets that brought down enhanced soldiers. Ferdinand had found the plans in Pops' books and created some weapons for us to use in emergencies.

This was an emergency.

I tried to control my tears but couldn't.

Gavin grabbed my hand. "Silk, relax. You are an excellent shot. She's hurt but will not die."

Gavin's words rang true. Rayne's breathing was shallow but there, and steady. I closed my eyes for a quick prayer. I handed Gavin Cameron's guns, which he took cautiously. I picked up my batch brother and carried him out of this place—or at least to a spot where I could check his wounds. We sprinted. I worked my way around the tunnel, stopping briefly to prevent Cameron's blood flow. While trekking down a recently made shaft, I found a large hole. I jumped inside first. It may have been home to someone at some point or another, but it was empty for now. This hole would be the best place I could use to hide Gavin and Cameron.

"Gavin, get in."

Gavin didn't argue. He jumped into the hole and helped me bring down Cameron's unconscious body. "Silk?"

I shook my head and placed a finger on my lips to stop him as I studied the area around me. My fingers shook. A knot formed in my throat, making it hard to swallow. I needed to protect them. They had to stay safe.

"Please, Gavin. Don't fight me, don't argue. Stay here. Watch over him for me. I'm trusting you, Gavin; please stay hidden 'til I come back for both of you. Understand?"

My voice cracked with every word. Gavin's eyes watered, reflecting what mine were like at the moment. He nodded without a word. He dipped his head down. I grabbed everything I could to cover the hole, stacking item after item over the opening. A man ran down the corridor, edging away from me. I stopped him.

He yelled, yanking his arm from my grasp. I stole the dirty coat from his body and threw it near the boxes that I stacked over the hole. Whatever I could do to mask the smell, I'd do. When I felt confident enough I could fool another genetic, I grabbed a shard of broken glass from the ground to slice my hand open. The blood dripped down my fingers, so I curled them into my palm to not let blood drip near their hiding place. I shook it off to spread around the beginning of the human-made opening and down the tunnel heading away from their location. Stretching out my hearing, I picked up commotion again from far behind. Either Rayne was back up, or her partners were.

I shook out my hand again and ran away from the spot I had hidden the two closest men in my life. Cameron, the man I thought I had feelings for since I was a stupid teenager, and Gavin, the man who had come into my life and refused to hide his feelings from me. With a burst of speed, I worked my way down the tunnel, ignoring the shocked looks and gasps of the people around me. Reaching a fork in the pathway, I shook the rest of the blood off my hand before it completely healed over. My eyes closed as I reached out my hearing. The person following me had passed the spot I hid the guys.

The tiny setules in my fingers came alive. I moved to the wall and climbed. I wasn't wearing the usual footwear I wore around the bunker, so I couldn't use the setules on my toes. Instead, I placed my covered feet in spaces to assist the climb.

I made it to a far corner of the vast area in another part of the subway system, watching from my vantage point—waiting. I didn't care how people looked at me or how they gave my position away. All I needed was the one place I knew they couldn't get the jump on me. Within minutes, Trevor Dallas, the green-haired cowboy, showed up. The drifters gave me away. He immediately blinked up at me and studied me from his spot on the ground.

"Well, I'll be damned. The elusive Silk."

I didn't move nor speak. Trevor Dallas enjoyed riling up the sleeping bear. We all knew better than to give him any sort of power over us. But he was right. I never left the safety of Safe Haven. It wasn't because I couldn't fight or lacked in the supernatural department. My emotions were volatile, and Thunder knew it, but he had chosen me to protect Gavin. I saw why he had done it. It was time for me to stop hiding and join them.

Trevor admired me from the ground where he stood. Several things crossed his eyes—capturing the elusive black widow, kissing the elusive black widow, and stomping his booted foot to destroy the black widow spider.

He crossed his arms. "In case you're wondering, Rayne is alive and well."

I gave nothing away, merely watched.

However, inside, I was a raging mess of emotions. Grateful I hadn't killed my sister. Thankful she didn't die. I'd had to make one of those crazy last-minute decisions. Either I lost one of them or two of them, or hopefully, no one at all. By mentioning it to me, he was trying to rouse my emotions. Unfortunately for him, I had worked on mine for quite a long time before him.

He leaned against a graffitied wall. "I'm terribly sorry about the fish."

God, I wanted to punch him so badly, but I remained where I was and did nothing to give away my feelings. Gavin had clearly stated several times that Unit 13 barely knew a thing about me. Bringing up Seaa's death was a ploy, an underhanded tactic to get me to give away my weaknesses.

He would not figure me out.

While he worked out another way to piss me off, I reached out to make sure the guys were safe. Satisfied they were, I grinned at Operative Dallas. Watching him made me pity him. He tried every underhanded method to get his way, so secure was he in his spot in Project Hercules? The fact that I could see it in the way Dallas stood. In the way he watched me. And how his nerves twitched whenever he said something that excited him. The man enjoyed a good fight and might've even enjoyed good torture.

The sicko.

"You know, you're a lot hotter in person than in those file photos."

I silently dropped to the ground. "And you look a helluva lot older in person."

The cowboy grinned. He gawked at the spot I had perched on. "Interesting. You literally hung in that corner without assistance."

"I like to climb things. I've gotten pretty good at it." I shrugged. A move I learned from Gavin.

"I picked up Cameron's scent in the bloody residue left behind with Rayne. Where is he, Silk?"

I shrugged again. "No clue."

He nodded, fixing his hat lower over his brow. He was preparing to attack me, but the man was sadly mistaken if he thought he could. Trevor ran forward, so I side-stepped him. Trevor stopped by the wall with one side of his mouth lifted. The man merely played a game.

"Let me enlighten you to one of my abilities, operative Dallas. I can see your every move in slow motion. It's loads of fun for me." I bit my lip and grinned. "Maybe not so much for you?"

He didn't like the new bit of news.

"I can do this for hours. So, let's make a deal, cowboy."

Trevor crossed his arms again. "A deal, you say? I'm a bettin' man."

"Yes. I leave, and you leave. Neither one of us has to fight right now."

He walked to the side with his arms in the same position. "You think you could beat me if we fought one on one?"

His team tried to surround me, but I heard where each one waited, and each one watched. "I can beat you one on one, Trevor. But we both know you're not the fair-fight kind of guy. I hear them all. None of them will get the jump on me."

He snickered but didn't bother confirming or denying my words. In his downcast eyes, studying me from underneath the brim of his hat, Trevor Dallas wasn't confident about fighting me. Not because he hadn't before, but because he had nothing on me. Trevor enjoyed a fight, which was evident in how he moved with careless abandon, but he didn't put himself in an altercation he couldn't win—not without backup, cheap tactics, or assistance.

The cowboy pulled his hat back with a look of disgust on his face. "I captured Seaa, you know. I tortured her and beat her. And I enjoyed every single second of it."

Cheap tactics, indeed.

The more significant thing to do was ignore him again and not play into his goal, but I got so pissed off I flew forward at a speed the operative could not achieve. My hand wrapped around his neck. His feet dangled in the air. The man tried to pry my hands off himself. I yelled down the hall: "You either shoot him to try to get me, or I kill him, and then, in turn, I kill you before you even make the shot."

Unit 13 had not dealt with me in person. I'd studied them from vantage points for years. I knew how they moved and how they reacted—the time between cocking a gun and firing it. My abilities allowed me to process in a faster time than the others. Although I wasn't at a hundred percent, they didn't know.

"Trevor Dallas, those two guns won't work on me, and the blade in your boot will only be as useful as decoration. We can end this right now, and you walk away with your team, or I end it for you."

One side of his mouth lifted. "So, if we fight right now. You'll kill us all?"

He sounded dubious, so I dug deep and controlled my entire being for the next words out of my mouth. "I shot my baby sister. Do you think for one second I won't do it to you?"

For one minute, Trevor Dallas stood in front of me, unsure. Before long, he grabbed the walkie at his waist, struggling for air at the same time. "Remember, Silk, this ain't over 'til the fat lady sings." He pressed the button and told his group, "Fall back. Grab Operative Rayne."

I couldn't do anything about Rayne right now as much as my mouth wanted to tell him to leave her be. I had Cameron and Gavin to save. At least Rayne was alive. Her life wasn't in jeopardy. We at least had a better understanding of what had happened to her and could better prepare ourselves to bring her back. I owed it to my little sister. No matter what I had to do, I'd get her back.

Trevor Dallas walked past me. I watched for any sign of betrayal. The rest of the team moved from their spots and walked toward a different location down the corridor. Rayne got checked by a medic and taken back down the other side from what I gathered.

Before Trevor left, he turned around to say, "I've heard lots of rumors about you, black widow. Other than a regular lusty blow to my libido, you aren't as all-consuming as they make you out to be."

I gave him the deadliest of my smirks and dropped my shield. Trevor seemed visibly disturbed by the onslaught of my power. He reeled back, grabbed his chest as if at a cross between ripping off his shirt or keeping it on. His eyes glazed over. Pupils dilated.

"My pheromones cause the equivalent of an undead outbreak within a certain radius," I said through a smile.

He took one step toward me unable to hold back. "Crawl to me on your knees, cowboy."

Trevor dropped to his knees doing as I commanded. When he reached the half-way point between us my shield went right back up. The cowboy blinked, picking himself off the dusty ground. He sucked in air, holding his weight against the tiled wall. Trevor had finally felt the pure, raw power of a Batch 001 experiment.

"Leave, Trevor Dallas. Don't turn around as you walk away. Take this moment as the only gift you'd ever get from our kind."

I could talk the big talk, but inside I was a wreck. It was starting to become difficult to hold anything in, and I didn't know why. Something was changing inside of me. The military trained these men to find the one small hitch in our voice or twitch in our eye. Being "on" was depleting all the energy I had left. If he stayed any longer, he'd catch me in a web of my own making. Trevor had the upper hand. If he even had a clue he did, I'd be long gone right now.

I didn't even have a good meal in my stomach. My body felt weaker, and using my power would deplete my last reserves. Holding my energy back had the same effect. I'd fallen out of buildings, crashed through glass windows, bled, and almost died in a

Gidget shaft. I'd run from bad guys, hid from them, and made sure Gavin was safe at every waking moment. Add to all of that, I fought with my altered sister and couldn't have made it if I had to do it one more time with him.

But he didn't suspect a thing. There was a fine line of concern between his brows. He hadn't even noticed his Stetson was askew. Instead, Trevor stumbled out of sight—only turning back once to look at me.

I didn't breathe.

I didn't move.

Not until they were long gone.

Afterward, I collapsed.

-69-

CHAPTER SEVEN

Sector Charlie
Old Subway Tunnels
Gavin Foxhand
New States Citizen ID: CH.JJ49.GF-Rank A

THE DARKNESS IN the hole where we sat hidden swallowed me up like rogue tidal waves in the sea. The earth had layers of rot. My fingers slid over substances I couldn't describe, let alone decipher. If my KeViewer worked, I would've used the light to see if it seemed as bad as it smelled in here. Cameron's breathing came in slow and shallow. The swelling on his face left behind by Rayne had distorted his features. I didn't know what Cameron, known as "the chameleon," resembled underneath the bruises and wounds. If Silk hadn't intervened when she did, my friend, Rayne, would've destroyed him.

The thought of her brought fat tears falling from my eyes.

She wasn't herself, and I knew it the moment I saw her fight Silk. Those two became inseparable at Safe Haven. Rayne, in her right mind, wouldn't have attacked her sister. The relationship those two females had rivaled anything I had seen in person. I most certainly didn't have that kind of relationship with my sisters, let alone my father. When I first met her, she was lost—a woman trying to find herself in this kind of life.

Simply put, I felt a pang of jealousy. Rayne had parents that weren't her flesh and blood and yet loved her unconditionally. I mean, what wasn't there to love? She was a beautiful person, inside and out. I couldn't even get a man who shared the same blood as me to show me off as his blood-born son. Or was it because he'd had an affair and the woman had died in childbirth, leaving me as the evidence of his infidelity. I shook the morose thoughts away. Rayne didn't have that with her siblings.

Not for the first time, I wondered how Silk was doing. She acted bravely on the surface, but the woman was horribly fragile, like thin glass. The main thing I worked on was my expression when she'd spew out venom from those exquisite, plump lips. The sting briefly hurt, but like an aloe balm, it would dissipate, and I'd see again those harsh words were a façade behind which she hid.

Her super-hero shield.

The minutes had extended into hours. I moved Cameron's head from my lap so I could stretch out my legs. Noise from above us caught my attention. Dozens of things went through my mind, and none were pretty. I searched around in the dark with my hand, but nothing stuck out as big enough to protect us.

Shit!

It wasn't like anything I put in my hand could hold off these super soldiers. When Rayne showed me her strength that day in my apartment, I was intrigued and baffled.

These super soldiers were experiments created in a lab to assist the United States, now New States, in the final world war. We called it Ragnarok because it became the fight of the gods—the end of the world as we knew it. Each country tried to dominate through fear. Every country had its ammunition, whether nuclear or through the use of chemical weapons.

What remained of the United States perfected what they dubbed "The Herculean Cocktail," a scientifically fortified drug that caused enhanced abilities in volunteer soldiers. The rest of the world knew what those volunteer soldiers were and cheered them on when they ended the war singlehandedly. But what would society do if they knew that these super-soldiers had started as experiments like Silk and Rayne? Regular humans with guns could do nothing to a genetically altered human.

But in these circumstances, something was better than nothing.

I had no clue where we dropped his guns. My hands

patted down the sides of Cameron's body looking for any other weapons he might have. It was hard not to notice that these men were built like tanks. Snow and Guy had a smaller build than the rest of the male super-soldiers I'd come in contact with, but they were muscular and built to stop a car with their bare hands. I worked out in my home gym when I had the time, but I wouldn't achieve their fat-to-muscle ratio no matter how much I tried.

I stopped imagining what I couldn't reach and kept seeking a weapon. After thoroughly searching, my hand finally landed on a dagger placed methodically between his boot and jean-clad leg. I held the weapon tightly in my hand. The noise level outside increased.

A bright, blinding light shone into the gloomy chamber.

I squinted against the light and saw a hand reach out for us, but I couldn't tell who it was. I waved the dagger, but the stranger knocked it out of my hand without a second's hesitation. I opened my eyes and jumped up to grab the person. In a bent position, they'd fall into the hole, and I'd subdue them before realization dawned on them. My hands made contact. The light moved to the side. All I got to see was a blur of black hair, and weight pressed itself against my chest, straddling my legs.

"You stupid, son of a..."

Silk cussed like a nineteenth-century sailor. Through the dim light above, I could see she was angry, relieved, and undoubtedly one of the most exquisite creatures I'd ever had the pleasure to know. I leaned up to wrap my arms around her back. Her entire body froze within my arms, but I didn't care. She was here, and she was safe. It had been hours since I last saw her. Cameron was knocked unconscious and bleeding. I was no help to anyone right now. If Silk had never come back...

I'd... I couldn't even finish the thought.

"Gavin, if you don't get your hands off of me, it'll be the last time you ever get to use them."

The threat may or may not have been fact. I couldn't fully tell when it came to Silk. She hated me, then tolerated me. I got her to relax enough to cry in my arms, but then she'd spit out venom from her mouth like no other person living on this planet could. Silk was an anomaly. Here was a woman who I needed but who sure as hell didn't need me.

"I'm so glad you're safe." I dropped my hands from her back, but they burned as I lay them on her thighs. They landed there, and at first, I thought about moving them again, but if she didn't realize it, I wouldn't bring it up. The woman straddled my thighs. My entire body was on fire, but I did my dandiest so she wouldn't notice. If I gave her any indication she did amazing things to my body, I'd probably not have bits left to use.

"Of course I am, fool."

She got off me without issue. Cameron groaned from his spot on the ground. At the moment, I felt sick and unsure. The man hadn't moved or said a word since she dropped us into this hole. I knew better, of course. These warriors healed quickly, but he had lost a lot of blood. I didn't think he'd make it. Silk stared at him as she did with Rayne. There was a whole lot of affection in the expression—a lot more than a familial bond. I tried not to let it get to me. I closed my eyes and took a deep, relaxing breath.

I sat up. "He hasn't moved since we got him down here. But I made sure he was still breathing evenly."

She nodded but didn't look at me. "We need to get out of here, Gavin. Rayne did a number on him. He needs Dr. Ferdinand." I didn't want to say out loud that she'd been through the wringer too. Typical Silk, she took the worries for herself and cared more for the well-being of others. She didn't want people to call her on it and would more than likely deny it if we did.

I climbed out of the hole first. Silk placed Cameron over her shoulder and jumped. It was physically impossible to jump out of the hole with another human hanging off your shoulder, but there it was, right in front of me. She landed on the ground with a resounding *thump*. Silk had many more talents than I could ever hope to achieve. Gradually, I realized I could never be enough for her. But damned if my heart would let me forget her. I shied away from human interaction in my old life, preferring my introversion and using it as a shield to keep the riffraff away.

We ignored the gawkers standing around and ran out of the tunnels as fast as I could. The drama unfolding the past few days had done a number on my sanity. Selfishly, I believed having Silk in my home for a few days would help bring us closer together. Like Rayne, Silk didn't look at me with the eyes of a gold-digging, connection-seducing hussy who wanted nothing to do with me but with my dad's money and pull. *No, that's unfair of me.* Not all women were like that, but the ones around me were.

I was the heir of a vast amount of money in a world with barely any of it left.

For years my father had a parade of females come into my home under the pretense they were there for something entirely different. As a hacker, my job got better every time I broke into my father's technological devices to find out what he was doing. Gregory Foxhand III would seek out the most influential female, displaying her around me like a common woman. In a sense, he was hiring the girl to hook me in and get him the heirs he needed to keep the line of Foxhands going.

A complete load of shit.

I was a Foxhand by name only. Not in a million years would I be able to take on the burden that comes with being a Foxhand heir. Not like I wanted to. My father owned the companies that designed and manufactured high-tech medical equipment for the hospitals and military. Ultigraphs and Hydro Chambers, to name a couple, were designed with ease and function in mind. Although the world suffered after the wars, technology progressed in several ways.

Manufacturing companies for high-tech devices weren't the only thing we undertook. Biology and chemistry started their own trend when scientists created superhumans out of Petri dishes. We were already well-known as a country full of debt and civil battles. Now we were known for our superhuman technology.

Making a name for myself was the only way not to lose who I was within the chaos of the world. I took the bad guys down with knowledge instead of money and muscle. I didn't need Foxhand's title to give the globe its much-needed break. I used my skills as a hacker to see behind the government's curtain in front of the remaining New States' citizens' eyes. If I had an inkling of bad practices against the people, I made sure to shut that company down.

We didn't need any more enemies within our lands.

My new friends suffered because humanity was greedy. We had an innate, overwhelming urge to be better than everyone else—to give off the illusion "America was great." That, too, was another load of shit. We could only be as great as the greatest person, and everyone thought they were the better one of the deal. Humanity forgot working together got us progression and morale. I mean, how many times did we fail at playing Simon Says or Follow the Leader? With failure came the ability for exceptional success. But don't tell General Braggart that type of wisdom. His idea of success stemmed from his inability to fail.

Or so he thought.

I didn't blame Rome for distancing himself from his father's corruption. He was better off with the first batch in Safe Haven. And now we knew for sure Rayne had been brainwashed; he could at least come up with a plan to get her back. Those thoughts buried deep that they tortured Rayne to death were appeased today. It may not be great news to see my friend used and manipulated, but she was alive. The rest could be taken care of with a well thought out plan and execution.

Silk walked ahead of me as we weaved around fallen beams. She dragged her feet, refusing to complain. I didn't hear her sigh or grunt or mope about. The woman carried the chameleon on her back as if he weighed no more than a feather. Silk stayed between the old metal rails of the subway system. We hadn't had electricity down here for years since the war started. The squatters knew steel, iron, and alloy melted and could sell for good money. I shook my head. I needed to fix my KeViewer system and get back online. It was time to stop being watched over and be more productive in this fight. I had thugs willing to kill to get to me. If Silk weren't around, I would've been theirs in a heartbeat.

They planned for everything to get me.

Unfortunately, they didn't plan for Silk.

We exited the underground system, taking a similar route that I had when I first went in search of their hideout. Silk kept to the sides of the crumbling buildings as the night dragged on. Daylight would be out soon, so it would be better to be near Safe Haven when it happened. The area got more familiar. Safe Haven wasn't far away, but with the light of day making its ascent beyond The Waste, we couldn't afford capture.

In front of me, Silk collapsed on the ground, exhausted. She panted but made no other sounds of distress. I ran to her, almost losing my footing from the lack of coordination. We were both tired and we'd had no real food or sleep for quite a bit. Any more of this, and we'd both be useless.

"Silk, let me help."

I waited to hear her argument, but she gave no reply. Silk had passed out on the ground with Cam on top of her. My entire body quivered. Exhaustion crept through every crevice and absorbed itself through my bloodstream. Silk needed my help, so I would not let her down. I dragged Cam off to the side and hid him behind a couple of metal trashcans.

Silk's dark hair lost its luster and bounce as it draped over her face, limp like soggy noodles. And then, out of the blue, my body felt hot. It slowly doubled in heat. I took off my jacket. My fingers felt stiff while my entire being sought the source of the flame.

The strength of the fire ripped through me like a wrecking ball.

I keeled over, breathing rapidly from the hit. My brain couldn't place coherent thoughts. I watched Silk like a kid in a sweets shop for the first time. I shook it off. This ability of hers was the guard others said she kept up. Silk had dropped her shield when she had gone unconscious. The phenomenal amounts of pheromones she excreted could bring any sane man to his knees. Now I knew why Silk didn't need a weapon.

She *was* a weapon.

Knowing she didn't need this type of perversion from me, I stuck my head in a trash bin with God knows how many years of filth and sucked in the horrid smell. I gagged a few times before I felt comfortable enough to suck in more of the putrid air and hold my breath. Silk didn't move. I could barely tell if she was breathing normally. There wasn't enough time for me to check. Holding my breath for long periods wasn't a significant accomplishment of mine.

No pedestrians hung about because The Waste was off-limits, so I dragged her next to Cam and threw debris and dead bushes around them so no one would spot them. Thunder had mentioned he had a team member posted in the last tunnels near Bravo, another ten-minute walk. So, I ran. My feet pounded on the dusty ground, echoing between the old buildings. When I was far enough, I let out the air in my lungs and sucked in more. My chest felt heavy. The heartbeat behind my ribcage tripled its rhythm.

Silk needed me.

I'd do anything to help her.

My legs wobbled, and my vision blurred. I stopped right before a utility hole, calming my frazzled nerves. This wasn't the time to drop unconscious again. Silk could attract people with the energy she let out. If that happened, and something happened to her, I'd never forgive myself. With my vision back and my legs under better control, I went down into the tunnels' darkness by the metal ladder bolted from top to bottom. Hardly anyone stuck around the beginning of the tubes, so I knew my best bet would be to run down these corridors yelling at the top of my lungs.

And pray someone could help find me.

And hoping no one who could kill me did.

I beat down the old concrete floors and crushed tiles and yelled out for Thunder. I yelled out for Rome. I called out for anyone that mattered with no response back. The drifters and residents of the tunnels called out to me, beckoning me to shut up or back off. I didn't care for them. I only cared for her. My voice cracked with the force of my scream. My throat was raw from the strain.

All I needed was one person from Batch 001.

One.

With the strength in my legs depleted, I dropped to the ground in a tangle of limbs. My face hit the ground. The sting of the cuts in my face burning. Not meant to assure me from the looks on their faces, strangers got up from their spots on the floor to loot or hurt me. I threw my arms out and yelled for them to back off. No one cared.

And they sure as hell didn't fear me.

"Move," I heard from behind the gathered bums.

The crowd parted without fuss. The strangers who hovered over might have feared me, but they definitely feared him. Thunder came forward with a regal presence; no regular person could amass. His long, dirty blond hair rested behind his ears. He wore a large coat over a white shirt with strong arms crossed over a massive chest. Uncontrollable tears rolled down my face as the weight of my worries washed away. I hated to feel so vulnerable, but people's lives were on the line.

"Thunder, thank God."

CHAPTER EIGHT

Sector Bravo
Safe Haven Headquarters
Seaa – ID: PH049.001

THE ENTIRE FACILITY erupted like a long-dormant volcano. The madness consumed us in its grasp, refusing to let go or loosen its powerful hold. One part of the bunker had crazed madmen arguing about the new reports, while the other end had brothers hovering over Dr. Ferdinand—immune to Silk's pheromones because of their familial affection—waiting for news about Cam's health. Hours earlier, Thunder had come into headquarters with Silk over one shoulder, Cameron over another, and an exhausted, frail man standing beside him. For my sister's pheromones to have exploded like they did, meant she had depleted all her energy. The worst thing we could do to ourselves was to consume our vitality.

Each one of us had abilities. These powers were exclusive to Batch 001—a gift given to us by our creator. When we accepted our skills, we could easily control them without issue. Thunder had the advantage of static energy. He controlled the discharge he released. The man could shock an individual or fry them to a crisp—his choice. Hail could freeze things with the touch of his fingertips, but lately could cause an entire line of sight to freeze over. That new boost to his power came from Dr. Plumboy's experimentation when they captured him at Unit 13 headquarters.

I could control water when it flowed. I wasn't sure why it worked that way, but I couldn't make water in a cup move for the life of me. I knew I could move moving water during a reconnaissance trip to the Charles River. My little sister Rayne altered her body, turning it into liquid. But no matter how exciting these powers were, Silk's gifts were a lot more precious than any of ours combined.

Dr. Sebastian Lester had taken various DNA strands from wildlife and injected them into a cocktail he created for Project Hercules. I had strands of the fairy wrasse fish and manatee, while my brother Thunder had elements from the electric eel. Guy got his speed from the peregrine falcon. Hail drew his abilities from the artic wolf. Rayne had a chemical variant of the mutable rain frog. We all carried one or more creatures in our blood, helping manipulate and manifest our genetic coding.

Silk was the exemption.

Our sister Silk didn't carry the strands of an animal or fish. She held the strands of various arachnids. We didn't know why he used the spider for Silk's coding, but we hoped something would turn up in his plethora of journals. Pops wasn't a very organized individual. Each notebook had notes on all of us at different intervals of our day or random thoughts. There was nothing organized by section or a journal specific to one of us, and because Dr. Ferdinand could understand Pops' writing, we left it to him to find out his reasoning.

But Silk had been created with another intention altogether—we weren't sure what, exactly. I could cast temporary illusions on others, but Silk had a strong shield she used to hide from the world. The barrier prevented her pheromones from leaking out and attracting males and females to her. She could make someone put down their guard, allowing her to sneak up on them undetected, silently, and with extreme prejudice. Using up all of our energy dropped us for days into an unconscious state—no one could awaken. If Silk were in that state, any man or woman around her would suffer if they couldn't control their baser instincts.

Several of the residents in Safe Haven had built an immunity to Silk's pheromones but not by choice. She had unwillingly taken the option from us. We had to have an intense affection toward her or another person to outdo our bodies' primal reaction to her siren call. If she wanted to catch us she would, with the use of that one cuticular power. At her fingertips and toes, tiny hairs gave her the ability to stick to surfaces both vertically and upside-down. We could keep no secrets from our sister. Silk could use trichobothria to sense sounds and movement at one ten-billionth of a meter like a spider.

Braggart's obsession with Rayne baffled me.

Why did Rayne make him so hyper-aware of her every move when there are super-soldiers like Silk?

If anyone at Project Hercules was valuable, Silk was the best and most primal form of bio-genetic warfare. I grabbed my hair and pulled on it. Trying to think in this absurdity was like trying to stick the end of a freshly spun web through a needlepoint. Useless and disappointing. There had to be a link between Rayne and Braggart and an even bigger one between Dr. Lester and Silk. But who the hell could figure it out with the chaos claiming the fugitive first batch's once somber headquarters?

Screams echoed down the corridor of the bunker. The house was in an uproar. Silk was so far from consciousness; the ones suffering were those who claimed to love her. It was those times that made Silk so dependent on no one but herself. She barely opened up to us or others, and in times like this, matters were ten times worse. Debris crashed against the wall. More screams swallowed up the space—the anguished cry graining on my ears.

"I need to see her," Guy screamed to the rest of the group holding him hostage.

Guy was the only one of the entire group who couldn't control his baser instincts. The man would sleep with any female who gave him the thumbs up. He had slept with them all and had also left them the next day as if they'd never existed in the first place. Guy was the most average of all of us. He resembled a regular "American" man. He had a muscular physique but not overly drastic like the one's Thunder, Rock, or even Rome carried. His smile always warmed the receiver. Guy had strength like us, enhanced hearing and smell, but he was incredibly faster than any of us—even Silk.

Silk was very fast. The ways she moved was calculated to perfection. Her spider-like abilities could make her see things as if they were in slow motion. In The Arena, a fight between Guy and Silk always ended with her standing the victor. Most of the time, it had more to do with his idiosyncrasies than anything else. Plainly put, Guy Gust was a hornball, and the moment breasts or a butt came in his general line of vision, the man would choke. Because of his high sex drive, situations like this made it difficult to live with him. I couldn't imagine living with Guy in a two-bedroom apartment with paper-thin walls.

Shoot me now.

I slammed my hands over my ears. The words Guy spoke had an underlying sound that was horrendous on sensitive hearing. It resembled a frequency only animals could hear and humans couldn't. My head pounded. The wails increased in pitch. No longer able to take it, I slammed against a firm chest on my way out of the mess hall.

"Are you okay, Slug?"

Steady cool hands held my shoulders. The scent

of worn leather and a little myrtle consumed me. My skin absorbed it as if it were the very water I needed to breathe. Ordinarily blue, Hail's eyes were teal, a sure sign he had gone aroused. But his feelings for Rayne hadn't allowed him to fall for Silk's pheromones as badly as Guy. As shameful as it was to admit it, I had hoped at one time or another he'd lose control, at least because it meant his feelings for her had died down.

I mentally slapped myself.

Being the ugliest creature in this compound came with unpleasant thoughts. Apparently, Pops hadn't built me as pretty as Silk or as genuine as Rayne. I had fish parts and a dirty mind. Sometimes I felt it was better to leave Safe Haven to do things by myself than spend it around the people I cared about with feelings of jealousy or envy.

Hail never directed eyes like those to me. Although the color of those irises matched most of my scales perfectly, our romantic connection hadn't clicked. It never fell into place. He cared about me like one would a little sister. I didn't want to be his sister. Brashly, I wanted Hail to throw me down and caress the lousy and more delicate parts of me.

I slapped myself again, but this time, not in my head.

Hail gripped my wrist. "What the hell, Seaa?"

I didn't need him to see me in this state, so I walked around him after yanking my wrist away. He pulled me back again. I stared numbingly at the forceful fingers wrapped around my skin. Why did this have to be the only contact someone gave me? Granted, my sisters held my hand. The men in this place had no problem putting their hands on my forearm or shoulder. But not once had someone touched me romantically. Not like what I heard Rome did for Rayne. Or Rock did for Beatrice. Hell, not even how Cameron felt Suzanne as if she were the frailest creature in the universe. The hard knot of rejection blocked my airways.

My body wore scales like armor.

The digits on my hand and feet syndactyly connected.

Gills marred the skin behind my ear and directly below.

My hair was vibrantly colored like the hair of a socialite New Citizen, but I was anything but that.

No one here really understood my growing pains, and I had to live with them consistently. The howls of a frustrated Guy rang in the corridor once more, sending the chaos through my mind like millions of tiny lightning bolts. My body raged from within as my blood pressure soared freely through my veins, injecting me with a stimulant unlike I had ever felt before. The room grew hotter. The words jumbled together. The high-pitched sound of a jet engine overtook my hearing. Hail's mouth moved. The vision of his gorgeous features faded from my eyesight. The energy burst through me faster than I could stop it.

When I could finally get my eyes to open—to see what the hell happened. The teal had disappeared from Hail's eyes. He watched me from the eyes of an arctic wolf. The grayish-blue studied me from top to bottom from his spot over me. One arm had wrapped itself around my back while he leaned down to the ground. The strength in his eyes made my insides flutter. They left me raw and naked.

"Seaa, did you do this yourself?"

Did I make myself collapse? I probably did. With the craziness going on in this bunker and then the drama inside my head, it be enough to bring the strongest warrior down. Just because I was built as sturdy as an oak didn't mean I was indestructible.

I moved to stand but found I could not do anything but sit up straight. "What the hell are you talking about?"

He gestured to all of me with his free hand. "Seaa?"

I cast violet eyes to my lower body. Piercing screeches erupted from my throat had filled the corridor of the bunker, so loud Hail dropped to the floor in tears. His hands covered his ears. Drops of blood trickled from his palms. Waves after waves of sound pushed against the metal walls and down the tunnels.

Safe Haven went quiet.

I closed my mouth, apologizing profusely to Hail as he blinked back consciousness. My clothes lay tattered on the ground beneath me because my legs had fused. The scales had melded together with the shiny skin between my legs. The stunning ombré of turquoise and purple shades glimmered from one end to another. I didn't have human legs anymore. Slapping the dusty ground of the rocky interior in a wavy effect was the mesmerizing tail of a fish.

THE HIGH-PITCHED sound of a threatened animal jolted me from my slumber. I shot upright, staring at the contents of my bedroom. The light above my head hummed. My boots lay scattered on the floor. My old clothes settled in one corner of the room. I studied my wardrobe. Someone had wiped me down and dressed me in one of my many tunics and stretch pants. This tunic was black with gray stripes—a high elastic waist cinched the shirt into two connected pieces. I felt my curls bounce and knew that it had been more than a wipe. Beatrice must've bathed me while comatose.

How the hell did I get back?

I threw my legs over the side of the twin bed. The feel of the cold stone underneath my bare feet brought shivers up and down my spine. The nest of curls on my head scattered over my shoulders. Shaking off the stupor, I reach my hearing out to the entire bunker to decipher the different bits of chaos before I ran out there.

The Planning Room held Thunder, Rome, and Snow in a debate about Cameron's health and the reason for his wounds. I closed my eyes and pinched the bridge of my nose. Thinking about Rayne right now would not help me figure things out. Cameron's breathing came in regularly as Dr. Ferdinand fidgeted around with controls on the medical equipment in the medical wing; it seemed Suzanne sat waiting. Beatrice hummed in the kitchen as she chopped vegetables on a cutting board.

I reached out for Hail. He tried comforting Seaa in the hallway.

Holy shit! Seaa's alive?

I tried to focus on their conversation, but Guy wouldn't let me concentrate. Guy hollered from the cells. He banged on the wall and pulled at the bars like a raging maniac. Rock tried to persuade him, but nothing could get through to the man. Seaa wasn't dead. I wanted to run to her, but I needed to deal with the madness in the cells. I shoved my feet into a different pair of boots. The yelling ground on my nerves, so I burst through the bedroom door. The kitchens were on the way, so I stopped to peek my head inside. Beatrice smiled as I snatched an iced croissant from the baking trays. I devoured the sweet fare and headed down the corridors until I got to the small prison.

"You'd think he'd better control himself by now," I muttered to Rock as I licked my finger.

Rock seemed disturbed and tired as if he'd been dealing with Guy's nonsensical ramblings for days.

"Oh, thank God you're awake. Turn it off, Silk."

An eyebrow shot straight toward my hairline. Guy yanked on the bars, his eyes glazed over. His arm reached for me from between the metal, touching air. I kept the barrier down long enough to take in his madness. Men were all predictable. Rock had a mate, so it didn't apply to him. Thunder and Snow thought of me as a little sister. Dr. Ferdinand saw me as a younger daughter. The rest had strong feelings for someone else. They were able to control their inhibitions.

Guy Gust was a walking penis.

Guy raged again. Rock slapped his hands over his ears. Guy had predictably fallen for my pheromone ability because, like all men, he didn't know how to be respectful of a woman's flesh. The familiar pangs in my chest slithered over my veins. I hated creeps like him. The reason I tolerated him and everyone else here was because we came from the same genetic cocktail.

"Please, Silk. He's been at this for almost two whole days."

I felt stiff all over. No matter how bad I got, I had never drained myself to the point of oblivion. Two days was more than I had ever gone in that state of mind. My mental barriers went up. Rock visibly relaxed, which showed me that even though he was in love, the ability broke him up inside. I sighed because I didn't mean to hurt them. This power was usually in control. To feel so out of control made my stomach clench. I may be broken, but I sure as hell wasn't defective. Guy stopped moving. His eyes shot toward the back of his head before he dropped to the ground, unconscious.

Rock watched me give Guy the cold shoulder. I turned to walk out of the cells before Rock grabbed my hand. The overwhelming urge to punch him washed over me. I turned to face him and punched him in the face, satisfied. Blood sprayed from his nose as his head whipped back from the force.

"I don't like being touched, Rock."

My batch brother keeled over with a hand over his face to stop the blood. "You're one sick, twisted bitch," he mumbled between fingers.

With one hand, I flipped my hair back, ignoring his harsh words. They were mean, but they weren't untrue. Instead, I zoned in on the ruckus gathering in the main corridor. The facility seemed more lively than usual. I trotted down the worn path. Gavin came out of his temporary room beside Rayne's. He had seen me because his breathing hitched, and he stayed frozen in place. There was nothing I wanted to say to him. The past week had been one big emotional roller coaster ride I refused to get back on. He was safe. My job was done.

The group gathered all talked at one time. No one dedicated their conversation to Cam or planned a way to bring Rayne back from Braggart's hold. They didn't comment on the fact that Guy had stopped hollering. Or that I must've been awake because my pheromones were no longer pulsing in the air around us. The group before me was plenty preoccupied with something else.

I pushed between them, disregarding the dirty looks shot in my direction. By the time I got to the center of the problem, my innards had curdled. There was brilliance before me but also so much antipathy. Not for what I saw, but for who had done this to her. My big sister lay on the ground with her scales in full view and the most exquisite tail I had ever beheld.

Seaa was a mermaid.

CHAPTER NINE

Sector Bravo
Safe Haven Headquarters

PEOPLE GATHERED IN the corridor, bickered, influenced, and discussed the new situation before them while I fought with my self-control. My sister was alive. The blood in my veins felt clotted and heavy. A hot, pulsing rage came over me as they argued before her, while tears rolled down her dust-covered cheeks. We'd always had to fight the vile stares for being genetically enhanced freaks. Seaa more than most. She was stunning with those wonderfully vivid colors in her hair and a smattering of freckles over round cheeks.

Seaa had the cutest button nose that twitched when

she was angry or confused. Her ears were aligned evenly on her head but only came away slightly. It made a stunning view when her long, multi-faceted hair settled in waves in front of her ears by her temples and behind them, hiding away her gills. It was her smile that did it best. When she was happy, she had all these laugh lines that settled on her face. It made staying stoic impossible. We wanted to laugh with her if she was pleased and sigh when she found the most mundane things beautiful.

She may not have seen it, but I sure did.

Being able to see her right now spurred me on.

I shoved the two closest people to me away. Snow slammed one side of the wall, and Hail landed on top of Rome and Thunder. The group died down. The gawkers averted their attention from her to me. Snow mumbled how many ways to hurt me, while Thunder asked Hail if he was okay. I ignored them, more worried about my older sister.

"Are you alright, Seaa?"

Seaa's lavender eyes went wide. I didn't let her say anything because I knew deep inside she felt horrible being the center of attention. If we were honest, I would've stared at her too, but only because the last thing I knew was that she was dead, and they were recovering her body. It was too bad these jerks didn't have a sense in those big heads of theirs. I leaned down and lifted her into my arms. She wrapped an arm around my neck. We turned. The group behind me spoke amongst themselves as we rushed out of the area.

Now in my arms, I could feel how thin she had gotten. God knows what she had gone through in that facility. Now in my arms, she weighed practically nothing. Her waist had dwindled—every body part thin, almost brittle. I was afraid to squeeze her. If I did, I was sure that I'd break her. Physically we were very fit. She may feel light and fragile, but I knew better than to think she wasn't capable. Seaa had survived the outside world longer than I had and was living proof that she had nerves of steel to withstand whatever Braggart dished out.

It only took me seconds to get us into her bedroom beside Hail's. I gently placed her on the bed. Once I knew she was safe from prying eyes, I ran back and locked the side door. A knock filled the air as I approached the main door to her room. Twisting the lock closed, I turned to stare at Seaa, who had tears streaming down her face. We both knew it was Hail, but I wouldn't open the door unless she asked me to. When she shook her head, I walked away and left him to his own assumption.

I knelt on the stone floor before her bed. "Seaa, what the hell happened to you?"

She visibly shuddered. "I don't know, Silk. It just happened. One minute I was angry and confused, and then it got hot, and this..." —she pointed to her tail— "happened to me."

It's not what I meant, but I let her control the conversation. After she vented, I'd get to the subject that most interested me.

She's alive.

"Can you turn it back? Does it hurt?" I stared at her exquisite tail, unable to ask anything else at the moment.

It was riveting. No one person could imitate the way her colors flowed together. The shimmer in each polychromatic cerulean, periwinkle, and rose-colored scale glittered under the neon lights of her room. Her fish swam to the edge of their fish tank, watching us from their spot on the dresser. Their perusal riveted me. The neon fish watched Seaa as men and women watched me when my pheromones gob smacked them. Why did I get the mob of puppets? I stared at the magnificent colors in her tail. The swirls of her fins almost curling outward.

Seaa lifted my chin, staring into my eyes. "A-are you envious?"

I smiled, shaking my head as I moved away from her hand. "I can't hide anything from you now, can I?"

Seaa snickered. The sound so melodic it was like a fairy. "You are the leader in hiding things in this facility, Silk. But when something really does fascinate you, then you look like a young child seeing something beautiful for the first time."

I grinned, turning around with my back to her bed. The stone floor felt cold underneath my rear as I sat back and stared at her bedroom. Seaa had loads of little lights strung around her room. The glowing fish tank on one end with neon green, pink, and orange fishes kept staring in her direction. I gave my sister a side-eye. I was envious of Seaa. She didn't see how gorgeous she was. How she drew people (and fish) to her and how badly I pushed people away.

My thoughts went back to my original question. "Seaa, you're alive."

I heard her run a hand down the scales of her new tail. "Yes, Rome saved me."

Shocked, I twisted my body to face her so quickly I almost snapped my bones. "What do you mean?"

Seaa took a deep, calming breath. "Rome made sure that the soldiers taking my body to Alpha didn't get far. He brought me back to Safe Haven, and when I awoke from the medicine that put me under, he was the one with the foresight to shove me in the Hydro-chamber before I suffocated to death."

There's been so much going on that I tried to process this new information as best I could. The last time I was here, we were in a meeting discussing how to bring Seaa's body back. We all thought she had died there. Who put her under? What did she mean?

"I'm so lost."

Seaa ran her hand down my unruly curls. "Rome's friend Zane injected me with a drug that imitates death. He pretended to kill me to get me out."

I grabbed her hand, seeing that her long fingernails matched the colors on her scales for the first time. "And Rayne?"

She shook her head. "He couldn't with her, but he did it to take the pressure off her." She cleared her throat when it cracked. "They used me to break Rayne." Hearing her words made my heart tighten. I closed my eyes, preventing myself from breaking down. Having her again brought me much-needed peace, mostly when I felt so stressed out about everything.

"I'm so glad your back with us, Seaa. I really am."

She leaned over to place a wild curl behind my ear. "Me too, Silk."

Unfortunately, the sadness on her face told me differently. Why did I feel like she would've preferred to have died than come back to us? Seaa always hid away around New States, studying and researching—trying to find a way to bring Hail home. I didn't know if she paid much attention to the goals she claimed to make or if she preferred to stay away from us. It wasn't hard to see that she had fallen in love with a man who might not love her back. It also wasn't too hard to point out that her anomalies made her uncomfortable. If only she knew I'd trade her any day.

I pointed to her tail. "Is this from Foxtrot?"

She shook her head. Her long, colorful waves swayed with the movement. "I don't think so. The only thing they did to me was try to control me with this new drug, but it didn't work on me. They resorted to torture and a new cocktail instead to break Hail and probably Rayne."

When she mentioned Rayne, my entire insides solidified. My chest shook as I took in a large lungful of air. "Yeah, I noticed."

"You noticed?"

She seemed puzzled for a second before her violet eyes went wide. "You saw her, didn't you?"

I nodded. "We need to all talk, but not before your—" I pointed to her tail "—legs normalize."

She laughed. "Silk, this is a lot more important right now than me. I can handle this. It doesn't bother me, and the choker allows me to get my nutrients. Granted, I feel a little dry and prefer to be in the water right now, but this doesn't hurt me. Let's get the group together. You can tell us what you know."

BY THE TIME I got into the Planning Room with Seaa in my arms, all of the Safe Haven residents had sat or stood in their usual spots around the room. The most out of place event happened when Rome and Hail both came forward to grab Seaa from my arms. The guys both looked at each other, about ready to rip each other's throat out. They had no idea I was almost ready to do it myself. How in the world could this scenario be happening again?

I remembered how not too long ago, Rayne got a cut from a spring on the old couch by the edge. Both males had run over to check on her. Both of them coddled her. Rayne smacked them both away then. I stared at both men now, trying to gauge their intentions.

Hail cared for Seaa like a sister, but the bond between her and Rome had grown during my time away. She idolized him, and he felt protective of her. There weren't any romantic feelings involved. He well and truly wanted to make sure she was safe. I studied Hail's eyes, which were a cross between gray and azure.

Hmm. So does Hail, it seems.

I put my foot down before a fight occurred. "Both of you better back up now, or I'll hurt you both," I growled through my teeth.

Rome and Hail simultaneously put their hands up in surrender.

Seaa patted my back, so I stared down at her. "Leave

me with Rome, Silk. Don't worry. He won't hurt me."

Oh, sweet sister. I know he won't.

Rome walked forward a tad as if asking for permission this time. I clenched my jaw. With one swift nod, I moved my arms to place her into his. He carried Seaa with no problem. I stared at him for a long time. Maybe I waited to see if he'd cringe or look disgusted by her mermaid form, but he didn't. He fitted her snuggly to his chest while Hail watched in pain. I don't know when it happened, but their friendship had changed at some point.

Maybe it was bound to happen, or it appeared after she returned, but their animosity toward one another wasn't all there anymore. Seaa didn't even look back at Hail. It was as if she was mad at him for something he had or hadn't done. I studied the smooth rock under my feet. I shouldn't even dwell on it. So long as Seaa was safe and content, I would be too. Rome stood near the wall in the back. Seaa was perfectly alright in his arms. She also didn't seem to be as uncomfortable as I thought she'd be.

With those two, their relationship changed when he saved her life.

Maybe he isn't as horrible as I make him out to be.

Thunder caught my attention when he cleared his throat. I turned to stare at everyone in the room, only then realizing that I spaced out for a bit. Rock was in the far back of the place, with Beatrice sitting on his knee. His nose had healed as it did with all of us. Punching these guys had become a form of stress relief. Cameron wasn't in the room, but Suzanne sat in a chair, alone. She became my first priority.

"Why is she here? This place isn't for everybody. Whoever may be looking for her can eventually trace her here, and then we're all sitting ducks."

Thunder sighed. "Listen, Silk, that is a conversation I prefer Cam to be awake for, so please refrain from questioning Suzanne and tell us what went wrong on your mission to help Gavin Foxhand."

Gavin looked up from his seat on the old couch—the spot that Rayne usually sat on. He stared at me and then at the rest of the group. Before I answered, he did.

"We were attacked in the apartment."

I nodded to confirm it with the rest of the group.

"Do you know by who, Silk? Was it Unit 13?" I heard Snow ask from his perch on a chair.

I walked closer to the large table. "No. These were regular humans. Mercenaries, maybe."

Thunder watched Gavin's reaction, but he didn't even blink. The twenty-year-old was not acting like himself. In situations like this, he was usually uncomfortable, especially with confrontation of any kind. "Gavin, did you know them?" Thunder asked him.

Gavin shook his head. "No, I didn't." It was as if the fight with the mercenaries had changed him.

Thunder turned to me. "Silk, what can you divulge about them?"

"The group was tactical and very well prepared. If I weren't there, Gavin would be in their possession. Now, their leader Viktor isn't solely human. He seems more."

"Super-soldier?" Guy asked.

I placed my palm on the surface of the wood. "He

smelled off, but not one-hundred-percent enhanced. At least, he doesn't have the same Herculean cocktail running through his blood we all do." I got lost, staring at the large pendant lights that hung from the ceiling while in thought. "He doesn't have super speed, and if he did, he didn't use it. I'm not sure about strength either, but he can definitely track. He sniffed Gavin out and heard me on a perch far from his location."

"Damnit!"

We all studied Rome. He showed no signs of wear holding Seaa. His points with me increased. "What do you know, Rome?" I questioned.

He shook his head and cracked his neck. "Viktor is Dr. Plumboy's nephew." The whole room remained silent. Seaa watched him from her position in his arms. "You mentioned Viktor, but I didn't put two and two together 'til you spoke of abilities. Do you remember when I told you guys about making sure nothing gets into Alpha?"

I did recall that conversation. Rome had mentioned that we must ensure grabbing Seaa's body beforehand because we could never make it back out of Alpha in one piece. He didn't say precisely what he meant. None of us ever remembered being inside of Alpha, even though we were sure Seaa and Hail had been taken there for implantation.

"Alpha was Foxtrot's joke of a house of horrors."

"What do you mean by that?" someone asked from the other side of the room.

I didn't catch who said it because terror ran through my veins. Viktor had fangs. He may not be exactly like us, but he was genetically superior. That meant that

Alpha was a testing ground for General Braggart and his military.

Rome sighed again. "General Braggart let Dr. Plumboy play with his own versions of the Herculean Cocktail before finally getting the correct chemicals after Dr. Lester died. Viktor and a few others became guinea pigs. All 1 can say is that Alpha's residents aren't all human. Or at least they weren't. Braggart made sure to clean up that mess before trying to clean up Batch 001. We all joked around that the wails of creatures in that facility could still be heard. We weren't allowed access to Alpha. I've never stepped foot past the Receiving Station beyond the gate. And those walls were too thick to listen through."

It meant exactly as 1 thought. There were more of us, and from the sound of it, some more beast than human. Braggart may have thought he got rid of the genetic experimentations, but it was clear to me that there was more to Alpha than meets the eye.

Alpha *was* the house of horrors, and this time, Braggart wasn't its only ringleader.

CHAPTER TEN

Sector Foxtrot
Unit 13 Headquarters
Operative Rayne – ID: PH064.001

MY BODY JOLTED from the cot inside the medical lab within Foxtrot. The inside of this room brought a cold sweat down my back. Technicians and doctors milled about doing one job or another. Not wanting to spend another minute here, I ripped out the IV line buried in my skin and yanked off the electrodes attached at different points on my body. The machines beeped incessantly. Doctors and their nurses noticed I had awakened, moving toward me at a swift pace. Some tried to stop me from moving while the others took heed of the drawn brows and pursed lips.

I hated this lab.

I hated it even more that one of the fugitive genetics had landed me here.

"Move."

They didn't even question me, preferring to stay alive. A fresh pair of clothes lay on a chair by the cot. Finding it necessary to remove the medical gown, I changed into the borrowed clothes and burst through the slightly open door. Trevor Dallas stood with a booted foot against the wall, his arms crossed.

He grinned as he said, "The boss didn't like finding out you had your ass handed to you by a first batch freak."

The blood flowing through me burned hot. Instead of heading toward my room, I stood toe to toe with the cowboy wannabe. "First of all, I happen to be one of those freaks, cowboy. Second, I've landed you on your ass several times already, and lastly, I had taken Cameron down before Silk showed up." I leaned in closer, taking in the smell of his cheap-ass cologne. "Besides, where the hell were you when she knocked me out? Were you too scared to face her on your own?"

Trevor gritted his teeth; his jaw was taut. I studied his body language, grinning when I hit the nail right on the head. "You were scared, weren't you? Did Silk beat you so badly that you ran for your pathetic life?"

He pushed away from the wall. The drastic move pushed me back slightly, but I didn't back down.

"I'm not scared of anything, little girl. I know when to make a tactical retreat to prevent unnecessary loss. Not something you know how to do, Operative Rayne.

If it weren't for my forces, you would've died in those tunnels."

The anger boiled and festered, but there was nothing I could say to that. I could have died in the subway tunnels after Silk shot me. Opening myself to that type of attack meant that I needed to train harder. I couldn't fail the general.

I couldn't fail my father.

Sector Bravo
Safe Haven Headquarters

AFTER ROME'S SUGGESTION, the room refused to quiet down upon hearing that the mercenaries' leader trying to grab Gavin was: a) Dr. Plumboy's nephew, and b) an experiment from Alpha. According to their records, the most confusing part was that Viktor Veracruz had died after the experimentation in Alpha— terminated by Braggart to clean up his dirty mess. For me to have spotted him very much alive and well, it meant that he either broke out from Alpha without getting caught or someone on the inside released him.

Whatever the reason, gaining that kind of knowledge might be very beneficial to this new plan put in place during my time away.

The Rayne Project.

With only a brief explanation from Seaa, I agreed that fighting back was the best thing we could do right now. We'd hidden away for far too long. It was about time we brought the fight to him. And not just to him, but to all of New States. They sat around, oblivious to the happenings beyond their comfort bubble. Knowing that there are more of us out there and fighting against Ground Force and government immorality, we might finally bring perspective. I hated that we were making our presence felt and had to do it under Thunder's command.

I didn't know if I could trust him.

Thunder sat in his chair, listening to everyone talk at once. I saw him there, and that hatred for what he'd hidden all these years rose to the surface. Remembering how Rayne looked as she beat Cameron close to death, the way she almost choked out Gavin, and how she fought me made me clench my fists at my sides. Deep breathing kept me put. Everyone trusted Thunder, but he had let us down. He had let all of us down. I worked to ignore the shaking anger buried in my bones. Thunder smiled at something someone said, and I broke.

My sanity snapped.

The raging anger within me took me over the table and on top of Thunder. I heard gasps from the rest of the group as one clenched fist slammed into Thunder's face. His hands held on to my waist, but he didn't move me as I beat him over and over again.

"If we knew about Rayne earlier, we could've prevented all of this," I yelled as I punched him once more in the nose.

Yet another fist made contact with his cheek. "She wouldn't be in this hell!"

I felt hands wrapping around my arms, trying to

jerk me off of Thunder's lap. I yanked them down to the ground. The two holding me flew over one another, landing on the others.

"You don't understand how painful it is to see what she has become," I cried.

Strong arms banded around my waist, lifting me off Thunder. I worked my body around to hurt the person holding me when I realized it was Gavin; fresh tears rolled down his face. His baby blues with a hint of green in them comforted me in a way nothing else could. Behind those pained eyes were trust and understanding. His arms didn't let go. The strength in them reassuring me that he was on my side.

"It's okay, Silk. You're allowed to be angry right now."

He stopped looking at me. Instead, focusing his attention on our leader, who stayed sprawled on the floor, staring back at us—blood covering his face. I could feel the heat of his hand splayed over my stomach. It made the butterflies flutter freely. "Rayne is under Braggart's control," he began. "She almost killed Cameron, me, and she went for Silk with an unbridled vengeance. There was no recognition on her face. She cared for no one."

Before I gave away the pain I felt stirring deep inside, I pulled Gavin's arms from my waist and stomped out of the Planning Room as loudly as I could. Chairs flew to one wall, and the large round table we had used for several years slid to another wall, crashing and splintering into little pieces.

I hated that damn table.

Sector Bravo
Safe Haven Headquarters
Gavin Foxhand
New States Citizen ID: CH.3349.GF-Rank A

THE BROTHERS CAME around to help Thunder off the floor while I stared in the direction Silk had disappeared. The delicate woman was falling apart, and none of them had a clue how close she was to breaking—splintering off into little pieces. Thunder was off the floor. Beatrice had come around with a wet rag to help him clean off his face. Her long wavy hair rolled over one shoulder. Everyone stared at the doorway. Miraculously, no one made much of a sound.

Roman Braggart and Seaa were having a conversation with their eyes, both taking glances at the door the woman I cared about had walked through. The new woman, Suzanne, had no expression on her face. She interlocked her hands together over her belly. She didn't move from her chair—only listened. As soon as I could get all the parts to fix up my KeViewer, I'd make sure to look into her thoroughly.

Clearing away the hacker in me, I studied the room once more. Rock seemed preoccupied as he watched his woman blot the blood off of the leader's face. Guy and Snow stared at one another and promptly burst out laughing. Taken back a couple of feet, I watched with narrowed eyes as they slapped each other on the shoulder. How could they be so cavalier about what had happened here just now? Afterward, when they released their pent-up frustrations, the guys all turned and stared at me.

"What the hell is your problem?" I asked them.

The majority grinned. The warriors' behavior confused me and enraged me all at the same time. My fists clenched, the righteous anger for Silk's feelings rushing through me like boiling water. Thunder sat down on the chair he had picked up from the floor, curiously watching me. He said nothing. The first to speak was Guy.

"Everyone else saw what I did, right?"

The three gave a stiff nod. "I'm so damn surprised I'm not sure what to do with myself."

Seeing Silk beat the crap out of their leader made them laugh from *surprise*? What the hell was going on with these men? I chanced a look at Rome, but he was walking out of the room with Seaa in his arms. The shock had already left their faces. His entire posture reflected defeat. He wasn't the same man I had met almost a week ago. Roman Braggart was breaking faster than Silk. I turned to look at the men in front of me.

"If you're so damn surprised, then why the laughter? You guys have no idea what the hell that woman has gone through."

Thunder replied, "Clearly."

I grimaced. "Seriously?" My fingers went toward the bridge of my nose out of habit. I remembered I didn't have my glasses on, so I dropped them.

Thunder shook his head with a ghost of a smile on his lips. He stood from the chair, placing a large hand on my shoulder. I naturally flinched but hoped he didn't notice. Not even using his strength, the man was imposing to look at—the feel of his hand heavy.

"I see you don't understand our shock, Mr. Foxhand. We weren't surprised to watch Silk's angry tirade. No, we were more surprised at the fact that she allowed herself to be held by you, and you're still alive after it."

What the fuck?

His words seemed like a punch to the gut. I took a couple of steps back, staring at the smooth stone under my feet. Silk hadn't yelled at me. She hadn't threatened to kill me this time either. The woman I cared about was finally letting me in.

My eyes came off the floor to seek the exit Silk had taken. A hand went to brush back my loose strands—a nervous gesture Silk hated with a passion. I dropped the hand instead. I wouldn't do anything to upset her. She didn't realize my feelings for her were genuine. She may be used to men falling all over her because of her ability, but I had spent four days in this bunker with her power at full blast and didn't go crazy as Guy had. That meant my feelings for her were real. I know I didn't care about her as a sister—like a majority in this hideout did. I had real feelings for her.

Real feelings for the woman with more secrets than the country.

I ignored the men and walked out of the Planning Room. But not before taking one last look at the dilapidated table. I know I wasn't the only one who thought it was a miracle that the table had lasted as long as it did. It was bound to go at one point or another. The hallways were empty. I went to Silk's room and knocked on the door. No answer.

Maybe she's not here.

I checked the mess hall. Nothing. I asked those I saw, and still, no one had answers for me. I spotted Suzanne walking out of the clinic with Beatrice's assistance.

"Beatrice, do you know where Silk might be?"

She didn't say anything but pointed to the door of the clinic. Suzanne didn't even register me. I put a hand up to acknowledge her help and walked through the medical lab's metal door. Inside I found Silk. She sat in a metal chair by the hovering steel table where Cameron lay healing. There were tears in her eyes, and it broke my heart. I felt the pressure squeeze behind my chest and shatter into a billion pieces. I didn't know what relationship they had, but whatever it was wasn't mutual. Cameron lived with Suzanne. The consensus around the facility was that Cameron hated being around Silk, so he went to live with his lover.

To see her so upset about his injuries made me angry.

"Why are you in here?"

She swung her head to face me. The curls on her head swirled with the movement. Silk didn't look sad anymore. She was pissed off.

"My being in here has nothing to do with you, Gavin." She pointed a slim finger to the door behind me. "You found your way in, now find your way out."

I gestured to Cameron. "Are you in love with him?"

Silk flew off of the chair so quickly it slid back and slammed against a medical table full of supplies—the items cascaded off the sides.

"What the hell did you just say?"

To anyone else, she'd spark fear—a fear so deep it shook our bones long after it was gone. But I'd been through enough with her not to be scared of it anymore. "You heard the question, Silk. Are you in love with him?"

She took measured steps to where I stood. I didn't back down. I watched as she approached and could only feel warmth at her nearness.

"I don't *love*, Gavin. I have no emotions for men, whether it is Thunder, Cameron, or you. No man deserves a piece of my heart."

A sharp pain burst inside of me. Not for her words toward me, but for the pain she felt deep inside of her. The secrets she kept to herself that no one in this place knew. My job was to find things out that others didn't want the world to see. That basis applied to this moment as well. I wanted to know everything about her: the good, the bad, the ugly. The only thing I wanted was for Silk to confide in someone—even if it wasn't me.

She was probably right. No man deserved her heart. But if she would give me a chance, I'd show her what true affections were, and I'd never intentionally set out to hurt her. She wasn't just alluring on the outside. There was real kindness inside of her. Sometimes I felt as if it was as innocent as a child, especially with how she set out to protect her sister from the hoard of curious onlookers.

In her eyes, there was a genuine intrigue. I could see how she cuddled her sister and admired her abnormalities. If we would only watch Silk's eyes when she looked at Seaa, we could see how much of a "girl" she wanted to be. She loved the colors. We called her the black widow when she was way more than that and hid it from everyone in this facility.

Everyone but me.

I shook my head. "You're right, Silk. I'm sure no man deserves your heart, but I wish I knew why. I wish I knew why you push us away when you secretly want us near." I gestured to Cameron again.

Silk stared at me with the most prominent, darkest eyes I'd ever seen in my life. They reflected the eyes of a wounded animal. Her nostrils flared. I knew the moment was coming, but I didn't prepare for it in time. Silk snarled in the most feminine way possible. Her hands made contact with my chest, pushing me away from her. I couldn't describe the feeling, it hurt so much, but I could equate it to a double paddle defibrillator on its highest voltage.

The strength of the blow landed me against the door. Sharp pain exploded from my back and head and all through my limbs. I couldn't breathe out or in. My eyes blinked as I watched remorse cross those pleasing dark eyes before the darkness took me down.

CHAPTER ELEVEN

Sector Bravo
Safe Haven Headquarters

THE SIGHT OF him crumpled on the white tile floor of the clinic undid me. It felt as if tons of weight from our gym had slammed into my chest crushing my ribcage. Dropping to my knees, I gingerly observed Gavin for any significant injuries and slowly slid him away from the door. I laid his head on my bent knees, brushing back the hair from his closed eyes. Bile sat like a solid lump in my throat—my chest heavy. Dr. Ferdinand was in the room next door and came running out when he heard the crash. My fingers shook.

"Silk, don't move him."

It was already too late for that. Fear must've been evident in my wide eyes so much that the older doctor had to pat my shoulder and console me. I watched Dr. Ferdinand as he joined me on the shiny floor with his equipment in hand. Gavin didn't move. What if I had killed him? What if I had broken his back? Gavin wasn't like my brothers or the super soldiers in Project Hercules. He was human. Average. My body didn't stop shaking. I reached out beyond the ringing in my ears and heard Gavin's heart thump steadily. At least he wasn't dead.

I watched Dr. Ferdinand checking Gavin. I swayed back and forth, unintentionally rocking Gavin's head in my lap. A groan from the steel table caught my attention. Dr. Ferdinand studied Cameron from his spot on the floor and then Gavin and me. "I'll take care of it, Silk. Go check on Cameron for me."

I debated whether I wanted to move but knew arguing with Dr. Ferdinand would bring up more questions than I dared to answer. Knowing the young man was in good hands, I gently placed his head down. After pushing myself off the floor, my body gravitated toward the floating table.

My fingers couldn't stop shaking. A single line of tears fell from one eye. I could've killed Gavin. My issues could've hurt an innocent man. Cameron opened his eyes, staring straight at me. He lifted a hand from his side to wipe the wetness from my face. At that moment, I heard movement and turned to see Gavin was off the floor and staring straight at me. The pain reflected in his eyes took my breath away.

"Mr. Foxhand, please, I need to make sure you are

not concussed."

Gavin helped the doctor from the floor with a brief smile. Not a genuinely happy smile, but one meant to ease the weak doctor's nerves. He glared back at me and down to Cameron's hand, now enveloping mine. Gavin studied the floor, ran a hand through his hair, and stopped. He stared at his hand as if it had done something he hadn't authorized. That was my fault too, because I made him question his movements. I was a walking enigma—a pariah—a curse. He didn't look back at me. Instead, he walked out the door without a second glance.

I clenched my fist, torn between staying and running after him.

"Silk?"

Cameron's voice filtered through my indecision. "Yeah, how are you feeling?"

I cautiously pulled my free hand away from him. He moved around as if giving himself a thorough body check. "I feel like a building fell on me." He flinched when he twisted his waist. "Two buildings."

He bent at the waist, the crisp, white sheet falling off his bare chest. "Enlighten me. That beast beating the shit out of me was Rayne, right?"

I nodded.

He shook his head, sliding his legs off the table. "Damn. Was she always that strong?"

I shrugged. Doing so made me think of Gavin, the corners of my mouth pulled down.

Cameron dropped to the floor, holding nothing but the sheet to cover his male parts. Turning around and acting coy was not in my genetics. I stared, unabashed, as he moved around the room to put some clothes on.

The doctor must've come back in because he chortled, running over to check on Cameron. I turned to the older man. "Dr. Ferdinand, were you able to catch up with Gavin?"

He shook his head as he followed Cameron around the room with his stethoscope in hand, trying to get a reading on his heart and lungs. If he would've only asked one of us, we could've told him everything was in working order. As it was, Dr. Ferdinand was human and a doctor to boot. It was in his nature to make sure. Cam was never one to stop and wait. He moved, and the older man followed.

"Gavin walked out of the hideout."

I froze. Gavin couldn't pull the same crap Rayne had. Letting her go to give her breathing space had been a mistake. Not one I was willing to make again. I turned to leave the room when Cam stopped me.

"Silk, we need to talk."

I yanked the hand he put on my arm, twisting it within my palm. He blanched but didn't pull it away. "Where are you going?"

"That's none of your concern," I uttered through clenched teeth, pushing away his hand.

"Silk, Suzanne's here. I need to talk to you about her. About everything that is going on and what brought me back."

I clenched my fists, about ready to punch him. "I know she's here. I've seen her, and she's not my concern, Cameron. She's yours. My priority is to keep the man that walked out of here safe."

He pointed to the door. "You mean before or after

you beat the shit out of him?" Cameron joked.

The fury I felt all over managed to gather in my fist. I punched Cam so hard he flew over the steel table and onto the floor on the other side. Dr. Ferdinand gasped, running to Cam's postern. He spat blood out on the floor. "See, this is the reason why I told Thunder you're not yet prepared to take on a mission." He then sought my eyes, his much more gentle. "Why I had to leave this place when all I ever wanted to do was stay."

That infuriated me further. *Is Cam blaming me for him leaving?*

"You only know how to hurt people, Silk. You don't know when to pull your punches." He pointed at the door. "When I woke up, that boy was practically comatose on the floor, and I'm pretty damn sure it was you who put him there."

Instead of taking his bait, I smiled pretty and went to walk out of the door. "I don't need to explain a damn thing to you. You weren't awake for the conversation that landed him there because *you* were comatose for the past two days."

"Two days?" Cameron swiped a hand over his bloody mouth. "Shit!" He ran around the table. "We need to move quickly." He rubbed his backside. "Damn, I think you broke my ass."

He grabbed my hand and rushed out of the room without giving me a second to pull back. Our immense speed brought us into the mess hall, where the rest of the group was sitting around trying to eat something. Seaa sat next to Hail, back in her leg form.

"We need to move quickly."

The entire group got up from their seats, staring at both of us. I yanked my hand from Cam's grip. The longer Gavin was out of my sight or hearing, the worse it might be for him. I was about to walk out when Cam said, "I was attacked by a beast-like man in Suzanne's loft."

My head shot up. Everyone remained quiet as if one sound would stop him from talking.

"Is everyone already in here?" He looked around the room.

I had already noticed that the only people not in here were Rome and Thunder. Thinking of them physically manifested both men. They walked down the hall only to stop when they spotted Cameron standing by the mess hall entrance. With his massive size, they'd notice him before ever noticing me standing right beside him. Cam turned to them.

"Oh, good. Get in here, please."

Both men walked in without much of a fuss. Gavin was a concern for me, but before I could make my escape again, Cam grabbed my hand and hauled me inside. I pulled from his grip, slapping him with the back of my palm.

"Stop touching me!"

He shook his head. "This is not the time for all your combative attitude."

About ready to argue, Thunder put his hand up to get everyone's attention. "Listen up."

I moved away from Cam. He noticed but didn't say anything about it.

"As I mentioned before, Suzanne and I were attacked by a man-beast. He wasn't at all receptive or cognitive, so he wasn't all human. The creature was powerful and controlled by a collar on his neck. Every time someone sent a signal to it, I could hear the high-pitched tone. It enraged the beast, almost doubling the strength of his attacks. We almost didn't make it out alive."

Thunder spoke from his spot by the roaring fire. "Do we know where the signal came from?"

Suzanne spoke from her spot at the table. "We were able to gain possession of the collar, but we need a technical genius to play with it and see what they could find."

"Fuck! Gavin!"

Everyone turned to stare at me.

Gavin's hacking skills could get us into those collars in no time at all. He was really good at his job. During my days at his apartment, he did two jobs, and each one was to the customer's satisfaction. I also noticed him reject jobs that didn't sit morally well with him. He refused *a lot* of those. Gavin Foxhand didn't need his father's big money. The man did it all on his own and then used that money to make his equipment even better. But without Gavin here. This conversation would be moot.

"Yeah, where's Gavin," I heard Snow ask.

I grilled Cam with my eyes. "I've been trying to catch up with him for a while now, but someone keeps stopping my efforts."

"Who the hell is this Gavin guy? You mean the Fox-hand kid?"

The way he spoke about Gavin filled me with rage. My stomach clenched. "That guy is a genius hacker and the Foxhand heir. He's significant to our mission."

Cam crossed his arms. "Significant enough to almost disable him?"

The entire room turned red. It felt like lava was coursing through my veins. My muscles no longer belonged to me. I had no control over anything anymore. There were no thoughts in my mind. No matter how much I tried to put together coherent reasoning, nothing could stop the immense rage rushing through me like a whirlpool burying its victims at the bottom of the sea.

One minute I was standing far away from Cam, and the next, I awoke from the crimson-infused disorientation with Thunder's arm covered in white around my neck, pulling me away. Snow and Guy worked on pulling my arms from around Cameron's neck, and they, too, were covered in a dense web.

Suzanne screamed for me not to kill him from her spot at the long table. Rome wasn't in the room anymore, and Seaa had joined Rock at my waist covered in a thick spider's silk. They were all on me, and all had the same dumbfounded faces. I immediately let go of Cameron's collar, noting the mark of my hands around his veiny neck. The same web-like material covered my skin. Every piece of exposed skin and clothing had been replaced by a form-fitting suit that protected me from nape to toe. It wasn't entirely white like our image of a spider's web. Under the fluorescent lights, prismatic colors refracted from it, turning it into soft shades of a rainbow.

Cameron wheezed and coughed. He glared at me, but there was no real menace behind it. "I was almost killed by Rayne, Silk. I don't need to be brought down by you too."

I thought I heard him mutter something about "psycho strong women" under his breath.

Thunder fought with the silk on his hands. Every time he pulled it off one hand, the other would get stuck with it. Seaa helped remove the silk off of Rock. The other two rolled it around like a ball.

"I'm sorry, guys. I have no idea how this happened."

The men in the group blinked, confused I had apologized.

Seaa came forward, ignoring their shock. "Silk, I always thought you were made special. Dr. Lester had a plan with you, but no one knows what that might be." She should be the one talking. Her entire body changed into a resplendent mythological sea creature. I covered myself in a web.

"What makes you think that?" I pulled on the suit, but it didn't even budge from my body.

Seaa touched the silk gingerly. "The material feels tougher than carbon fiber. I wonder..." She pulled the gun from Rock's waist and aimed it at me. "Don't worry, Silk. I promise not to hit anything vital." She yelled out for Dr. Ferdinand's presence.

I felt my heart squeeze, but I trusted Seaa. For that matter, I believed all of them to an extent. I've wavered with Thunder's deceit, but I had confidence they wouldn't intentionally hurt me. I nodded. The guys moved back—none arguing with Seaa's idea. No one moved. No one breathed.

The gun went off. Seaa aimed for a neutral spot in my stomach where no vital organs could be affected.

Not like I had to worry. The bullet, made specifically for our genetically engineered batch, didn't even break through the fiber. I wore a silk version of a Kevlar suit. The bullet stuck to the material and dropped right after.

"I have no idea how I did this."

Seaa placed a cold hand on my cheek. "Silk, the moment your eyes glazed over, the thread came out of your skin and wrapped itself around you—protecting you." She pushed back a lock of my hair. "Your body reacted in self-defense. Let's say it was a protective instinct." She sighed as if coming to terms with her own freaky morph. "Kinda like mine."

I shook my head. "I've been in danger before and never did this." I tried to pull it off me again. "Your morphing was mesmerizing. I... I...feel like a freak show."

She laughed. "You weren't protecting yourself. Like it or not, little sis, but you were protective of Gavin."

I pulled away from her. "Stop speaking nonsense."

Seaa nodded. "Why don't you try pulling it back in. I got rid of the tail when I willed it back earlier. You can do it too."

Knowing full well I needed to get to Gavin, I did as she asked, and sure enough, the web retreated under my skin. I had never done anything this extreme before, but I didn't have time to process the crazy. The others gawked at me as if seeing me for the first time. One of the biggest peeves of mine was being the center of attention. The red that I saw had become a warning. If I wasn't protecting myself and was, in fact, protective of Gavin, could I make it come out again?

I nodded to Seaa and ran out of the room in search of Gavin. One of the small boats to the bunkers was missing, so I jumped into the cold water and swam to shore. The moment I made it to the rocky beach, I inhaled traces of Gavin. His smell was strong around the woodlands. Tree branches whipped around as I walked through. He wasn't in there and had made it to the edge of The Waste.

I rushed through The Waste to get to the town—following the scent of roses and old books—the moonlight's glow my only source of light in the darkness. The smell of years of decay slammed into me, but Gavin's scent was more pungent—imprinted in me on a deeper level than I wanted to admit. If something happened to Gavin, I wouldn't be able to forgive myself. My shaking hand wiped down my face. Why did it matter to me so much? I turned the corner, slamming into a smell I recognized.

Viktor.

CHAPTER TWELVE

Sector Bravo
Edge of Ashur
Former Southern Camp Territory
Seaa – ID: PH049.001

THE ENTIRE ROOM blew up with a conversation about Silk's new ability and that of my own. My sister and I were obviously going through something out of our control. Maybe that something was what caused the change or awakening of the new ability. Cameron argued with Thunder about finishing the issue presented to us, but my brother only shook his head. Thunder was never one to do things without the rest of us present to have a say in it. I was lucky to have gotten

The Rayne Project underway without Silk's presence. I put a hand up to shut them all up.

"I know we have loads to talk about, but we need to do it with Silk. Give her a minute, please." Thunder agreed, walking out of the mess hall. I searched for Rome.

While Silk went off to find Gavin, it didn't escape my notice that Rome had made his retreat from the mess hall. He had been on a consistent decline since my awakening. Losing Rayne had changed him somehow. It wasn't something I was used to seeing. Rome had always been Braggart's top soldier. His love affair with Rayne softened him. What we had tried to do for years, Rayne accomplished in the few days he chased her around. For some reason, I felt it was my job to keep him alive, at least until Rayne came back to her senses. I tracked Rome to the edge of Ashur, where the old military forces had set up camp to track us down. We knew the risks of being so close to the Southern Camp, but the group firmly believed that the best hiding spot was hiding in plain sight.

I stopped moving, ducking behind a few crates.

From this spot, I could see Rome standing in the center of what used to be their central convergence. He screamed at the top of his lungs repeatedly. Each shout twisted me up inside. The man had utterly lost it. Tears ran down his face. The veins in his neck exploded as if trying to run away from the protection of his taut skin. Rome resembled a broken child. I couldn't bear to see it anymore. I was about to leave the cover of the crates when I saw a familiar-looking cowboy walking up to Rome. More soldiers surrounded Rome from every exit. My legs shook as it became harder to breathe. Trevor Dallas wasn't the person I needed to see right now.

"Well, I'll be hot-damned."

Rome stared at the awful man. "Where is she, Trevor?"

He laughed. "I don't have to tell you shit, traitor." He grinned again. "Or should I say ghost?"

Rome ran a hand through his hair. "I'm obviously not dead."

Trevor Dallas nodded. "Yes, you're right. Not yet." He whistled and that's when Rome noticed he was completely surrounded.

"Trev, you have to know things aren't right with Project Hercules. Listen to me, man. None of us signed up for this kind of life. Braggart lied to all of us."

The cowboy didn't even bat an eyelash. After the endless rounds of torture I had endured by Trevor Dallas, it was easy to see that he enjoyed this life.

The next moment, Trevor and everyone else who had surrounded Rome shot their weapons. I saw Rome grit his teeth, clenching his jaw from screaming in pain. Amps of electricity rushed through him in large doses to subdue him. He glanced in my direction. While they beat him down, he took that moment to tell me with his eyes that he knew I was here and that he didn't want me to move—at least that's what I took from it. Rome wasn't too hard to figure out. One thing I knew for sure was that he would never allow someone else to get hurt on his behalf.

Rome took every beating, kick, and static blow. He bled from his lips and the cuts on his skin. The only thing he wanted was Rayne. If only I knew what that type of affection felt like. My love for Hail had always been one-sided. Hail wouldn't be out here screaming for the bad guys to come to kill him to find out about the woman he loved. Rome had achieved the goal he wanted. He needed to get their attention, and he got it. But dying wouldn't get him the answers he sought. Rayne would never know he loved her as much as he did if he let these bastards kill him.

Steeling myself for a fight, I turned to rush out of my hiding spot when my knees buckled—the group beating Rome senseless pulled away from him like a well-choreographed dance group. The man in a military beret and peculiar facial hair walked toward the injured Rome with one hand behind his back and the other curling the tip of his mustache. Bile rose from the depths of my stomach. I bit it back, praying from my little spot behind these crates that I could contain my bodily functions. If I retched right here, I'd immediately give up my location.

What the hell is Braggart doing out in the open?

I couldn't contain the quakes wracking my body. Tears fell from my eyes as reminders of my time in that facility rushed through my mind like photographs. I didn't feel pain anymore, but my body remembered every bit of it. My hands clenched around my belly, remembering how bad it felt when he cut me deeply and pressed in his fingers every time it tried to heal. Or when Trevor would beat me over and over again with a metal rod to see if fish bled red. The abuse could only be seen in the faint scars left behind after my body healed. The wounds, however, were permanently etched into my heart.

"I'm rather surprised to see that my son is still alive."

Rome tried to get up from the dirt, but his arms quivered. He dropped to the dusty ground, leaving a dust cloud in his wake.

"Well, no matter. We have loads of work to do, so let's see how well he does in the interrogation rooms."

Trevor belly laughed. Rome reached out to grab the cowboy's ankle, but one of the soldiers practically cattle prodded him with a military-grade taser. General Braggart turned to look when Trevor beat Rome in the head with his boot three times.

"W-where's Rayne?" he mumbled into the dirt.

Trevor lifted his foot to kick him again when Braggart's hand went up, stopping the cowboy from another punishment. "Rayne, you ask?"

Roman Braggart tried to lift his head to face his father. "Where is she?"

The general smiled, but there was nothing humorous about it. He whistled—a high-pitched shrill from between the gap in his teeth. The moment he did, a soldier came out of the shadows with long hair. She wore black military trousers and a tucked-in black tank-top. Although it was freezing outside, she wore nothing to keep herself warm. The look on her face held no warmth in it whatsoever. She seemed as cold as our surroundings.

"Rayne, your brother is asking about you."

Pyros could've put together a slew of fireworks and explosives to implode a building, but that weight wouldn't compare to the feeling weighing down on my chest and shoulders. I almost crumbled from its intensity. *Brother? Siblings? Is that why Braggart always had this unhealthy fixation with Rayne?* Not able to hold it back any longer, a whimper rushed past my lips. The noise didn't catch up to Trevor. However, it did reach Rayne's hearing. She turned quickly. I pushed my back against the crates and slapped a hand over my mouth. Seconds passed, and I felt her. She stood feet away from my hiding spot. I closed my eyes tightly.

I can't fight her. I can't do it.

I tried to control the shakes, all the while holding my breath.

"Didn't Braggart call for you?"

My lavender eyes shot open to see Zane standing right in front of me, preventing Rayne from moving forward anymore. There was a device in the hand behind his back that emitted a dull pitch. It made it harder for me to hear the conversation that was happening right in front of me.

"I didn't know you were up here."

He grinned.

I felt faint.

"That's my job. To stay unseen. Unheard."

She made a sound with her mouth. "Right."

Her presence disappeared. Zane didn't move his head to look at me, but he did acknowledge with his eyes that she was gone. He stayed put. I could finally inhale even though I didn't need to breathe to survive. I held my breath so no one could hear me. I turned slightly to look past the crates. Rome had passed out at some point. The men dragged him to their vehicle, leaving behind two lines in the dirt from his boots.

Rayne followed beside General Braggart. The doors opened and shut as they all disappeared from the abandoned camp.

Rayne was General Braggart's daughter.

She was the love of her life's sister.

I felt sick to my stomach and could no longer hold anything inside. My body retched over and over again beside the crates. It felt as if all my insides were trying to come out of my body. Zane's presence hung around me. He knelt beside me, holding back my multi-colored hair. When I finished, he handed me a clean, folded cloth.

"Seaa, why did he come back?"

My eyes sought his. "He left before anyone could stop him."

Zane sighed. "I had hoped he'd stay away, but I guess I didn't account for his feelings being so deep."

I shook my head. "He hasn't been the same since her capture."

He stood up from the ground. "The coast is clear." And he put a hand out to help me up. "This little box here is a gem for messing with our hearing."

I stared at the box as he threw it up in the air and caught it again. "Are those used to mask our proximity?"

"One of my hires uses it as a noise-canceling solution in the board rooms. I found that it blocks sounds that only we supers can hear. So, I took one to test it out." He studied me. "If I didn't have it on me right now, she would've picked up your heartbeat."

My deep breath quivered. Zane had saved me again. In need to change the subject, I openly searched the area they had vacated. "Zane, is it true?"

Zane groaned. "Unfortunately, yes. Rayne *is* General Braggart's daughter."

"He's not just lying to cause trouble?" I secretly hoped.

But before I even finished speaking, Zane was shaking his head in denial. "Nah, when he mentioned it a while back, there was this huge uproar in the facility. The general didn't need to prove anything to us, but Rayne seemed disturbed, so he confirmed the bloodwork right there in front of everyone. The girl is ninety-nine-point nine percent his kid."

"I knew there was some connection, but I'll tell you, I didn't think it was this." Zane stared at nothing in particular as I spoke. His being here right now with me was disconcerting. "By the way, why are you helping me? I thought the last time we got together you would've been killed for it."

He grinned, and I could see the set of sharp fangs in his mouth. "I'm a lot tougher than I look."

Zane's grin disappeared. There was a moment that I saw his ears move, and then his entire body vibrated and shifted. One minute I spoke to a live, breathing man, and the next, he was a large, ferocious cat, facing off with two outraged men. Thunder and Snow stood side by side. Sparks flew off Thunder's hands. His eyes shot lightning, a trait I didn't know he had. Snow had an arm folded by his chest with a blade sticking out, and in the other, he aimed his gun. The cheetah growled, positioning himself in front of me.

I laughed, and all three stared at me as if I had gone insane.

"First of all, put that away, guys. Secondly—" I shifted my eyes to stare at Zane's immense cat form "—you don't have to get defensive to protect me from my siblings. They wouldn't hurt me. Instead, you should've let me cover you. It would be the very least I could do for saving my life. Twice."

Thunder and Snow complied with only a few seconds of eye interchange.

Seconds later, Zane shifted back into his human form. "Before you ask, only two of us can shift into animal forms yet carry human traits."

Thunder and Snow looked at each other again. Snow mumbled. "Could that be the beast" —he pointed at Zane— "Cam was talkin' about?"

My brother grinned, acknowledging Snow's joke as he shook his head. Zane, all the while, watched their exchange as if wanting to trust Batch 001 and wanting to take them down. Thunder turned to Zane again.

"You and who else?" Thunder asked.

Zane lifted one side of his mouth. "Rome."

Snow slapped his knee, laughing. "Oh, I knew we smelled a cat in that man too, but I didn't realize he shifted."

Zane cracked his neck, rubbing the back of it with his palm. "Rome and I were tweaked. Unit 13 injected me before Rome, my cocktail a smidge different than his. When Braggart saw my physical abnormalities, he changed Rome's. You can't see his panther unless the man lets it out. I can change back and forth without effort. But if Rome shifts, his panther blood takes over. He's a pure predator. He can't control his actions, nor can he do anything to stop it."

"How do we get Rome and Rayne out of there?"

Snow added, "Yeah, can we do the same thing you did for Seaa?"

Zane shook his head. "No. I'm not allowed around the prisoners anymore. If they keep Rome there, I won't be allowed anywhere near him without getting caught. Braggart is watching me like a hawk."

I placed a hand on his forearm. "I can't thank you enough for getting me out of there."

He rubbed the back of his neck again, almost sheepish. "I hoped that by removing you from the equation, Rayne wouldn't crack under pressure. Unfortunately, the Mind Eraser wiped the slate clean."

"Is that what you guys call it?"

"It's not what the scientists call it, but it's what *we* do inside Foxtrot."

Zane pulled a crate free from the pile, sitting on top of it. The handsome man placed both elbows on his knees, using his fists to prop up his chin. He observed us.

"For what purpose do you help us?" Thunder asked.

"I'm no longer feeling patriotic. When my friend crossed sides, I knew that the real dark side wasn't with you guys but with Braggart's military. But with Rome inside, I can't leave quite yet." He got up from the crate.

Thunder nodded. "Very well. Please let us know if there is anything we can do on our end to retrieve our comrades."

The tall, dark-skinned man cracked his neck again as he stretched. "For right now, there isn't anything, but we'll meet right here in three days."

"Very well," Thunder replied. "I will meet you here myself."

"No funny business, asshole," Snow interjected.

"Snow!" both Thunder and I said at the same time.

Zane didn't even get flustered. "Trust me; if I wanted to catch you, I would've already." He wiped the backside of his jeans. "Right then, I'll see you here in three days." He turned to me. "Later, gorgeous."

Gorgeous?

I blinked a few times before Snow slapped me on the back, laughing as he walked away.

Ignoring my idiot brother, I moved to catch a glimpse of Zane. He moved so quickly; *we* had a hard time trying to pinpoint his location. Zane was faster than any of us. If he wanted to bring us down, he could've. His endearment floated to my mind once more. *Gorgeous.* No man had ever called me that. Was the super-soldier messing with me, or did he genuinely find me pretty? I shook my head to clear the petty thoughts. This wasn't the time.

"Thunder?"

He turned to look at me. I told him, "We have a huge problem."

Taking a deep breath, he said, "I'm sure I'll survive. What's on your mind?"

I didn't have a way to say this next line with tact. It was necessary to get it over with, like ripping a band-aid off. I sucked in a deep breath and told them what I had learned.

"Rayne's Braggart's real daughter."

The Thor-like man dropped to one knee.

CHAPTER THIRTEEN

Sector Bravo
Safe Haven Headquarters

SNOW AND SEAA rush into the bunkers with Thunder in their arms. They ran straight to the medical lab. The metal door slammed shut behind them. I came back to talk to Thunder, but something happened while I was gone. Why in the world was my brother unconscious? I ran to our small medical lab, pushing the door open. Dr. Ferdinand was already checking Thunder's vitals while Snow and Seaa watched from the sidelines. I'd never seen Thunder go down. He was the strongest of all of us. When he fought, there was no room for error. He had always come out of it unscathed.

"What the hell happened to him?" I rushed to the steel table. "What did you guys do?"

Snow was about to hold me back. The fury on my face left no room for argument. Instead, he dragged Seaa before me. A cheap ploy, but it worked.

"Silk, please. We don't know what's wrong, either. Let Dr. Ferdinand conduct his examinations." Her hands were up in surrender.

I stopped right before I plowed her over. "Where did you guys go?"

She twisted a strand of her hair around a slim finger. "I followed Rome, and the guys followed me."

I looked around the room. When Snow and Seaa came in, Rome wasn't with them. "Where is he?"

Seaa shook her head. "Rome's been taken. He gave himself up to find Rayne."

"That idiot," I raged.

"Will you please quiet down, Silk? I have a massive headache."

We turned to see that Thunder sat on the hovering metal, rubbing his head. Dr. Ferdinand extracted blood from his other arm. His features were paler than usual. The blond in his hair seemed dull—lifeless. Regardless of his stature and immense build, Thunder appeared smaller to me at the moment. Everyone was used to his imposing aura, so to see him like this made my chest tight.

It's not like I've made it any easier for him. I remembered my fight with him earlier. I rubbed my hands down my face. There was so much going on, and all stacked on top of each other. I've always let my anger out first, instead of processing the situation beforehand. For the people who loved me, I needed to do better. I just didn't know how to go about it.

"Thunder, what happened?"

He slid his legs off the side. "Silk." His hand sat comfortably on my shoulder nearest to him. "I am fine. Tired if nothing else."

I nodded. "When's the last time you slept well?"

Thunder stretched and rolled his shoulders. Snow watched him too, listening for his reply. Seaa swayed from foot to foot, anxious. There had been so many things falling on top of us the weight had become unbearable. We'd gained and lost Rayne all in the same breath. The attack on Gavin. Cam and Viktor's appearance. Seaa's tail. My silk barrier. Now we'd lost Rome to Unit 13—again. I didn't think any of us could handle anything else.

"Silk," Thunder began, "please get everyone into the Planning Room. Seaa has found out that Rayne is Braggart's daughter."

I felt my blood coagulate—my muscles close to rigor mortis. Other than the short intake of air, there was no other sound in the room. My mouth finally remembered how to move, so I asked, "Say again?" As if the first time he spoke, I could've misunderstood.

"Rayne is General Braggart's daughter. Rome's sister."

I shook my head in disbelief. "You must be fucking kidding me. What the hell, Thunder?"

Seaa stepped in right before my body leaped on its own toward Thunder. The joke wasn't funny. Snow took a step back in self-preservation.

"Please, Silk, I heard it myself and confirmed it with

Zane."

I slowly turned my head. "Zane?"

She nodded as if it all made sense. "He's Rome's friend. The man who saved me."

"You mean to tell me that you are basing these facts on Braggart's soldier?"

She seemed to deflate a bit, and I wasn't sure if it was because she wanted to trust the soldier or that I couldn't. "As a matter of fact, I *am* Silk. You have no idea what it's like on the inside of that place, to step onto the wrong side of the tracks. For that moment" —she straightened— "for that one freaking moment, one person came to my aid. One person helped me." Tears fell hard and fast from her eyes. "Imagine being locked in a dark room with nothing but your misery, and then out of the darkness comes a brilliant hand to lift you." She wiped away a tear. "Zane is that to me right now. I'm going to believe him. Even if it ends in my death, I choose to follow him."

Her words, so sincere, made my chest tighten. I grabbed her hands in mine. They were cold but soft. "Seaa, I'm sorry. I'm just going through so much right now." I looked up at Thunder, who watched us both. "Gavin was captured."

Thunder squeezed his temples with one hand— thumb and forefinger. "As if we didn't have enough on our plates. We can't get The Rayne Project off the ground without him."

I nodded. "I know. Let me find him. I can track Viktor down."

"Wait!" We all turned to Seaa. "We need to be in better contact with one another from here on out. No one is allowed to leave unless they are reachable by KeViewer."

We hardly ever used gadgetry because it could triangulate our location. But if it was time to bring out the reconnaissance kits, I would oblige. Thunder might be a different matter.

Thunder placed a hand on her shoulder. "We will figure it out," he stated. He turned to me. "Was there blood?"

I shook my head.

"Good. Then that means they need him alive."

"Do you think this Viktor guy is working for Braggart?" Snow interjected.

I shook my head again. "I don't think so. They seem more mercenary to me."

Snow and Seaa nodded, but she was lost in her mind. Without a word to any of us, Seaa walked out of the medical lab. We followed closely behind, unsure of her trail of thoughts. She walked down the stone hallway with determined steps. Her exquisite hair flowed around her head as she poked inside each common area—seeking, searching for something. We passed the mess-hall when what she sought wasn't inside. Snow and I shared the same puzzled look while Thunder's eyebrows creased in concern.

The inside of *Tutus Portus,* the Latin words for Safe Haven I used on the card I gave Rayne when we first met, used to be filled with calm energy, no matter the abundance of destruction and instability left on the outside for us. Now, we walked around with so much weight on our shoulders we questioned whether our bones were strong enough to withstand the pressure.

Did our super strength have a cutoff line we were close to crossing? Suddenly, Seaa stopped, and it took the right amount of our abilities to move around enough not to plow into each other. She walked into the Planning Room, so we followed.

Once inside, I cringed, seeing for the first time the mess I had left behind. The round table that had stood in the middle of the room lay in pieces by the metal wall. All I had done was push it away. I didn't realize that my anger may have caused more devastation inside our home, but the pain inside me had only grown more prominent for years. I stayed away from those I didn't trust and kept my heart safely tucked away where no man could reach it. It still didn't matter. Standing before me was a man I had once cared for who could never care for me—not in the way I needed. Granted, I was a stupid little girl who fell for all those fairytales her father told her about men on white steeds doing anything for the woman they loved.

It happened about a year before our escape.

Pops taught me that no man or woman in that facility was allowed to touch me inappropriately like they had done years before. With proper knowledge in mind and my powers under better control, I walked around the facility in less fear than I had when they'd touched me and follow me everywhere I went. The feel of their clammy fingers on my skin or the look on their face when they reached exposed skin repulsed me. I could feel their lust hit me like a tank and roll over me, over and over again, burying me with its weight and intensity. Afterward, I was left behind, battered, beaten, and bloody. My fear of their lack of humanity increased, encompassing me like a thick, impenetrable wall.

Until the day Cameron saved me.

No one in the facility knew about my powers but Pops. He told me never to expose them to anyone, so I didn't. Once I had better control of it, the advances slowed down, but they never fully extinguished. A male soldier had gone into The Garden as part of his patrol, spotting me by the small pergola covered in flowers. Seaa was there, as she always was, plucking flower petals and blowing them around us.

I didn't know why he got angry. I didn't know why most of them got mad around Seaa. They treated her crudely. Later, we realized Seaa scared them and disturbed them, all because of her slight deformities. None of that mattered to us. We loved her regardless of all her differences. Seaa had always been more beautiful than I could ever hope to be.

The soldier used the back of his hand to push Seaa away from me. He yelled obscenities, pointing at Seaa as he told her words that pierced her deeply. Pops warned us not to fight back. He didn't want to give General Braggart enough ammo to rid himself of our group. So, I sucked it in like I did every one of their transgressions. When he kicked her on her side was when I exploded. I grabbed the man's ankle when he came in for another kick on a small girl who had withered and curled into herself to escape the pain. The fury broke, and when it did, his ankle had snapped with it. He dropped to the ground, screaming in agony. By then, I had climbed over him, beating him to an inch of his life.

Another soldier had walked in then and attacked me with one of those damn tasers, and it was all I could do not to turn on him too. The pain inside of me had boiled over, and I saw nothing but their lives in my hands. The adrenaline within my blood burst like a firework. I leapt over the body lying on the floor and had almost landed on the other soldier with his high-pitched scream when Cameron caught me in mid-air. He held me tightly to him, cooing in my ear with soothing words Pops used on us all the time.

Pops walked into The Garden with General Brag-gart. When I came to my senses, I came to several re-alizations at once. One: I broke my promise to Pops. Two: I almost killed the man on the floor. Three: It was the first time I saw genuine fear on the faces of the people I cared about, and four: Cam came to my rescue. He didn't ride in on a white steed, but he did stop me from killing the two soldiers unlucky enough to have seen me break. I was the black widow. I was the woman who ate men who thought to fall for me.

That was all in the past.

Today, I stood beside the shards of a table we'd worked on for years and watched the man I cared about kneeling on the rock-hard ground between the legs of his lover. Suzanne sat on one of the unbroken chairs with one slender hand swallowed by Cameron's large ones. The other ran her fingers in his straight locks, pulling them away from his face. At one point in my life, it would've bothered me. Lately, my mind and heart had faced one thing too many to bear anything more.

She heard us come in and glanced over in our direction, not seeing us. Cam turned with her, immediately dropping her hand and standing from the ground. He grimaced when he saw me standing behind Seaa and Thunder. I smirked. Seeing them together no longer bothered me. I'd come to grasp that Cam had been a folly a little girl believed in. He wasn't my fairytale ending anymore. He belonged to Suzanne.

"Hey, guys." Cam shoved his hands into the pockets of his jeans. "What's going on?"

I snorted. Snow stared at both of us with a huge grin as if expecting us to get into another fight. Guy and Snow always sought a little action and took great pleasure in other's turmoil. I glared at him. He pretended not to notice. My beautiful big sister took to the spot Cam vacated, kneeling in front of Suzanne.

"Sue." She held the woman's hands in-between her own.

Suzanne faced Seaa, recognition crossing her features at the sound of her voice. "Seaa. We haven't chatted much. I'm sorry for everything you have gone through. I'm glad you came back to your family safely."

The smile Seaa sent Suzanne told a story I had yet to read. These two had a friendship of sorts when I had barely given the woman a second thought. Suzanne had saved my sister from real death. Her intel had brought us to Seaa. She got Seaa back home, whether it was in a body bag or not.

"Thanks to your *eyes*, Sue." Suzanne smiled.

I watched their little exchange while I felt Cam and Snow's eyes on me. It wasn't too hard to figure out why they watched me. They thought I would step in and cause a scene, but I didn't have it in me anymore. Seaa was a grown woman who made her choices based on the hand we had been dealt. Cam was also a grown man and did what he thought was best.

Even if it was to stay away from me.

Seaa rubbed Suzanne's hands, shrouded within hers. Suzanne didn't flinch. Not once did I notice her seemingly repulsed or disgusted by Seaa in any way. For that respect, I guess I could cut the woman a break. "Sue, we need to find Gavin. It seems a mercenary group may have abducted him."

"How can I help you?" she replied.

"We need to know if Gavin's father hired this group. If they are working together at all."

She seemed to contemplate Seaa's words. "Gregory Foxhand is Gavin's father, right?"

We all nodded, even though she could not see us.

"I can get my network to follow Foxhand to garner his routine. They would be able to tell me if something fishy is going on and if he's any if at all involved."

Seaa squeezed her hands. "Thank you."

I walked forward, turning to face Thunder. "Please, let me find Gavin."

"Are you nuts?" Cam yelled out. "You aren't capable of espionage, Silk. You are too damn hotheaded."

I could feel the heat he accused me of coursing through my body. With fists squeezed at my side, I thought of Gavin and how I owed it to him to find out his whereabouts. He was my responsibility, and I had ruined it. I would get him back. I *needed* to get him back.

"Thunder, he is my responsibility. I can track Viktor down myself. You can send a different team to Gregory Foxhand once Suzanne's network gets back to her. We'll coordinate. Please." I felt a number of emotions well up inside of me. I bit my lip, almost as if holding it back. "I need to find him," I whispered.

My brother nodded, placing one steady hand on my shoulder. "Go, Silk. Take Cameron with—"

"Cam? Why the hell Cam?" I cut in.

He squeezed tighter, silencing me from saying more. If Thunder was letting me go, I needed to shut my mouth and do as he said. "Yes, I understand."

Thunder nodded. "Good. I want Cameron and Silk to find Gavin Foxhand while Suzanne gets her network of people to place tabs on Gregory Foxhand. Once we have that intel, I want Seaa, Snow, and Rock over to Foxhand's with a plan to get in and a plan to get out." Thunder walked to Cameron, who watched over Suzanne as if trying to figure out how to leave her again.

"Do not fret over Suzanne." He placed a hand on Cameron's shoulder and one on Suzanne's. "She is safe here. No beast will come for her and no man either. Guy, Hail, and I will keep the base protected."

"I know," he replied.

"Good. Now, go ready yourselves. You leave tonight."

CHAPTER FOURTEEN

Sector Bravo
Bravo Antiquis Warehouse District

HAVING TO PROCESS and decipher all the scents surrounding me is stressful in itself and now made more difficult with Cameron hovering so close behind me. We walked within striking distance of one another, but neither of us spoke a word. 1 know he had loads to say from the way he looked sideways at me, but the stone-cold, fuck-off look 1 had on my face told him to keep his comments to himself. 1 didn't have time to mess around with Cameron. Gavin's wellbeing was my first and foremost priority.

Afterward, 1 could worry about Rayne and Cam and

everything else in-between.

Gavin, please be okay.

I sniffed the air, trying to eliminate all of the scents I didn't recognize and all of the scents I did. Viktor's fragrance grew smaller, diluting itself among the rest of the smells permeating the area. He was getting harder to track, and we weren't even out of Bravo Antiquis yet.

"I still have no clue what you are tracking, Silk."

As I climbed over a large, jagged rock, I stared at Cameron, watching as he sniffed the air like an animal. The bewildered look on his face left no room for misinterpretation. Cam couldn't pick up anything.

Exhaling loudly, I asked, "What are *you* picking up?"

His nose went back into the air, giving me a perfect side profile of his angular, Asian features. Cam had a long, veiny neck that was usually covered by his straight, black locks. He hardly ever brushed his hair, but it fell around his head as if he did. The rest of him was pretty standard for the genetically altered boys of Batch 001—tall, muscular, and incredibly full of himself.

"I'm gathering a lot of animal species."

I walked past another building that had deteriorated with time. Dead vines crept up one side. The glass that remained had yellowed. "That's Viktor. As I said, he smells like us, but there's something there that isn't quite Batch 001 or 002."

He tried again. "I've lost it."

Cameron had many heightened senses that we did, but because of his ability and having had more chameleon to his genetic coding, his sense of smell wasn't as strong as ours. His was pretty limited. "I'm switching from Viktor to one of his men."

"One of his what?"

"His men." I leapt from one high ridge down to the bottom without issue. Cam followed. "Baker's his name. I had him hostage for a bit to get some answers, so his scent is pretty much imprinted in my system. Viktor may be able to trick us with his cocktail mix, but Baker is all human."

Cam jumped over a rotting log, the smell momentarily nose-blinding me. "How did these guys come at you?"

I looked back at him as I answered. "Like a regular militant group. I sensed them before they hit the floor, and once they did, they opened fire on the front door guards. Everything just went by quickly."

We moved in silence again, but it was nice to have a conversation for once that didn't involve us at each other's throats. The attraction I used to have made Cam the only singular person in my vision. The sun and moon rose and fell with Cameron. Probably why we fought so much; I couldn't control those volatile feelings. I felt dirty for having them when I should've embraced them instead. He never did wrong to me, but I took out the entirety of my hatred on him and the others.

We entered The Waste. Here, the people loitering around minimized, and the destruction maxed out. Baker's smell intensified, so I moved through the rubble with renewed purpose. The men had a few hours on me. Viktor may not be entirely human, but he advanced at the same pace humans did. I wouldn't charge in without a plan, but I was going to get to Gavin as fast as I possibly could.

I ran. Cam didn't have a problem catching up as we moved around debris and jumped over concrete boulders. I only had one goal in mind. Nothing was going to get in the way or stop me from achieving it. The mistakes of the past wouldn't haunt me in the future. Finding Gavin and bringing him back safely was the first step in breaking the cycle I'd been bound to for so long.

Thunder ripped through the cloudy sky above us as if an omen of what was to come.

The Waste
Red Line Subterranean System

THE NIGHT GAVE way to morning, giving way to the midday hustle inside the red line subway tunnels. Bodies pulsed in various directions as Cam and I pushed through, trying to keep our wits about us. The smells in the pits were poison to humans. To us, they were entirely toxic. More than once, I had to stop and regroup because Baker's smell would elude me. I believed Viktor knew precisely what he was doing by making it down here. But he was mistaken if he thought he could make it out of here with Gavin, unscathed.

My body hummed with energy the closer we got. I could almost feel Gavin near. It wouldn't be long now. The many tunnels in the subterranean system wouldn't scare me away. They couldn't.

In the time of the running subway system, the red tunnels were long, with many stops in-between. Although Charlie was habitable, the other end of the red line was not. Down by Ashmont and Braintree, dilapidated buildings, homes, and businesses had disappeared entirely. There wasn't a foundation leftover to decipher where a building had stood. Everything on that side of New States had been vaporized by nuclear weaponry. After the surface burst, the fallout was immediate. But after almost half a century many made their way back to the areas that could be of benefit to them.

This entire area was considered The Waste. Ground Force rarely patrolled this spot. Even with all of their hazard suits and masks, humans were fragile creatures. Average humans not only carried physical frailties but mental ones too. Radiation was a significant factor in their lack of appearance on this side of the world. For the homeless that traversed these parts regularly, it was a blessing. For us, it could prove a hindrance. The massive number of unwashed bodies, multiplied by a thousand, assaulted us from every direction. There was so much movement going on that we split apart more than once.

A woman holding a basket of blankets ran toward a man hollering from a maintenance hole farther ahead. Her shoulder slammed into an older gentleman with bicolored hair. The box he held dropped to the floor. The contents inside the open box wafted out in a delicious allure. He looked around himself as if he was making sure no one noticed that he carried treats inside. Cam and I exchanged glances. The Market didn't sell treats like these. Baked goods like these were only sold in Delta. So, why would a baked goods vendor be traversing the subway tunnels of an unauthorized zone?

The smell reminded me of the food in the facility when we were younger. A woman had baked us treats all the time. She didn't converse much with us, but she always paid close attention to what we enjoyed and any ideas we had about her baking. If one kid thought chocolate would be great, she made chocolate chip muffins the next morning. Her mouthwatering treats smelled like the ones in the box. I studied him further.

He passed the bickering couple. My nose simultaneously took in the smell of sweat, ammo, and herbs that I've come to recognize as Baker, and now the scent of cinnamon rolls and yeast. The man walked with purpose, tightly gripping the box in his hands.

"How can you concentrate with the smell of bread hitting us every twenty seconds?"

I didn't have time to answer him. The man with the box stopped in front of another I recognized from Viktor's group. The guy, dressed all in black, pushed off the graffitied wall, peering into the box. He took it from the older man. The man in black turned in our direction. I pushed Cam against the wall, pressing my body close to his. Cam's body welcomed mine. His arm wrapped around my lower back, while the other hand cupped my cheek. We were so close to each other it almost seemed as if we were kissing.

"If you move your hand any lower, I will cut off your

pecker and shove it down your throat."

He grinned mischievously. "Oh, I love it when you talk dirty to me."

Ignoring his sarcasm, I peered to the side and noticed they had both disappeared down the tunnel. I immediately moved away from Cam, pushing forward down the same path. I no longer had to concentrate on Baker's male scent. I was chasing down the cinnamon roll man instead.

Cameron grinned from beside me. His massive body camouflaged with each person that passed me. It gave the illusion that I walked on my own. "Don't those baked goods remind you of something?"

He was on the same train of thought that I was, so I nodded. He didn't stop moving but cleared his throat, trying to grab my attention. I briefly checked him out. His face was turning a few shades of red.

Annoyed, I asked, "What is it?"

A dirty man with a lot of girth around his waist bumped into my shoulder but kept moving. I could feel his eyes on me and grinned, internally laughing at what he might've been thinking. A man that size would've knocked anyone else out of the way. Instead, I had almost demolished him and not budged an inch.

"You have a good-looking smile, Silk. Use it more often."

I glared at him, dropping the smile off my face.

His hands went up in surrender. "Or not."

We kept moving. Cameron didn't say anything else, but I knew something bothered him. He pushed to one side, following the scent of fresh baked goods. His stomach growled in response. Cam turned sheepish with a massive smile on his face as evidence. I shook my head, a husky laugh coming from my throat.

"Hungry?"

The man I had once loved shrugged, but it didn't have the same effect on me as Gavin. The baker and thug walked together ahead of us. Soon I'd be with him. Soon he'd be back at my side where he was supposed to be. Nothing would bring me down from that high.

"Silk, Suzanne's pregnant with my kid."

Nothing but that.

Sector Charlie
Downtown Trēbeta
Seaa – ID: PHO49.001

SUZANNE CAME THROUGH for us in a big way. Her contacts had called, giving us the exact time to make our move. Gregory Foxhand liked to partake in a little alcohol right before going home from work. He entered an underground establishment where women paraded around in costumes full of glitter and glamour.

Before leaving the bunker, I had gotten dolled up to resemble the women in the club. With the help of a lot of costume jewelry and makeup, I looked exactly like a New States resident but with less class. A wide rhinestone choker with tassels covered the majority of my neck, hiding my breathing apparatus. On my ears dangled a pair of earrings that had rhinestones and tassels, similar to the choker. The rings on my middle fingers were connected by a dazzling thread of gems that wrapped around my wrists like a bracelet.

I blinked false lashes, remembering the moment before heading out—my heart still in an uproar. Beatrice had handed me my long, hooded overcoat to cover myself until we got to the spot and a bag with clothes to change into afterward. Nightfall rapidly approached, so we moved quickly, or we'd be too late.

Hail walked in through the open door of my bedroom. His entire body froze right before crossing the threshold separating both our rooms. I know I must've looked ridiculous in the outfit. The way he stood there, mouth agape, made me withdraw into myself in an awkward uncomfortableness. I squirmed in my frilly tutu covered in sequins. Blood rushed to different parts of my body, sloshing around like a drunken sailor. Its familiarity stilled me, taking deep, calming breaths. I didn't need to turn into a mermaid at this point.

"S-stop staring at me like that, Hail. You're making me uncomfortable."

Hail shook his head, all the while blinking repeatedly. "Sorry, Seea. You look really good."

I look good?

Ignoring him, I grabbed the silly little bag sitting on my bed that contained some make-up, a KeViewer, and a fake sector pass, ready to get this job done and over with. It took a long time to convince Thunder, but he finally agreed to use the technology. Instead of being excited about the news, being in such revealing clothes put a damper on my mood. I felt better wearing the oversized clothes I was used to. People didn't comment on my scales or the color of my hair.

The magic I used only helped so much. It didn't change my appearance like Silk could change hers. Mine only covered my insecurities. My wild magic only made the people around me think I was beautiful—not that I was. Hail was only being friendly when he said those kind words earlier. Zane a gem for saying his. Neither saw me as anything more. Hail only saw a sister and an adjacent roommate.

Done feeling sorry for myself, I marched out of the bedroom with renewed purpose. Hail followed close behind me. The halls were eerily quiet as the onlookers stood and stared at my gaudy outfit. No matter what I did or how far I ran, I felt like a freak on display. My insides stirred. My heart beat furiously. If it weren't already cold in here, my hair would have stuck to the sweat on the back of my neck. The need to control my emotions increased. I couldn't afford to screw things up now—all of this mermaid magic needed to stay hidden. Our bodies were changing every day. Dr. Ferdinand had locked himself in his office, trying to find anything he could in all of the journals our Pops left behind.

Thunder stood by Snow and Rock, loitering by the exit. All three heard me come and stared unabashedly—not like I could've hidden the sound. Being quiet is a job we took seriously, but wearing five-inch stiletto heels and sparkles defeated stealth's purpose. No, my outfit screamed, "Look at me in all my flash."

"Seaa?" Thunder questioned.

Snow's silence unnerved me. They always had something to say between him and Guy, and it usually grated on my nerves. I didn't realize his silence bothered me more.

"Yes, brother."

He shook his head. "Wow. You are beautiful."

I had my forehead parallel to the stone ground, staring at my feet rather than at my family's faces. His words made my head shoot up so fast I thought I got whiplash. As if sensing the unease in my neck, Hail's hands rubbed that one section in such a manner that it left my insides in more of a chaotic mess. I squirmed away. Not because of his prodding, as he touched me without discomfort many times before. I moved because this time, his touch felt different. It felt possessive.

"You are kind to say so, Thunder."

He rubbed his neck in a nervous gesture. Thunder was never antsy.

He put his hand down and approached me. His tan, large hand grabbed hold of both of mine instead. Feeling the warmth of his fingers encompassing mine brought tears to my eyes. I blinked them away. We didn't have our Pops anymore, but Thunder was always the father figure we looked up to since Pops' death. He was the rock of our little group—the solid foundation we relied on.

A smile reached his eyes, showing me faint lines at the corners. "When have you known me to be kind, Seaa?"

My eyes blinked, stupefied. Thunder was right. He never told us things to be kind. He was brutally honest most of the time and told us the truth, even if we didn't want to hear it. I stared at him, seeking his face for the truth that lay there. When I saw it, I burst out in tears—uncontrollable tears that flowed down my cheeks in steady streams. His calloused thumb wiped them away, gingerly missing my bottom lashes. I felt Hail's body get closer, but one hand up from Thunder kept him back. He grabbed my chin with his thumb and forefinger, lifting my head to face him.

"Seaa, you are more than you see yourself. You walk into that club tonight with your head held high because no other woman there will match your beauty or your strength." He dropped his hand. "Got it?"

I nodded.

Flipping the bag over my shoulder, I called out to Rock and Snow. "Let's go, boys. We're going to be late if you guys keep dawdling."

There was laughter behind me, but this time it didn't swallow me up in self-pity. I was a super-soldier who had survived an underground military prison, and neither this club nor Foxhand's father would scare me. My sister waited for me. Silk was out there proving herself, so I would do the same.

Nothing was going to stop me. Not even myself.

CHAPTER FIFTEEN

IT WAS TIME to find Gregory Foxhand. I signaled to
the guys to stay close and made my way to the club's
front doors with those final moments in my mind.
Thunder had helped me see something I kept losing
sight of—myself. Although the years of laughter and
whispers had taken a toll on my heart and mind, tonight would be different. I was in disguise. Wearing
this disguise, I could be anything I wanted to be, and
today that would be me.

The music behind the wide double doors thumped
and wailed, graining to my sensitive hearing, even
though one ear held a tiny earpiece to communicate
with the rest of the team. Fixing the piece deeper into
the canal, I watched the people standing around the
club and the two bouncers standing in front of the

doors. They watched the loitering humans and pedestrians on their way home.

The night sky had hidden behind thick, gray clouds.
A man in a three-piece suit walked arm in arm with
two females dressed similarly to me. Getting inside
this place would be a breeze. I dropped the large cloak,
feeling the weight of it being pulled back by Snow. No
one saw him do it. Hidden in the shadows, my brothers moved with diligence and purpose. We'd lived life
on the run for far too long. We may have found comfort in our anonymity today, but yesterday we were
trained military soldiers, and tomorrow we'd face the
world.

It's that part that should scare them.

The singer's lyrics swooned through the open door
as the man walked in with his women. A couple beside
the doors necked like young teenagers. I sauntered
forward after taking several deep breaths. I crossed
the cobbled path in front of me, whipping the deep
purple mixed with blue turquoise strands of my hair
over my shoulder. People stopped when they saw me.
Others stared as they walked, hitting people as they
went by. I made sure to keep my heart in my chest as
it rose in my throat.

My slender, curvy body swayed with each step,
enough that it caught the attention of the two guards
standing by the door. My long legs took me closer to
the entrance faster than I had hoped. The clacking of
the heels reminding me I was indeed doing this. The
men took one look at each other and opened the door
as I made it to the halfway point on the cobbled path.
They didn't stop staring. My usual insecurity rose from

within, but I buried it down with only one thought.

I am perfect for this job.

My heels clicked against the stone as if a Siren call to men only a few feet away from me. Some women slapped their partners as their men stared flagrantly. I turned to one of them with a wink. The guy shivered with a goofy smile on his face. His actions brought me a new thrill I hadn't ever felt before.

"Damn, Seaa's eating these guys up," Snow muttered through the earpiece.

Rock's gruff grunt was the only reply.

I squeezed my hands into quick fists to help with the nerves, releasing them when I stepped foot on the dirt path that led to the club's front doors. I winked again to one bouncer as my sweaty hand slid over the cloth of the other's shoulder in a lame excuse for a caress. I knew I botched that, but he didn't even notice my unpleasant move. He smirked lasciviously. The music turned to static noise as I focused my senses on finding Gavin's father. The doors closed behind me. Although I made it inside without any issues, finding Gregory Foxhand was another story altogether.

I descended the stairs down into the depths of the club. The music changed, and the dancers swayed with their hands in the air. The various colored lights made it difficult for me to get my bearings, playing havoc with my eyes. I blinked to focus. When I finally opened my eyes, I was able to decipher their faces better. Not knowing what this Foxhand guy smelled like, I used my hearing to pick up his name and my sight to acknowledge when I'd found him.

Couples grounded perversely in rhythm with the

music. I watched as the men showed several signs of enjoyment each time the woman got closer, swayed deeper, and touched them. I studied women's movements. Each curl. Each dip and turn. And each titillating sound of approval. I wasn't regular Seaa right now. I was in disguise and playing a role.

A man like him wouldn't be sitting around with the others. If he had snuck in, then he would stay out of sight. I stared at the balcony above me, lined with booths and glass. I rarely saw a person walk across it, so he had to be sitting in one of them up there. I watched ravishing women getting turned away from the spiral iron-wrought staircase. It wasn't enough to know where he sat. I needed to be invited.

What better way was there to find someone rich and powerful than to make them come to you? I used what I learned from the dancers around me and found my way to the middle of the dance floor. With my arms up in the air, I swayed my body in a dance that complimented my assets. My long, styled waves curled around my arms and waist as if they couldn't part with me.

Dancers moved away, watching me in rapture as I moved the attention to myself. Being a superhuman kept me from falling on my face as my heel caught several times on the holes in the wooden floor. Each time I got caught, it moved me in a new way, drawing more attention to my body. For the first time in forever, I felt so incredibly charming that not even I could keep myself from stopping to gauge the onlookers' reactions. Tonight, I felt different even though I looked like a more dolled-up version of myself.

One song drifted into the next. I kept my eyes closed, swaying to the music, feeling it deep in my core. I felt my body move around as if caught in a wave. The movements were fluid. I went with the motion of it instead of struggling to break free from its embrace. I could feel the men and women on the dance floor swarm me as if they couldn't get enough of my euphoria. I barely even registered Snow in my ear as he said that I'd been spotted. Once the song finished, two men approached me and led me to the back of the club.

"Our boss would love it if you joined him at his private booth."

I giggled and batted my fake pink lashes. It wasn't long before the men stood in front of the bouncers blocking the staircase. They nodded to one another and let us through. The women dying to be a part of the club royalty upstairs pouted and whined. The noise quieted down as we moved through a hall at the top, separating the booths from the rest of the dance floor below.

"Keep an eye out, Snow," I heard Rock tell him.

The sounds of the club rang through my ear as Snow replied, "I am following close behind. By the way, Seaa, I think Silk's pheromones got nothing on that dancing of yours. Good god, woman!"

I clenched my jaw to keep myself from laughing or arguing with him. Snow's sense of humor was a hit or miss most times. Right now, I couldn't afford to get caught by the guys taking me to a back booth surrounded by three similar couches. Sitting inside was the man I wanted to see.

One man leaned down to whisper, "We've brought her Mr. Foxhand."

Gregory Foxhand III sat in the middle of the enclosure, with three women in clothes less vulgar than mine clinging to his every word. Money lay scattered on the table with three open bottles of liquor and wine. The women were draped in fine jewelry. Whether they were from society or the working class, these women were expensive.

"You wanted to see me?" I asked the man garnering all the attention of the people around him.

Gregory Foxhand was an older version of Gavin Foxhand. While Gavin had short dirty-blond hair, senior had salt and pepper strands instead. Both had bright blue eyes that bordered in green, and while Gavin's seemed more innocent to our failing world, Gregory Foxhand's eyes had seen more than he could handle.

I turned away from the man to study the other booths. They sat empty. His two men stood at the end of the box, watching the area around me. They wouldn't make a move unless Foxhand gave the word. So, the only thing standing in my way from having a heart to heart with the older gentleman was the three women before me.

I leaned over the table as he gestured for me to take a seat and join him. But I didn't have the time to sit idly by until an opportune moment became available. Silk would check in any minute now with news, and I would be dang sure I was ready to give her what she needed to get Gavin back and help our group.

"Send them away."

The music changed again as he stared at me. The

women pouted when I spoke but didn't bother moving. "Send them away now," I repeated.

I wasn't sure what was going through Foxhand's mind, but I didn't have time to wait and find out. I got up and affixed my eyes on both of his men. Quickly, before anyone was the wiser, I grabbed one of the bodyguards' heads and whipped it against the back wall separating the booth from the rest of the room, and by the time the other had turned, I'd wrapped my arm around his neck and squeezed until the man hung limp in my arms.

I slowly dropped him to the floor. We didn't kill innocents. The women screamed, rushing to leave the booth as not to get killed by me, but I didn't let them get too far. One side of my mouth lifted in a smile as I grabbed one's scarf from her neck, wrapped it around her wrist and around the other's ankle. Both women fell over one another in the booth. The last girl tried to slip past me, so I grabbed her hand and threw her back into the pile of limbs in front of me. I took the rest of the shiny scarf and wrapped it around her wrists as well, tying the pieces together. The girls screamed and groaned from their uncomfortable positions as Gregory Foxhand watched in horror.

The music blasted from the speakers. No one would be the wiser.

Bending at the waist, I placed a finger to my lips to quiet them. At this point, Snow came in from behind me with his black gear and guns in full view. They simmered quickly.

"Gregory Foxhand, where's your son?"

Gregory narrowed his eyes and seemed to have

gone into thought. "How do you know of my boy?"

I stared at a fingernail, pissed that it had broken at some point. "There's a lot about Gavin that we know. Consider me his friend, and right now, you are my enemy. Where's Gavin?"

He seemed to have stared into space again as if trying to figure out how real my words were. All of a sudden, he shot up from his seat, almost pushing the table away from him. "The explosion at his building was for him? I assumed my son was on one of his wild trips again because he wasn't home. You're telling me someone has Gavin?"

I stared at Snow, who was better at telling if his words were lies or not. He gave me the nod, so I watched Gregory search for his KeViewer. The moment he pulled it out of his jacket pocket, I snatched it from his hand.

"If you didn't hire mercenaries to grab Gavin, then who did?"

He ran a hand through his hair like I've seen Gavin do. "No one's really supposed to know about Gavin. It's my way of protecting him. The fewer people who know Gavin exists, the fewer who would come after him."

"Right," I replied without any real vigor. This man knew nothing about his son. Gavin was an excellent hacker—a veritable genius. Hiding him away wouldn't help with a damn thing.

With crazy eyes, the man stared at me. "You said you're his friend. Find him. Find my son. I'll do anything." He shoved the cash from the table toward me. "Find him. Find him, please." Gregory Foxhand tumbled out of the booth to face me. He was not that much taller than me, but he had enough height on him that I had to look up. He tried to grab my hands, but I pulled them back. I didn't want to be touched. Snow judged the man's body language for all the signs of a liar.

Snow whispered, "The man is downright distraught. He's not faking it. His pupils, hands, and gestures are all signaling he's not lying."

I nodded. "Fine, Mr. Foxhand. Now that I know for sure it wasn't you, we can proceed with finding Gavin and getting him back."

He went to grab my hand again. Instead, I smacked it away. "Listen closely; keep your KeViewer on you at all times." Snow had already connected to Foxhand's technology. He gave it back to me to hand back to the older gentleman. "We'll be in touch. Do not contact anyone about his disappearance, or we won't be able to get him back. You saw my skills here today. We are the very best at retrieving him, so don't make the mistake to double-cross us."

He studied me for a moment, his eyes raking over me from head to toe. Foxhand's eyes then took in Snow, recognition crossing his features. "You're Project Hercules, aren't you?"

Snow and I didn't even nod. My brother crossed his arms, grinning as he studied the tied-up girls instead. The music in the hall was deafening. The girls whimpered from their awkward positions. They were too scared to follow the direction of our conversation. As long as Foxhand stayed alive, then that meant they wouldn't die either.

He put his head down. "This is my fault. I treated him like a disease to push him away from the corruption. Instead, I brought the apocalypse to his front door."

"Gavin is a grown man who can make his own decisions and a real asset to our team, Foxhand. He has a perfect circle behind him right now. We'll find him. But don't make us regret letting you live. Do as we say, and he'll come back alive."

He shook his head, agreeing. "I just don't get how you all came to be."

My voice dropped to a whisper. "Call it serendipitous. Now, I mean it. Call no one, do nothing, and he'll come back alive."

"Anything," he replied as his eyes turned misty.

I nodded. "Stay by your KeViewer. We'll be in touch."

I wasn't sure if Gavin Foxhand knew this or not, but Gregory Foxhand loved his son very much. He might not have known how to show it, but there was definitely a paternal feeling emanating from the older man. Hopefully, we'd be able to get Gavin back fast enough for him to know it too.

CHAPTER SIXTEEN

Outskirts of Sector Delta
The Waste

CAMERON AND I watched from our vantage points at the camp set up by the mercenaries. It was a home laid out in the open with tents for the fighters and their families. Women washed clothes together by a well while kids ran around, chasing one another in glee. The guys sat at a table, clinking their cups together in celebration. The younger group of children gathered around the pastry man as he gifted them a baked good each. The mothers washing clothes would occasionally look up and smile.

How could mercenary families live so carefree?

Their men killed and kidnapped and came home to their families as if it were nothing. Did they not understand the baggage they brought with them? We lived in a world with less humanity in it. Like us, soldiers could track others better than trained humans, so why put them at such risk? I couldn't understand it. Right now, though, I only cared about Gavin. If they gave him back without trouble, then I'd leave the rest of their group alone. Viktor said he cared about the well-being of his team. If that was so, I truly hoped he understood that I'd do anything for mine.

I glanced at Cam without turning my head to see him.

His news earlier was a shock to my system. The woman who came and went from his bed now carried a baby. I didn't even think we were capable of bringing life into the world. Guy never got any of his female companions pregnant. Rock and Beatrice were more in love than anyone I had ever met, and they never ended with a product of that love.

Our conversation in the tunnels came back to the forefront of my mind.

"Are you seriously telling me this now?"

Cameron scratched the back of his head, his face a few shades closer to crimson. "I've been trying to talk to everyone, but with everything going on, it just hasn't happened."

I nodded, biting my lower lip and keeping an eye on the two men, oblivious to our trailing. "Thunder knows then." It wasn't a question.

"Yeah."

My head moved up and down again on its own. "I

don't know what to say. Congratulations?"

He sighed, leaning slightly to stare into my face as we walked. "I thought you should know, Silk. I..." The man's eyebrows shifted. He seemed weighed down by the words that came next. "I loved you, Silk."

I was in such shock I bumped into a squatter. The woman tipped over and fell into another. They both fell, causing the two we followed to turn back and see. Cameron moved faster than I did. He pulled me into his body, hidden in the shadows of his camouflage. Cam watched me from mono-lidded red phoenix eyes that slanted down in the inner corners but curved upward at the end. He was dazzling. He also just admitted to me that he "loved me."

The people all righted themselves and kept moving. No one the wiser. I let go of him to see where our two guys had gone. They had turned down another tunnel.

"Did you hear me, Silk?"

Was he saying something? "Huh?"

"I left the facility because I didn't think you were ready to be in love. The thing with Suzanne happened, and I promised to take care of her."

I shook my head, trying to process his words. "You're saying that you loved me, but instead of helping me heal my wounds, you left and got another woman pregnant?"

He cussed. "Shit, it's not what I meant."

Instead of trying to understand what he meant, a throaty laugh burst from me. It didn't matter that Cameron left or that Suzanne was pregnant or that at some point, he had loved me as I loved him. All I knew right now and at this moment was that the only man on my mind and probably engraved on my almost non-existent heart was Gavin Foxhand.

We walked. I put a hand on Cam's wrist. I didn't look at him, but I could see him watching my hand. "Cameron, the past is the past. I'm not anymore changed than I was before, but I do feel—" I searched my mind for the right words "—happy for you."

My KeViewer vibrated, bringing me out of the memory. I gingerly pulled it out of my pocket as to not alert anyone to our location. Cam and I were pretty far away from the group, but I didn't want to risk Viktor's sense of hearing being as sharp as ours with him being such an anomaly.

"Seaa?"

My sister's sultry voice came through the line all breathy. "Gavin's father has no clue who'd grab him. Snow said the man told the truth."

I nodded as if she could hear me. "Well, we know where he's at and where the mercenaries make camp. Cam and I are watching from a vantage point pretty far off from their location."

She seemed to be talking to someone. I waited with the phone to my ear. "We're in Downtown Trēbeta. You guys?"

I looked around. "We're in the outskirts of Delta. The Waste. Deep into The Waste, where normal people shouldn't tread."

She told the rest of her team, then came back on the line. "We could probably be there within the hour."

I stared at the camp, knowing full well that we should wait for backup, especially when we didn't know what we were working with. Plumboy's nephew meant a connection to Project Hercules. Nausea churned in my stomach. If we waited any longer, Gavin might not be alive. Worse yet, he could be experimented on. I couldn't allow that.

I turned to look at Cam, who sighed, knowing very well my thoughts at this very moment. "Sorry, Seaa. I can't wait that long."

"Silk!"

Her last word before I hung up the KeViewer. "You ready, Cam?"

He cracked some bones as he stretched his muscles. "Yeah, I guess so."

We jumped off the vantage point and made a beeline to the mercenary camp. Although I looked straight ahead, I felt Cam veer off to the side to stay hidden as my backup should I need it. I'd dealt with Viktor before at my worst. I could deal with Viktor now at my best.

Dust from the ground rose in the air as a gust of wind picked up. I walked through the menacing cloud with eyes on one goal—getting Gavin back. A woman glanced over in my direction. She squinted to see through the field of dust, her eyes then opening wide. A finger pointed in my direction as she screamed for everyone to run. All the women ran toward their children. The pastry man and another elder gathered with them. The mercenaries grabbed their weapons, threw themselves off the picnic table, and righted themselves before facing me. I knew they couldn't see me clearly because of all the floating soot.

Their guns aimed at my shadow.

I watched as Viktor ran out of a tent, searching for the disturbance. The scar on his face seemed less imposing now. Gavin was near, but I couldn't see him. Viktor's men ran forward with their guns aimed and ready. They squeezed their triggers and fired. The bullets did nothing to me. I felt them pierce my skin and then fall off me. My legs moved forward. Viktor's brows narrowed, then widened with recognition.

"It's the super! Worst case, fellas," he called out.

The men dropped their weapons like synchronized swimmers. One arm came down around their backs, and what seemed like homemade guns were pulled out from their belts. My body had cleared the smoke. The women and some of the men huddled in one corner. For a split second, I wondered why they didn't run, and saw Cam standing right behind them. They slowly moved back, another scream rendering the air. But not before one of Viktor's men shot off one round of his homemade gun.

The bullet could barely be seen flying through the air. I didn't have enough time to move out of the way. The unusual bullet hit me above the knee, right past bone and muscle. I dropped to one knee. The pain burst through me in one blow.

"Son of a—" I yelled through gritted teeth.

Viktor was about to holler when one of his men landed on top of him. I briefly glanced at Cam, who held the pastry man by his neck—his body changing colors to blend in with the group. The moms crouched on the ground with their children, refusing to move. Cameron used his speed to get to the rest of the men standing off in front of me. Viktor joined the fray.

I got off the grime, ignoring the pain in my leg. There was so much going on around them that they briefly forgot that one bullet wouldn't bring me down. Viktor was the first to look at me. When he saw me get up, he turned away from Cam and his men to aim his gun at me. There was a feral cry from his lips, fangs exposed through his Balbo beard. I remembered how powerful my new power could be, so I willed it to cover me. There was no way I would outrun those bullets. Images of the suit and how I felt when it first sprang up coursed through me. A similar sensation took over, and I could feel the webbing seep through my pores. It covered me from my neck to my toes.

Viktor shot three times. Each bullet hit me in different areas, not once penetrating the armor. He grabbed one of his men's guns from the ground to point it at Cameron. In an instant, Cameron placed the pastry man as a shield. I remembered the words Viktor had told me about keeping his men alive. When Viktor saw the man pulled up, he hesitated, and that one second of pause was all it took for me to make it right in front of him. I grabbed Viktor by the neck and lifted him in the air.

"Put your weapons down now!"

Viktor grabbed me by the wrist and squeezed. I felt pressure from underneath the suit, but he didn't breakthrough. I had a feeling that if I wasn't wearing this suit right now, Viktor might have been strong enough to crush my bones. He noticed that his strength couldn't penetrate through the armor, so instead, he wrapped his legs around my waist. He clenched his thighs so tightly I felt myself lose balance.

We both tumbled to the ground. Viktor came around first, kicking me in the face. My head blew back, and my curls bounced forward into my face. The moment I moved them away, Viktor was already aiming the gun at my head. I moved just as two men fell on top of Viktor.

Cameron grinned as he tossed the human males like sacks of potatoes—one on top of the other. I got up from the ground at the same time Viktor did. We were about to run toward one another when a tortured howl rendered the air. The piercing scream was so high pitched that we all flinched and looked toward the last tent of their camp.

Cameron took the moment to end this little battle by grabbing his guns and aiming them at the women. I felt my insides churn. The women and children should never go through something like that. Viktor noticed, as did his men. They screamed for him to leave them alone.

Viktor faced me. Fear in his eyes.

"Cam, put the gun down," I told him.

He seemed to consider my words and then realized why I had said them. Cam sheepishly rubbed the back of his neck. "Sorry, ladies," he told them.

I turned to Viktor again. "You told me once before that your men are important to you."

Viktor deflated. "Men, put your guns down."

Another scream.

Viktor shook his head, but he wasn't worried about the sound. Cameron didn't like surprises, and this seemed like a whopper of one.

"What the hell is that?"

I nodded, thinking the same thing.

"That is the reason I fight back against you mutant freaks," he spat.

My arms crossed. I stood there thinking, *he's the kettle calling the pot black.* "I'm the freak, you say?" I pointed at myself.

Cam laughed. "Dude."

Viktor pointed at both of us. "You chose this life!"

Cam snorted and pushed a human in front of him out of the way. "Dude, we were created in a fuckin' lab from fuckin' Petri dishes. We had no choice in the matter."

Viktor narrowed his eyes in thought. "You're Batch 001?"

I smirked while Cam spread his arms out beside him. "In the flesh, buddy."

The leader of the mercenaries paced the ground in front of us. "Then why were you protecting Foxhand?"

This time, Cam crossed his arms over his chest and stared, letting me answer the question. For a second, I didn't know what to answer. Was I protecting Gavin because it was my duty? Did I not finish that quest when I brought him safely to the bunkers? That deep, gut-wrenching feeling percolated in my belly again. *Yes*, I brought him to Safe Haven, but I didn't keep him safe. Gavin may have briefly been safe from these mercenaries, but he wasn't at all safe from me. The one who caused that man the most harm was me.

I was his *real* threat.

But instead of feeling remorse, all I felt was a deep, crawling fear that if I ever walked away from Gavin, never to see him again; I'd die inside.

Instead of answering his question because I didn't feel like I protected him, I replied, "Where is Gavin? And you better hope on your life and of those around you" —I heard the women holler, squeezing their children tighter to them— "that not one hair is out of place on Gavin Foxhand's head."

Before Viktor could answer, I heard Gavin's voice coming from one of the tents. "Silk! Silk, I'm in here."

At that moment, I saw the rest of my siblings come out from different directions. Seaa walked toward the group of huddled women, children, and what seemed like some of their elderly from behind. Rock came in behind Viktor, while Snow appeared from within the tents with Gavin standing beside him. Gavin was pulling the ropes off his wrists as I ran toward him. I stopped right before him. My eyes roamed his entire body, seeking any sign of an injury.

Gavin's hand rested gently below my chin, lifting my face to meet his eyes. Something snapped inside of me. The pain I felt deep inside hid behind the calm balm of his gaze, and I felt all my worries and dreaded past disappear. My suit receded into my skin. He deeply stared as if asking me something I couldn't understand. No one had ever stared deep into my mind, talking to me from such a deep level before. I didn't know what he was asking me until I saw his eyes drop to my lips, and then I knew.

Gavin was going to touch me in a way I'd avoided all my life.

I felt the pain stir again from within, but this time I willed it back down. For the first time in a long time, I waited for him to lean in closer. The dread of such intimacy brought sharp butterflies to my belly. My mind kept screaming that all men were scum. No man should be trusted.

You aren't good for Gavin, Silk.

But my heart wouldn't let my mind ruin this now. I felt my lacking heart beat furiously in a way I hadn't felt in years. Gavin's hand slid ever so lightly to the side of my face, his strong fingers cradling my head. The other slid around my waist and up toward the middle of my back. He leaned in closer, now having gone farther than any man had ever gotten. My mind and heart warred with one another. I ignored it. I wanted to ignore it, at least for once in my pathetic life.

Gavin licked his lips and came into mine. The touch was very cautious. Feather light. His lips were warm and slightly chapped. I could feel them abrade mine, but it didn't feel wrong. The wings of the butterflies stilled as if they waited to see what came next. He slowly pulled away, watched me and what he must've seen in my eyes gave him pause. Tears flowed down my cheeks. His thumb wiped one away, but they kept coming. Instead of kissing me again, I felt his cool forehead touch mine. Forehead to forehead and nose to nose, we didn't say a word to one another. There were collective gasps around me, but all I wanted to hear was Gavin's hitched breathing. I knew that the sound he made meant he wanted more but respected that I needed some more time.

No man had ever given me a choice.

Gavin did.

The more I was around this man, the more I realized that Gavin didn't want me because of my pheromones or my looks. Gavin Foxhand wanted me because of me. Whether I was the black widow or a genetically enhanced superhuman, Gavin didn't see any of that. He saw the girl with all the scars.

He saw beyond them and to the real me.

He whispered, "I'm sorry, Silk. I shouldn't have run out of the bunkers."

His deep voice soothed me. I shook my head slowly, rolling my forehead from side to side on his. "It was my fault. I failed to protect you."

My eyes were closed; I sensed his smile. "Let's talk about how wicked strong the woman I'm in love with is later."

My heart jumped. *Is Gavin really in love with me?*

Holding on to those feelings, I tucked them away to analyze later. My legs shook, and my mind went blank. I could feel the blood drain from my face. I opened my eyes to see concern cross Gavin's features.

"Silk?" I faintly heard him call out.

The world spun. I briefly caught sight of the others around me before I dropped hard to the grime-covered ground. My world went black.

CHAPTER SEVENTEEN

Sector Foxtrot
Unit 13 Headquarters
Operative Rayne – ID: PHO64.OOl

FOR THE THIRD time since we captured Roman Braggart, I couldn't keep myself from his cells. Part of me hated him for being a part of our father's life since his youth, while I rotted away in some mindless oblivion I couldn't crawl away from. The other part of me wanted to know more about him. Why did he call out for me like a man deprived of water in a hot, scorching desert? I didn't know him. All I knew about him was that he was my brother but that we had never met. He had betrayed Unit 13.

That was his biggest mistake.

No one failed Braggart—my father—the reason the world functioned. I curled my fingers again and watched as the man lay on the cot inside of his cell. His large chest rose and fell with his breathing. The bright, single light from the middle of the room barely bothered him. There was motion on his face, so I turned to see.

His lips curled into a half-smile. Eyes the color of green moss stared back into mine. I was conditioned to see beyond the person in front of me. Being a soldier could do that to a person. But my insides didn't get the memo. I cleared my throat to hide the rush of blood running rampant underneath my skin and the heavy thuds of my heart. Roman Braggart shifted in the cot, sliding around into a sitting position. Even that simple move seemed so effortless for such a big man. He didn't turn to look away or blink me back into a more comfortable position beyond the clear glass. He only stared, and I could only stare back.

"My beautiful Rayne."

I couldn't help it. I blinked. Questions ran through my head like coordinated locusts on the prey for food. I mentally shook away everything he made me feel with those three words. Roman Braggart was a traitor. He was also my brother. Nothing else mattered but that.

"Save your strength, soldier. You're going to need it when you are being questioned."

He leaned his elbows on his knees with his hands hanging between his open legs. Chains attached to his wrists and ankles clinked against the metal. "I don't care what happens to me anymore. I've seen you. That asshole can torture me to death for all I care."

Roman shrugged as if nothing could bother him anymore. How couldn't it? I felt all sorts of different ways, rising from anger to fear with only those uttered words. It bothered me, and I didn't know why. I fixed my facial expression, making sure not to show the traitor any weaknesses on my part as he talked.

"I'd gladly die happy now."

I felt my heart shatter, and it took all I had in me not to collapse on the floor like a rag doll. I was short of breath. Inside my body, a war of emotions raged. But no one could see the mangled pieces inside. Outside, I was the very picture of calm. Nothing seemed to rattle me. Why did Roman Braggart's words cause me harm?

"Why you here, doll?"

Trevor Dallas's words made my skin crawl. He was the only one who couldn't keep me composed. I detested the squirming rat with my entire being. Turning my head, I glared at the cowboy as he sauntered over with two more guards behind him.

I crossed my arms. "I didn't think I needed your permission to be here," I replied.

He grinned as if mocking my words. "I'm sure the general prefers you don't get brainwashed by that traitor."

I heard Roman scoff. Without looking at him, I could tell he had straightened on his cot. "*I'm* going to brainwash *her*? Right. Like you guys did?"

His words made me face him. What did he mean about being brainwashed? A sharp pain started in the center of my skull, radiating outward. I flinched from the onslaught but immediately composed my features. Ignoring the massive pain in my head, I turned back to Trevor.

"You need to pay more attention to yourself and stop worrying about me. I have the general's ear, you wannabe cowboy."

Roman's laugh sent shivers down my spine. I didn't know if it was good or bad.

I watched Trevor squeeze his fingers into a fist. I'd love to fight him again, but I didn't think I'd be able to hold myself back from killing him this time if I did.

He gave the guards behind him a gesture with his chin. They both came around him, unlocking the cell. I took a step back but couldn't get my body to leave. Instead, I watched as they both entered the cell. One aimed his gun at Roman, while the other cautiously approached with the key to his chains.

"One wrong move, Rome, and these guys have orders to put you down faster than you can blink," Trevor muttered from his safe spot in the pristine white hallway.

My headache pounded harder, almost debilitating. Thin brows furrowed as sweat dripped from my temple. What the hell was happening to me? My breathing turned choppy. I placed one hand against the wall behind me for support. Luckily, Trevor didn't notice a damn thing, too obsessed with the traitor in front of us. However, as the guard dealt with Roman, Roman's eyes were only on me. He had a mixture of regret and concern in full view of everyone else. There was no way Trevor wouldn't notice now.

He turned just as I composed my features. I stared back at the freakishly green-haired cowboy as if nothing mattered—the picture of extreme calm. He turned around to Roman, not giving me a second glance. The guard walked Roman out of the cell. I moved closer to the wall when I felt my entire body want to melt into his. The chains screeched and rattled against the floor tiles and swished when they rubbed against the material of his pants.

Trevor had a gun in his hand. To anyone else, he seemed undisturbed. I saw more than any other soldier in this unit. Trevor equally hated Roman Braggart and feared him all at the same time. The moment he stood right beside me, Braggart stopped and stared at me. His penetrating gaze had locked on mine—I couldn't look away, and I sure as hell didn't dare to move.

"You're so beautiful, Rayne. I missed you so damn much."

One guard shoved a gun into his back while the other yanked on his chains. I could feel the eyes of Roman Braggart eat me up in a delectable perusal of forbidden fruit. My mouth watered, and a foreign ache inside almost dropped me to the floor in a puddle of goo.

What the hell is wrong with me?

Before I could even form coherent words, Trevor pistol-whipped Roman Braggart in the face. A fierce growl erupted from his throat, animalistic and primal. The intensity of it vibrated inside of my head and heart. Blood trickled from a cut on the side of his almost luminescent eye. His eyes briefly glowed before he gained control of them again and stared at Trevor.

"You're a fuckin' shithead. You know that?" Roman spat.

All that got him was another hit in the face. More blood trickled. I squeezed my fingers so tightly I could feel my nails breaking the skin in my palm. I wanted to wipe the blood off Roman's face or punch Trevor in his. One of the two would happen if one of us didn't move away from here. Thinking it be better if it were me leaving, I straightened out and walked down the hallway. I didn't look back at Roman Braggart, whose eyes I felt watching me, nor at Trevor Dallas, who watched him with equal intensity.

Right before I turned the corner, I could hear Trevor tell Roman, "She'll never see you the way you see her."

My first inclination was to tell Trevor not to speak for me, but my pounding headache worsened, and as much as I refused to enter the medical wing, I knew I had to get rid of it in some form or another. The facility's halls were alive with the sounds of guards walking from one area to another in patrol or soldiers training in the arena. I walked past another room with the sound of exercise equipment banging against the weights.

General Braggart walked with Dr. Plumboy, both speaking in confidence. I always kept an ear away from meddling, as we were trained to do, but today I defied others and listened in on their conversation.

"Trevor Dallas will deliver him for—" he paused, cracking a smile "—interrogation."

He meant torture. The inflection in his voice gave it

away, and for some reason, it upset me.

"Very well," Braggart began. "Make sure that you get as much information out of him as you possibly can."

General Braggart looked up and stared at me as I approached. He squinted his eyes to study me. He motioned for Dr. Plumboy to go on without him. The general stopped before me. "Rayne, I can see something trouble's you."

I was practiced in the skill of hiding my feelings. What he was seeing had to be because of our parent-child bond. "I have a migraine, is all." I nodded as if it all made sense.

One thing Braggart wasn't was a doting parent. I remembered the conversation I had with the bartender days before. A lot was going on in this place that confused me beyond reason. Nothing had felt right since the moment I awoke in that medical lab. I refused to believe anyone over my father, but I knew better than to tell him of the things I'd witnessed and learned.

That bartender talked to me like a man who knew me. He said I had parents who I adored. The man told me about the mother's illness and the father's position in a university. The bartender had even said to me that I loved to collect things from the past. The way he spoke was not like that of a man building a lie on demand. Unit 13 trained super-soldiers to tell the difference. Thomas told the truth, but if Braggart did too, then who was lying to me?

Oblivious of my thoughts, Braggart nodded, curiously watching my every move. I kept my posture loose and my eyes on the spot in front of me.

"Very well, my little Rayne. Carry on."

Taking that as my cue to go, I walked as straight as I could toward my room. My head pounded harder with every step I took. I walked into the rec room as if in a fog. The other members of Project Hercules laughed and ate in pleasant camaraderie. I knew none of them, nor did I care to know them. Once deep inside, I turned down the right side. I felt eyes on me—deep and penetrating. I shifted and saw operative Zane Mueller watching me from his seat at the bar.

Zane wasn't like the other operatives in our facility. He followed orders and at the same time, marched to the beat of his own drum. He'd caught me off-guard earlier when we snatched Roman Braggart from Sector Bravo. I wasn't used to feeling ineffectual. I heard the sound of a woman and the smell of something familiar. When Zane appeared in front of me, it took me a second to compose myself and walk away from him, although I wanted to seek the familiar sensation.

Letting out a lungful of air, I made my way to the room, and right before I opened the door, Mueller appeared right beside me. He was the fastest in the facility. It didn't surprise me to see him approach as quickly as he did.

I took a deep breath, ignoring the hammering within my skull. "You saw Rome."

There was something about the name *Rome* that drove another nail into my brain. I grabbed my head, squeezing to ease some of the pain, then glared at him. "Move," I rushed out through clenched teeth.

He leaned in instead. "Not everything around here is truth, Rayne." He pounded on his chest and then tapped the area where his heart belonged. "Sometimes, the truth is right in here."

The roaring pain grew. I gritted my teeth harder and shoved him against the wall. "Move," I bit out.

Zane grinned, putting his hands up in surrender. I dropped him and opened the door to my room with my other hand. The moment I saw him move aside, and I was safely enclosed in my solitary chamber, I crumbled to the floor in a pile of limbs.

I awoke to the sound of banging. My eyes opened, staring at the ceiling of my room. Blinking the fatigue away, I picked myself off the rug, briefly noting on the clock that it read a little over three in the morning. Someone knocked again on my door, and then a slip of paper rushed from underneath. I knelt down to grab it. The scent reminded me of Mueller.

Why in the world is he knocking on my door at this hour?

The pain subsided. My neck popped as I moved it from left to right. Once my eyes adjusted, I read the note he had slipped under my door.

He's in bad shape, Rayne. It would help if you re-membered him. Don't let him die like that.

For a split second, I almost tore out of the room without a second thought to consequence. Then the more stable part of my brain told me that I had no business thinking of the traitor, my brother, the man who meant nothing to me.

Or did he?

Before I lost my nerve, I threw on a different tank top and finger-combed my hair into a tight ponytail. The paper now crumbled, I threw it in the mini-incin-erator bin by the door and stepped out. The rec room had gone quiet. Barely anyone ambled around at this time. I walked with renewed purpose to the holding cells. Mueller didn't tell me who to go to in his letter, but I knew deep inside he meant Roman Braggart.

I took the halls swiftly. Some soldiers wanted to question me, but none dared to stop and approach me. There was some comfort in being the general's daughter. No one asked or dared to stop me. After a few winding turns down the clean, white hallways, I made it into the lower cells where they kept the stronger criminals. A pained groan stopped me from moving farther inside. I heard a curdled rasp of air and then another cry. My heart tightened. For some reason, I didn't want to see him. I didn't want to see him hurt, but I couldn't understand why not? Even if he was my brother, we had no real sibling bond. I barely knew him.

Ignoring my wavering thoughts, I walked into the room with my head held high. I took one step after the other and then faltered when I saw the state Roman Braggart was in. Blood stained his clothes, sticking to his skin. The metallic smell overwhelmed me. I could no longer see his tight tan skin covered in tattoos. His slick, black hair dripped with a mixture of sweat and blood on the floor. Roman held his gut, blood trickling from between his fingers.

He turned his head. One eye was red with burst blood vessels, but the other held a vibrant fight within him. Whatever they did to him hadn't broken him yet. I wanted to know why he fought. What was so important that he couldn't just give up?

"Rayne," he whispered between cut, bloodied lips.

I watched him. Afraid to move. Afraid to speak.

He tried to straighten but instead settled on watching me from a reclined position on the cot, the pain evident in his face and movements. "As long as you're okay, then so am I," he coughed out.

Somehow, his words upset me. "You are a fool, Roman Braggart. A fool and a traitor."

He smiled. "I guess I'm a fool in love, but I'm no traitor, Rayne."

His confession sent an arrow straight into my heart. The plethora of emotions was draining. If the general or anyone in this facility knew what went on inside me, I'd be opened up and studied without a second's hesitation.

I grimaced. "You're speaking nonsense. What do you know about me other than I am your sister?"

A kind of laugh and cough ripped from his throat. It pained him, but he ignored it to stare at me with his one right eye. "You are not my sister, no matter what that asshole says."

The words of the bartender at Traces came back to me. Someone else raised me, but I wasn't sure who or why. That brought a flush of cold sweat down my back, anger heating my blood instead. "How do you figure?" I replied, avoiding asking him what I truly wanted.

His eye never left mine. "Because the way I feel about you is not that of a brother to his sister, but of a man to a phenomenal woman."

I felt my heart kick up speed. The best thing to do was to ignore it. "As I said, you are a fool. What's worse is that in your delusional world, you don't consider us family nor yourself as a traitor."

He shook his head, the mixed blood and sweat dripping around the floor before him. "I chose to leave this place because I knew that the cause I was fighting for was wrong. I know you feel it inside, Rayne. The things they do here are not right. There was no way I could betray something as corrupt as this place. I chose to leave and fight for the right side. That doesn't make me a traitor, Rayne. That makes me a realist."

I shook my head. The headache coming back. "I don't understand."

Roman licked his lips. "I love you, Rayne. Understand that."

The migraine exploded in my head, taking the very breath from my lungs.

CHAPTER EIGHTEEN

THUNDER DID A sharp whistle with two fingers in his mouth to call everyone out of the cafeteria. The staff moved back into the kitchens. I took my time getting up because today I had clean-up duty in the cafeteria. While my siblings moved on to their next schedule of the day, I stayed behind to clean up their leftover food and trays.

I moved quickly. Grabbed a few trays, stacked them, and placed them in the appropriate spot by the conveyer. The heavy weight of someone's stare made me stop and involuntarily shiver. I hated being around the guards without Pops or my siblings present. It made me uncomfortable every time I was in the room with someone of the opposite sex. The skin at the back of my neck prickled. The hairs on my arm shot up. My arm immediately shot out to the side, firmly grabbing on to a guard's wrist.

He stared at my fingers on his skin. He blissfully shuddered as if my touch had done something to him. Lately, my nearness to some of these men had done something to them. I swallowed the lump in my throat, releasing the instinctual hold on his wrist.

"P-please don't touch me," I tried to say in a firm voice.

The guard grinned, exposing a set of tobacco-colored teeth. "You felt it too, didn't you?" He asked. He was already making his way closer to me, pinning me against the tray return bin.

Bile rose. My insides curdled. He slithered closer like a snake seeking heat. I pushed back farther, feeling the pressure of the metal edge piercing into my skin. My fingers shook as I placed one hand on the bin and the other in front of me. Where was Pops when I needed him?

I gawked at the other guards, who watched with equal parts curiosity and anxiousness. They weren't going to help me. We weren't allowed to fight the soldiers on duty—every rule in this facility obeyed. Even Pops had warned us that we shouldn't make the general mad. The ache in my back woke me up. I sidestepped the guard but slammed my shoulder into another. The one I slammed into ran his clammy hands down the exposed skin of my arm. I shuddered, repulsed at the feel of his touch.

"Mmm," the other sniffed my skin with the scent of his arousal slamming into me.

I gagged, but nothing came out.

My knees buckled, but I didn't have time to fall to the ground. The one behind me had grabbed me by the armpit, pulling me closer to his excited body. Tears fell from my eyes as they touched parts of me that made me uncomfortable. I wasn't allowed to fight them. Pops told me to follow the rules. The chant encircled my mind reminding me to be good. The rest of the group did as they were told. I had to, as well.

But I couldn't help the crushing weight of fear on my body.

A whimper escaped my lips, and it only excited them further. I held my pain back. I couldn't show them it hurt. A soldier against the wall watched, unmoving. He didn't follow the others, but he also didn't stop them from their onslaught. I moved away from one, but kept slamming into another as if it were many instead of the two. Anywhere I went, one was there to gain access to a body part I possessed amid reproductive growth. Pops told me my body was changing and with it more attention from the opposite sex. But what he didn't explain to me was why I had to endure it.

More tears joined the fray as the soldier's arm came around from the back, sliding right under one of my breasts. I jerked away, feeling a rush of anger coalescing within me. They could see the flush of embarrassment and the wave of pain on my face, but they only *laughed.*

"Leave me alone," I rushed out when I could no longer tolerate their touch.

If I couldn't show my fear or the pain they caused me, then I would show them an emotion I kept in check. Righteous anger tore through my veins like the blood that flowed in it. I blinked several times to dilute the red haze covering my sight.

Their laughter haunted me. The sound echoed in my head like an awful song stuck on repeat. They didn't bother to move. I could easily subdue them. I was stronger than a lot of the soldiers used in this facility. But I wasn't allowed to touch them. We weren't allowed to fight them.

The rules were always obeyed.

My fist curled. I'd no longer succumb to fear. They wouldn't hurt me anymore.

"What on God's green earth do you think you are doing to that girl?"

The baker lady who made us the treats came around the doorway with thunderous eyes and a large metal soup spoon in her hand. The males parted as quickly as they had gathered. I tried to move but the rage inside of me kept me firmly rooted. The woman got closer, her ample body shielding my small one. I blinked again, recognizing that she had come to my rescue. We were always happy to see the baker because she had sweets ready for us every morning in the cafeteria, but I was never more pleased to see her than I was right now.

"The trainee was having difficulties with the trays. We were only helping."

She didn't even look down at me as I stared at her with wide eyes. No one ever believed us. But for some reason, the baker didn't believe the soldier's words. She waved her spoon at them.

"I will report you," she threatened.

The men laughed and walked away. The one by the wall who did nothing to help only stared at us. He shook his head but said nothing. The baker lady grabbed me by the shoulder, turning me around to face her. Standing this close to her, I could see one eye draw toward her nose while the other stared straight at me.

"What did they do, Silk?"

I shook my head, afraid to voice the issues out loud. Project Hercules created warriors. We weren't allowed to complain. I was a weapon and needed to act like it. The baker lady only held them off temporarily. Her interference wouldn't stop the assaults. The rage burned through me. I was unable to dissuade it. The red haze never fully dissolved. It only recessed deep into my mind, waiting for the day it would come back out.

Outskirts of Sector Delta
The Waste
Gavin Foxhand
New States Citizen ID: CH.JJ49.GF-Rank A

THE MERCENARIES RAN around the camp, pushing away from Silk's pheromone radius of expulsion. Seaa and the rest pushed everyone as far back as they could, fully expecting Silk to bring the entire camp down with her ability. I watched from my spot on the ground as I held Silk's body to mine. Although unresponsive, Silk's body thrashed and seized. Blood poured from her leg wound the more her body convulsed.

Seaa screamed for medical help. A woman who looked to be in her mid-forties with strands of gray in her hair came forward. Seaa stopped her. "If you feel weird at all being around Silk, you need to tell us immediately."

I didn't know if I had become entirely immune to Silk's pheromones, but I felt nothing coming off of her. The woman nodded at Seaa and ran over to where I held Silk close to me. She checked her leg. All the while, I watched the woman for signs of distress. Silk's body shook again, sweat beading on her forehead.

"Please, bring her into the medical tent. Follow me."

Seaa approached, but I put a bloody hand up to stop her. I didn't need her help picking up the woman I loved. I got up from the ground. Edging closer, I scooped Silk into my arms and walked over to where the woman waved us down. Seaa followed closely behind, while the rest of the team kept Viktor and his people at a good distance.

"Seaa, I don't think she's lost complete control," I said as I laid her on the cot provided.

The woman moved around swiftly. She made quick work of tearing off one pantleg to gain access to the wound. Seaa and I watched from the sidelines.

"Yeah, I don't feel anything either. I'm going to get Viktor over here. Give me a minute."

I nodded and watched as she exited the tent. The medic tore open a package with her mouth. Inside were the fixings of a suture kit. After cleaning the wound, she worked on stitching everything together. Within minutes, Seaa had come back with Viktor. We watched him for a reaction and nothing.

Viktor stared at us both. "You told me I might feel something powerful draw me toward her, but I feel nothing," he told Seaa.

We both exhaled. "Okay, good. Viktor, you can bring your people back in."

He nodded, running out of the tent.

We watched as Silk shook her head, clearly distraught over something out of our control. "Is she in pain?" I asked the medic.

The woman shook her head as her fingers deftly handled the needle and thread. "No, I don't think so. I have applied a generous amount of local anesthesia to numb her to the work." She briefly looked up just as Cam came into the tent. "I think she's having a nightmare."

"How is she?" Cam asked at the same time.

Startled, the woman looked back at him. "She'll be fine."

Seaa pushed him out of the tent. "Cam, there's enough people in here. Go make the people comfortable out there."

He snorted but listened. I watched him go, shoving down the feelings of jealousy I knew threatened to consume me. Silk had come over to me. She had allowed me to kiss her. It wouldn't make things with her better if I acted like some jealous jerk. Silk groaned but didn't wake. I grabbed the edge of my shirt to wipe off the sweat from her forehead. Victor came inside, asking to speak to Seaa.

The medic called out that Silk needed blood. Seaa put a hand up to Victor. But instead of waiting for her to volunteer, I told the medic I'd do it.

"I'm O negative."

The woman didn't even question it. She sat me on a chair and cleaned a spot on my skin. As she worked, Seaa turned to Viktor, finally acknowledging him. "There is a lot we need to discuss Viktor, but I don't want to do too much of it without Silk present. You kidnapped Gavin. If it has to do with him, I know Silk would want to be present."

The sound of the beast's howls made Seaa's head shoot up. I had already gotten used to the sounds. Viktor had told me that these creatures were created by Project Hercules. He wanted me to hack into their collars and then mentioned some other things, but I was too pissed that I got captured that I didn't listen. My only thought at that time was when Silk found me, and I knew she would, she'd be one pissed off super.

"They're beasts," I told Seaa.

"Beasts?" she questioned.

Viktor nodded. "Yes, we captured a few beasts during a mission. They had some collars we needed hacked. We found out about Gavin's abilities with technology and then dug deeper and found he was Gregory Foxhand's son..."

"I get it," Seaa interrupted. "You thought he would be an easy way to stop Project Hercules."

"Yes."

"Okay, so we're fighting on the same side."

Viktor stared at her.

"We have a mission we've titled The Rayne Project. We're working on getting all of Braggarts major financial players out of the game and bring our sister Rayne back from their compulsion." She sighed. "It's a long story."

"Then I want in. I need this stopped."

Seaa pulled out her KeViewer. She spoke to Thunder, coming up with a way to resolve the matter between our team and Viktor's mercenary group. As they spoke, I slowly disengaged from their conversation and brushed the hair back from Silk's face as the medic finished. I didn't even notice when she had pricked me and taped the needle to my skin. Blood poured from me to Silk intravenously.

The beautiful woman no longer moved or groaned. She seemed more at peace. Seaa and Viktor carried on with their conversation. Exhaustion consumed me. I sat closer to her, taking in her scent. Seeing her so relaxed now, made me sigh with relief. All I ever wanted to do was show her that I'd never leave her. I wouldn't walk out on her again.

No, I'll never leave her again.

CHAPTER NINETEEN

Outskirts of Sector Delta
The Waste

I OPENED MY eyes to see that I was inside a tent with medical equipment all around me. Gavin sat to one side, slightly hunched over a chair with an IV in his arm. I saw before I heard the blood pulsing from his body and into mine. My body tensed. I jerked up, knocking over a metal tray with bloody gauze and a suture kit. The three other guests inside the tent turned around at the sound. Gavin's head shot up—alert and ready for anything. I yanked the needle stuck in my arm, covering the small drops of blood with my other hand. One stranger ran over to Gavin's arm and pulled the needle from his arm too.

Seaa and Viktor stared at me.

"What the hell were you doing?" I demanded of no one in particular.

Before anyone spoke, I fingered the metal bracelet on my wrist that held the reminder of my days in Foxtrot hidden beneath. Now awake, the thoughts of my time there and the sweet baker lady who had intervened when no one else had were foggy—almost forgotten. It'd been a long time since those memories had risen to the forefront of my mind. I fingered the small wristband again. The feeling calmed me. It was a reminder never to forget my hatred for that place and the men in it. I stared at Gavin. Although the kiss lingered on my lips, I couldn't make myself hate it. I turned to my bracelet again, shoving the metal aside and caressing the old plastic band underneath. Noise in the room brought my eyes upward.

Seaa only shook her head. "I'm sorry, your highness, but you had a huge hole in your leg that kept bleeding out. We all noticed but were too absorbed in your little romance that we didn't want to disrupt anything."

The blood I'd been transfused with must've worked because I could feel my cheeks burn. Gavin stood by the borrowed bed. He seemed a little pale, but overall he was fine. I needed to make sure anyway.

"Are you good?"

Gavin smiled. "Of course I am."

I nodded. My fingers itched to touch him, but some habits were hard to break. It didn't take long for Gavin to read my mind, though, because he wrapped his hands around mine, dropping the fingers that held the plastic band. I didn't squeeze back, but I didn't pull away either. I left his hand holding mine while I addressed Silk and Viktor.

"So, you're not a threat now?" I gestured with my chin to Viktor.

Seaa's eyes almost popped right out of her head. "Oh, damn, Silk. You have to see this! Can you stand?"

Can I stand?

I moved my hand away from Gavin's, sliding my legs to the ground. One side of my jeans was cut up like a pair of real short shorts. The only evidence of a bullet wound was a clean cut of gauze wrapped around my thigh. To make both sides of the jeans look even, I grabbed some medical scissors from another side table and cut the other to match. I slid my boots back on and strapped them. On my feet, pain pulsed from the wound in my thigh, but not enough to drop me on the floor.

"I'm good."

Seaa nodded. When she turned around, I grabbed the plastic band underneath the bracelet and ripped it off. I could feel a weight lift from shoulders I hadn't known was there until the moment I did. I staggered. Gavin shot his hand out to steady me, thinking it had to do with the hole in my leg. If only he knew how grave this reminder was of the life I'd escaped from. Dropping the thin piece of plastic on the medical tent's ground, I moved to stand by Seaa.

Something in me changed, but I ignored it.

Gavin stayed behind us as we walked out of the tent. Outside was a different matter altogether. Rock had four kids hanging from his arms. The kids laughed as he rolled his hips like an old-school washing machine, flying them back and forth. The mothers watched with smiles on their faces. Cam sat at the rickety picnic table in an arm-wrestling match with Snow. The men boisterously laughed, slamming down coins and bills as they made bets on who would win.

One man watched us from his spot by the last tent. I recognized him as the one who shot a hole through my leg. We got closer. He looked down at the floor.

"Dusty, lookup, you idiot. You did nothing wrong," Viktor told him.

He straightened and stared right at me. "I did nothing wrong," he parroted.

I laughed. The man flinched but stayed rooted to his spot. With my hands, I created space between Seaa and Viktor so I was face to face with Dusty. Viktor tensed but one hand from Seaa on his shoulder comforted him somehow.

"It was a good shot," I smirked, and he saw there was no malice in my words. He visibly relaxed.

But then I leaned in, ever so slowly that he tensed up again. I reminded him that I wasn't one to mess with, my mouth by his hair. "But, if you ever aim your gun at me or one of my own again, I will rip through you faster than you could blink."

The man nodded.

I stood straighter, walking past Dusty and into the tent. Inside were three cages, two of them occupied by roaring half-human half-beast hybrids. They rattled the cells trying to escape, but each time their skin would make contact with the bars, the metal would burn them, and tiny plumes of smoke would rise from their skin.

"Oh, fucks."

Seaa put a hand on my shoulder as Viktor walked closer to one of the cages. The beasts screamed and growled, trying to grab him, but they couldn't. The metal would burn them so severely that they stayed in the middle of the cage, refusing to move forward or backward.

Viktor spoke first. "The bars are made of silver. It seems to be the only thing that keeps them from breaking free."

I shook my head. "What are they?"

"Alpha experiments, Silk," Seaa replied. "Apparently, Plumboy has been playing with a few cocktails of his own on Braggart's orders."

I shook my head again. Not in disbelief because I wouldn't put it past those assholes, but because the situation seemed to only get worse—never better for us. "Are these the beasts Cameron was talking about?"

Seaa nodded. "Yeah, Cam said they are very similar, and those collars" —she pointed to three broken collars on a crate— "were around their neck and seemed to be controlling them."

I watched Viktor as Gavin leaned a bit closer to take a look at the collars. "How did you come in possession of these animals?"

"My group and I were able to raid a caravan DBT unit."

DBT's were Dead Body Transports used to take dead prisoners from a military base to a base in Alpha. The units took dead bodies, but these creatures were very much alive. "Explain."

Viktor watched Gavin fiddling around with the collars. The young heir was in his own little genius world. It seemed that anytime he was near technology, he couldn't help himself. I enjoyed seeing it bring out a passion within him. The fighting, running, and death-defying experiences weren't Gavin's cup of tea. His job was to hack and read. It was my job to make sure he was safe enough to do it.

Viktor turned back to me.

"There were about five vehicles, and only one of them was a DBT. We didn't get to see what they were transporting if anything, but we were able to steal one of their vehicles and make it out of there with these cages and the beasts inside."

"Three cages."

Viktor nodded. "Three beasts."

I turned to him. "What happened to the third?"

Viktor sneered, turning to stare at the others. One growled at him, and Viktor growled back. "One beast escaped and killed one of my men. I killed it in return."

"Ah," I heard Gavin mutter.

We turned in his direction.

He pointed at the devices. "These collars seem to emit a very high frequency that may cause a kind of bloodlust in these animals, increasing their strengths." He touched the lining underneath. "This bad boy right here is silver. And these little holes here might be injecting silver into the beasts that get them to do their bidding." He shrugged and ran a hand through his hair like he usually did when thinking hard about something. "I'm throwing stuff out there. I wouldn't know for sure unless I had the tools to open these bad boys and find out for sure."

That's precisely what Cam had said when he mentioned the beasts before. He told us that the collars emitted a high-frequency hum that we could hear. Each time the collar hummed, the creature would get stronger and more ferocious. Gavin hadn't been at that meeting. For him to know by just looking at it was a testament to his talent.

I crossed my arms again, remembering my real reason for being here. "Why Gavin?"

Viktor stared at the roof of the tent. "Gavin Foxhand was to be used as leverage to stop his father from funding Project Hercules any further."

I narrowed my eyes, knowing full well he wasn't telling me everything. Viktor let out a long, deep breath as he stared in Gavin's direction. Gavin tinkered with the collars, oblivious to Viktor's line of sight.

"My uncle sold his soul to the devil. Unit 13 needs to be torn apart and buried away permanently, so I thought using the same beasts against them would cause mayhem in the facility." He clenched his fingers in the hand that rested by his thigh. "We got intel that Gavin was a huge dark web hacker. We thought he could hack these collars and make them work for us. But..." Viktor stared at the beasts and then Seaa and me. "We learned something better. We gained knowledge that he was Foxhand's son, and such, a tool to manipulate Gregory Foxhand."

I caged the rage rushing through me. "You wanted to forcefully use him?"

He put both hands up, showing me he meant no harm. "My men had strict orders not to hurt him. We didn't want to cause the kid pain, but we also knew that waltzing into his apartment to talk to him wouldn't get us an audience, especially when his father has done everything in his power to keep that boy under wraps."

I opened my mouth and licked my lips after realizing I had clenched my jaw so tightly it ached. "Then I ruined your plans."

A sound like a laugh and grunt escaped Viktor's mouth. "You aren't lyin'. We were not ready for a super, especially not a super soldier from Batch 001."

Viktor studied Seaa, who watched Gavin curiously. "Putting that aside, your sister told me that you all have a plan called The Rayne Project that involves nipping the major players for Braggart in the ass. We want a part too."

Seaa smiled. "I've already called Thunder. He agrees that we should partner with the mercenaries."

I grimaced.

"We were waiting for you to get up. Thunder is letting you handle this next mission. I have Gavin's father's whereabouts. I think with a little visit from his son and his new *girlfriend*, he might be amiable to our suggestions."

The word girlfriend made me nauseous.

"Yeah, let's just pay him a visit. And stop calling me Gavin's girlfriend."

Seaa giggled, and Gavin smiled. For some reason, neither one of them seemed to be too worried about my words. I narrowed my eyes at them. Gavin put his hands up in surrender, but Seaa laughed harder.

"I love you, Silk," she whispered.

I loved her too. "Yeah, yeah."

I HAD LOST track already of how many times Cameron apologized to the ladies and their children for pointing the gun at them earlier. The women didn't seem too disturbed. On the contrary, they giggled as he smiled that flirtatious little grin of his. There was a time in my life when that smile did things to me too. A long time ago, when I was younger and naive, but not anymore. I quickly glanced at Gavin, who stood with his arms crossed as Viktor explained some things to him, and realized it was that lean man that had my attention now. Cameron had someone else he needed to focus on.

He would become a father very soon.

Baker walked around a picnic table to stand in front of me. "How did you guys find us?" he asked.

I turned away from watching Gavin and seeing Cameron in a whole new light, to see Baker make himself comfortable on top of the termite-infested picnic table. An older gentleman walked beside him, leaning against the same table. For a second, I couldn't place him, but then I remembered the box of pastries and bread and knew he was the baker we had followed here.

The baker man watched with extreme curiosity. He handed me a wrapped blueberry muffin, which I took in my hand. It smelled so sweet and delicious my mouth watered. He passed another to Baker. I sniffed it, watching Baker take a bite first. There was nothing in it that stood out to me.

"First, I followed your scent because it imprinted in my senses, and then I followed the baked goods man here." I gestured to the old man.

He pointed to himself, questioning. I unwrapped the muffin, taking a bite, damn the risks. I loved sweets.

"Yeah, I saw you and one of Viktor's men meet in the tunnels. I knew you were both going to make it to the same spot, so I focused on the smell of fresh bread instead."

The older man laughed as Baker shook his head. "No one can smell those treats down there."

I pointed to my nose. "We can," I said through a bite full of sweet bread and blueberries.

The baker nodded emphatically. "My late wife had mentioned a few times that the children she cooked for had abilities unlike any other."

Memories of the baker lady came back to my mind. "Your wife was a baker at the Foxtrot bunkers?"

He smiled, but it was sad. "Yes. Unfortunately, my wife spoke up about some injustice at that place, and they killed her for it."

My heart stilled. The older man's late wife was the woman who came to my rescue. The nightmare I had, a reminder of that incident years ago. I wiped the left-over crumbs off my shirt. "I remember her."

The older man straightened, dusting off an imaginary piece of dirt from his apron. "Yes, well, that's why I joined Viktor and his men years ago. I found out those children escaped that cruel place, and I hoped to see them again one day and see why my wife refused to leave them when things got bad."

"I'm sorry it took you this long to meet us," I added.

The baker shook his head. "No, I saw one of you not long ago in Delta. A young brunette. Lost and alone. My late wife had shown me photos of these kids she worked with. The girl was immediately recognizable." He sighed. "I tried to give her advice and make it as nonchalant as possible in case she was being followed."

His description reminded me of Rayne. She mentioned she was in Delta looking for information. It was the first place she went to get a new pair of clothes, and food. I stared at the scuffs on my boots. "If you're wife was the baker at Foxtrot, then I'm probably the reason she was killed." My insides felt heavy. My fingers shook. "She helped me once, and I never saw her again."

Those brown eyes had tears falling over ashen cheeks. The baker came over and grabbed my hands, enveloping them in thick, callused palms. "No, oh, dear child. She was a righteous woman, and what she saw that day would never have let her sleep at night if she had done nothing. I'm the one who's sorry I kept all this to myself for so long. When the government knocked on my door, insisting she told me of confidential things, I denied it all." He sniffled. "My wife was the brave one. I hid away for years in my little market baking bread and pastries instead of going to someone, anyone, to tell them of the things she had talked about in private."

Baker shook his head as he followed the conversation. "No way, Carlton. You have supplied us with the necessary foods and items from the market we couldn't gather ourselves. You've kept this group alive."

Feeling an urge to comfort him, I stepped forward, wiping a tear from his cheek. The salty drop transfixed me. "You did right. Besides, you are making amends for it now." I gestured to the entire camp. "For everyone here."

"I'm only a baker."

I shrugged, shoving my hands into the pocket of my cut-off jeans. The wind blew more dust around us, whipping my curls around in a frenzy. "No, you're more than that."

Baker agreed. "Yeah, you're the movers and shakers of our era."

The older man smiled. "No, that's where you are wrong." He pointed at me, the camp, and the rest of my siblings. "That's what *you* guys are doing."

I stared one last time at my siblings and the new group of mercenaries standing by our side. This group standing here was what stood in the way of the government. We were the only ones who could bring an end to General Braggart and his Unit 13 regiment.

We would influence a change.

CHAPTER TWENTY

WE LEFT THE mercenaries back at their camp with the agreement to call them the moment we needed them. Viktor spent years trying to stop his uncle and General Braggart. Some of his men died for the cause. He hadn't been enthused about staying but knew his place was protecting the rest of his people. If we could find him, Batch 002 would have no problems either. He had our group fighting with him. Unit 13 would not hesitate to kill them if they posed a threat. With us at his side, his people wouldn't suffer if ever anything happened to him.

I won't allow their families to experience any more hardships.

Seaa, Gavin, Snow, and I made our way to downtown Trēbeta where Gavin's father lived. The rest of the group headed toward Safe Haven to prepare for our next fight. We kept close to the crumbling buildings, far away from the people walking around in layers of clothes. The winter wind blew more vigorously, but we barely felt the weather. Our adrenaline kept us warm enough to survive the winter months' elements. Gavin was the only one of us in a thick coat, blowing warm air into his cupped hands.

I watched the dense clouds above my head, covering the smattering of stars I knew hung farther above. The night was quiet but alive all at the same time. Couples canoodled in dark alcoves, while others walked swiftly to their next location. No one stared at us nor paid us a second glance as we passed. Seaa shuffled around in a hooded robe, hiding her luxurious hair beneath. Snow, too, wore a hoodie to cover his platinum hair. I didn't bother changing my complexion this time around, but I did borrow a different pair of pants from one of the females at the camp. Walking around in shorts was way too conspicuous around these parts.

"Uh, Silk?"

Gavin caught up to me. I turned briefly to look at him, acknowledging his call.

He almost tripped over broken cobblestones. My hand shot out to steady him without breaking our stride. Gavin grinned timidly, running a hand through his hair.

I sighed.

Gavin jumped, dropping his hand from his head. "Sorry, Silk. I keep forgetting you hate it when I do that."

I shook my head, curls bouncing from cheek to cheek. "It's fine, Gavin."

The young man crossed over a rusted metal pipe. "Think we could talk about what happened. You know, before you passed out and ended up in the medical tent?"

My stomach clenched, and bile rose from my throat. Memories flooded my mind. I shook my head, trying to absolve myself of them. A male medical technician whose face I couldn't remember came to the forefront of my mind. He would stare at me with the same eyes as the soldiers from the cafeteria. His fingers would touch my skin in gentle caresses instead of using a professional detachment to perform his job.

He'd whip my hair over one shoulder, sniffing my neck as he leaned over me to check the machines located behind me, illuminating my vitals. The nearness of that man made me squirm. Goosebumps would litter my skin as if protecting me from his touch. Why didn't I fight it before? How come I didn't know then about the consequences of my power or its effect on men around me?

I knew what Gavin wanted to talk about, and I'm sure I owed it to him, but for right now, all I wanted was to put these bad memories behind me. I shook my head, placing a brief hand on his shoulder. "Not now, Gavin."

He stopped walking without saying a word. I didn't turn to look at him but kept on. I knew Snow was right behind us and would make sure Gavin kept moving. In time, he kept walking as if he hadn't just gotten turned down again. I didn't want to hurt him. That was the furthest thing from my mind. I could only hope that he respected the challenges I faced. We were near Gavin's father's penthouse condo when Gavin stopped walking again.

"Oh, hell no."

I turned to look at him as Snow hovered behind him. Gavin stared up at the high rise, glinting like a beacon in the darkness. There weren't many buildings like this anymore, so seeing it in its grandeur must've been quite intimidating to some.

"I may have never set foot inside my father's residences, but I do know where he lives. Damn it! Why the heck are we here?"

Seaa turned to face Gavin. "We made a deal with your father, Gavin. He'd give us anything we wanted to bring you back safely. You already know we were confronting him at some point. Your capture only brought that upon us faster."

Gavin ran a hand through his hair looking at me defiantly as if waiting for me to argue with him for doing it. I kept my mouth shut.

"Yeah, but why did I have to be here? I could've just gone along with Cam and Rock."

Snow laughed, so Gavin turned around to face him with his fiercest glare. The expression on his face made me smile, so I put my head down to hide the smile with my hair, pretending to study the ground.

"Dude, your dad would be easier to convince if he saw you alive, duh."

Gavin blew out an aggravated breath, somewhere between a grunt and a growl. His warm breath puffed out every time he spoke. "Fine. Let's get this over with already." He walked, muttering under his breath, "Why don't y'all just stick a needle in my eye?"

His words brought me back to the medical room in Foxtrot when the same male technician had rubbed my skin with an alcohol swab before getting a shot. His fingers would scrape down the skin of my elbow intentionally. I'd squirm, trying to relieve myself of the awful sensation, but he'd only comment in a breathy voice how "needles aren't as scary as you think. You'd enjoy the sensation if you let it."

Sounds all around me grew louder, but I couldn't make them out. All I could see and hear was that male's face and voice repeating itself over and over again in my mind. I couldn't run away from the room. No one ever understood why I hated their visits. All I saw was their lustful eyes, could hear their hitched breathing, and could smell their arousal.

Hands shook me, bringing me back to the present. "Get a hold of yourself, Silk."

I shook my head, watching as Snow kept Gavin safely tucked away in a dark side alley while one Ground Force officer moaned from the ground and the other lit his wand up in a blaze of fury. In an instant, I bent down to grab the one officer by his collar, lifting him from the ground. The man squealed as I tossed him toward the other one. The one holding the wand accidentally zapped the first. He threw the dead weight off himself, jerking when he realized that he couldn't move the rod from underneath Seaa's boot.

"You can't do this to an officer of the law."

"Right," I heard Seaa say.

She grabbed the custom taser from his hand, snapping it in half. He leaned upon his elbows with his face twisted in rage. "I'll report—"

Those were all the words he could get out of his mouth before I punched him and knocked him out cold.

Seaa stared at me with those large violet eyes. Her button-nose flared out, almost mad at me. I smirked because why wouldn't I find it funny? The hauntingly beautiful mermaid-woman was quite intriguing when she was angry—especially at me.

"What?" I mock asked.

She grunted, checking both directions of the alley for any witnesses. "What the heck happened earlier? You didn't even sense them coming."

I don't know what happened to me. It was difficult for me to tell Seaa that these memories made me lose control of what was happening right in front of me. Instead, I shrugged, pretending not to know what she was talking about. My siblings were used to this behavior from me, so she didn't question it further.

We made it to the back of the building, avoiding the guarded front doors at all costs. Snow yanked on the locked back door, pulling it clear off the locks. Seaa stared at him. She clearly wanted to throttle him.

"You couldn't have used more tact than that?"

He grinned and stretched his arms over the back of his head, showing off pale abs above the waistband of his jeans. "Who? Me?"

She made a small garble from her throat. "Focus, Snow."

Gavin sighed and stared at the stairs before him. They wound to the top in a never-ending cycle with no end in sight. "We have to climb this entire thing?"

Before I could lend a helping hand, Snow picked up Gavin in a romantic way, winking as he sped up the stairs. We were supposed to have been a lot quieter than this, but all Seaa and I could hear were the cuss words of one very pissed hacker-heir. The building owners had the stairwell painted in a flat gray—the stairs comprised of cement and marble with wrought iron handrails. Once we got to the floor we needed, the view changed spectacularly. The dim light from the stairwell didn't prepare our vision for the brightness of the crystal chandelier hanging in a long hall with a bank of Gidgets to our left and one solitary Gidget ahead.

We walked to the solitary Gidget, taking a peek inside.

"Do you have access to Dad's apartment?" Snow asked Gavin, who was moody about his trip up the stairs.

"No, of course not. I told you all that I've never visited my father. Not like I'm welcome."

Seaa was the first to shake her head, replying, "I doubt that."

Snow pushed Gavin inside. We all followed. A high-tech security system covered the panel to the right. Gavin neared it, studying the mechanism in front of him. I could see the hacker in him trying to figure out how to go about messing with the system when the system turned on and started speaking out loud.

RETINAL SCAN READY

Gavin glanced at me and then at the beeping system. The security system emitted a red light that ran from the top of his eyebrows to the bridge of his nose. The system beeped twice then spoke again.

WELCOME, GAVIN FOXHAND

We all stared at one another as the bars of the Gidget closed. The machine whooshed upward at a fast pace. My siblings and I peered at each other, readying ourselves for whatever we'd come in contact with when the doors opened.

Standing in front of us with a tumbler of ice and a honey-colored liquid was Gregory Foxhand III. His eyes took us in quickly but remained on his son. The sight of him almost broke me. The man had been drinking, that was pretty clear from the bloodshot eyes and how he swayed on his feet, but he'd also been crying. Their eyes were the same, one more aged than the other. One brighter; the other dull and tired.

It was difficult to avoid comparing one to the other. The men's resemblance was eerie. And both were into technology. One hacked it, and the other created hordes of it. Seaa said the father would do anything to get his son back. I had a feeling the conversation here between both men would change something in them.

The room we stepped into was beyond spectacular. While Gavin's apartment was posh with a Mediterranean flair, his father's was brisk, sleek, and modern. The interior was comprised of metal and glass, in dark, subtle tones. It didn't seem like a place for a man who had four children. The home resembled that of a bachelor with nothing in his life but his money.

"Gavin," Gregory whispered as if he couldn't believe his son was standing right in front of him.

I sensed Gavin's discomfort and couldn't help but

stand in front of him, protecting him as only I could. Gregory stared at me with bloodshot eyes. Gavin placed a shaking hand on the back of my shoulder. If he was trying to convince me he was alright, controlling the quivering limb would've helped.

"We brought Gavin back as promised."

Gregory turned to Seaa, nodding so hard I thought his head would roll right off his shoulders.

"What can I do ever to repay you?"

His behavior was not of the man Gavin made him out to be. I put a hand up to stop Seaa from saying anything else, gauging Snow's reaction, as he could tell better than all of us if the man was an excellent actor or not. Snow knew what I wanted to know.

"He's good," he answered.

I nodded, turning back to stare at the older man as I walked around him. Gregory Foxhand stared back. I gave him credit for not flinching. I never did give off a welcoming vibe. Anyone who stood near me felt anxiety deep down to their toes.

"You know what we are then?"

He nodded. "I do. Project Hercules' failed experiments."

Snow grunted, but Gregory's words didn't bother me. I stopped Gavin from speaking up. I could tell his father's comments bothered him also. My heart skipped a beat, so I willed it to stay calm.

"I don't see where we have failed, but we did belong to Project Hercules."

The man grimaced. "It's not what I meant."

I smiled, but it wasn't a pleasant one. "You've pretty much made our lives miserable, Foxhand. I think it is about time you do something for us."

He sucked in a deep breath, shooting back the last in his tumbler. He placed the glass on a side table— the ice cubes clinking against one another. "You have my word. I told her" —he pointed to Seaa— "that I'd do anything if you brought my son back. I meant it."

"Don't act like you care about me," Gavin cried out, his hands fisted at his sides.

Foxhand Sr. gave his son a tired look, exhausted from the hours of worry he no doubtingly went through. "Son, I've told you a million times before. I did this for your own good. You are my only boy. I'd do anything to keep you safe. Even make you believe I didn't care about you."

Gavin snorted. "Well, you succeeded."

The older man took another deep inhale and one long exhale. "I'm here now, Gavin. Tell me what I can do."

"With me, nothing. But you will pull your funding from Project Hercules."

Gregory squinted, his brows meeting between his eyes. "Project Hercules was designed to create a better place to live for you, Gavin. If I pull my funding, I am taking away the very service that I wanted to keep you and the world around *you* safe."

We all made a noise through our noses.

"You don't get it, *Dad*," Gavin spat out. "The government is using private funding to create bizarre creatures. They are taking the power of this project to their heads. People are dying, and families are living in the sewers. Not everyone is benefiting from the government's assistance."

Gregory ran a hand through his hair. I glanced at Gavin, who was doing the same. It seemed the move was less a habit and more a genetic trait.

"Fine," Gregory bit out. "I don't really understand it, but I will trust you, Gavin. I will make the call right now and relieve Project Hercules from my money."

Gavin smiled, exhaling, his hands no longer shaking. "You have no clue how much that helps."

The KeViewer in Gregory's pocket went off. He stared at the screen, frowning. He put one finger up, silencing us. "Yes, this is Foxhand." Silence. "Yes, I understand. Thank you."

He hung up the line, staring at all of us. "You are about to get ambushed. Someone noticed you getting into the building and has gotten Ground Force to surround the building from every exit available." He walked up to Gavin and me, placing a hand on his son's shoulders. "My insider in Unit 13 also alerted me of the presence of Batch 001 experiments roaming the entrance of Sector Bravo."

Seaa, Snow, and I stared at each other. "Cam and Rock," we said at the same time.

Seaa grabbed her KeViewer, punching in a few buttons before putting it up to her ear. "Where are you guys?" Silence. "Don't go any farther. You and Rock need to lay low. Find somewhere to hide right now. We've just gotten word that you were spotted."

After a few nods, she put down the phone and punched in another set of buttons. "Viktor, we have a problem. How quickly can you get to Trēbeta?" Silence. "Very well, we will see you soon."

Seaa stared back at us. "Foxhand Sr.?" She stared at

the older man. "How long do we have before they get antsy?"

Gregory paced the marble floor in front of us. "I'd say they saw you go in, and because you activated my private Gidget without signing in out front, the valet must've told them you are in my penthouse. If that was the case, then you have about thirty minutes before Ground Force requests access to my penthouse."

"Can they make it inside without your permission?"

He shook his head. "No, no one can but those whom I've programmed on the Gidget."

I folded my hands over my chest, getting ready for one hell of a fight. "I guess we'll wait until Viktor gets closer, and then we'll make our way down and say hi."

Seaa and Snow smiled.

The Rayne Project had begun.

CHAPTER TWENTY-ONE

AFTER ABOUT AN hour or so of uncomfortable silence, waiting in Gregory Foxhand's penthouse apartment, Viktor called Seaa to let her know that he and his men were taking their spots outside, surrounding the Ground Force officers that surrounded us. We decided to fight unarmed because of the multitude of innocent people wondering what was going on inside the building. Gregory wanted to speak to his son, but it wasn't the right time for them to share each other's woes. Gregory wanted to bond with his son, while Gavin only wanted to be far from his father.

I also wasn't going to ask Gavin to stay. I knew better than to force that man to do anything he didn't want to do. Gavin would've been safer staying in his father's apartment, but he wouldn't remain regardless of anything I said unless I made him promises I couldn't keep. My fingers and muscles tensed as a memory of promises flittered to my mind. The first medical doctor that had assisted Pops in our health and performances always leaned in, breathing his coffee-infused breath in my face with promises of anything a girl could dream of if I promised myself to him.

My heart beat so hard it reminded me I was alive. The rhythm didn't sit well in my stomach. The fingers on my hands quivered uncontrollably until I squeezed them into a fist. I sat on a hovering bar stool. My leg shook, bouncing in tandem to the ticking of the clock. Bile rose and fell in a game of cat and mouse.

"I think I'm gonna puke," I muttered before teetering to one side—off balance.

Gavin reached me before anyone else, leading me to the bathroom. "Are you...you know, okay?"

I took a deep breath. "I'll be fine." Of course, I didn't know for sure. I wasn't sure at all what the hell was going on with me. I went from never thinking of my time in the bunkers to consistently having memories better, long forgotten. My emotions were volatile. My fingers touched the skin where my plastic band used to be. Had taking off my small little protection done this to me?

There had to be a reason why all these memories kept coming back up. I didn't want to think of the past. If I wanted to change along with the change we were making in the world, then I needed to let go of all the hatred I pushed down to the core of my soul. I'd be lying, though, if I didn't think it was just better to be a bitch. I pursed my lips at the crude thought. Why did I label myself so disgracefully? Why couldn't I be the woman my sisters thought me to be? I gnawed on my bottom lip. When I thought about it, I was never mean to my sisters. If I had it in me to be friendly, why couldn't I stop the prejudice against men?

I splashed water in my face as my hearing picked up Snow's comment to Seaa. "She pregnant or something?"

His comment made me think of Suzanne and Cameron. The citizens of New States had been doing a fine job ignoring the chaos surrounding us and living with what they had. We, of course, didn't accept that. Unit 13 created us to fight, and we'd done nothing but hide. It was time we changed the world for the better. Suzanne and Cam were going to bring a baby into the world. I couldn't allow that child to come into a fight. When that baby came, it wouldn't be to be poked and prodded by government hands.

The sound of light footsteps moved closer.

Snow needed a butt-whopping for his "pregnant" comment, but today wasn't the day. I stared at my reflection in the mirror, water dripping from my chin. A knock on the door pulled me away. "Silk, you ready?"

I opened the door, smiling. "Of course I am. Oh, remind me to kill Snow after this, okay?"

Seaa laughed.

Before heading into the Gidget, I channeled the web from within to the surface of my skin. In front of everyone, the armor covered me, keeping my body protected from any real damage. The colors transitioned as the lights of the penthouse hit the suit.

"That was amazing, Silk," Gavin whispered by my

ear.

His voice ran down my spine, tightening around me in an exhilarating embrace. I ignored it, working on keeping my facial muscles relaxed. I never had to hide what I was thinking, but because my feelings for Gavin felt raw and new, I didn't know what to do about it yet.

Gregory watched with trepidation as his son got ready to move. Gavin carried a backpack that had once belonged to one of the mercenaries. He fiddled through them, grabbing some trinkets from a desk in a corner that belonged to his father. I watched, studying Gregory's every move, hoping he didn't betray us in some way. All that man wanted was to sit with his son and bury their problems. Gregory sighed.

"Listen, before you go. I know that you are trying to end this project, but pulling my assistance won't get you what you desire. You need at least one more contributor. I don't know the name because we keep ourselves anonymous, but I know that one of the financiers owns a shipping barge located at the end of the Delta Financial District by the Boston Harbor. But because there are so many barge owners shipping and receiving on that end, I'm not positive how much this information helps you."

Gavin turned to his father. "It helps. Trust me. Thank you, Dad."

With that excellent piece of news, we made our way to the Gidget as Seaa sent word to Viktor that we were headed down. Snow and Seaa loaded first but not before Snow grabbed a piece of chocolate from a side table. I snatched it out of his hand as he unwrapped it, shoving it into my mouth and savoring the sweetness of the cocoa. Everyone laughed as if we weren't just about to go out to battle.

Behind me, Gregory tensed. A hand gripped Gavin's shoulder—the one holding the backpack with his things. My hand instinctually dropped on top of the one squeezing Gavin. Gregory stared at me. Gavin stared at Gregory.

Gavin turned slightly, using both his hands to remove Gregory's. "Dad, I'll be fine. The least you could do now is trust me to make the right choices for myself."

Assured Gregory wouldn't be a danger to Gavin; I let go too. A lone tear dropped from Foxhand's right eye, glistening underneath the immense metal light fixture.

"I never meant to make you feel unwanted, Gavin. You are my boy. I didn't" —he pointed to me and the others— "want you to get involved in all of this."

Gavin stared at Seaa and Snow. "They are my friends," he smiled. Then he studied me. "And...uh, hopefully, more."

Gregory's eyes went wide. The blue in his eyes brightened as if seeing something fresh, new, and exciting for the first time in his life. He peered into Gavin's eyes, blinking when he saw what he was searching for. He then turned to me with the same expression. His perusal made me uncomfortable, but all I could think about were the words Gavin had uttered. It didn't take long for Gregory to find what he saw inside Gavin within me. Just thinking about it made me hyper-aware.

Familiar sensations ran through my body, but the

blood pooled in my cheeks, making it evident that his words did something to me. One side of Gavin's mouth lifted, sending me into another mental tizzy. I blinked it away, turning to Gregory Foxhand.

"I will protect him with my life," I reassured him.

Gregory nodded, keeping his hands placed beside him. His fingertips squeezed the material of his pants as if begging it for help to keep them there. Gavin placed his hand on the part of my lower back— not quite low enough to touch my rear and not high enough to reach the middle of my back. He tactfully placed it right between both. Gavin pushed gently, ushering me into the Gidget.

I stared at Gregory Foxhand. The older version of the man I'd grown to care about. "We will keep him safe," I reminded him.

With one last look at his father, Gavin closed the bars, and we made our descent in the Gidget. Snow sniffed the air, taking off his hoodie and releasing his bright whitish-silver hair from its confines. The Rayne Project wouldn't only kill the funding keeping Unit 13 active, but it would also put us more in the open. We wouldn't be hiding from people anymore, nor would we be keeping to the shadows.

Seaa's fingers shook. She fingered the colorful strands of her hair and then the jeweled choker around her neck that kept her hydrated. I hadn't noticed before, but she wore false colorful lashes that brought out the violet in her eyes. There was some makeup leftover on her face. I thought Seaa was magnificent without any of that, but seeing her now made her seem more confident and poised—none of the things she had been comfortable with before.

Of all of us coming out, Seaa would be the one having the worst time. She didn't complain this time. This plan was entirely her idea, so she stayed quiet. If it weren't for the fact that we knew her so well, no one could have noticed her anxiety. Her hooded robe dropped to the floor beside Snow's. Her chest shuddered with an anxious breath.

"You ready for this, babe?" Snow asked Seaa.

She nodded, fluttering her mink lashes.

I turned to Gavin. "Stay in that corner. Do not come out until the Ground Force officers on the floor are subdued."

He didn't fight me. Instead, Gavin lifted the bag he carried higher on his shoulder. "I understand."

The Gidget dinged, and through the mounting bars, we saw four Ground Force officers with their wands lit up in front of them. If Vuwands were their only fighting method, then this would be a lot easier than we thought. I stepped out first because I wore my armor. My siblings were behind me while Gavin stood to the side behind them. The first officer jumped forward, aiming his wand at me like a fencer. I smacked it to the side, giving him credit for hanging on to it. I stepped forward, thrusting a palm up into his nose. The man dropped to the ground in tears, screaming through a puddle of blood already pooled in his cupped hands.

I shifted my feet. My hand came down to the back of another's neck. My leg shot out to hit the last one in the gut. The man hacked, dropping to the carpeted floor. Seaa and Snow laughed. They grabbed the first two officers' wands, cracking them in half.

Snow joked, smashing the third Vuwand against the wallpaper-covered wall. "Silk, you should've let them zap you."

I gave him my dirtiest glare. "You first," I replied.

Snow's piercing light blue eyes—almost white, sparkled under the bright, crystal chandelier. "What I mean is that you now have this wicked suit of armor made from the tough strands of a spider's silk. I think it be good to see if it protects you from the strong electrical output."

He grabbed the final Vuwand from the ground next to an unconscious officer. The wand lit up. The colors too bright to visually endure. The crackle popped in front of my face. "How 'bout it?" he asked again, lighting up the wand once more.

Seaa jumped between us. "You guys forget that these wands don't just create fire sparks but have those Strychnine tips at the end of them that inject poison into the body."

I stared at my suit. The armor built from my engineered body's web worked as a barrier between my organs and painful weapons. These wands were a hindrance to all of us. I leaned down, opening one of the unconscious officers' coats. Inside were three injectable vials of antidote for those severely injured by the Vuwand's shock and poison.

"Okay, Snow. Here." I handed him the antidotes. "Use these just in case."

Snow grinned like the cat that ate the canary. He gave no word he would start. The Vuwand aimed straight for my chest. I waited for the pain, but it didn't come. Snow zapped me over and over again, then stared at the tip of the wand—almost disappointed. The thin needle they used to inject the poison had bent beyond repair.

He laughed, the sound echoing from the walls of the room. "That's one awesome-ass suit."

"It'll serve its purpose," I added.

His grin then turned into a frown. "How is it that you females have been banging out these incredible powers lately?" he muttered under his breath. "I can't even figure out what mine is other than the cold weather really does nothing to me." He pointed to the hooded coat crumpled in the Gidget. "I only wear that thing because I'm kind of recognizable. Long white hair and I'm young as hell with eyes that look demonic."

I got where he was coming from, but having a suit that poured out of one's skin didn't make me any more normal. Rayne could turn into liquid, and Seaa turned into a mermaid. I'm pretty sure we all would've rather chosen to be more regular than freaky. That made me study Gavin's reaction to me. He didn't seem to care about my web and did think it amazing.

Gavin grabbed my hand when he drew near. "So long as you're alright."

His kindness unnerved me, but I welcomed it nonetheless. I gently squeezed his fingers back, hoping to convey that I was trying, albeit unsuccessfully. He took it as affirmation and laced our fingers instead.

I blinked away the ache in my chest. The one deep down behind my rib cage that blossomed every time this guy was near me. "So, shall we come down on the Gidget or take the stairs?"

Seaa sucked in air. A reminder that she was going

to be on display to the rest of the world. If I held her close to me, I was sure I could feel her heart beating furiously. But the mermaidesque woman didn't surprise me when she replied, "I'd rather take the Gidget. Let's get this over with already."

I snickered as Snow smacked Seaa on the back. Gavin powered the Gidget, ushering us forward. We made our way to the lobby, which was sure to be full of Ground Force officers ready to pounce. The area around me was tense with unused energy. We were ready to get on with this show and finally throw Unit 13 for a loop. I let go of Gavin's hand, letting him know with my eyes that I wanted him to stay in the Gidget, safely tucked away until we could decommission the officers below.

Gavin did not attempt to fight me. He knew his place in this "relationship," just like I knew mine. He was made to change me. I was made to keep him safe. The thoughts sobered me up. We started this as enemies. I couldn't see myself anywhere near this man or any other for that matter. In the time we'd shared, I'd learned that not all men were built equal. Some deserved my actions, but I realized others did not. Cam came to mind. One minute I hated the man, thinking he'd never grow the hell up. Now Cam was going to be a father. He changed the way he thought to support the woman bringing his blood-borne to the world.

The air from the moving Gidget pushed us down from the top. We were anxious about the fight ahead. Gavin ran a hand down his face, staring at the ceiling of the Gidget. Snow shifted on his heel, rocking back and forth. His long, straight hair swished in the same rhythm. Seaa was the most distressed of us all. Not because she couldn't fight. *No*, that wasn't the reason she glowered. Seaa would be fighting in front of spectators.

An anxious energy pulsed in waves around our little group. Our powers heightened as the adrenaline within us coursed through our blood. A warm blast of air hit us the moment the Gidget made it to the lobby. The number of officers was insurmountable.

Snow made a sharp, shrill sound. "Good God," he muttered.

My heartbeat tripled. The blood within me boiled in anticipation. The tension of the situation lifted me. Fighting was what I was good at. I stared at my siblings as the wands in front of us lit up the entire room with their luminosity and crackle. They created us to fight. The other countries no longer picked a fight with the remaining New States because of the superhuman, genetically engineered humans.

Because. Of. Us.

CHAPTER TWENTY-TWO

SEAA'S HAIR STRANDS flew with the breeze of this cold early winter morning. Pedestrians hedged the streets as they made their way to work or the market early in the morning or back from their late-night shifts. Although she wore leggings covering some of her scales and a long-sleeved shirt that looped around her middle finger to hide the scales visible there, she kept her illusion magic up and fought against several officers.

Like me, our ability to use our powers without an expiration date was highly beneficial. So long as we kept our energy up through nutrition and rest, our capabilities never caused us any trouble. A cold shiver ran down my spine. We got lucky that Gavin had

found Thunder. Cameron and I had been utterly disabled, running the risk of dying, getting killed, or dis-
covered.

Now we intentionally ran that risk.

The people watched, openly gawking at the scene
unfolding in front of them. Some feared us. Their
hands covered their faces to keep us out of sight and
out of mind. But we weren't make-believe. The government created us first. The only thing people knew was
of the super fighters that ended the wars and only because they were perfected after the military claimed
to have failed with us. We weren't the problem around
here. The problem was these immoral officers taking
advantage of what little humanity we had left.

I blocked an attack, grabbing the man by the wrist
and staring into his face. He yanked repeatedly. The
bystanders collectively sucked in their breath, waiting to see what would happen next. I watched him,
gauging his fight with my own eyes. I saw a determi-
nation to win from the depths of his brown eyes. I saw
no malice there because he was just a boy wanting
to make a difference. Instead of breaking his wrist, I
pulled him into my body, cracking my head against
his. The boy dropped to the ground unconscious but
very much alive.

"T-they're freaks," I heard someone call out.

The area in front of me disappeared. I was back in
The Garden at the compound, beating on a faceless
soldier repeatedly. Seaa wasn't a freak. None of us
were. The inability to control my emotions showed
on the soldier's face. There was blood everywhere. I
could only see red in a room of animated flora and

foliage. Cameron was there, pulling me off of him.

I had this memory before.

However, this time it felt entirely different. I wasn't looking in detachedly. I felt every raw emotion of the situation as if it had just happened. A sharp pain burst through me. Lights flickered in front of my eyes in a kaleidoscope of colors. I blinked. A Ground Force officer had punched me in the face after realizing that his Vuwand wouldn't bring me down. From behind him, I could see Viktor coming in to bring him down.

I punched the man in the nose as I came back to my senses. The sound of his bone crunching underneath my fist was louder than those of his screams. Viktor grinned as he watched the man squirming around on the floor.

"And here I thought you needed help."

Another man came from behind Viktor. The surprise attack didn't work. Viktor knew he was there without me saying a word about it. He turned in time to grab the wand as it came down and yanked it from the man's body. With both hands, he snapped it in half over his thigh. A few onlookers cheered, clearly excited that we were winning, while the others stared at us in consternation.

I smiled, but it wasn't a friendly one. "I don't need help, Viktor."

He nodded, punching one officer in the face and tossing another. "Could've fooled me. I've sparred with you before, black widow. Not once were you distracted."

His words hit me square in the chest. He's right. There wasn't one time where I allowed anything to distract me. I had been under extreme fatigue with injuries close to fatal, but I didn't space out like this before. What's worse is that I didn't even know I was under attack when we supers relied on our superior hearing.

Viktor went off on another Ground Force officer. Red pulsed in front of me. The blood in my veins heated. Red throbbed again in front of my eyes. My muscles tightened. Two Ground Force officers came around with heavier artillery than their usual Vuwands. I noticed one of them aim at Gavin as he watched from the doors of the lobby. The red covered my entire line of sight, highlighting the two men with guns in their hands.

I used my ability to get right in front of them, yanking a gun out of one's hand and kicking the other so hard in the knee I heard it snap. A growl ripped from my throat—animalistic and primal, like a mother with her endangered cubs. My strength intensified. I took that energy and squeezed the weapon in my hand, hearing the metal bend and the plastic crack. The officer on the floor let out a blood-curdling scream when he noticed his lower limb sitting at an awkward angle.

RED.

The standing officer grabbed his Vuwand when his gun could do nothing for him. He repeatedly zapped me, whipping the weapon across my face. I felt the blood drip from a cut on my lip. The bright red would heal before I even paid it any attention—*all reds would heal.* My hand found his collar. I lifted him off the cold ground. People cheered; others cried out in despair. I didn't care. My blood throbbed harder, the sound filling my eardrums. I tossed him and then slowly stalked over to him as his body crawled away in fear.

These humans had no idea who they were up against. Why should I worry about what these people thought? I spat on the ground beside me. If the humans wanted to fear something, it *should* be me. I was the black widow. My father created me with a purpose. I didn't know what that purpose was for a long time, but I did at this moment. I was a weapon. I got built the way I did to weaponize and destroy anything that stood in our way, like in this moment. He meant my loved ones' harm. I'd protect them with my entire being if I had to.

"Silk!" Gavin called out for me, bringing me into the moment.

Blinking back my troubled thoughts, I sought his voice. The red haze disappeared, and I could see how scared these men were of me. Our job was to show them we existed—not for them to fear that existence. I turned to Gavin, who ran a hand through his hair. His eyes grew wide, and I felt three shots in my back, and one grazed the top of my head. The brief pain shot down to my toes. I took a hand to my head, coming back with bright red blood.

"Oh my gosh, she was shot," I heard a woman call out.

A young child yanked on her dress. "Mama, she's alright."

Indeed I was okay. Not because the bullet didn't hit me in the back of the head, but because their ammo couldn't do much damage to us. Plus, the ones in my back got blocked by my suit. The only ones with real weapons to inflict pain were the military. We'd always hidden before. They didn't feel a need to give Ground Force access to specialized weapons because the wands could be enough if they hit us sufficient times.

Electrical discharge turned into a considerable weakness for us. No human could withstand getting shocked by high electricity outputs, but it was another thing entirely for us. Our abilities didn't work. Muscles would contract so tightly we couldn't move to defend ourselves. Our strength would deplete. Through the years away from Foxtrot, we forced ourselves to build a tolerance for the weapons. As much as Braggart thought Ground Force was equipped with the right kind of weapons, he didn't account for our resilience against them.

My hand touched the spot where I bled once again. Underneath, I could feel my skin stitching itself up. The cut wasn't intense. All the pressure did was further piss me off. The breath in my lungs burst. Three men tackled me to the floor. One seemed like a civilian with two Ground Force officers. I felt their hits on my armor and the jabs of their wands on any available surface. I knocked one down with my leg. The civilian grabbed the Vuwand and triggered it right below my cheek. I felt my entire body burst from within in an uncontrollable ripple that dropped me to my knees.

The armor receded. The crowd gasped. One officer kicked me in the stomach. I choked on my tongue, grunting and instinctively holding my side. Gavin screamed for me, but I wouldn't look at him. If I showed them he was my weakness, they'd hurt him. I got kicked again in the same spot. My body fell to the side as nausea rose. I gritted my teeth to keep quiet. The civilian came back in to shock me once more.

A shoe hit his head.

Then a KeViewer.

Then a few rocks.

He yelled at the small cluster of humans standing behind us pelting him with whatever they had on hand. The strength of their wills floored me. They had no weapons but the minuscule objects within their reach. I carefully watched their eyes as they glared at the men before me. The citizens didn't retaliate against me. They retaliated against the humans that had lost their humanity. I felt like our world wasn't as trampled as we thought it was. I quickly scanned the area. Many saw us as the virus that plagued their world, while others saw us as the cure.

"Leave her alone," one yelled.

Another joined, screaming, "It's about time Ground Force got what they deserved."

I took their distraction to my advantage. I tripped the officer to the cold ground then slammed my leg on top of him. He stopped moving. The civilian who had interfered, clearly on the side of the Ground Force officers, probably an off-duty one himself, stared in shock at the disabled officer and then back at me. He went to use the Vuwand on my available body, no longer encased in its armor. This time, I gave him no opportunity to get near. Getting control of my limbs again, I snatched the wand from his hand, throwing it far from him. He ran toward the group standing on the side, grabbing the small child who had earlier spoken in my defense.

"Stand back," he hollered with a small blade at the boy's neck.

A sneer crossed my features. I narrowed my eyes at the thug. The people screamed at the man, but he didn't hesitate to draw the blade closer. The boy whimpered, calling for his mother. She cried with hands over her mouth as others around her pulled her back. I took small steps toward him.

"Let go of the boy, you coward."

He shook his head. "I'm no idiot. He stays right here."

"Silk!"

Gavin threw a gun at me. At that moment, I grabbed the weapon, aimed, and discharged before the man could even blink. I hit him on the top of his shoulder, the one holding the knife. The blade fell to the floor, and the civilians who had gathered jumped him. The mother cried with her boy back in her arms. More cheers encircled our little group of warriors. I turned to see that we had won over the gathered Ground Force officers. We all stood above the groaning or unconscious individuals on the ground. None of them were dead. The people who gathered cheered while others walked away from us—trepidation in their eyes and tension in their bodies. We couldn't make them like us, but we weren't going to hide anymore.

I felt a tug on my jacket. "You're like one of the super-soldiers, right?"

I knelt down. "We are better," I said with a wink.

The boy grinned, clearly entranced. "Then I want to be like you when I grow up." He smiled once more, showing me a mouth, sans primary teeth. He made moves to punch, rolling his wrist around. I put my palm up, and he happily struck it.

No one ever wanted to be like me before. The thought humbled me, filling me with a euphoric bubble that only grew from within and encompassed my entire body from outside.

Gavin approached me, pulling me into his arms. For one second, I wanted to fight it. I tried to push him away and keep him at a distance. The feelings he stirred inside of me were making trouble for me. But I didn't want to move. I didn't want him to pull me away or to keep me at a distance. It warmed me every time that man fought to be with me—to care for me. He gingerly petted my unruly hair. His fingers gently touched the back of my skull.

"I'm so glad you're okay," he cooed in my ear. Goosebumps of the best kind rose from my skin. I couldn't contain the warmth percolating inside of me. That bubble grew even more significant. It covered Gavin within its glee.

It seemed I wasn't as cold-hearted as I thought.

AS A GROUP, we walked toward Safe Haven. Everyone stared and studied their surroundings, making sure to prevent an ambush by government soldiers. We knew they had to be around the area, but we couldn't afford to be caught off-guard nor lead them to our home. Seaa got off the KeViewer, whipping her hair across one shoulder.

"Cameron and Rock will meet us by the Ashur warehouses. The old Southern camp."

Gavin held my hand as if it was the most natural thing in the world. I waited to feel wrong about it, uncomfortable or disgusted. Nothing. The only thing I felt was awkward. And only because I had never held a boy's hand before. Embarrassed because I waited for Snow to make fun of it or for someone to make me feel as if this wasn't the right thing to do.

Snow turned to us but sought beyond us. "Yo, Viktor?"

Viktor grunted in response.

Snow grinned. "I'm not used to taking it slow. How do you do it?"

I gave Snow a face for his idiocy.

"Seriously?" Gavin questioned.

My brother shrugged.

Viktor only shook his head. His men laughed, joining in on the ribbing.

"He can't help it," one said.

The other agreed. "Yeah, man. We slow as hell."

After about a few more hours of trekking the subways, taking the red line to the orange line, and getting out of the silver line tunnels to Ashur, some of Viktor's men seemed tired, but not one of them complained. Viktor often stopped to make sure they were okay, offering water or snacks. He was a great leader. The men on his team trusted him implicitly. The same way we trusted Thunder.

Thunder.

Damn. The last time I talked to him, we fought hard.

I felt guilty, but a lot of that rage was uncontrollable. Suppose we knew things ahead of time. If he hadn't taken this secret to himself, we wouldn't have lost Rayne to Braggart's forces. She wouldn't have lived a life of mystery. The wind whipped around us, bringing a chill straight down to my bones. Flurries fluttered softly to the ground. We all turned to look at the gray clouds.

I missed the sun. We all did.

"Well, I'll be damned."

We all tensed. The entire group stood stock-still as if not moving gave us the ability to become invisible. I took a deep swallow, letting go of Gavin's hand as quietly as I could without being noticed. As if choreographed, we faced the right of us, hoping not to see what was right beside us.

Trevor Dallas stood tall in his wranglers, boots, and cowboy hat that we knew covered the most god-awful greenish-brown hair. About four other operatives stood beside him. He didn't come unarmed either. All of them carried special calibers with the right amount of force to penetrate our thick skin.

He whistled.

Movement came toward us from behind, in front, and to the left of us. Regular agents covered the front, but there wasn't a place to go—it being a dead end. Turning back would only throw us into a maze of alleys that would cause more harm than good. That left the rest of us, and it wasn't any better. Standing between two operatives and regular soldiers was the one I was dying to see but not in these conditions. She stood with her arms crossed. Her hair in a high ponytail. She wore cargo pants and a tank top as if the cold did nothing to her body. Her hazel eyes glistened in the falling snow.

Rayne.

CHAPTER TWENTY-THREE

WE WERE CLEARLY outnumbered. Viktor maintained his composure. His men gawked at the threat with wide eyes, their hearts almost audible over my own. Gavin tried to squeeze my hand, but I avoided the touch. I didn't want them to see him as a way to get me. I wouldn't jeopardize his safety like that. I moved slightly away. Trevor jumped off the roof. He landed on the snow-covered ground with a loud thud.

We stared at the issue presented to us and realized that we all had worked an angle for the best outcome. Snow stared at the men in front of us, ready to alert us the moment they tried to pull the trigger. Seaa avoided eye contact with Trevor Dallas, instead maintaining a constant visual of Rayne and her group. Viktor and his men had already turned to study the ones standing behind us. That left Gavin and me to watch Trevor and his operatives.

It seemed we weren't going to get out of this unscathed, but we also wouldn't go down without a fight. Viktor's men came into the battle with eyes wide open. They trained to fight for their cause. I felt Gavin's presence beside me, strong and assuring. He didn't sign up to get killed. He came to us to help a friend and stayed for other reasons. But he stood beside me as a strong presence and fighting will. No matter the circumstances, Gavin Foxhand wouldn't regret the choices he'd made thus far.

Would I regret it for him should anything happen to him?

"Rayne," Seaa called out. "What have they done to you?"

"We've done to her?" Trevor replied. "Last I checked, you were dead, fish girl."

Seaa flinched, but she didn't take the bait; instead, she focused her razor-sharp sight on our little sister. "Rayne, please, remember me."

I wanted to see Rayne's face, but I didn't dare take my eyes off the scheming, twisted Operative Dallas.

Rayne didn't say a word. I could feel her watching us from her perch. Trevor laughed out loud, his voice graining to my ears.

"I'm stupefied that ugly fish thing is still alive and kickin'!" Trevor took a step forward. "Wait 'til the big man hears about this."

It was then that the entire area erupted into chaos. The soldiers all came in from every direction. They ambushed us. We had no place to go but fight. I shoved Gavin between two large crates.

"Stay," I yelled at him.

I didn't give him enough time to argue back or a moment to gauge his reaction. I acted on impulse. Gathering myself, I brought the armor front and center again and took the first person who dared put a hand on me. I flipped her into a group of soldiers ganging up on Viktor's men. We heard gunshots going off, but no clear direction where they came from.

Two soldiers came toward me. I dropped down to trip one and then used my fist to hit the other in his solar plexus. While he bent in pain, I spun him into an operative about ready to shoot me with their weapon. I briefly looked for Gavin but couldn't find him. I turned again when a growl rent the air. Viktor tore through an operative as if they were made of butter. Viktor's scar highlighted the rage on his face. We didn't need to worry about him. The man could take care of himself.

I sought out Trevor Dallas. We had unfinished business.

The area around me had erupted into another big quarrel. One man caught me off-guard with a blunt metal object to my face. It briefly drew my shield back into my skin. The disfigurement on my face shot pain through my entire body. I blinked and grabbed the metal pipe as the bones healed and my skin mended. I yanked him toward me and then over my shoulder. His body slammed into two other soldiers fighting one of Viktor's men. The guy smiled at me and saluted. These men may have been all human, but they fought with a true warrior spirit.

It made me think of all the challenges we'd faced up until now. We won the battle against Ground Force, but would we win the war against Unit 13? The spider inside of me hissed to get in on the action. With eyes over the people fighting, I knelt to yank the boots off my feet. I called on the silky thread of my web to the exterior of my body again. It comfortably encased me. Trevor Dallas grabbed one of Viktor's men. I knew before it happened. The man's neck cracked with only one twist of Trevor's hand. Fury briefly blinded me, but I blinked it back.

I couldn't afford to lose myself right now.

Instead, I jumped up onto a building, using the setules in my fingers and feet to stay perpendicular to the wall. Trevor watched with glee, grabbing his gun from its holster. I felt the bullets hit my legs, but the armor remained put. He briefly dropped the smile, but then it was back up and ready to deliver menace. Trevor Dallas always had the wrong things to say.

"You stick to walls and now are impermeable to our bullets?"

I shrugged, adoringly imagining Gavin doing the same thing. "Amongst other things."

The cowboy tipped his hat with the barrel of his gun. He briefly stared at the onslaught behind us, probably thinking the same thing I was—would we win or lose? "I'd have to admit, spider girl. Ya'v quite impressed me."

The cold wind breezed between the buildings. I didn't know if fighting in the middle of the day would be helpful or a hindrance. We weren't used to it. Batch 001 kept to themselves at all times. We fought or left the base at night or made sure to be in disguise during the daylight hours. With our fight out in the open, I couldn't help but think that at some point, this would prove a problem.

Trevor scratched the scruff on his face with the tip of his thumb. "I see my gun won't do a damn thing to you, unless maybe if I aim it at your head." He said "head" louder than the rest of his words, aiming his gun at precisely that. I slunk across the side of the wall, watching as each oversized bullet meant for my head only just barely missed. I whipped back my head to clear the hair from in front of my face, watching as the snow fell in small bursts. One minute it would be heavy and the next nice and slow.

Like this very moment.

We locked eyes. Trevor knew we were at an impasse. He stared, smiling at the gruesome fight before us, watching as both family and foe dropped to the ground. I couldn't keep to this wall all morning. My duty was to my family but leaving Trevor right now meant that he would be more than available to join the fray and probably pick at least one or two of us on his own and definitely enough of Viktor's team.

"How about we cut a deal, you and me," I began.

A side of the cowboy's mouth lifted, clearly amused. "I'm a bettin' man."

"I beg off the side of this building..."

"I'm listenin'," he cut in.

I dropped to the ground in front of him. To his credit, the man didn't flinch. "...And we fight close combat. No weapons. No powers."

He turned to the sky, smiling as the snow gently

pelted him in the face. His eyes, no longer hidden by the brim of his hat, had vertical slit pupils that glowed a reddish hue when the light hit them in just the right way. The man cracked his neck from side to side. If it weren't for the raspy hiss out of his mouth like those of a snake preparing to strike, I wouldn't have expected the round kick to my face. Instead, I flung myself backward. Back pressed against the stone wall. His booted foot barely missed the front of my face. I could feel the dirt and snow from the bottom of it, spraying me right below the chin.

My body curled, swirling low to the ground. I spun to the side, avoiding a subsequent jab. Trevor recovered, kicking down to where I had moved. By then, I had already turned to the other side. Trevor growled through clenched teeth. I moved again. My body didn't stay motionless, and it frustrated him that he was always a second too late. Batch 002 was built using similar dynamics to us, but Pops made us significantly better in some areas more than others. Although Trevor was fast, it seemed I had one up on him.

"Stay still and fight," he yelled over the sounds of clashing.

I surprised him by standing still. His eyes grew wide, the slit more prominent. His jaw dropped. It was brief, but I took advantage of it, nonetheless. I thrust the heel of my palm into his nose. The sound of his nose breaking made it clear the man would have to deal with the blood at some point. I swung my leg around, hitting him on the side. Trevor lost his balance but quickly gained his footing. When he went for his nose, I kicked forward.

Trevor Dallas jumped back, boots sliding on the mud and snow. He smiled, teeth now red from the blood dripping in blobs. "Has anyone ever told you that I like to cheat?"

Before I could counter it, three operatives came from behind. One held me around the neck, threatening to cut off my air supply. The other two yanked my arms to the side, almost popping them right from the socket. I screamed, moving in place as much as I could. That did nothing for them. The one at my throat squeezed tighter. I felt my body grow weaker. Before I could do anything about it, my armor receded into my skin.

Trevor took his hat off and, with the same arm, wiped the blood off his face. "Interesting. I'm sure the general would love to see what makes this..." —he touched the length of my arm with his finger— "work."

I gritted my teeth. Males touching me were one thing I hated the most. Trevor Dallas didn't even give me enough time to rage. He kicked me in the chest. The operatives holding me barely budged. The only thing that moved was my chest, and it felt like it would rip me right from my arms. The only air left in my lungs exploded from my throat, bursting through the tight hold the operative had on me. I gasped but could not suck in the air. My vision blurred—the blood in my face reaching my brain. Through the fog, I could see Trevor aiming his gun at my head. I yanked once more.

He cocked it.

And fired.

There was a burst of air. I felt my body move but

not because of Trevor's discharged weapon. The bullet missed me entirely. My throat cleared up. I sucked in air like a fish out of water. The sounds around evaporated. One arm dropped. Garnering my bearings, I watched as the only operative left holding me tried to bring me down. Instead, I countered and dropped him to the ground myself, punching him in the face for good measure.

My eyes focused on the fight before me. Trevor and the other operative fought to keep one man off of them. Cameron raged from one to the next, almost ripping the arm of one and cracking the skull of another. Trevor tried to get his movements under control, but Cam had shifted against the wall, camouflaging into his surroundings. He came out again and disarmed the operative. If Cam had shown up in the heat of the battle, Rock would be here too. My eyes shifted. A large howl rendered the air silent. We couldn't help but look toward the sound.

Amid the chaos, a beast emerged from a gaggle of bodies. It was fierce and deadly, taller than all the rest of us, and quite capable of tearing us all limb from limb. Trying to make sense of it, I quickly turned back to Cameron, who had his situation clearly under control. The one operative lay dead on the ground. On his rear, Trevor Dallas hunched over awkwardly against the building, unconscious.

Cam and I didn't say a word to one another. We ran toward the rest of the fight. Rock assisted Seaa. She held her own against Rayne, neither one of them trying to hurt her. There were bodies everywhere. The beast stood in the middle, roaring against the sky as if crying for something entirely out of his control. I flipped over a soldier headed my way. My vision was consumed only by the creature lifting Braggart's soldiers into the air, ripping them open with its sharp claws.

The animal seemed part bear, part wolf, and part something else I couldn't describe. The one thing that did stand out the most was that it was all humanoid. Pieces of what must've been a shirt clung to its broad, hairy chest. The remnants of jeans were the only thing that covered its lower half. It had fur from its head to its clawed paws. The eyes were jaundice, canines too big to stay inside its snout.

Cameron put one hand out to stop me. "Go back and finish Trevor, Silk. We need him gone. I'll handle this thing."

I wanted to fight it, especially when the colossal monster could hurt Gavin. But I also knew Cameron was right. Trevor Dallas posed a big problem for our group, and getting rid of him now would be the right thing to do. I turned around, running back to where we had last left him against the building. The animal roared again. The sound of it made me shudder. I made it to the spot where Trevor lay, but he was no longer there. My eyes roamed the area, looking for him.

I couldn't see a damn thing.

"Damn it," I cussed.

Making my way back, I watched as the beast slammed his arm into Snow, knocking him into the crates I had shoved Gavin into earlier. My brother hung from one box with his hair sweeping the ground below. Nasty butterflies threatened deep in my belly with the promise of vomit if 1 didn't control my nerves. My legs pumped harder. 1 made it to the crates and moved them around. My eyes took in everything around me at once.

"Gavin," 1 hollered.

1 tossed another broken piece to the side. "Gavin!" 1 screamed louder.

Snow slid down the wood and metal box. 1 grabbed him before he hit the ground, placing him down gently. 1 couldn't find Gavin. The only thing left underneath the debris was his backpack and some blood.

The red consumed me once more. 1 saw the soldier's face laughing at my sister's deformity. 1 saw those facility guards touching me all over. The male doctors putting their hands on me longer than it warranted. And that one last male technician trying to put his hands down my pants.

The locked cage door holding back my rage burst open.

Energy radiated in a crescendo.

1 felt my heartbeat behind closed eyes. There were no sounds around me but the blood rushing to my head and a faint hum in my ears. A rumble started in my stomach, ripping through my esophagus. The words out of my mouth were a cross between Gavin's name and a frustrated scream. My head and upper body whipped back and forth. Soldiers fought. My sisters fought. Rock had been knocked unconscious on the ground—snow covering him in a thin layer.

My eyes searched.

Rayne's hair was wet and longer than 1 had last

seen it. Seaa, too, had damp hair dripping down her round cheeks. The cool air surrounding us made her freckles come out. Viktor was nowhere I could see. His men lay dead on the ground before me. Soldiers and operatives deceased or senseless. But no Gavin. My eyes narrowed, long lashes almost caressing the cold skin under my eye. Fingers clenched. I couldn't get a grasp on his whereabouts. There was too much death around me, too much blood.

The fighting blurred together. My emotions volatile. I only wanted to find Gavin. I wanted the war to end. The sounds blended into one high pitch. The ringing so loud I covered my ears. I screamed louder, feeling the helplessness consume me. My throat raw. My mind blank. The only thing keeping me alive disappearing from my view, pulling further and further away. I, incapable of reaching out and touching what I needed.

What I craved.

The area spun. I tried to focus on something, but the world went round. I got dizzy. My head felt as if it would float right off my neck if it weren't attached. My legs moved on their own accord to keep me balanced. I caught sight of Cameron getting lifted into the air. Then I went back around. Cameron fought to get the beast's clawed hand off his neck. It spun again.

The beast thrashed, sending Cam into the wall.

His body crumpled haphazardly in the most disturbing angles.

I screamed again.

CHAPTER TWENTY-FOUR

IN THE CONDITION of the world in which we lived, some things were entirely out of our control. We were safe from the pain of this world, or we thrived in it. Death and life went hand in hand—one for the other. It hurt like hell to live as we did. Some never experienced love. Others experienced only heartbreak.

I faced both.

Cameron lay unmoving. His breath didn't come in and out like some of the bodies around me. There wasn't any blood. *No.* He didn't shed a drop of blood but for a few cuts on his arms and face. But he was dead. However I packaged it, however I turned it around in my head or let the words marinate on my tongue, Cameron had died. My screams tore through the alleys of Ashur, reverberating within the vast emptiness of the warehouses. The vibrations pouring from within me blew out windows.

Cam was going to be a father. He wasn't supposed to die out here. The man had a plan to protect the woman carrying his child and bring a new future to fruition. But he wouldn't make it home on his own two feet. Snow dripped from my hair, mixing with the blood and dirt on my face. I wanted to scream again, but my throat went numb. Nothing would come out but a wheezing bit of breath.

I sucked in air, my voice quivering with unshed tears.

I cried for him at that moment. I cried for everything we had gone through and for our last moments together—for the fact that he loved me once. For the life of a father he'd never experience. I clutched the shirt on my chest with trembling fingers. I couldn't breathe. I couldn't suck in air.

"Silk!" I heard Seaa cry out for me.

Eyes red-rimmed from the tears, I shook away my stupor and focused on my sister. She was pinned to the ground by Rayne. Trevor stood over her with a gun pointed to her head. No more death. I couldn't see someone else I loved die right in front of me. My sanity snapped at that moment. The fine threads keeping me together audibly splintered, and the pheromone shield I worked hard to maintain dropped as if released from its shackles.

I could feel the power I held back pour from me like a dam bursting, the water overflowing and flooding everything in its path. All of the men and women in the area visibly shook. Their legs quivered, dropping them to the ground as I took one step closer to my sisters. Trevor's entire body trembled. The fingers holding the gun let go. Seaa flinched. Trevor watched as his gun fell beside her head. Rayne yelled at him, but he could do nothing but look at me.

I took another step.

His head tipped to one side—cloudy eyes, unfocused. Rayne tried again to grab his attention, but he couldn't. Trevor Dallas was ensnared in my web and could no longer break free. Seaa escaped Rayne's hold as she distractedly watched Trevor. Trevor took a step toward me. The men around me crawled toward my feet. They reached out as if my very touch could free them from their rapture. I took another step forward. Trevor shivered, his face turning bright red. His fingers wouldn't stop moving. He used them to scratch every part of his arms and chest. The cowboy squeezed his skin.

My hold on him was potent, which meant his lust for me went deeper than the asshole wanted to admit out loud. That enraged me further. I let every ounce of my power out of its cage, reveling in the feel of my hair floating around me—my skin tingling with a potential it had not felt before. More men crawled toward me, briefly skimming their fingers on my bare feet. They shivered as if that touch consumed them. I saw very few women, but some blinked, stupefied by my raw power. Two more steps closer. Trevor dragged his feet, sluggishly making his way past groveling men and dead bodies. One more step in the snow, and I finally stood right in front of Trevor Dallas.

I leaned down, not breaking eye contact, to grab

a weapon from the frozen dirt. The moment I stood up, Trevor slowly reached out to me, entranced. Pupils dilated, his eyes glazed over. The pheromones in my body consumed his very soul. Before I could sink metaphorical fangs into him for all that he'd caused up until now, Rayne tackled him from the back. We all tumbled to the ground. The beast behind us roared again. Rayne tried to snap Trevor out of it—literally slapping him with a closed fist to the face. I took that moment to stare at the hybrid creature. It had both hands holding its head.

Interesting.

The beast tried to fight my pull, which meant the creature was more human than animal. I didn't divert my attention for long. Trevor wasn't going to break free from my hold. I grabbed Rayne from the waist, pulling her off him. She fought me. Her brown eyes were full of emotion.

"Can you feel it," I yelled in her face as we fought to dominate each other.

She pinned me down, my head slamming against the dirt. "Feel what?" she countered.

I spun her, pinning *her* instead. "My power!"

She shook her head, grunting through clenched teeth, fighting my physical hold over her.

Rayne spat in my face. "No. Your power does nothing to me."

The snow washed away her spit, both dripping over her forehead.

Seaa stood over us. Without willing it to, my body felt pulled to the side. It tried to break free from me. So I turned my head and felt my insides quiver when

Gavin pulled himself up from the ground. He was fine. My being knew he was there before I had even set eyes on him. Other than a few cuts on his body and a bruise on his face. Gavin would make it out of here just fine.

Rock regained consciousness at some point, and he, too, walked over to where we grappled on the dirt and pebbles. The beast waged war with himself. Rock briefly stared at it as he tried to decipher whether it would pose a problem or not. The rest crawled over one another to get to me—to do my bidding. Snow didn't move, but his chest rose and fell.

I turned to the entranced horde. "Keep to yourselves," I commanded them. The humans crawled over to each other instead of coming toward me. Relief flooded my veins. I didn't need all of them on me at this moment.

My mind snapped back to Rayne.

"Take a look, little Rayne. Only those who truly love me are free from my spell." I wouldn't tell her that Guy still fought that losing battle. "Don't you see? Look around you, damn it! Everyone here can handle my pheromone ability and that's only because they have genuine feelings for me. If you didn't know me. If you weren't my sister. Then you'd be right under the spell like everyone else here."

She didn't move, studying our faces as we hovered over her. I only hoped that she could really see that our group didn't have to fight the ability, and as much as I was loath to admit it, my brothers, who happen to be males, did care about me. Trevor groaned, mumbling how he needed me and other profane descriptions of what he'd do for my body. "Don't you see it, Rayne?"

Rayne blinked several times. She moved from my face to Seaa's and back. She blinked again, grinding her teeth harder as if fighting a building migraine. Her chest heaved with the effort. Trevor carried on with his adoration, clawing at my feet and moaning from his spot in the mud. Rock placed a heavy-booted foot on the man's back. Her eyes swam to the back of her skull.

"He's gonna beat himself up for this shit as soon as he comes to."

The man deserved death, but Rock was right. It might be better to let him live with his weakness and insecurities. Then another part of me wanted to put the man out of his misery and ours.

Seaa leaned down. Rayne gritted and cussed, raging with the hold on her mind. Seaa took gentle fingers to Rayne's forehead, wiping her hair back from her eyes. "Look at me, hon. We're your family. It doesn't matter what Braggart fills your head with. Come back to us, Rayne. No man can tell you how to live and who to love."

Rayne, drenched in mud and snow, cried from her spot on the ground. She screamed, pulling her hands from mine and covering her head as the beast had done moments before. I stood off her, letting her fight her way through whatever compulsion took her from us the first time. Seaa wrapped her arms around herself, distancing herself from the cowboy on the floor. His treatment of her washed over me again. I grabbed the weapon once more, reaching behind my head with it in my hand.

I struck down at the man who had caused us so much unbearable heartache.

But it didn't connect.

Rayne held the blunt object with her left hand right over Trevor's head. We all stared at her. The muscles in her arm bulged. "That's enough," she whispered. Her voice was raspy.

No one said a word. The only noise in the area were groans from the compelled victims on the ground and the agonizing howls of the beast-man.

Letting go of the weapon, I stood straighter, waiting to see what would happen in the next few moments. Rayne leaned up on her elbows, staring at the chaos all around us. She blinked a few more times. "Oh, good gods, Silk. What have you done to all of them?"

No one could speak. Seaa dropped to the ground, pressing her body against Rayne's. She squeezed the girl so tightly I thought she'd break her. Rock garbled out a kind of laugh, his boot holding Trevor down on the ground. I couldn't help it. My eyes darted to Gavin, who smiled, one side of his face swollen. I shook, dropping down beside them both and holding them in my own embrace.

We smiled, but it was short-lived.

"Guys," Rayne's muffled voice came from somewhere inside our little bubble.

We all pulled back at the same time. Rayne lifted off the dirt, wiping off as much as she could from her cargos and top. "I'm going to need a really long shower."

I laughed, feeling like a weight had lifted from my

shoulders. "What are we going to do with that one?" I pointed to operative Trevor Dallas. "While we are on the subject, what about the rest of his motley crew?" I pointed to the raging, clothed orgy on the ground. My nose scrunched up.

Rayne stared at Trevor. "He seems to be too far gone to know I've broken from their little mental cocktail." She stared at us. "I need to save Rome. They're torturing him." Tears flooded her eyes. "Trevor needs to be alive to make this believable. If I come back without Trevor, my...my..." —she got lost in her words. Taking a deep breath, she said— "...father won't believe I lived and Trevor died here."

I nodded. "He'll remember some of it, Rayne. Make sure you don't twist much of what happened here."

She nodded. We then studied one another, reading each other's expressions and agreeing without saying words aloud. The beast roared again, now on its knees. It stared at me with pained yellow eyes. Gavin noticed my line of vision and jumped up.

"I've got it."

Gavin crept over the grinding bodies until he made it to Snow's spread-out body. He put an ear to his mouth and then again to his chest. Our supernatural powers allowed us to know these things from a distance, but Gavin was all human. He didn't realize Snow lived.

I felt Seaa tense beside me. "Oh, God, Cameron," she whispered behind her hand.

I didn't want to witness her reaction. The words out of her mouth were enough to remind me that Cam hadn't made this fight. I watched Gavin as he nodded over Snow's body. Once Gavin got confirmation, he nodded to himself again and then crossed over Snow's body. He made it to the crates, and from the debris of wood and metal, he grabbed his backpack, unzipping it. We watched as his hand went inside and pulled out one of the collars.

Rayne stared at the beast. "I've never seen one of those before," she pointed at it.

The animal didn't take its eyes off me. Its stare told me it felt tortured and out of control. Something about its eyes was very familiar. Gavin neared the beast. It growled at him, exposing sharp fangs. Gavin jumped back almost as fast as I jumped forward.

"Seaa, come hold this thing down," Rock grumbled.

Seaa shook her head. "I-I can't."

Rayne's eyes went soft. "Oh, Seaa. Trevor can't hurt you anymore. We won't let them."

Rock emphasized Rayne's words by pushing Trevor deeper into the mud with his boot. I wanted to ease my sister's fears, but this was something she needed to do herself.

Seaa nodded but did not attempt to move. Rock understood more than he let on. Instead of forcing her, he punched Trevor on the back of his head. Trevor Dallas dropped to the muddy ground unconscious. Rock leaned down and turned Trevor's face slightly. The man lived.

"There. He ain't going nowhere." My brother stared at Seaa with dark, beady eyes.

Seaa stayed put, her clothes soaked through. Some of the iridescent colors of her scales were showing through the thin, wet fabric of her clothes. Rock moved around the bodies. Once with Gavin, he cracked his neck a few times, then jumped in with the beast. The animal pulled around, swiping at Rock. His giant body moved faster than it looked capable of. Rock's arms, which hung from the elbow at a weird angle, rolled in a circle, tightening around the monster's arm.

Seaa made a move toward Rayne, holding her hand. The beast made another swipe, almost cutting off the antennae-like knobs on Rock's head. My brother moved like a dancer. He was more genetically mutated than Seaa, but he never let any of it bother him. We never brought it up to him either. He annoyed the hell out of me, but I cared for him in my own way. Seaa and Rayne gasped, deeply mesmerized by the battle. I turned back to Rock. My brother came around the creature's back and held its arms behind it with one foot in its back. The animal screeched in pain. Seeing his opening, Gavin moved toward it with the open collar.

The animal wailed. Its screams pierced the sunless sky. The collar came around the animal, clicking into place. Immediately the animal calmed. Rock let go of it. He came over to Gavin, pushing him back away from the animal-like man. We watched as the creature dropped to all fours. Heavy breathing. Whimpers of an animal in distress. Finally, after about a minute of watching it, the beast transformed back into a human. We couldn't take our eyes off him. Within seconds, a half-naked Viktor dropped to the snow-laden ground, exhausted.

"Oh, shit," Rock cursed.

Gavin turned to me. "I saw it happen, Silk. All of his

men died here today."

He didn't need to explain further. I stared at Cameron's snow-covered body. A lot of people died today. Rock picked up the exhausted half-man half-beast from the ground and slung him over his shoulder. The collar now too big to stay on his neck. I watched as Gavin grabbed it again, placing it in his bag.

Rayne broke in. One hand on my shoulder. "I'm sorry, Silk." We stared at Cameron together. "But we can't let his death go in vain. Let's end this."

Seaa squeezed my free hand. All three of us connected by the beautiful mermaid. "Please be careful, Rayne. Don't let anyone know your back to normal."

She shook her head, some of the water in it spraying on me. "He won't know a damn thing. That place felt wrong even in my altered state of mind. Nothing will give me away. I'll escape with Rome. I promise to come back."

We trusted her.

Seaa hugged Rayne. "We love you, little sister." She wiped Rayne's tears mixed with melting snow and moved away from her.

Walking to Cameron's dead body, Seaa picked him off the ground. Her tears dropped on his chest. My tears fell in steady streams as I watched. We lost someone important to us today. The air I sucked in quivered. It wasn't the time to break down.

We left Rayne alone in that throng of despair. This time, I was the one to grab Gavin's hand in mine. We'd lost enough already, so I wouldn't lose him too. I made my way to Snow. Gavin assisted me in placing him over my shoulder. Rayne waved to us one last time. I threw my shield back up to prevent innocent stragglers from getting hit with it.

Once out of the old Southern camp warehouses, the town of Ashur was alive with people. Women watched their children playing through open windows. Some workers cleaned up the debris from the streets. Kids kicked an almost deflated ball around. Ashur wasn't very pretty. Not like Beta Antiquis. But it was home to a lot of people in Sector Bravo. We didn't want any of them to see us holding three unmoving bodies, so we stayed close to The Waste and into the underground system.

Some things never changed.

It didn't take long to make it home.

But when we walked in like fragile pieces of glass about ready to break, our brother, the leader of our group, could do nothing but sob with us.

We all cried for our fallen brother.

We wept until there was nothing left.

CHAPTER TWENTY-FIVE

Sector Bravo
Town of Ashur
Former Southern Camp
Operative Rayne – ID: PH064.001

STRADDLING THE COMATOSE cowboy, I lifted him by his collar. How easy it would be to kill him right here and right now. As tempting as it was, I knew for sure that if I came back to headquarters without Trevor or Unit 13 soldiers, General Braggart wouldn't believe the story I was going to tell him. I slapped operative Dallas across the face. He didn't rouse. I heard rather than saw the others in our group gathering their bearings. I stayed in character, making sure not to give away that I was no longer under the control of General Braggart and Dr. Plumboy.

I back-slapped him this time. My head shot up to see the others helping one another from their roll in the mud.

"Get your sorry asses off that ground. Make a note of all the bodies. Make a note of friendlies and foes."

A female operative walked over to me, watching as I smacked Trevor again. He finally stirred.

"What the fuck," he yelled, wide-eyed.

I got up, putting pressure on his chest. "What's the last thing you remember," I asked, crossing my arms.

He shook his head. The female helped him off the ground. I watched him with the same disdain I'd had since I first found out we were partners. That part didn't change.

Trevor patted the top of his head, more than likely looking for his stupid hat. He flinched, then gingerly touched the giant knot on the back of his head. The cowboy hissed in a breath. "Fuck happened?" He gawked at the mud-covered soldiers, shaking his head. "One minute I was fittin' to put a bullet in the fish, and then I'm drawn to that black widow."

I nodded, giving him an expression of sheer annoyance. "How could you all have gotten so hung up on that creature?"

Trevor watched me. "You weren't?"

Here is where I needed to be extremely cautious of what I said. "Did you not hear me trying to bring you back?"

He shook his head, then stopped. "Yeah, I think I do remember you calling out to me. You started fighting with the fish, and all I could do was walk toward Batch 001's secret weapon."

I sighed. "You left me to fight her on my own. Then all of a sudden, I felt this tug toward that same woman. So did everyone else here. It was as if I were no longer in control of my actions."

He nodded, clearly in agreeance with my admission. Trevor turned to the woman beside us. "What did you experience?"

The woman stared at the group, watching as they moved the bodies to clear the area before civilians crossed to this part and saw them. "Same. One minute I was fighting, and the next, everything was out of my control. I remember being drawn to her. Nothing else. Next thing I knew, my head was under operative Johnson, and operative Ramone was on my legs." She shook her head. "It was the damndest thing."

Trevor Dallas pulled out his KeViewer. "Operative Dallas reporting."

A soldier came and placed a KeViewer unit with a holographic image hovering in the air in my hand. The count showed twelve enemies dead and twenty-one allies. I moved it to show Trevor.

"Yes, sir. Operative Rayne has just shown me the report. Twenty-one Unit 13 soldiers dead and twelve foes." He stopped to listen again, then looked me up and down. "No, sir. She seems fine. Probably in better shape than all of us," he added. He moved away from me. "General, we encountered a beast here. Humanoid." Trevor narrowed his eyes. "But, sir?" He nodded again. "Understood."

The KeViewer went back into his pocket. I moved

toward him. "What did he say about the beast?"

Trevor Dallas kicked a rock on the ground. It slammed into the side of the brick building. "Nothing. He said it was over our clearance level."

At a time like this, I'd defend General Braggart, so I did. "General Braggart is the one in charge. We obey at all times."

Trevor snarled at me. I pretended not to care as I usually did in the barracks. Faking I was entranced might be easier than I thought. None of them would be the wiser. I would get Rome and hightail it out of that place. Thinking of him stirred feelings I hadn't voiced before and now probably never would. Roman Braggart was the love of my life, and because of our relationship to Braggart, neither of us would ever be able to indulge in those explosive feelings.

I'm in love with him.

The soldiers grabbed their comrades from the ground, dragging them over to a waiting DBT van that would then take them to the facility in Alpha. I watched as the last person from our group was loaded into the vehicle. Trevor stomped over to the van.

"Where are you going," I called out.

He flipped me the bird and got into the passenger side of the van. The rest of the group made their way out of the clearing, leaving behind the dead men who fought with my siblings.

"Ma'am, we are about to head out."

I nodded, standing among the dead, remorse churning in my stomach. "Go on. I'll be walking back."

It wasn't unusual for us supers to walk or run to places in New States, so she didn't question it. The woman called out to the rest of the soldiers and loaded into the last vehicle. I watched as they left. As soon as they were out of earshot, I sensed two warriors coming toward me. One a leader. The other a former flame.

"Hail, Thunder," I called out to the empty space.

Both men appeared. Their eyes were swollen from shed tears. Neither seemed imposing; their size almost curled and withdrawn.

"We're here for the men that died. I'm sure when Viktor wakes, he'd like to send them off the right way," Thunder replied.

I bit my lower lip. "I'm sorry guys."

Hail smiled at me. "It was out of your control, Rayne. We are glad you're back."

I nodded, blinking back unshed tears. "I need to go in case someone comes back. Is there anything you need me to do before I leave?"

Thunder leaned down to one fallen man. "No, we've got this. Stay in touch."

Turning away from both of them, I made my way to headquarters as fast as I could manage. The lives of those men couldn't go in vain. I need to get into headquarters and get Rome out of there quickly. We had to do something. The run back cleared my mind. Zane's image floated to the forefront of my consciousness. Talking to Zane would be the best thing I could do to move forward. He'd already helped us before, and I know he'd do anything for Rome.

At least, I hoped so.

Back at Unit 13 headquarters, I went straight for the small dorm I used behind the rec room. We walked inside the recreational area, and the rest of the group that hovered in mid-laughs or games stood and watched our mud parade. Some of us were bruised, others cut. Some had rips in their clothing, and others dripping wet. Before I was sent to assist Trevor Dallas on his mission, the powers that be sent operative Zane Mueller to a different clean-up job in downtown Trēbeta. He sat at the bar, watching the same parade the others were until he made eye contact with me.

I knew Zane had been trying to knock me from my spell for a long time now. He was Rome's friend and confidant. He had also saved Seaa from this horrible place. I kept my eyes on him, not breaking contact for a minute. I shifted them, ever so slightly, hoping he'd understand that I needed to talk to him in private. Zane didn't move. He didn't smile. His face entirely impassive. I turned the corner, out of sight. If that didn't get his attention, then I'd have to try again later.

Now at my door, I shouted to another operative that I'd see her later for a practice round in the ring. She went into her room. I pressed the keypad to unlock my door. On the second button, I felt Zane's presence standing right next to me. I twirled to face him. Other soldiers were coming, so I pinned him against the wall. His shirt crinkled within my fists. The men passed by as Zane acted amused by my move. The guys didn't stop staring, probably waiting for a fight to break out.

"What the hell are you all looking at?"

They rushed off. With drawn brows and a pinched mouth, I stared into Zane's eyes again. "We have a lot to talk about."

He pulled my hands off his shirt. "Do we?"

I swallowed hard. "Yeah, Zane, I'm back."

He didn't even blink. "I have no clue what you mean."

The man thought I was lying. I dropped my hands to my side, thinking of the best way to put this to him without him thinking I was trying to trap him. I remembered our conversation. "You told me not to give up the others. To protect Rome."

His eyes widened.

"I'm back, Zane." I fingered the tiny scar in his hand where I had stabbed him with a girl's hair clip.

He nodded. "I have a job in the private sector this evening. A paltry protection detail for some super-rich asswipe. Can you get out of the compound and meet me?"

I nodded. "I'll make it so."

Zane pushed me away. The move had me against the back wall. "Next time you got a problem, don't blame me for it." He winked at me, side-eye staring at the stragglers in the hallways.

Punching in the last digits of my door lock, I walked inside to grab my shower items and clothes. I had a practice spar with one of the operatives in an hour. Afterward, I'd go to General Braggart to get a pass off the compound. But I needed a good enough reason to be let off. I thought about it as I gathered my things. What would be a good reason that wouldn't tip Braggart off? Being around him made me uncomfortable. Whatever I came up with would have to be quick, simple, and straight to the point.

An hour later, I was sweaty again as I sparred with

a female operative. The woman came around with a roundhouse kick to the face, but I blocked it with my wrist. Training and fighting all came with whatever they did to me. I may have remembered everything that happened before it, but unlike Hail, I didn't lose everything I'd gained. She punched with her right. The movement seemed slow to me, as it usually did. I moved out of the way before it landed, noticing General Braggart walk over with two other soldiers. He seemed absorbed by their conversation.

I needed to make him feel incredibly proud of my actions so he wouldn't question me when I asked to get out of here for a couple of hours. The girl came back. I did a backflip away from her, dropping into a crouch. Flipping over again, I smacked her in the chest with both feet. The crowd cheered. There was no emotion on my face. I spun, hitting her hard on the side. She grabbed where I hit her, regaining her balance. I noticed Braggart had stopped. His two lackeys right beside him. I turned in time to avoid the operative, instead getting right into her face. I punched her three times and then kicked her with my left, balancing with my right.

I kept the position as she flew into the crowd. I didn't put my leg down until the crowd's cheering had slowed. Ignoring her, even though I wanted to help her up, I walked over to General Braggart, the man I shared blood with.

"Job well done," he praised.

I held all of the anxiety and rage inside of me. He was about to walk away when I called out, "General." Braggart stopped. I walked toward him with my hands clasped behind my back. "I have a request, sir. I read the report Mueller brought back from the supers fight in Downtown Trēbeta. There's something about the report that doesn't sit right with me. Permission to investigate on my own."

General Braggart curled his mustache. Anxiety rushed through me. I pretended to watch him like a proper soldier. Instead, I looked over his shoulder.

"Very well. Report to me immediately." He didn't say anything else. Braggart walked away with his lackeys, their conversation picking up where they had left off.

I went to walk away when Trevor Dallas grabbed a file from one of the technicians. He skimmed through it and shut it with vigor. His face went blank. Whatever the man read in the file had shocked him. Afraid it was something about me, I marched over to where he stood. Instead of stopping in front of him, I slammed into his shoulder, hoping he'd drop the folder. The jerk didn't even flinch.

"Watch where 'ya going," he sneered.

I turned and smirked. "Oops," I teased.

Plan failed. I really wanted to know what was in those files, but I couldn't get him to drop them. Hopefully, I'd find out soon enough. For now, I had permission from the general to leave the compound. I'd head to the same place Mueller did for the investigation to assess the area myself, but all I wanted was to speak to Zane in private. We needed a plan to leave this place.

With Rome in my arms.

Sector Foxtrot
Unit 13 Headquarters
General Brockton Braggart

THE BODY VIDEO surveillance that I had a few soldiers wear before they confronted Batch 001 proved fruitless. The images we were able to garner showed my men fighting against the first batch. I was able to see my daughter keeping up with her pack as she fought the one woman who was already supposed to be dead. Trevor got slammed around by the one they called Silk, a man who seemed familiar, but I couldn't place him assisted. Then a beast appeared out of nowhere.

The animal tore my men apart as if they were made of paper, then killed one from the first batch. The last thing we caught from the video was an intense supersonic explosion, and everyone went still. The next thing I knew, we were staring into the mud and then darkness. The only sounds audible were groans and the swirling of materials rubbing against the camera.

According to the report, everyone in the group had been bewitched by Silk, even my daughter. They only remembered being pulled in by her, and that was it. The video went for about thirty-five minutes of darkness before they all got up from the floor to wipe themselves off. By then, the experiments were all gone—the beast too. I turned to ask what else the analyst had for me when operative Trevor Dallas stomped down the hall toward me. I dismissed the men instead. The snake hardly ever came out of Trevor Dallas, but the gleam in his eyes told me the snake was loose and very much alert.

"Operative Dallas," I murmured. "To what do I have this pleasure?"

The shifty man stared at me, loads written in only his eyes. I briefly scanned the material in his hands, noticing he held a file for Roman Braggart. My insides raged, eyebrows drawn. The cowboy had looked into the wrong kind of information.

"I know he's not really your son," he spat out.

I placed my hands behind my back, the picture of ease. "Did I ever say he was?"

Trevor shook his head. "Everyone here knew he was your son."

One hand came forward to touch my curling mustache. Doing so made it all seem inconsequential. "I adopted Roman years before. He *was* my son. Now he's more of a nuisance."

Trevor Dallas studied my face as if trying to read the words clear as day. Roman Braggart would ruin me, especially if he found out Rayne wasn't his sister or Rayne found out before he did. Even more so if he dug deeper and found out who his birth parents were. His being here and alive would ruin all my plans. Before Trevor could get a word in, I grabbed the KeViewer from my pocket. I narrowed my eyes at the holographic screen. I hardly ever received a call from defense financing for the W.D.A.

"General Brockton Braggart," I opened.

The voice from the other line came in on one rushed breath. "Sir," he began. "I have gotten word from the higher-ups that funding from Gregory Fox-hand was terminated."

The blood in my veins raged. "What!?"

Trevor Dallas stood steady. I didn't walk away from the cowboy. The man told me that the other partners were baffled by the news and had tried since to convince him to rescind the termination. The image of the man in the video I couldn't place came to mind. I remembered now where I had seen him before. According to our Intel, Gregory had a son he kept hidden away in a large, elaborate apartment. The man in the video was Gavin Foxhand, and he seemed very friendly with the supers. I hung up the call and threw the KeViewer at the wall for good measure. The soldiers around me watched as it splintered into pieces. Knowing full well things were falling all around me, I switched my attention to operative Dallas.

"End Roman Braggart! You have my full authority to get all the information you can about Gavin Foxhand and then kill him. Kill him *dead*. Kill him *gone*, Operative Dallas." I leaned into him with all the power of my title behind me. "If he lives, then you die."

I walked out of the open room.

I can't be brought down. I am a king. I am God around here.

I was untouchable.

CHAPTER TWENTY-SIX

Sector Bravo
Safe Haven Headquarters

DOING A PERIMETER check around our small bunker area had to be better than dealing with the insanity inside of it. No one had been able to control their reactions to Cameron's dead body, especially Suzanne. I had noticed her hand wrap around her belly as if it were the only way that poor child would be protected. I would've run to her as Cameron would to reassure her that they'd both be fine, but I wouldn't know how even to start. I never assuaged anyone before; even my sisters understood that consoling was foreign to me. I also didn't want the group to know of the baby news until I spoke to Suzanne first or if Thunder would divulge it.

As it were, we didn't stop crying and hadn't been able to absorb the news. It came as a shock to us because it wasn't from a maniacal general or one of his minions. The death came at the hands of our allies. Thunder didn't blame Viktor. Neither did anyone else living in the bunker. In our line of work, we understood the term "friendly fire."

Suzanne was tight-lipped. We couldn't get her feelings on the matter, but we assumed she blamed him. Viktor surmised the same because he had willingly locked himself in one of our cells. He had unwillingly exploded into his beast when he saw all his men lying on the ground before him. He didn't have it in him to think of the consequences rationally. He raged into his beast and lost all control over his mind. He didn't remember a thing.

His mental state seemed to take an even bigger blow when Thunder and Hail arrived with all of the dead mercenaries. He asked Thunder for his help in bringing the bodies back to their families and went back into his prison to keep from harming anyone else. It would take some time, but hopefully he'd see that his men engaged for a cause and died fighting for it. We wouldn't let their hope for a better world end there. We also wouldn't let Viktor shifting into a beast consume him.

Viktor Veracruz hadn't shifted into his beast since escaping Alpha's Project Hercules Facility 2. The creature was a separate entity from Viktor, but both lived in the same body. When his beast took over, he had no way of pulling him back, so he said. Many soldiers who had been experimented on faced the repercussion of death if they couldn't control their beast. No one in that facility made it out alive. Viktor surmised that they were no longer creating shape-shifting soldiers like Zane Mueller from his discoveries of the location.

Braggart and Plumboy were creating creatures that performed on blood lust.

Feeling guilty, he remained inside the cell as he offered his information to us. He wasn't sure if a memory of his men or having to face the remainder back home would trigger the beast, so he stayed inside to protect us. It was evident that his animal was stronger than we were. We've been thrown into walls, coming from it almost unscathed. To hit the wall and come out dead like Cameron did was a foreign thought for all of us.

I should be doing the same thing. Judging by my actions the past few days, I deserved to be locked in one of those cells alongside him. My siblings no longer questioned my actions, even though some wanted to throttle me for it. The only ones who ever saw beneath the surface were my sisters. My thoughts were forgotten when I heard movement approach. The sound of footsteps lightly crunching seashells underneath their feet told me the person was lightweight.

The cold breeze blew her scent right at me. "Hello, Seaa."

I waited until she came around the bend, passing one of our little boats pulled onto the shore. The bunkers were underground but for a small building above ground, nestled between several giant oaks and pine trees. Once an essential part of the city, our small human-made enclave came about the wartime—an almost non-existent town within a larger one, built by the military before Braggart to assist the war. They were the first line of defense if any enemy water transports came in through what was once the Fort Point Channel, now spread wider with no boundaries to stop the harbor's flow.

The small island was encircled by water, and then the nearest large landmass to Bravo was enclosed by thick woods and, after that, The Waste. I took a more in-depth look at the area before me, now made barren with our war's force. We were pretty protected here, although in plain sight of the enemies. Loads of proverbs Pops used to read us fluttered to my mind. He'd say things like "out of sight, out of mind," and "hiding in plain sight," all idioms with similar connotations.

Seaa picked a large rock, strategically placing herself right beside me. "Is the night quiet?" she asked.

I encompassed the area beyond the walls with my hearing. There weren't any soldiers or operatives headed our way in swarms or a mob of New State citizens marching with weapons to end our lives. As it were, the people in Bravo went about their day. Word of our appearance had been on everyone's mouths since the fight in Charlie. No one spoke of seeing us in Bravo. The cold air blew again. The hair on my head flew back away from my face. Seaa watched with a small smile on her face.

"Yes, the night seems quiet."

She nodded and took a large gulp of air. Seaa didn't

need to suck in oxygen like one of us, but she did so anyway as a habit she formed to seem normal around others. "I wanted to talk to you about...well, you."

It was my turn to sigh. "What about exactly?"

The wind kept blowing from the North. I stared at the sky, seeing the thick clouds moving with the force of the weather. It had snowed earlier, but the temperature dropped incredibly. Our bodies already prepared us for the blizzard that would soon cover the world in its solemn brightness. Seaa shifted uncomfortably on the rock. She pushed some of the snow off of it.

"I've noticed the change in you, Silk. It happened the moment that boy kissed you."

I cringed. The weight of Seaa's reminder made me want to curl into myself. Being away from the drama indoors wasn't my only reason for patrolling tonight. Avoiding Gavin had been another. He didn't push me for answers like I thought he would. The moment we came to the facility, he had locked himself in his room with many gadgets and gizmos to fix his set of computers and the collars controlled by Alpha. I would check on him every once in a while to make sure he was okay. I'd hear his breathing and the way his fingers would brush into his hair, and I felt a sense of calm wash over me.

My body curled against the same rock. "I don't want to talk about that, Seaa."

She took advantage of her spot above me. Her hands pulled some of my hair up, fingering the curls. "I don't want to talk about the kiss either."

I stiffened. *Then what the hell else does she want to talk about?*

"I meant the behavior since then. You've spaced out more often than not, and it's not like you. I feel like you are stuck here and somewhere else, Silk."

I snorted. If Seaa only knew how right she was about her theory. Ever since I took off the bracelet in Viktor's camp, I felt like all of the memories I had deeply buried had opened up and spilled forth. There was no way to lock them back, and I couldn't afford to let them consume me. My sister sat behind me, playing with my hair, and I realized that she "consoled" me. Mere moments ago, I'd thought of how I didn't know how to care for others, but I realized that maybe I'd been doing it in my own way.

Maybe it was about time I shared with another person.

Maybe it would be easier to handle if I did.

Another sigh mixed with the cold air around us. Seaa patiently waited. I used my hearing again, spreading it away from me and past the water, through the trees and wasteland, and into Beta Antiquis district. There was nothing new that needed my attention, nor anyone around us sneaking in an ear.

"What I'm going to share with you is hard for me."

Seaa didn't stop playing with my hair. Her fingers rolled around my hair, allowing the coils to tighten to them. She'd let the ring go, and it would spiral its way back with the rest.

"I...I was a victim of sexual assault since we were very young."

I couldn't ignore Seaa's sharp inhale. "I-I'm..." My heart beat ferociously. Bile rose. The acrid taste filled my mouth. I pulled from my sister's nimble fingers, hurling toward the water. All of the sustenance I held now lay bare before me, floating back and forth unto the shore. Seaa dropped from the rock, gently rubbing my back and holding the hair from my face.

The water before me wavered until it no longer existed. Before long, I was back in Foxtrot. *I stood in the center of The Garden in nothing but a white thin-strapped dress. The color of my curls was a dark contrast to the bright white of my clothing. I fingered the dress with thin, trembling fingers. The full-spectrum, ultraviolet lights hanging over my head felt like a paltry imitation of the sun we barely saw. I shielded my eyes from the gleam with a hand over my brow. I didn't remember why I walked in here. I couldn't remember how I had come to wear this dress.*

The lemon tree swayed, its golden lemons fighting to hold on. The two guards from the cafeteria came from behind the tree. Their hands no longer held fingers, but long moving snakes swiveled and swirled, extending themselves toward me. My chest got tight. Sweat dripped from my temples. I felt my feet step back in self-preservation. No wind blew in the indoor garden, but I felt a cold shiver crawl down my spine. I cringed. Noise from behind me twirled me around. A male doctor appeared. He had a stethoscope around his neck and another one in his hand.

"Inhale deeply," he whispered between closed lips.

The guards behind me spoke too. "We only want to assist you," they hissed.

My entire body shot through a rose bush. The thorns scratched me. I ignored the pain in favor of getting out of the twisted nightmare. I pulled free from a branch of blood-red roses, twining their thorns around the fabric of my gown. Finally free, I grabbed the front of my dress, willing my heart to stop its drumming. The laughter of a crazed man drew my eyes up. Through my lashes, I could see a technician strolling toward me. He had a large needle in one hand and a tourniquet in the other. Bile sat in my throat. I couldn't speak. I couldn't scream with fear that I'd throw up all over myself.

I shook my head as he mumbled, "I only want to make the hurt go away."

My knees buckled as I threw my hands over my ears. "G-go away," I gasped.

The skin holding me together rippled with goosebumps as movement crawled through the back of my hair. I jumped forward, almost diving into the technician's arms. My legs stopped me before impact. Behind me, the men with snakes for fingers drew nearer. Heartbeats grew louder. The men spoke at once—all of them murmuring their delight in my skin or their adoration to me. The room spun. Everywhere I looked was a man drawing closer.

The only exit I saw shimmered before my eyes. A red haze moved and contorted until it resembled a man. I fell to the ground, my legs no longer able to support my weight. I stared down at my dress and saw that it was covered in bright red blood. My throat constricted as screams gathered in the large, enclosed space. I rocked back and forth on the grass as the guard I had beaten slithered closer. He had bruises all over his face. Cuts with dripping blood adorned swollen cheekbones and lips. The blood from his crushed *nose trickled in thick torrents down his chin and onto his uniform.*

I turned to see all of them close enough to touch. The weight of the blood on my dress pulled me down, keeping me in place. I hollered for help, my throat raw with the nightmare. They drew closer. I maniacally waved my hands in the air to dispel them. It got harder to breathe. I inhaled, but nothing would work. I felt my throat constrict again. Hands cradled my shoulders. I flinched.

Seaa had her hands on me now, pulling me back from the nightmare. Tears ran down my cheeks as the flashbacks tried to dominate my emotions once more. "No," I yelled out loud. "Not anymore," I hollered to the memories driving me insane.

Seaa forced me to face her, holding me tightly to her chest. "Don't worry, sweet girl. They can't hurt you anymore. No one can hurt you anymore."

I sniffled, my body shaking.

She held me tighter to her. Her embrace was so comforting I felt my tense muscles relax. Her hand got lost in my hair. The other curled on my back from underneath my arm. The warmth helped me feel at ease. The soldier in my head. The doctors. The technicians blurred before my mind's eye. They lost their form until they were completely unrecognizable. Before I knew it, the shadows had lifted from my eyes, disappearing from my view—the pain along with it.

I pulled away from her body. We walked beside the shoreline. She quietly followed. "I didn't know I was unintentionally attracting others to me. The pheromone ability was new to me and even newer to Pops.

But for the entire time it started, I faced constant uncomfortable situations from them making advances at me through disgusting words, the scent of their lust, or physical reactions." She quietly listened. "T-then the interactions became more forward and even more unpleasant. Hands touched me in places no young girl should experience."

Seaa wiped a few tears away but made no noises. She inhaled. "Did they go far?"

I shook my curls. "No. Other than a few caresses over my clothes, no one had ever gotten far enough to do more. Not until one of the technicians got caught going into my pants by Pops." I both cringed and smirked at the memory. "That was the last time anyone ever did. Pops taught me about assault and molestation, and he figured out my abilities. No man ever touched me again."

She nodded as if understanding my meaning. "I remember. You went from aloof to full-blown frigid." Seaa pulled her long waves over one shoulder. "I don't blame you, Silk. I wished I'd known."

No one knew my horrid past because I liked it better that way.

Rayne took pleasure in exploring our past. She enjoyed learning about the way they lived or how they ate. She spoke about her book and magazine collections. If we were curious about the most mundane things, then Rayne possessed the knowledge. She'd tell me right now that when something of this nature happened to the girls of the old world, they'd spend time with a therapist, someone who could help them through the trauma. We didn't have anything like that anymore.

Telling someone our weakness gave them an advantage over us.

I turned to my sister, giving her the answer I felt she needed to hear. "Seaa, you had your own problems." I grabbed both her hands in mine. "You're not the only one fighting through a traumatic past." I dropped her hand and encompassed the entire area around me. "Hell, we are still struggling to breathe. There was never *really* the right time."

I took a couple of steps back, feeling the weight of all our problems and my pent-up emotions bubble to the surface of my mind like a geyser. My fingers shook as I pushed a curl behind my ear. Seaa watched me from her spot. The anguish in her eyes undid me. My voice cracked as I cried, "You almost died, Seaa. I thought you were dead, and now Cam—and I just can't help feeling like I'm next. I'm just all sorts of messed up."

She dropped her head, her excessively lengthy hair falling over her shoulders to hide her face. "I guess we're both freaks," she sniffled.

"I'd rather be a freak with you than anybody else," I joked.

Seaa giggled.

My nose caught the scent of a male from batch 002 coasting toward me from the water. The senses I possessed extended from my body like invasive vines ready to bury anything in their path. He noticed me at the same time that I did him. I heard him say "I'm Zane Mueller" as if the name would appease me. Briefly lost in the conclusion of my past, I didn't immediately place his name. The muscles within me rigid. I stole a look at Seaa, who watched me with concern.

"Zane Mueller is coming," I muttered on autopilot.

Seaa's face registered the name before I could. She smiled, staring over the water as if expecting him to appear like a deity from its depth. It was at that moment that I remembered the man who had risked his life to save my sister in Foxtrot. Zane was Rome's best friend and currently our undercover ally.

At least, I hoped.

The surface of the water broke. In the darkness I could see a large body crossing the small body of water toward us. His arms broke the surface, one after the other. I stood my ground, placing my sister behind me. She grabbed hold of my hand but didn't go far. It was as if she expected him to come. I turned my head to scold her when a widely built, luscious black man broke through the water. The wet clothes he wore clung to him in all the right places, the cold water not bothering him one bit. In the concealed moonlight I could see the tear markings of a cat on his face— his eyes glowing in the night. I blinked a few times to clear my mind.

Seaa spoke first. "Zane!"

She ran under my arm and toward the man sloshing out of the water. She leaped into his arms as if she belonged there. I took in their demeanor. I studied his moves and scent. Seaa adored the man. But Zane... Zane Mueller lusted over the mermaid-woman.

As the cowboy liked to say: "I'll be damned."

CHAPTER TWENTY-SEVEN

ZANE MUELLER LIFTED my thin sister in his arms, smiling a set of sharp canines. Like Viktor and Rome, Zane possessed the higher expression of a wild beast in his genetic make-up. The group at home had mentioned he could shapeshift into a giant cheetah. I hadn't personally experienced it, but I also had never met the man in person. Seaa was foremost on that man's mind. My abilities and eugenics of an arachnid gave me higher senses than the rest of my brethren. I couldn't tell if Seaa knew about Zane's interest in her, but I was optimistic about it. The appeal was evident in how he held her and shielded her from the cold of the night—or how he protected her from unseen enemies.

"Zane, I am so glad you came back."

He smiled at her again, pulling down the wet beanie from his head. Zane's ears angled at the tip like those of the cat. Water dripped from his cargo pants, t-shirt, and hat. He hadn't worn a coat. "We agreed on three days, right?" he replied. "I waited at the rendezvous point, but no one showed up. I figured I'd find you."

Seaa pulled him from the water to where I stood watching them. "Silk, he's Zane Mueller. He's the one that saved my life."

Zane extended his hand to shake mine, but I didn't take it. I only stared at his face. "You're an operative for Braggart. Why should we trust you?"

Seaa flinched, indignation written all over her face. "Silk!" she cried out.

I turned to her, crossing muscled arms over my chest. "What? I am only stating the obvious."

Zane grinned. He placed a comforting hand on Seaa's shoulder. "I don't expect *you* to trust me, black widow." He turned to Seaa. "So long as she trusts me, then it's all good."

Seaa smiled.

He turned back to me, squeezing the water from his shirt. "I actually came with a word from Rayne. I know she's reverted." He then wrung the water from his beanie. "We're gonna try to break Rome out. I'm not allowed in the cells anymore since faking Seaa's death, but Rayne still has access. My job will be to distract them."

Seaa nodded. "Then you must come inside and speak to the group. Tell us everything you know all at once." She pulled on his arm.

Zane pulled back. "I didn't just come to tell you of

the plan to break Rome out, but rather to tell you guys he might not even make it."

His words hit both of us square in the chest. Seaa's eyes opened wide while her hand almost tightened at her neck. None of us believed that Rome would die there. When Rayne said she'd get him out, we all expected that it was exactly what she'd do without issue.

"Was he tortured?"

I watched my sister's reaction. Tears softly fell from her eyes. She blinked them away so rapidly they were there one minute and gone the next. Seaa suffered much during her capture. Rayne faced the same punishments. Rome was Braggart's greatest weapon turned traitor. I firmly believe Braggart would make an example out of him.

"He's in bad shape. The last time I saw him, he smelled only of blood. The man was barely recognizable." Zane shook his head. His hands fisted at his sides. "I don't know why he let them. All Rome needs to do is shapeshift into his panther and destroy them all." Zane slammed a fist to the surface of a large boulder. "Fuck!" he yelled.

Seaa grabbed the hand he had punched the stone with and held it to herself.

As I processed his feelings toward the situation and the fear he felt for his friend, I barely noticed the giant man coming from behind us at full speed. The ground shook beneath our feet. Zane's ear's twitched but not with enough time. Hail came over one of the boulders to my back, launching himself through the air. He slammed against Zane. Both men dropped to the shell-infused sand, grappling with dominance. Seaa hollered from her spot beside them. She would put a leg in to interfere and then another back as if thinking of it again.

Hail punched Zane in the face. The knuckles on his hand bled. Zane roared, flipping Hail over his shoulder. Seaa and I covered our faces as rock dust and debris flew all around us. The explosion was bound to call the rest of the group. I moved toward Seaa, whose feet moved back and forth as if debating whether or not to interfere.

"Damnit, Hail! Stop it!"

I could only watch the fight on the ground between operative Zane Mueller and Hail. It felt off somehow. Hail didn't fight him only because he was an operative of the first batch, but because of a much deeper reason I couldn't yet figure out. Did he hate all of the operatives working under Braggart? Did he not trust him? We were all told of Zane's switch. He'd been a great ally. I stared at the beautiful woman yelling at both the men.

He brought Seaa back to me.

The men roared at one another. Hail's eyes went white. I ran the rest of the way toward Seaa, pulling her back in time to avoid the blast of ice Hail released. The entire area froze over, covering Zane Mueller in the same block of ice that Hail had covered me in weeks back. Mueller stilled. Seaa yelled at Hail, asking him to release Zane from his power. Hail didn't have time to answer because Zane shape-shifted into a cheetah within the ice, cracking it from his body. The animal growled, fangs dripping saliva.

He launched at Hail. Our brother barely had enough

time to block him before the large feline ripped into his arm. Hail screamed, back-handing Zane. The former operative slammed into the boulder he had punched earlier. Ice cracked, crumbling off the sides of the surfaces Hail had covered. I held on tight to Seaa, who was quivering with rage. It took everything I had to hold her back. She could have weighed half of what I did, but that didn't stop me from taking it easy.

Zane shifted back into a human. The visual aesthetic of the entire moment was one I'd watch again. His skin rippled. The fur stood on end, moving in one direction like waves on water. His canines pulled back as his paws extended before him. Little at a time, digits appeared instead. Once the fur had receded, his dark skin appeared—clothes and all. His ability to alter his clothing eerily similar to mine. The moment seemed so slow, but it was done in a matter of seconds. Zane was back to normal and punching Hail repeatedly in the face with a closed fist.

I could hear Guy and Snow coming from behind. They saw me holding Seaa and then the battle in front of us. "Thunder sent us out here to check," Guy said.

I gave them both one of my nastier expressions. "And what do you see?" I said, words dripping in sarcasm.

Both men laughed. They saw the second half of what I did. I couldn't figure it out, but Guy didn't hesitate to point out, "Hail's hella jealous."

Both Seaa and I shot him a look of complete distress. *What the fuck?*

Seaa seemed to shutter within my arms. Hail knocked Zane on his ass. We watched as Hail created a sharp icicle with his hand and stomped over to Zane. The area had frozen. Seaa pulled free from my arms. Hail had his hand behind his head with the sharp object aimed at Zane.

"Seaa!" I yelled for her, but it was too late.

Guy, Snow, and I all ran toward her simultaneously, but none of us made it. Zane stared, wide-eyed at the Siren. His hands had gone up to stop her, but instead, she slammed into his chest. The next sound would be one we'd never forget. The tip of the icicle pierced the back of her shoulder straight through to the other side.

Snow and Guy tackled Hail to the ground, whose eyes had cleared back to normal. He stared in shock over the two bodies holding him down. Seaa collapsed in Zane's arms. I watched as the man's eyes glazed over, staring at the beautiful girl fallen in his arms. A growl erupted from his chest.

I jumped in quickly. Zane was about to launch at Hail, who lay silently on the sand. I held my hand up to stop him. "Don't you dare let her go," I warned.

Zane seemed to pull out of the rage of seeing her in pain. He blinked a few times, then lifted her into his arms, holding the frail woman to his chest. Zane Mueller had a severe crush on my sister. I watched my sister, so quiet in his arms. She bled from her shoulder and had passed out at some point after the stabbing. Seaa adored Zane—hero-worship I could only assume. I turned to Hail, who was off the ground, trying to get to Seaa. The boys held him back.

No, Seaa adored Zane, but the man she truly loved was the one who only saw her as a sister.

I waved to Zane to follow me. Guy and Snow must've been smacked together because I heard a crack of two heads coming together and then yelps from both. They cussed Hail. I didn't look. Zane held Seaa beside me. The other three followed behind me without a word. I sensed Hail's sadness and grief. He knew he had hurt her. Although Seaa wouldn't die of these injuries, I knew something inside Hail did.

We made it inside. Thunder had his hands crossed over his imposing chest. He pointed one finger at Hail, beckoning him to follow. Like a scolded puppy, Hail walked over to Thunder with his tail between his legs and one last longing look at Seaa. Zane followed me into Dr. Ferdinand's office. The other two knuckleheads laughed as they walked behind Thunder and Hail.

Zane shook his head, staring at his surroundings. "Never a dull moment in this place, huh?"

I gave a second look at everything he saw as if seeing it for the first time myself. The area had ceilings that were a cross between steel riveted into the stone or smooth stone itself. The floor was polished stone, smooth from any depressions. Military-grade hanging lights went down the hall in a row. They hummed with the power coursing through them. Farther down, I could see a few flash off and on after years of wear and tear. Empty crates and boxes sat on one corner.

We entered the large steel door that led into the clinic—the only room in the entire facility that didn't look like it was made of stone. The clean interior sparkled. The smell of antiseptics reached my nose. In his office, I saw the old doctor jump from a chair at his desk. He had one of Pops' books open before him.

"Oh, no. Please, place her on the table."

Zane seemed to think about it for a second, but he complied. He gently laid her down on the floating surface. The table didn't even move with the extra weight. Seaa had more weight on her since her rescue, but it wasn't enough yet to get her back to normal. Dr. Ferdinand checked her vitals as we watched from the door. He moved her gently, poking and prodding around the open wound. Zane didn't speak as he watched the old doctor work.

Dr. Ferdinand cleaned the area covered in blood after ripping part of her shirt. Although modestly dressed, the doctor drew up the sheet to cover her. Once the wound was cleaned, he stared intently at it with the magnifying glass attached to a device on his head.

"She's already healed." He poked around a little more. "Her skin is clean and should stitch up together nicely in minutes."

Zane took a deep breath. "Why hasn't she woken yet?"

The doctor clucked from his spot before her. "Seaa, although a genetic like the rest of you, is weak from her time in Foxtrot. Her immunity to certain things has not increased as quickly as the rest of the group."

I turned to the doctor. "Would that be because of the experiments they injected her with?"

The doctor sighed. "It could be."

We watched her for a few more minutes before a head popped into the room. Hail sheepishly stared at both of us, and then remorse crossed his features when he stared at Seaa, unmoving on the table.

"Dr. Ferdinand, will she be okay?"

The doctor nodded. "She'll be fine, Hail." He then scolded him as Pops had done to us. "Listen here, boy! That wound was clean straight through, the diameter of it wasn't at all typical of one of your usual weapons, and you have used them all. I should know!" he said in a raised voice. "I'm going to assume you had something to do with it." He placed his hands on his old hips so hard I thought he would snap in half.

Hail nodded. "I created an icicle."

The doctor nodded again. "Yes, adds up."

He ripped the gloves off his hands, gave us one last look, and went back into his office. We all stared openly at Seaa, whose chest rose and fell. The silence thickened. But before I could say something to diffuse the tension, Zane uttered words I wasn't sure I'd ever hear.

"I like her," he began.

Both Hail and I stared at Zane. "She's interested me since Foxtrot. The way she held her ground against the assholes in that place. How she survived when all the odds were against her." He took a deep breath, smiling roguishly. "I'm plenty interested in that woman."

I felt Hail's chest puff out. He looked as if he wanted to yell at Zane. Instead, I watched as he bit his lip and inhaled. Hail shook his head as he walked out of the clinic, and Zane and I followed him to the hallway. Hail headed toward the Planning Room. I gestured for Zane to follow. Once inside, he stared at the residents of Safe Haven. If I were Zane Mueller, at this moment, I'd be thinking I was a guest in a lion's den. One wrong move. One moment of hesitation. One wrong word. And Zane Mueller would cease to exist.

He cleared his throat and grinned. "I'm Zane Mueller. You can call me Zee."

The group muttered to one another. Thunder spoke, and they all quieted down. "Zee, thank you for meeting with us. I know it is at the risk of your life."

Zee shrugged. "The facility instills fear. Braggart kills on command, especially when shit don't go his way. I've been blessed to work the private sector lately, so I don't head out to wars or on clean-up duty—" he held his hand up "—no offense. But things gotta change. Rome's one of the best, and seeing him there, suffering..." He left the rest unsaid.

Thunder nodded. "We understand."

"I'm following Rayne's flow on this. Right now, she's got the man's trust."

Snow interjected, "Then why doesn't she just kill the bastard?"

I gave him a dirty look. "He's still her father, dumbass."

Snow shrugged.

Thunder added, "She's right, Snow. Rayne may not think of him as a dutiful person to look up to, but she still carries the man's blood. Us asking her to kill him would be asking too much of her." He sighed. "Don't forget that Rayne has only briefly come to us. She didn't suffer the time with us. She didn't know of any of us before now. Besides, to kill a snake we can't just cut off its head; another will grow back in its place."

"What are you trying to say?" Snow asked.

"I'm saying we starve the snake by cutting off his

funding as Seaa mentioned at the start of this project. We need to take away what nourishes that bastard and watch as it crumbles all around him. Getting Rayne or Zane to kill him won't end the fight." He turned back to Zane. "Zane and Rayne will do what they can."

"Exactly. Don't worry, Rayne and I will get Rome out of that place. It won't be easy, but we'll get it done."

"Does she need us?" Rock asked.

Zee nodded. "You guys remember the river by facility one?"

We all assented. The river saved a lot of us.

"Rayne will be moving Rome through the back tunnels. Although they are closed down, I'll be causing a huge explosion for her to exit."

"Seems ironic," Gavin said from behind us.

I hadn't even noticed he wasn't in the room. The man had his hair all in disarray as if he'd run his hand through it one too many times. We made eye contact, and I couldn't help the girlish shiver that went through me when I saw those blue eyes stare right into my soul. He gave me a little half-smile. When he walked by my side, he briefly twined his fingers through mine. The jolt of excitement came in like a wrecking ball. It was there one minute and gone the next. He let go way too soon. Gavin sat on the arm of the sofa, oblivious to the agony he left me in.

"I think it's a great idea," Gavin continued. "Hit them again in the same spot as the last time. General Braggart will be furious."

Thunder stared at all of us and then finally at Zane Mueller. "Zee, we will have some of our own waiting by the rapids. Make it into the water, and we will make sure you make it out alive."

"That sounds cool, man." He put a finger up as he turned. "Oh, and when I come back, it'll be for that little lady in the clinic." He winked and sped out of the Planning Room before anyone could process his words.

Seaa's knight in shining armor had arrived.

I didn't need to glance at Hail to know he was seething inside. Hail lost Rayne years ago and had come to terms with her feelings for Rome. Now, the woman he had gotten closer to the last five years before his capture was about to be swept away by another. If Hail didn't pull his head out of his ass soon, he was going to lose Seaa to Zane "Zee" Mueller, another member of batch 002 volunteers.

CHAPTER TWENTY-EIGHT

Sector Bravo
Safe Haven Headquarters
Gavin Foxhand
New States Citizen ID: CH.3349.GF-Rank A

ZANE RUSHED OUT of the Planning Room before anyone could let his words sink in. When they did, the room erupted into chaos. Everyone talked over the other in an effort to be heard. Zane had pretty much admitted that he was very interested in Seaa. Some of the warriors in the room laughed, while others processed what that meant. I happened to glance at Silk, who watched me with a light tint to her cheeks. I smiled at her. She was an enigma, but one I planned to stick to for the rest of my life.

Silk turned away from me, her blush brighter. She punched Hail in the arm. He grimaced. She whispered something in his ear, and he blushed deeper than she did. The room didn't contain itself until Seaa walked into the room as if nothing had happened. I heard she got stabbed by an icicle moments ago, but now I couldn't tell the difference in a fresh shirt.

The room went still.

"What the heck is going on in here?" she asked.

The room exploded again. Seaa was unprepared for the giddy parade. Some told her about the plan to free Rayne and Rome. The irony in using the tunnels. Simultaneously, others couldn't wait to say that Zane was more than interested in her. Her face went through a range of emotions: happiness, relief, surprise, disbelief. Blinking away the gaggle of voices, she turned to Hail, who stared at the floor before him. He didn't say a word, nor did he look at her.

Hoping I could get them back on track, I remembered the real reason why I had come in here. I had spent all the time I could working on those collars and was finally able to bypass their firewalls and hack into the server. Hacking this server wasn't the same as it was getting into Foxtrot. Alpha had security measures upon security measures that had me fighting to break through the system. I was finally able to, and the information I took from it was disturbing, to say the least.

"Hey, listen," I called out. Thunder reeled them all in an instant. "I was able to hack the collars. Their server led me to Alpha's communications system. Everyone needs to be in here."

Seaa jumped up, taking one look around. "1-1'll get Sue." She ran out of the room before anyone could stop her.

Rock volunteered to grab Viktor. We only waited about a minute before Viktor and Rock came into the room. Viktor seemed worse for the wear. He barely looked anyone in the eyes. He silently sat to one corner in one of the rickety chairs. The guy blamed himself for killing Cameron. He also had to contend with sending word to his camp about the loss of his men—their husbands, sons, and brothers. Viktor thought it best to leave another in charge for the time being, feeling unfit to help them at the moment. At least, those were the last things he said to us. A little later, Seaa walked into the Planning Room with Suzanne right beside her. The redhead seemed like she'd preferred to be swallowed up by the stone beneath her feet.

Suzanne's face had lost its pallor but for the blotchy marks of tear bouts. No one called her out on it. Cameron had been her mate. The man she loved. Now he was gone, and she was alone. I knew the feeling. I had no one when a lovely, mousy girl named Rayne came to me with one question. My mind went back to that moment.

I had been sitting on the rug of the library, reading through some information for one of my jobs. Rayne had spoken to me, and I'd looked up from my reading to see a brunette with hazel eyes wearing a god-awful green outfit. She made an immediate impression on me. She hadn't seen my money or my title; all that girl saw was the boy in the glasses.

My eyes swept over the beautiful Silk. It felt like a

lifetime ago that I had gone off on a journey to find Rayne in all my confused innocence and had since grown into a man willing to give his life up for the right cause. For the right woman.

"Listen, I was finally able to get some information on Alpha. They are creating these beast-men" —I looked at Viktor— "for no apparent reason but to instill fear." I leaned over on my perch. Everyone paid full attention. "I found a folder titled 'Terrorlution.' I found it appropriately titled for what I found inside. Braggart gave Dr. Robert Plumboy authority to experiment on several humans that would increase Project Hercules soldiers' strength almost three-fold. He's been messing with these experiments for a very long time. Around the same time that Dr. Lester perfected his genome.

"Everyone he has chosen has been a prisoner or—" I stared at Viktor "—family."

Viktor nodded. "Yes, my brothers. My mother, his sister, died in a fire. We didn't have any other family. It was just my brothers and Uncle Robert and me. He promised us a life where we'd be stronger. I didn't realize what he meant until it was too late."

Thunder placed a hand on Viktor's shoulder.

"I'm sorry for your loss," I voiced out loud.

Viktor merely nodded. The pain of losing the family he had left after his mother died to these experiments written on his drawn brows and watery eyes. Silk moved to the wall behind Suzanne's chair, leaning against it. I was aware of everything this woman did. She observed Suzanne's back as if making sure the woman didn't collapse from her weakened state. The woman listened to us, but the reminder of her loss turned her beet red as she held back the tears.

"These creatures are used as a tactic to intimidate and instill fear in the rest of the government and people. He's used them several times already. I specifically searched for the reason why they were sent to you, Suzanne," I said as I faced the woman.

Her head came up to face me, although not really seeing me.

"You were on their Terrorlution list. They wanted you dead, but I don't understand why?"

Suzanne sniffled. "Probably because of my mother."

We all watched and waited. She pointed at the center of the room. "When you all came back from that battle that killed Cam, I heard someone mention to Thunder that Foxhand's father made known that another Project Hercules supporter worked at the harbors. I didn't put two and two together then, but now I know for sure. My mother is trying to k-kill me," she blubbered through tears now released.

Guy shook his head. "Why would your own mother want you dead?"

Suzanne cried harder. I placed a comforting hand on her shoulder as Seaa held hers in her hands. The outpour was more than any of us could bear. She cried tears over the man she lost, and the one's over learning of her mother's betrayal. Finally, she wiped at her face, taking deep breaths.

"My mother doesn't want anything to do with me," she started. "That's nothing new. Having a blind child in this day and age is a sign of weakness for her." After sucking in a shaking breath, one side of her mouth lifted. "It also doesn't help that my 'eyes' know everything. The last time we spoke, I threatened to go public with her dirty little secrets. The woman has lots to her name and none of it done legally. She's critical in her line of business. My mother will eliminate anything that threatens that reputation, including me."

The entire room processed that bit of information. She shook her head as strands stuck to her wet face. "I didn't think she'd get Project Hercules to do it for her."

I sighed. "She must be contributing a huge chunk of money on the condition that they clean up any messes she leaves behind."

Suzanne snorted. "I'm definitely that."

Seaa squeezed her hands. "You are not, Suzanne. You have been such a blessing to our group—to Cameron. You aren't anyone's mess. She doesn't deserve to be a mother. One day, you'll show her!"

Tears fell again. Her breathing came in choppy. Silk leaned toward her, whispering into her ear. Suzanne cried even harder, turning in her chair and throwing her arms around the woman I loved. The room stayed quiet. Silk didn't move from her embrace. Slowly I saw the change in the beautiful spider woman. She became more than I could have ever thought possible. When Suzanne was done, and Silk assisted her back into the chair, she turned to face the room once more.

"I'll be showing her sooner rather than later." Suzanne wrapped her arms around her belly. I stared. The room grew even quieter. The only sound came from the low echoes of water dripping in an unused tunnel at the base's end. Suzanne's green eyes came into focus. "I'm carrying Cameron's baby."

ALARMS BLARED THROUGHOUT the interior of Foxtrot as explosions rippled through the facility. I ran past soldiers and medical personnel as they rushed away from the explosions. I went down another level, knowing full well that the torture rooms were near the fire. Rome wasn't in his cell when I had gone to see him. When I got information from one of the transport soldiers, I learned that General Braggart had sent Rome to the gas chamber.

The chamber sucked out the life from inside a genetic soldier and released a poison so deadly it killed the weakest of us after hours of torture. Braggart ordered Rome two consecutive blasts. He might not even survive the first in his weakened state. Zee had survived it once. Rome wasn't strong enough. Our plans to wait for the right time went up in smoke, when I heard what they planned. Zee had only arrived moments before with word from the group. He ran off in the opposite direction toward the explosives.

Not five minutes later, blasts reverberated through the interior. The entire facility shook and groaned. I took to another level, almost tripping over an unconscious soldier on the floor. The lights down here went out. Emergency lights came on, barely illuminating the interior. The sirens wailed. I slowly walked down the empty hallway. The smell of blood hit me hard. I peered closely and saw it sprayed against the white interior.

What the heck happened here?

I slowed my pace as the sounds of screaming reached my ears. The growls of an animal drew closer. My heart skipped a few beats. I held to the walls, hoping to keep my balance. As I turned the corner, the sight before me made me retch. There was blood and gore everywhere I could see in the dim light. A small pile of shredded clothing in the center of it all. I saw a body of a medical staff member moving, but too late, I realized it wasn't of his own volition. A black creature ripped through him. I took a step backward in self-preservation and bumped into a strong body.

Zee put his finger up to his lips.

The animal heard us. Its ears twitched and straightened. The animal looked right at me with glowing green eyes and bared its fangs. I felt faint, but Zee held me steady.

"Oh my gosh," I gasped. "What if that thing attacked Rome?"

I could feel Zee shake his head behind me. "That thing didn't attack Rome, Rayne." He pulled me aside, taking the spot I vacated. "That creature is Rome."

I hadn't had time to conceive the nature of his news when Zee shifted into a cheetah. He was as big as Rome. The animals growled at each other, their bodies poised to react. The black creature came into the light, blood dripping from his mouth. The panther roared, the muscles in its body flexing each time it moved. Another blast tore through the facility. Both animals jumped at each other.

With hands over my mouth, I threw myself to the side as the creatures rolled over one another beside me. The cheetah yelped when the panther took a massive bite from its side. That didn't stop it, though. I saw the cheetah use the wall for leverage. Zane's cheetah jumped on top of the panther, gripping tightly to the back of his neck. I heard them whine. I rolled the other way when their battle made it to the spot I vacated again. The panther slammed its weight on the cheetah. The cheetah slid, hitting the wall with such force he burst right through it.

The panther with its glowing green eyes stared at me, licking his chops at his next meal. I tore my eyes from the slick black animal to see Zane morph back into a human. He was unconscious. I had guns on me, but if what Zane had said was true, this panther was Rome. I couldn't hurt him.

"Rome, please!"

The animal didn't even flinch. In seconds, the creature pounced on me, dropping me to the ground with his fangs bared. I screamed, holding him back with all my strength. The animal snapped at me, trying to go for my face. I pushed back. It reared back a little to take a swipe at me with claws. I felt it tear through my arms, but I kept them up even as they bled all over my clothes.

"Rome! Damnit, Rome, come back to me."

It snarled and snapped, dripping blood and saliva all over my face. I screamed harder, asking Rome to hear my voice, hoping he'd finally snap out of it. My heart thrummed loudly. My body felt numb. It kept trying to break through, taking a bite out of my arm. I moved away in time, but it took enough to feel the world tilt on its axis. I could no longer hold it. My arms dropped. The animal didn't expect the move and fell on top of me. I felt weight one minute and then gone the next.

I turned slightly to watch as the panther readied itself to kill me. Tears rolled down my face. Gathering all the power inside of me, I shifted into liquid the moment he jumped. The panther slid and slammed into a wall. It shook its head but stared right back at me as I resumed my shape.

"Rome, I love you. Please, don't leave me like this."

The animal screeched a deafening sound. It ran toward me again. I shifted, drowning the creature briefly as I drew back into a solid figure. The animal shook its head, whining and growling all at once. It pawed at its head when finally its skin rippled, and the fur dropped to the ground like the leaves in fall. I grabbed my throbbing arm. Zane moaned from his spot on the floor debris. The alarms in Foxtrot blared. As they sang of danger, I watched in awe as Rome lay utterly naked on the ground.

What was once a ferocious cat now lay a vulnerable, naked man.

Zane came around me. His clothes were on as if he'd been wearing them the entire time, so I wondered briefly why Rome was naked. Was this a part of Zane's mutation? Did anyone else have this ability? Zee grabbed a pair of medical pants in one hand.

He dressed Rome, who groaned from the pain of his wounds. There was another explosion, this one close enough to feel. The wind blasted toward us. We dropped to hide behind the debris.

"That's the last of it," Zee called out. "We need to go now."

We both held Rome between us, running toward the opening Zane had made with the explosives. Memories of my time in these tunnels came back to me with such force that I staggered. Zee waited only momentarily but then pressed on. We ran faster, the pain in my body hitting me hard. I struggled to move.

"Let's go, Rayne. We are almost there."

I took a deep breath. Blood dripped down my arm. We saw the early morning sky covered in dense, gray clouds. No sun. Nothing but a cold, biting wind and snow everywhere.

"We're almost there!"

I saw ahead. The river was indeed there. The current moved with ferocity. I had once fallen in this river and been carried to an entirely different world. Not once did I think I'd be doing this a second time. We shuffled through banks of snow. Rome's tattoos all seemed to lack luster from the blue tint on his skin.

He was dying on me.

I ran my hand not holding him over his chest to help with heat friction, when Zane yelled out, "No!"

He spun us around behind him. I tried to gain my bearings, but it was too late. A hauntingly frustrated scream burst from my lips as I watched three bullets hit Zane in the chest. The man dropped to the ground. I lost my grip on Rome. He, too, fell. I cried, staring at

Trevor Dallas from tear-soaked eyes. He aimed again as more soldiers gathered behind him. I had rushed forward, turning into my liquid form. He shot into the water.

I sucked him and the tired soldiers around in the wave. They all flew to different spots around the ground. Trevor hit a tree as I pulled myself back into my human form. I ran toward Zane and Rome. Zane was still breathing. I lifted him and dragged Rome. My injured arm was too weak to carry him as I did Zane. I felt my muscles stitching themselves together, so I wasn't afraid of losing anything vital other than the fact that I could feel the blood loss.

My vision blurred. The desolate area spun around me. I cried as I pulled the men toward the river. I fell. Both men landed in the snow. I heard both Trevor and Zane groan. I looked over at Trevor, picking himself off the ground. Zane grabbed the gun from his waistband and shot at Trevor.

"G-go," he stuttered.

I shook my head, trying to drag him back too. He took another shot toward the cowboy who was trying to grab his weapon from the snow. In minutes, the soldiers I had pushed around were back off the ground, running toward us with weapons. Zane pulled his arm from me.

"I said go, Rayne. Tell Rome I'm sorry."

He got up from the ground with enough forced to push us back over the edge of the ravine. As I waved my arms around in the air to gain some leverage, I watched, in slow motion, as Zane flipped the switch on one of our modified incendiary hand grenades.

It was the last image I had of him before Rome and I fell in, smacking against the walls of the small gorge. I heard a grenade blow up above us. The sound of the blast rippled through the ground. The heat smacked me in the face before the cold, frigid water soothed the burn.

I pulled Rome into my body as the water drove us farther down the river.

Will we make it?

CHAPTER TWENTY-NINE

Sector Bravo
Safe Haven Headquarters

NEWS OF THE baby made the entire facility on edge. They thought about the same things I did when I found out about the baby from Cameron. How were we able to conceive? How would the baby turn out having these abilities? Would its growth affect the human mother? Seaa left the room with Suzanne. I noticed Dr. Ferdinand make a beeline toward the distraught woman. My promise to Cameron came back to my mind.

Instead of letting the older adult walk past me, I held him back with one hand to his chest. He stared at me in concern. I shook my head. "Let her come to you first, Doc."

He sighed but agreed. The older man was on our side, but it didn't diminish his need for the study. Dr. Ferdinand took every moment, ache, and wound to learn more about us. He looked longingly at the woman carrying the first super baby. Wanting to be a part of her baby's growth was tantamount to self-discovery. He couldn't help himself.

I walked back into the Planning Room, where it had erupted in conversation. The guys talked about the baby and the fact that Suzanne confirmed that the person we were looking for was her mother. How hard was it to have someone like that woman as your mother? Gavin thought his father wasn't capable of having feelings for him, but it was the complete opposite. Here came a woman who didn't have her mother's love at all. Who, if it weren't for Cam's appearance, would have died to appease a woman embarrassed to have birthed her?

We were all a victim of that. It's not like we had parents who got experimented on and birthed us to give us up, but we were still parentless. The only one who had become a father figure to us was an old doctor who couldn't help but warm up to us. Pops treated us like his children and died helping us have a real life. I couldn't see how someone could be so cold to their child. I had tendencies of being just as tough-skinned to others around me but never to children.

They are precious.

Children meant that we strived to move beyond the war and fighting. It meant that at some point, things would have to get better. If not for us, then for them.

I noted nothing would be resolved now, so I walked back out of the Planning Room. The walls of the bunker were alive with voices. I ignored the commotion in search of Seea and Suzanne. Suzanne didn't have a room of her own. She slept in Cameron's room, so I headed there first. Through the door, I could hear Suzanne crying. Seaa's words were barely a whisper as she consoled the human woman. Her pain rushed through me. Memories of Cameron crawled over my skin.

I wiped at it as if I could make the pain go away. Cameron's smile when he got his way. The way he teased me. How he both hated and loved me. All of the memories we had together since childhood rushed through my mind like a movie reel. A young version of himself, play-fighting with the other guys in the training room. The excitement was written on his face when he first learned he could blend in with his surroundings. The day he knocked Hail on his ass. The anger on his face as I cussed him out for leaving our bunker to stay with Suzanne. The way his Cheshire grin widened whenever I threatened to hurt his male parts. The way he acted the moment he told me his true feelings—the peace and relief on his face when he spoke of the baby Suzanne carried.

Tears fell from my eyes as I pushed my back against the wall beside the door. I couldn't go in now. Not until I controlled the ache within me. I thought I had cried it all out already, but the loss of Cameron felt raw. He left us. It was hard to believe he even could. I didn't want to question why things happened, but I couldn't help staring up at the ceiling, hoping it would reveal the answers I craved.

I cleared my throat. The palms of my hand became makeshift napkins. Instead of thinking more about it, I knocked on the door. There were a few whispers, and then Seaa's voice welcomed me inside. Seaa brushed Suzanne's hair back from her face, placing it in a high bun. The woman's bright eyes stared straight at me.

"I came because I wanted to apologize."

Seaa stopped messing with her hair. Suzanne stared at me. I felt it appropriate that I stay within her gaze. "Why should you be apologizing to me?" She was clearly confused.

"I've been nothing but nasty to you."

Seaa's lavender eyes widened. I wasn't one to apologize, so this came as quite of a shock to her. I ignored it and bit the bottom of my lip. Apologizing wasn't my strong suit. "I couldn't save Cameron either. For that, I'm sorry."

Suzanne didn't cry. Her chest held in a shaky breath, but tears didn't fall. "You aren't at fault. I know Cameron loved you, Silk. I know he left because he couldn't bear to be around knowing how he felt and waiting for you to heal from whatever prejudice you had toward men."

Am I that transparent?

She kept talking, oblivious to the fresh tears falling from my eyes. "I knew he cared about me, but not in the same way he cared about you. Did you know he relished those fights with you because it meant you cared enough to fight?"

I shook my head. Suzanne couldn't see it, but she

smiled nonetheless.

"Cameron and I had an agreement. We comforted each other. Neither one of us knew I'd end up pregnant with his baby." She sighed. "I cared about him so much, but I didn't want to tie him down to me when I knew he felt so much for you. But you know how he is."

I nodded, blubbering from my spot on the floor across from them. Seaa, too, had tears, wrapping her arms around Suzanne.

"No matter what I said, he refused to leave me to raise the baby on my own. He told me that we would get married and build our family and that he knew that in time he'd love me as he loved you."

I threw my hands over my mouth—the last of my self-restraint breaking. "I'm so sorry, Suzanne," I whispered as tears made my voice crack.

She got up from the bed. Her confidence in her whereabouts took her straight to me as if she could see exactly where I stood. Suzanne found me and wrapped me in her arms. "This baby is as much mine as she'll be yours, Silk," she whispered in my ear as she petted my curls down.

I shook my head. "I could never, Suzanne. You and Cam built something together I could never do. I did care about Cameron and, in time, learned that I had feelings for someone else. It took me a long time to break through my ache." I held her back by her shoulders, rubbing my hands down her arms as a way of comforting her. "But he has made me feel alive again. I concluded that Cam belonged to another woman. You both—" I placed a calm hand on her belly "—have created something beautiful that will always belong to you both. I will be a great aunt, Suzanne. I promise to protect you and that baby for the rest of my life."

Suzanne's knees went weak, so I held her to me. She cried, we cried for a long time. No one said any more words. Seaa joined us on the ground. We supers held the fragile human woman between us, knowing that from here on out, that baby would come into this world with the toughest aunts and uncles on the planet.

I would end Braggart and Project Hercules if it was the last thing I did.

FOR THE FIFTH time in the past two hours, I once again walked over to Gavin's door, situated next to Rayne's bedroom. Each time I raised my hand to knock, but I'd freak out and walk away. Then I contemplated kicking the door in but thought that would be too forward. No matter what I did, the result would be the same. I wanted to see Gavin. I wanted to be near him. We'd been forced together for so long that I felt sick to my stomach if I didn't see him.

I inhaled deeply. The entire group had been exhausted, having spent the majority of the night and early morning dealing with the news of Alpha and Suzanne. We waited on word from Rayne or Zane, but nothing had come forward yet. So, the best thing we could do was rest to keep our energy up. Except, I spent an hour in bed tossing and turning. I realized it was because I needed to see Gavin. I knew he was safe. When I extended my hearing, I could hear him tinkering around in his room. The man would pace the floors. He'd get exasperated and run his hands through his hair.

The next two hours, I came up with every excuse in the book to go by his room. I wanted to knock on his door and demand to know what he was doing. Some habits were hard to break. No matter the reasons, the main point was that I couldn't stand to be away from him for too long. I sighed for the millionth time. Instead of making a fool of myself, I turned back around and was about to walk off when his door slammed open.

Gavin Foxhand wore nothing but loose-fitting pajama bottoms. I'd seen him a few times in his apartment with his shirt off, but back then, I hadn't appreciated the way he was built. He wore glasses that he had found in his father's apartment. His hair was in disarray. Gavin was lean but cut in all the right places. He was by no means as big as the men in our circle, but he was perfect enough for me.

Something inside of me wanted to release the power in hopes that he'd gravitate toward me. It was a primal feeling. One I had never felt before.

Gavin turned to look both ways down the hall. No one else was around. When he saw that the coast was clear, he reached out and pulled me into the bedroom. Gavin closed the door, and all the while, my heart beat ferociously out of my chest. It was so hard and so loud that I swore he could hear it. I imagined him memorizing the beat, knowing how his nearness made me feel, and it filled me with an entirely new sensation.

He turned to me, pulling me close to his body. I let him. The moment my body touched his burning skin, I felt weak in the knees. Not ever had a man's proximity made me vulnerable. I had beat them at every turn. But not now, and not with Gavin Foxhand. I felt my weight grow heavier. I buckled, but he had already reached around and scooped me up into his strong arms. My arm came around his neck to hold on, but I didn't need to worry. Gavin held me tightly to himself.

Our eyes locked—my deep ones to his blues. My entire body shivered. The butterflies came back. This time, they didn't feel threatening. They didn't pierce my stomach, tying it into knots and making bile rise in my esophagus. The butterflies fluttered like those in a flower garden. They were happy, and so was I.

Gavin Foxhand laid me slowly on his bed. The old springs groaned with my weight. He grinned, but it didn't get awkward. I smirked, gingerly taking my shaking hand to the side of his face. I expected him to flinch, but he didn't move. Instead, he leaned into my hand. My palm felt the warmth of his face and the scruffy beard that he hadn't shaved. He drew closer to my body, leaning over me until we were parallel with one another.

My fingers didn't stop shaking. I wanted Gavin to touch me, but then I didn't want him to touch me. Gavin must've read the tension in my body because he didn't put his weight on me. He merely hovered. The goosebumps rose from my skin. Even those little traitors wanted to touch Gavin. The smile on his face drove me wild. His head leaned into mine. Instead of kissing me on the lips, he placed them on my forehead, then rolled to the side of the bed beside me.

I turned my head to face him. Gavin fingered a curl that had fallen in my face. The ring fell on top of the rest. "I felt you at my door for the past couple of hours. If you walked away one more time, I thought I'd explode."

An unladylike snort bubbled out. "You'd survive."

He smiled again. The glasses came off. The light above us flickered once and then steadied. The entire bunker was quiet. The only sound was the one of our breathing in this little room. Gavin reached over to pull me closer. I turned to face him, nestled more snugly against his body. His chin rested on the top of my head. I inhaled his scent of rose oil and almost an almond undertone.

Even breathing gave me peace.

I relaxed my body, letting the world slip away.

For this one moment, I felt at complete peace.

My eyes jolted open as a warning siren blared within the interior. It was only one long blast, which meant that an emergency awaited us, and we needed to gather in the Planning Room. Gavin had already bolted over the edge of the bed to grab his glasses. He slipped them on, but it was more out of comfort than necessity. If I recalled, he only used them to read, and rarely needed them. Once they were on, he drifted to the dresser, pulling out a white shirt to cover his naked abs. I bolted to the door, opening it wide as Gavin came in behind me, wrestling with his shirt.

Guy walked past the room at that exact moment.

He took one long look at us, grinned, and whistled a jaunty tune on his way to the meeting. "Fuck," I cussed out loud.

Gavin peeked over my shoulder, watching as Guy walked away. "Don't pay him any mind."

I sneered at Gavin. He merely laughed. The man grabbed my hand, leading me toward the Planning Room. There was a brief feeling of annoyance which coursed through my body, but then it was replaced with the warmth of his hand, and I couldn't stay mad. We entered the room at the same time as the last stragglers, rubbing the sleep from their eyes. Few noticed Gavin holding my hand. No one said a word.

The room was loud as it usually was when we were in it together. Thunder put his hand up, and that was all it took for all of us to quiet down. There was an immense concern in the depth of his eyes. Something had happened. Thunder's hair swept over his shoulder and back as he paced the smooth floor. I stared as he picked up one of the splintered pieces of the broken table.

"I need two volunteers to join me in a rescue mission."

Rescue?

"I'll let Suzanne explain."

I saw Suzanne rocking back and forth with a KeViewer in her hand. "My network received word that two bodies were found in the mouth of the harbor. They believe the two floated in from the river. One male: Caucasian, black hair, and tattoos all over. The other a female: Caucasian; long, dark brown hair."

Rayne and Rome.

"Are they alive?" Hail asked.

Seaa blinked a few times. Her entire body went rigid with the news. Hail neared her, placing a comforting hand to the back of her neck. I watched as she leaned into his touch as if it made all the problems go away.

Is that how I am with Gavin?

Thunder spoke up when Suzanne clammed up. "For now. They were pulled out of the water and hidden. They've had no medical attention, which is why we need to head out and get them here right away." He pointed to the old doctor. "Dr. Ferdinand, I need you to prep two tables. We need to make sure they get better."

The older man nodded and ran out of the room to prepare.

Hail put the hand not rubbing Seaa's neck up. "I volunteer."

"Me too," Seaa added.

Both stared at each other and then at Thunder. He nodded at them both. "Fine then, we leave at 1700 hours."

Thunder cleared the room as if he hadn't dropped a bomb on us. Rayne, Rome, and Zane were supposed to have escaped together. They were supposed to have called us before they left the facility. We were supposed to come in to assist if necessary. Where was Zane? What the hell happened? Why were Rayne and Rome on the verge of death?

The answer lay with Rayne and Rome.

If they survived the next few hours.

CHAPTER THIRTY

THE NEXT FEW hours went by in a blur. Everyone in the facility grew somber. No one spoke. No one laughed. All of us waited to hear news from Thunder as if his words could relieve the tension from our minds and bodies. Not knowing if they were alive or dead filled me with terrible anxiety. I paced the bunker, wearing the stone even further than we had these past few years since moving in here. Gavin tried to get my attention a few times, but I ignored him. I didn't feel like talking to anyone. All I wanted was to know that Rayne was alive and well.

Or, as well as she could be.

I paced the entryway once more. Rock ran from the surveillance room. "They've been spotted past the water."

I reached out my senses, and indeed they were. Five different heartbeats were coming back to us. Three were strong and steady, only slightly agitated from their long travel. The other two were not quite audible. They were alive, but barely. We rushed out the front doors of the bunkers. Thunder had driven the boat into our shore. Hail jumped out, helping Seaa over the side. All of them seemed tired from their hunched-over postures and pallor.

Thunder lifted Rome, placing him in Hail's arms. Hail walked away. Rock held the door open for him. I rushed over to Seaa, who had grabbed Rayne. I walked with her back to the doors, leaving Thunder behind to tie off the boat. We walked inside as a rush of movement caught my attention. The entire area lit up with people and conversation. I didn't see who was there, but I knew Gavin watched from a short distance.

We made it inside the clinic. Doing precisely as Dr. Ferdinand wanted, we left them and walked out to give him the space he needed to work. I took one last look at my little sister. There were unhealed cuts all over her face and neck that distorted her pretty features. Her skin no longer one tone. The blue and purple bruises changing her complexion. The swelling in some parts so extreme that I couldn't even remember how it was supposed to look. Her face was unrecognizable.

The two had gone through hell.

And it was only the beginning.

With Rayne and Rome back within the folds of Safe Haven, our group could better focus on the next task at hand—dealing with Sue's mother, another of Braggart's major financial players. We had the information we needed. Barbara Benedict had married a politician in the time before the war. When he died, she had taken the money to run military weapons to and from different nations by ship. The woman had earned enough to run New States on her own.

Suzanne Benedict had come into the world with a disability, and that drove Barbara insane. To all the political, wealthy figures, Barbara Benedict had a perfect life. She owned a successful company. Lived in lavish luxury. And had no children or husband tying her down. Suzanne lived in squalor. She had been banished to a sector and babysat by a nanny and some thugs until she broke free from that life, met Cam, and started her own network.

Now that very network, run by Suzanne, had every illegal dealing her corrupted mother had financed and run on record. All Sue needed was a little push and she'd bring her corrupt mother down. After thorough research, Gavin found proof that Barbara needed Suzanne gone before she leaked any of that information. Project Hercules had been funded quite a large amount in exchange for Suzanne's disappearance. Cam's interference messed with that plan. All we needed was the right moment to get to her mother.

Barbara Benedict didn't make trips to the shipping yard anymore. But one phone call from Gregory Foxhand advised us that she was making an unscheduled visit to the docks tonight. That meant this was our chance to end her business with Unit 13. Thunder spoke from the hallway as the entire underground residents bombarded him with questions. He seemed ragged as if he'd seen enough to last him a lifetime.

There's been enough to last us all a lifetime.

"Guys! 1 know you are all curious about Rayne and Rome. All 1 can say with certainty is that they are still alive. For how long? 1 don't know. Will they be the same? 1 don't know either. Their injuries were very severe."

Suzanne spoke up from her spot by the corner. She may or may not have noticed, but ever since the baby news, the men in Safe Haven unintentionally hovered over her like a protection detail for a mega important client. "Gavin's father gave us a huge leg up for my mother. If we don't take advantage of tonight, she'll head back to her lofty private residence with her crazy security measures. 1 say tonight leaves her open and vulnerable."

Thunder nodded. "She's right. Rome and Rayne are a part of our home, and 1 know that affects all of you, but we need to focus on tonight's mission." He pointed to some of us. "Rock and Snow will stay behind to watch over Safe Haven. The rest of us have a fight to get to tonight."

No one argued.

Each of us walked off to get ready. Gavin followed me to my room. His anxiety smacked me with each step 1 took. Frustrated, 1 turned on him with drawn brows and pinched lips. Gavin threw himself closer, pressing his lips to mine. My mouth opened in shock, and his tongue tenderly snuck in. His hand on the back of my head pulled me closer. My body tensed, but then he did this thing with his tongue over my bottom lip, and I melted. Gavin held me tighter, angling my head for deeper contact.

I couldn't think of a damn thing as he devoured my mouth with his. I was no expert, nor did I know what the hell I was doing. It felt right, though. My body relished his and pressed itself closer. When a tiny sound of appreciation trickled from my throat, Gavin lifted me into his arms. My long legs wrapped themselves around his waist. He walked only a few steps before bringing us into my room and slamming the door behind us.

At that moment, all I could think of was Gavin and the way I felt held by him. I didn't notice the crowd of gawkers smiling at our little spectacle as the door closed on their faces.

All I could think about was him.

Sector Delta
Old Boston Harbor

WE SPLIT INTO two groups of two. Thunder refused to let us fight alone. I had the unfortunate circumstance of getting paired up with Guy. Thunder stood at a vantage point, watching the workings of the shipyard from above. Seaa and Hail were strategically placed on the other end, closer to the water. With Seaa's ability to control water currents and Hail's ability to freeze it over, that left Guy and me to take on the muscle on the opposite end.

Guy hadn't stopped grinning since we left the bunkers. I know it had something to do with me—his eyes took me in from head to toe at every chance he could. But for the life of me, I couldn't figure out what it was that tickled his fancy. All I knew was that I would beat the snot out of him if he didn't stop.

Thunder came back on the line. Our earpieces picked up the connection loud and clear. "Three black SUVs have pulled up. Stay alert."

I ignored Guy and peeked around the shipping container. There were three vehicles in my line of sight, precisely as Thunder called. These weren't cars of the times before the war. These vehicles hovered about three feet off the ground. The affluent society used them often. Middle/working classes used the shuttle. The military preferred the older models because those weren't easy enough to hack.

The harbor lit up with expensive ships and people hollering from the docks. They lifted huge loads of crates into one ship and shipping containers into another. The port was alive with people and machines doing the jobs they were ordered to do. The job that earned them food to eat or coal to heat their hearth. No one paid attention to the vehicles. Not even when movement from the first caught our attention.

The first vehicle let out about eight men. Each one of them held a Vuwand in their hand and a gun on their hip. The last car let out eight more, but two operatives were included in that eight, which meant that they had been hired for private sector duties like Zane. No one exited the middle vehicle.

Guy snickered but didn't mention what made him

laugh. I shot him an annoyed face. He only laughed louder, but low enough that no one would be the wiser. Two average men walked by us, oblivious to the danger standing right next to them. They smelled of fish and seawater.

"Wait for confirmation on the last vehicle," Thunder called through the earpiece.

Everyone acknowledged.

I studied the way the men moved or how advanced the operatives' senses were. So far, none of them was the wiser.

"Tell me, Silk. How does it feel to be a *real* woman now?" Guy's eyebrows wiggled up and down.

Mine dropped. "What the hell are you talking about, Guy?"

On the line, I could hear Hail and Seaa tell Guy to shut up. Thunder told him to drop the nonsense. I didn't understand what he was talking about. What did he mean when he asked how I felt to be a "real woman?" As opposed to a spider? As opposed to a genetically enhanced human? I thought we were beyond this point already. Clearly, Guy could only act like an immature jackass with nothing else to do with his free time.

Guy snickered. Thunder came back on the line to tell him to stop. Seaa warned him once more. I stared at Guy, trying—unsuccessfully—to understand what made him laugh. He inspected my attire. I wore leggings and one of my usual tunics.

"What the hell are you looking at?" I half-whispered, half-growled.

Hail came on the line. "Don't ruin this Guy!"

Ruin what?

Too late, 1 didn't realize the reasoning of his laughter or the way he examined the way 1 moved and carried myself. Guy opened his mouth and my head filled with blood so quickly 1 couldn't contain what came next.

"1 was looking to see if the frigid woman 1 grew up with appreciated her body now." Guy wiggled his eyebrows again and the meaning sunk in.

The group all spoke at once, but 1 heard nothing but the blood boiling over in my ears. My arm pulled back. A fist full of embarrassment and pissed-off righteousness struck him in the mouth. 1 saw Guy's face whip back first, and then his entire body slammed into the edge of the metal container. He flipped about three times between the other boxes and landed into a pile of old pallets and tubs full of fish and water.

"Fuck," Thunder roared. "Get out there now," he called to the rest of us.

1 jumped on top of the metal container, avoiding two shots sent in my direction. The suit beneath my skin came forward, covering me from neck to toes. An operative sped over to where Guy landed. 1 blasted him with my pheromone charm. The man dropped to the ground. The shield came back up. Guy shook off the punch and grabbed the guns from the operative on the ground.

"Hail, the middle SUV is trying to get out."

Hail's power could be seen from the other end of the pier. The ability skimmed over the wooden planks, over some of the guards, and on the cars. All of them froze in place. We had a few minutes before it thawed. I jumped off the container. One guard lit up his Vuwand as he grabbed his gun with the other. With a roundhouse kick to the face, he dropped to the ground. His weapon and Vuwand skittered in two different directions.

I made it to the last SUV at the same time Guy did. "Not cool, Silk," he teased.

I growled. "You want another punch to the face?"

He laughed. "No, this is the face that drives the women wild," he joked.

We both made it to the middle vehicle and punched the back windows on each side simultaneously. The woman and two males inside screamed. Suzanne was the spitting image of Barbara Benedict. Both women had red hair. One was cropped short while the other was pulled into a severe chignon with giant feathers and birds sticking out of it. The men in the car opened fire. The woman screamed, covering her head, flattening the stuffed birds. Guy and I realized that the bullets were for genetically enhanced superhumans.

Luckily, we turned from the window in time to avoid them. I heard a grunt and saw Seaa flip over the other operative. She placed him in a chokehold. The man struggled. I did a quick check and saw Hail freeze guard after guard, but not once did he turn a blind eye to Seaa.

With him around, she'll be fine.

When the guns clicked, both Guy and I ripped open the car doors where the men sat. With the other hand, we pulled the men out as they reloaded. Barbara cried again. The men flew off and hit different areas of the harbor. My guy landed in the same tub I had sent Guy.

His guard flew in the air, spiraling and dropping into the cold water. The other humans ran when the fight started, preferring their safety to the job at hand. None of us worried about them, and if they did pose a problem, we knew Thunder was watching our backs.

Guy and I had this synchronicity thing going. Both our faces poked into the back window at the same time. The woman jumped. "What's up, babe? You can either talk to me, or you can talk to her." He motioned to me with his chin. Barbara shook, glancing at both of us. He grinned, the nasty bruise on his mouth growing darker. "Keep in mind, though, she's the one that fist-shot me in the buckets earlier, so I recommend coming out on my side."

I bared my teeth at him.

Barbara didn't think twice about it. She vehemently nodded and came out of the car willingly. The moment she made it out of Guy's side, the earpiece in our ears crackled and then went dead. We all turned when we saw Thunder fall from his vantage point. I squinted, seeing Braggart's soldiers where Thunder once stood and watched.

I yelled out, "Braggart's men are here!"

Before we could cover from the spray of gunfire, Barbara Benedict got hit twice in the chest. The one aimed at her head, entering Guy's shoulder instead. "Shit," Guy gritted through the pain. "They fuckin' shot her, Silk," he added.

The soldiers had made it to the pier, headed straight toward Hail and Seaa. Both fought off several soldiers and operatives. Behind me, I saw the current of electricity flow like a cloud storm over the harbor equipment. Many screamed. I hadn't realized that my heart pounded loudly until I confirmed that Thunder lived. I ignored Guy, and Barbara's body, preferring to help my other two siblings. Guy followed. We got there in time to subdue the extras and drop an operative on the wooden planks.

An operative who wouldn't seem to die came around from behind a packaged pallet. He wasn't wearing his hat this time. Trevor Dallas had been disfigured. Half of his face had healed like a burn victim's. It hid under the collar of his shirt but went over the entire side of his head. The hair on that side was completely gone. His eye was barely visible, swollen under the folds of skin. His mouth lifted on that side as if caught in a permanent smirk. The other side seemed untouched. Trevor Dallas's eyes had lost their humor. His gun pointed at my siblings. Eyes dilated, Trevor was out for blood.

I ran toward Seaa in time to push her out of the way. The bullet hit her side before she fell into the frigid, dark ocean water. My body hit the ground hard. I gritted my teeth on impact. Another shot rang out. Hail touched the ground, freezing a path toward Trevor. The man hid behind the loaded pallet, avoiding the freeze. He shot again. Hail was fast enough to create a block of ice with his abilities. I crawled over to the edge of the pier as another shot ran beside me. Debris flew into my face. I spit out the matchstick-sized pieces that flew into my mouth.

"Seaa," I called out.

She didn't answer. I couldn't find her anywhere. I threw myself into the water. The cold water hit my bones before I could prepare for it. I swam deeper, trying to see myself in the darkness. I held my breath. The only thing I could see were the bubbles in front of me. I swam farther down, moving around in circles. My sister wasn't anywhere. I could feel the panic set in. I didn't know what I would do if anything happened to Seaa. She meant the world to me. Both of my sisters did.

I screamed for Seaa in the water with the remainder of my breath. I felt my body react. It forced my lungs to inhale. They sucked in water, making me choke. As fast as it happened, I felt my body yanked from the water from above me. My head broke through the surface first. I coughed up the water, sucking in air like a vacuum. I coughed and sputtered again. Someone helped push the hair from my face.

"Are you alright?"

I stared with wide dark-brown eyes at Seaa, who swam in the water in her mermaid form. Her tail shimmered. She seemed so at home with it. Incredulous, I flapped my mouth like an idiot. Gunshots rang over us. I flinched a few times but realized they weren't shooting at us. A light flashed from our right. That electrical charge belonged to Thunder. He had joined our fight. I heard Hail scream out for Seaa.

"Seaa, can you control the water in this form?"

She nodded.

I swam under the pier as I watched the fight continue through the cracks between planks. I gestured for Seaa when a massive ship approached the harbor. The black and white boat blasted its horn. The side read "World Defense Assembly."

What the hell is that?

The crew from the ship aimed their weapons. These people weren't here to help us. Braggart and his men had outnumbered us big time. I looked over at Seaa. She saw the ship and then glanced back at the battle above us. We would lose someone versus lose this fight, and right now, we couldn't afford it. She called on the water. It lifted like a giant wave from the surface. The current pulled her high enough to see the area. She summoned a wall of water to block the ship from view. Another wave went toward the pier.

Soldiers ran to the side. Trevor blinked. Seaa commanded the water over to our group. The water wrapped around Thunder, Hail, and Guy, who wore their fatigue on their faces. The other ends of the wave pushed the others away as it yanked my brothers into the its depths like the hands of Poseidon. Seaa whistled. The pitch was so loud we covered our ears. Large water mammals came toward us.

There were three dolphins and a shark. The animals didn't fight one another. Instead, they obeyed Seaa's command and swam near each one of us. The shark approached Thunder. The rest of us got a dolphin. My hand went for a dorsal fin as the water from the pier receded. But before any soldiers could come after us, we were rushed through the water on the backs of sea creatures.

I might have had the power to create hordes of devotees or slightly change my physical features, but in this case, Seaa's abilities far surpassed mine. Being able to control the sea and its creatures was far more useful.

Seaa saved us this time.

CHAPTER THIRTY-ONE

Sector Bravo
Safe Haven Headquarters
Seaa – ID: PH049.001

THE SEA ANIMALS took us as far as the channel before I released them. The group didn't utter a single word, and I felt the usual insecurities flutter through me, attacking me from the inside. I kept to my mermaid form, swimming beside them—keeping up with the sea mammals like one of their species. Some parts of the broken channel were too shallow for the creatures, so we climbed out of the water after I shifted back into a pair of legs. We stepped foot into The Waste. No one walked the area. It was desolate, and because we hadn't been gone long, the night still reigned over us.

Hail had given me his long jacket to cover my nudity. *Why couldn't my morphing be as clean as Silks?* I wrapped it closer to me, inhaling the lingering scent of leather and camphor. I shuddered. The fingers on my hand felt numb. I shook them off. I wasn't cold. Being out here in the winter with nothing but a large jacket wasn't the problem. The memory of seeing Trevor Dallas and now the image of him in his burnt state crawled over my skin like millions of ants. The back of my eyes burned with unshed tears. In the water, no one saw me cry. But here on land, I'd be a nuisance.

I watched my sister from my spot in the back. She stood shoulder to shoulder with Thunder. Her strong legs took her over broken debris and large concrete blocks. Once in a while, Thunder would turn to her to help her over a huge building that had crumbled during the wars, but she refused help. Her strength and agility took her over these hindrances as if she walked over pebbles on the ground. Even her hair fit perfectly around her heart-shaped face. The curls were long and spiraled down her shoulders—some even curving around her bicep as if refusing to let go.

Mine hung straight down my back. I had uneven layers of multi-colored hair that did whatever it wanted. When I walked with my hair in disarray, it would get stuck between my arms and side, yanking my entire head back. I couldn't place it in a ponytail because my gills would show or stretch the skin by my ear with scales.

No one spoke about my metamorphosis or the fact that sea creatures came to our rescue. No one commented that I could build a water wall with the ocean and move it like a claw in a vending machine. My siblings had to be more than a little freaked out with my abilities. The *freak* part of that word was one I had gotten called since birth. Trevor and Braggart made sure to remind me every single day of my capture.

Cold seeped into my bones.

Ever since the tortures at Foxtrot, I couldn't get myself to forget the pain and humiliation. All of the tears I cried and the prayers for a quick death. I tried to be strong for Hail. He, too, had been brought in there and treated the same as me. Hail didn't break free. His mind broke first, and he'd let their experimenting change him. What reason did I have to live? Then Rayne showed up, and I couldn't let her see that they'd broken me. I stayed strong for her.

Then I died.

And even though I was alive and well now, I couldn't shake the deep-rooted fear inside of my bones whenever I saw either of those two men. I couldn't shake what they had done to me. My throat constricted, and my legs failed to function. The bones in my body rattled. My mind drew a blank. What kind of hardened warrior was I? I was nothing like my siblings.

To add to my melodrama, the sky opened up and dropped a slush type rain over us. The cold water dripped from my hair as we neared the forest near Safe Haven. Thunder crackled in the sky. I glanced a few times at my brother, who drew away from our group. The clouds came together like banging pots. I wondered what he was up to until a lightning strike came down, immediately targeting my brother. He lit up like a roman candle. I shielded my eyes from the blaze.

The strike disintegrated. Thunder glowed and rippled in waves of static energy. While electricity did significant damage to all of us, Thunder so happened to revel in it. He was immune. The clouds crackled again. The sounds so loud I gritted my teeth each time it reverberated in my skull. I took one look at the sky. It made fun of me too.

ONE OF THE lights hanging from the ceiling popped. The light bulb glass shattered, cascading all over the smooth stone floor. My siblings walked around, avoiding the glass all over the dark interior. We were already underground. The interior had gone from gloomy to oppressive with the loss of one light—like my mood. Ever since the horrible mission on the docks, I'd felt the fuse inside of me refuse to light. I couldn't get myself to smile. I couldn't make myself feel proud that I saved my siblings from Braggart's men. Seeing Trevor Dallas go from cocky cowboy to some cross between 21st-century villains like Freddy Krueger and Two-Face made my insides harden.

It wasn't because his deformities made me sick. We weren't built to discriminate because of the love Pops showed us, but rather because now his outsides matched the inside. It scared me. I already knew he was evil. To see it mar his skin felt surreal. It felt like everything I had in me stopped existing.

I kept to the wall—slick with moisture and cracks from years of abuse and humidity. The underground bunker was cool most days, but sometimes it could become a bit uncomfortable. While my siblings cleaned the sharp glass, I volunteered to talk to Suzanne about her mother. I wasn't sure what I'd say to her or how I'd say it.

"Hey, Sue. By the way, your mom's dead." Or, "Sue, I thought you should know that we never got to negotiate with your mother because Unit 13 shot her three times."

A deep breath left my chest. Either way, this woman had lost her man and mother in the same short timeframe. It didn't matter how I said it; Sue wouldn't take it well at all. I nervously fingered a strand of hair. My legs rounded a corner, bringing me closer to her room. Here, the lights flickered, being an old part of the bunker. I rapped my knuckles on the solid steel door, picking up the sounds of light footsteps. Sue opened it. Her eyes were red-rimmed from bouts of crying. I couldn't blame her. Cameron's death would forever haunt us. The only difference between Sue and us, other than the genetically altered part, was that they trained us to be emotionless machines that obeyed orders. She was all human.

"Hi, Seaa," she called out.

I shuttered, blinking a few times to sway the fog from my mind. "How did you know it was me?"

She smiled. "You have this unique scent about you. It reminds me of ocean breezes."

My lips curved. "Guess your nose is as good as ours, huh?" I joked.

Sue waved me in, opening the door wider. "Oh, nothing like that. I can only smell it if it's close by and only because losing one sense increases the others," she laughed.

"I can't stay, Sue." I shook my head. "Unfortunately, we have loads going on right now and constant meetings. I..." I searched for the right words again, but nothing came. "Thunder asked me to tell you, um..."

Sue leaned closer. Her soft, frail hand touched my shoulder. "My mother didn't survive, did she?"

I shook my head. Sue couldn't see me. Of that, I was sure of. But she nodded as if we had spoken out loud. "I understand."

I watched with apt curiosity. When we'd told Sue of Cam, she'd broken down and cried as if the death had happened to her. Hearing her mother had died didn't sway her one bit. How could someone feel ambiguous to the person who gave them life? What was wrong with the world I lived in that the children couldn't find righteousness with their parents? Roman Braggart had gone through that with his father. Rayne had to endure the same torture. Suzanne with her mother or Gavin with his dad. *I didn't get it! Why couldn't this world be better?* "I-I don't understand," I exclaimed.

She gave me a soft smile. "The woman only gave birth to me, Seaa. Not every parent is born to be a parent. Some of them don't have to give birth to a child but still love them unconditionally." Sue placed her hand on my cheek. She didn't flinch when she felt the scales beneath my ear or at my temple. The one who moved was me. Sue remained still, waiting for me to settle. "Take Dr. Sebastian Lester, for example.

The man loved you all as if you were his own children of flesh and blood. Rayne, too, had adoptive parents who doted on her for five years of her life. We all have someone."

Tears fell from my eyes. I didn't even know I cried until Sue pushed some of them off my face. She made absolute sense. We talked for a few more minutes, her words running through my head. By the time we finished, Sue had fallen asleep on Cam's old bed, and I stepped out of the bedroom, closing the door slowly behind me. Hail's presence slowly washed over me. He stood to the opposite side of the long hallway with one foot against the concrete wall.

I nodded at him in acknowledgment but didn't stop to chat. I knew why he was here. He wanted to talk about my abnormalities or the incident at the pier. I didn't have it in me tonight to deal with more drama. I walked faster. He silently followed. *What does he want from me?* I turned the corner. Rock moved quickly down the main tunnel with his woman in his arms. Their expressions left no room for doubt. The love they shared for one another defied everyday existence. Rock had more abnormalities than any of us, but he never carried it in his posture. He always stood proud and tall as if nothing could faze him.

Hail snickered. "Those two won't be out of their chambers until tomorrow night the earliest."

Thinking of it made me blush. I made a non-committal sound with my mouth and turned another corner down the hallway where my room sat next to Hail's. He followed. When I got to my door, I could tell my body lingered for longer than necessary, but my mind told me I needed to get in and lock the doors. I didn't need this conversation, or any of them for that matter. What human being could handle the strain we'd had to endure these past few months? It was as if I could no longer carry that weight anymore. My mind cracked. Soon it would crumble completely.

However, Hail didn't want to talk. It was the complete opposite. Hail rushed out a breath. A shaking hand ran through his short hair, and I noticed it was wet from a recent shower. I let my senses take him in and his usual scent. I could feel my gut tighten—the blood rush to my head. A gruff sound tore through him before he embraced me, rushing me through the open door of my room. He lifted me into his arms. His foot slammed the door of the room closed. The sound smashed into my brain, bringing me to my senses.

I slapped his shoulders, wiggling out of his arms. He growled. My feet touched the floor, and his head fell on top of my shoulder. I heard him take deep breaths. The feel of his chest against mine made me shudder.

What the heck almost happened?

"H-Hail?"

He took a couple more relaxing breaths before he faced me. "I couldn't help myself anymore."

What the heck?

I shook my head. "I don't understand."

His face jumped to mine. Eyebrows squeezed together as apparent confusion crossed his features. "What don't you understand?"

Did he want to mock fight like we usually did? Did he want to be playful or stay with me as we used to do? I couldn't wrap my head around it. Nothing made sense to me.

Before I could open my mouth, we heard the single blast from the alarm. "We have to go," I said instead.

Hail grunted, following behind me.

The moment we reached the end of the small hallway that led into the main tunnel, I stopped. Hail slammed into me. Thunder walked ahead of us toward the Planning Room. Behind him was Silk and beside her Rayne. She turned her head when she saw me. The beautiful brunette had swelling around her face—a bandage at her temple with dry blood. She smiled at me through the swelling and stopped walking. I could sense the pain that coursed through her, but that didn't stop me from rushing into her arms when she opened them up for me.

"I missed you," she whispered in my ear.

I whispered back, holding myself back from squeezing her tighter. "I missed you too."

She looked up when Thunder cleared his throat. "Come, we will all talk now."

Silk, Rayne, and I giggled. She held her stomach, flinching in pain but not wanting to stop laughing. She turned slightly to Hail, who stood behind me, her beautiful profile marred by bruises.

"Hail."

He smiled at her. "Good to see you again, Rayne."

The Planning Room was full of the residents of Safe Haven. Gavin walked in last with Sue. He helped Sue into a chair and then took a spot next to Silk. The innocent romance between those two warmed me and made me jealous all at once. I couldn't be happier for Silk. That woman had faced more than I could ever comprehend.

Thunder quieted the room. "I know all we do is meet here. I understand how tired you all are of this war. Although some of you might think of the last mission as a failure, we won't allow it to change our overall goal. With Barbara Benedict gone, we'd have to assume that her money might still finance Project Hercules and Unit 13. We are in the final stages. Let's go on the offensive."

Some of the men whooped.

"As you can all tell, Rayne is with us again. She'll explain what happened." He put a finger up. "Please keep your questions minimal. She's still recovering."

Rayne smiled again, stepping forward. We expected a grand start to her speech, but her first words only made the entire room laugh—not one of those laughs that only tickled the surface, but the kind that went deep into the funny bone.

"Who broke the table? I liked that old creaky thing."

After the laughter died, we all pointed at a blushing Silk. "It was righteous anger," she pleaded. "I don't remember the specifics, but I know it had to do with your capture."

Rayne smiled again. Her hand squeezed Silk's upper arm. She took in Gavin and Silk's nearness, and an eyebrow rose. "Oh, I have got to hear about this."

Silk studied her boots, rolling her eyes, while Gavin smiled.

Rayne turned back to face the rest of us. "I've definitely missed a lot. In time, I'll catch up, but right now, you all have to know that Foxtrot is gone."

The room roared with cheers and questions. Thunder glared. Everyone quieted.

"Zee and I came in after our missions and immediately found out that Braggart ordered Rome's death. We didn't have time to call anyone or plan accordingly. Zee ran to the armory, and I ran off to find Rome."

The sound of Zane's nickname made my stomach churn. He wasn't here right now with them. *What happened to him?*

Rayne moved her hands around animatedly. "The entire facility crashed down. Zee made sure to blow up whatever he could and then helped me get Rome out." She shook her head. "I tell you, though, it wasn't easy. Rome had shifted into a massive panther. It took everything to get him to recognize us, but by then, he had passed out, so we dragged him out of the old mines."

The reminder of the mine tunnels that Pops had saved us with the first time made my heart beat wildly. The irony of it wasn't lost on us. Some nodded, others smiled with recollection. Pops was a subject we all connected with.

"Unfortunately, we didn't make it out safely. Rome was out cold." Tears fell from her eyes in steady streams. She sucked in a shaking breath. "Zee took three bullets in the chest. Trevor hit vital organs because I could sense death taking him." She shook her head. "He pushed Rome and me past the pitch. The last thing I saw was him flipping the lever on one of the modified incendiary grenades and then the resulting explosion."

"Do you think Zane survived it?" Thunder asked.

Rayne shook her head before he even finished asking the question. "Not after feeling the explosion as close as I did falling into the gorge. I don't think he did."

The news tore through me. The room swayed. Zane had died. He wouldn't be here anymore to see me. Zee wouldn't be around anymore for Rome. He wouldn't be able to see this war end. I gasped with a hand to my mouth. I saw faces stare. I couldn't be here any longer. The crack in my mind grew like a sinkhole, sucking everything I had in me to the deep recesses of the earth, never to be seen again.

I died too.

CHAPTER THIRTY-TWO

Sector Bravo
Safe Haven Headquarters

I WATCHED SEAA float away from the room on a dark cloud. She didn't have to say anything. I knew the news of Zane's death affected her on a deeper level than we understood. Hail rushed out after her, but I wasn't sure anyone could help her right now. She needed time to get through her demons as I did. It took me the majority of my life to get through the pain of my youth. All I could hope was that Seaa saw and conquered hers before it was too late. Rayne watched Seaa walk out also, and she gave me a regretful look. I shook my head, ushering her to continue and let Seaa deal with things her way.

The group asked Rayne a few questions about the incident. She emphasized that after the explosion, she couldn't focus on much else. All she could do was try to save herself and Rome as the water consumed them. She didn't remember how she ended up on shore or who found them—thankful it was one of Suzanne's "eyes."

"It makes sense why Braggart and the rest of Unit 13 showed up at the docks. It wasn't a battle with us they were looking for at that moment. Braggart was trying to make his escape," Thunder surmised.

Rock moved toward the center. "Then why not head to Alpha?"

I was curious about that same question. Thunder shook his head. "I don't know the clear reason, but Braggart was never an idiot—an asshole, yes—but he never made choices that weren't in line with his plans. If Foxtrot is down and that was the major base of operations, then heading to Alpha would only bring his enemies to that door."

Snow interjected. "So you think if he's off-grid, then we'd focus on finding him versus lighting up the next facility?"

Thunder put his hands up, almost in surrender. "As hard as it is to understand, I don't know everything, Snow. I can only speculate." Before anyone said anything, he kept his hand up. "But what I can say with certainty is that Alpha goes next. I want that place destroyed and their business exposed. We need New States to know the truth about Unit 13."

Thunder searched the room for someone. His eyes

landed on the man who quietly sat toward the other end of the room. "Viktor, can you please explain to Rayne what you know about Alpha." He turned to Rayne. "Viktor Veracruz is Dr. Plumboy's nephew. He was unwillingly experimented on by Braggart and his uncle."

Rayne flinched. I could see the reminder of her father cross her eyes. She stared at Viktor as if she had seen him before. "You seem familiar."

Viktor nodded. "I was the beast-man at your last fight with the team here."

Her eyes widened. "You're one of those experiments from Alpha. We heard horror stories of that place," she admitted. Then she shook her head. "I didn't have clearance to Alpha. None of us but some medical personnel did, but we heard that monsters were made there. The soldiers banking there heard all about the attacks throughout New States caused by massive bipedal beasts."

Viktor smiled. His scar and sharp canines behind his Balbo beard a confirmation to me that he could indeed seem scary. I'd fought Viktor before. He wasn't an easy nut to crack. Gavin must've thought the same thing I did. He pulled me closer to him. I nestled along the length of his strong leg as he wrapped one arm around my side.

"I'm one of my uncle's firsts. I didn't know what I was getting into. He had this innate nerve to be better than Dr. Lester. After our mother died, he told us that we would be made stronger. He took us to Alpha and made us to exercise and train. He told us the shots were a cocktail of different vitamins and nutrients that would help our body grow stronger." He sighed, his shoulders bearing more weight than they could hold.

I felt Gavin's hand tighten around my stomach as if protecting me from the same kind of pain. My hand rested over his, and I felt him relax.

"My eldest brother changed first. He turned into a creature without understanding or reasoning. I couldn't get through to him. It was night and day. Both my younger brother and I started feeling changes around the same time. He couldn't handle it. He changed far less than me but fell into a comatose state. I heard my uncle talking to Braggart one night. They discussed all of their experiments. I wanted to know what they did, so I followed in secret one night and found a room of horrors. The sound of the animals coming from that room permanently engrained in my ears and soul."

He closed his eyes. A shudder ran through him. "The creatures were not of this world. I couldn't bear to be near anymore, so I ran. I tore through the medical wing where the doctors worked and slept. I found a ramp that led up, so I took it. I didn't realize my speed could take me out the top of that ramp and into Sector Alpha."

Snow snorted. "He fuckin' ran out of the front entrance."

Viktor shook his head. "I caught them off-guard. The facility is guarded heavily now. But I still think coming in through the front door is a great idea."

A great idea?

Viktor had regrets. I get that. I may have had a few

too, but for us to risk our lives so he could get his revenge didn't sit well with me. I pushed away from Gavin to face Viktor. Rayne stood by me as a steady presence.

"I get you feel some way about Plumboy, Braggart, Alpha... Hell, I think you're madder that you left your brother behind..."

Viktor growled, and the entire room erupted. My siblings went on-guard faster than I could've ever thought possible. Every individual in this room was one unit. We grew up together. I felt all of them get ready to intervene if necessary, but none made a move forward.

"I apologize, Viktor. I didn't mean to sound so blunt." I shrugged. "Old habits die hard."

Thunder coughed to stifle a laugh, but the rest of the group wasn't as courteous. They laughed out loud. I glared at them all. The old me would've torn them a new ass.

Viktor nodded, sighing once more. "I didn't mean to get upset, especially when you're right." He stepped closer to me. "I did leave my brother that day, Silk. I've been trying to rectify that ever since."

I understood. "I get it, Viktor. But you can't put my family at risk to get vengeance. We all want the same thing, but we need to go about it differently."

Rock intervened. "Hold on a sec, Silk." He placed a quick, comforting hand on Beatrice's shoulder as she stared at him adoringly. I was briefly captivated at the love those two shared and the unspoken words shared between them. Rock nodded at her and then turned to the rest of us. Beatrice stared at her lover as he stepped forward.

"I think Viktor is kind of right. A frontal assault would be something they wouldn't be expecting. I say we come in through the front doors."

Thunder crossed his arms. "And how do you suppose we do that?"

From behind me, I felt Gavin move forward. I turned to him as he spoke. "With me, of course. I've already broken through their firewalls. Going through the lock mechanisms would be a piece of cake." He stared at me. "All I need is to get close enough to read their security network. Once I have that, I can open up the front door." He put his finger up. "But if you want me to break into the system as a whole, then you guys need to take one of my devices inside and connect it to the main copper cable for the security system."

Thunder nodded, licking his lips in thought. "Very well. Rock and Snow, head out immediately to Alpha. Do some reconnaissance. We will join you in two days to end Alpha and all of their experiments. Braggart will think we are focused on getting to him. He'll never see this coming."

TWO DAYS LATER, precisely as Thunder called it, our batch made it to Sector Alpha. As a precautionary measure, he didn't let us make our presence known to the public not to tip off the military. We had all geared up with all the weapons we could muster in such a short time frame. Thunder also preferred to keep us split apart to not draw attention to ourselves. I refused to be in any group other than Gavin's, so here we were, walking to Alpha, Project Hercules' second facility, together.

Rock had called to tell us that other than guards posted on the outside fenced perimeter and a few by the doors, the facility had not shown any increased military presence. He gave the specifics. The number of guards. The times they changed shifts. Vehicles or DBT's entering or exiting the facility and the protocols and measures they took for someone to enter or exit a gate or door.

Alpha was made up of medical facilities and homes to predominant political figures like Washington D.C. to the old world. However, unlike D.C.'s abundant tourism and homes for middle and low classes, Alpha didn't get visited by anyone who did not live or belong there.

Alpha didn't have The Waste within its walls, but rather The Waste surrounded Alpha from the riffraff, enemy, and the like. There was only one way in and out—the orange line. The tunnels on this end had been purposely destroyed to prevent anyone from trying to enter. The only way in was through a series of checkpoints on the surface. But none of us had time for that. We took the silver line instead to the very end and walked through the wasteland until we made it to Alpha.

Anyone with our abilities could do it without a problem. Although Gavin had a harder time than us getting over massive, crumbled buildings and keeping pace, he didn't complain. I stayed close to him the entire time, helping him over areas that were too inconvenient for him. A few times he'd crack a joke about being "out-of-shape," which in turn made the solemn mood lighten. And each time, I'd see him differently. He was no longer a young kid in my eyes. This time, Gavin was more of a man.

Once at the rendezvous point, we gathered to hear Thunder's plan to infiltrate an unbreakable fortress. Each of us had our orders. We had our weapons and technology. Earpieces kept us in touch with each other. Knowing full well our time was up, Thunder wished us all good luck and split the group. Gavin and I were sent up high on a building that overlooked Braggart's facility.

I studied the building. There was no way of us making it in there without alerting someone. The building's bellman walked in and out, assisting people out of their cars and taking luggage inside. There were two Ground Force officers posted in front of the double doors. Another walked the side of the building. The man bent to tie his shoe. I looked at Gavin.

He'll do nicely.

Channeling the energy inside of me, I imagined my hair the color of gold bars—my eyes the subtle beauty of a blue sky. The birthmark under my eye disappeared. I stretched my muscles. The energy couldn't make massive changes to my body, but I had always been able to manipulate my looks and clothing.

"Holy shit. I still can't seem to wrap my head around that nifty trick of yours," Gavin whispered from beside me.

I grinned at him, placing a chaste kiss on his lips.

"Now watch me work."

Sashaying toward the side guard, I caught his attention on the way up from tying his shoes. I pointed over to the side, where Gavin hid from view. "I need your assistance, officer. I believe there is some ruffian over there that may not belong in this area."

He stared at me from head to toe. "Yes, ma'am. I'll be happy to assist you."

We walked over to where Gavin hid. He sat there with his bags beside him. Gavin grinned, not once shocked that I brought the officer over. The Ground Force officer went to grab his walkie-talkie but didn't have time to squeeze the call button. I clubbed him over the head. The man dropped to the ground unconscious.

"Silk, more tact than that next time," he teased.

I shrugged, bending to the ground. We stripped the guard quickly. Gavin gave me his bags, and in his new uniform, we walked to the front entrance. The two guards stared but said nothing to us as we walked straight through the front. My fake heels clicked on the marble tiles as we walked to the bank of Gidgets. No one paid us any attention. He did a great job of acting aloof. When the Gidget opened, we made it inside and to the top floor. Once at the top, we took the emergency staircase to the roof.

The door had a lock. I snapped the lock with my hand and opened the door. Once at the top, I barricaded the door from any humans walking astray. We hunkered down behind some HVAC equipment, seeing the facility from this spot. I shifted into my usual attire, dropping the glamour from my eyes and hair.

"Good, I've always liked your look." He took a dark curl in his hand. "These curls are a favorite."

His words made me blush and, at the same time, punch him from its cheesiness.

"Silk to Thunder. We are in position."

"Very good," I heard him call back.

Gavin turned on his small KeViewer, which turned into a bank of holographic computer screens that came around him in a half-circle. I watched him inside of his technological bubble work his fingers across the keyboard with deft preciseness. My job was to protect him and stay on-guard. Gavin had the fun job of opening up the front door. He worked and talked to the others. I stared at the dark sky as the colors of the sunset broke through the clouds. There were some oranges and reds, but a purplish red fought for a moment in the sky's aesthetic. I took a piece of chocolate from my pocket, savoring it in my mouth as I took in the scenery.

It felt like a long time since the last time I watched the sun set in the night sky. I had sat on Gavin's windowsill, thinking how very high up we were compared to the small world below. Now, once more, I stood over the people as they robotically went about their lives as if nothing mattered. Except, this time, I wasn't wearing the bracelet underneath the metal band around my wrist. The medical bracelet was gone. I had freed myself from that torture. No one made that happen but me.

I couldn't help but watch Gavin as he worked.

I had to admit that he helped a lot.

Gavin rushed out a "Yes!" He grinned at the monitors.

Through the earpiece, I could hear the group subdue the guards posted upfront. Gavin opened the first gate, and the team walked inside and straight for the rest of the guards before they even had a chance to defend themselves or call in for assistance. Gavin worked faster and prepared. Thunder could be heard grabbing a keycard from a fallen soldier and swiping them into the facility.

Alpha Project Hercules, home to all of their doctors and scientists, would no longer exist after tonight.

The facility blared with emergency sirens. The jig was up. I smiled as we watched from our vantage point. Tonight would be the end of Braggart's projects, even if we got hurt in the process. My eyes left the facility. The door at the top-level banged as someone tried to break through the barricade. The debris holding the door blew over the edge and down to the bottom of the building with a loud crash. I shoved Gavin behind the large HVAC.

"Stay here, understand?" He nodded, working feverishly on the computer to get access to the entire security surveillance network.

I stood straight as operatives with beasts standing behind them took the space of the roof. They were equipped with controls on their wrists that more than likely controlled the beasts' collars. They had weapons at their hips and in their hands. I took a deep breath. It was time to face-off.

Time to dance with the devil.

CHAPTER THIRTY-THREE

Sector Alpha
Project Hercules Facility 2
Rayne ID: PHO64.001

THE SIRENS IN the facility wailed, echoing off of the pristine white, tiled walls. I rushed in through the front doors with the rest of my siblings in a blaze of glory. No one expected us as the doors opened. The alarms went off, and now the soldiers inside came around different corners of this maze-like facility. We didn't have bullets to spare, so we made sure to make our one shot count.

Two days before, I stood in the middle of the Planning Room, only partially recovered from the death-defying fall over the ridge into raging, cold waters. The lasting ache in my muscles reminding me of the moment.

My entire body ached—from head to toe. I had been close to death before, but it seemed it wasn't my time yet. Both Rome and I had survived, but at what cost? Sure, Foxtrot was gone, but so was a good friend. Rome was in a coma and would probably land in one again when he woke to find Zee dead.

Oh, God. Rome's another matter altogether.

I found that I had deep feelings for a man I couldn't have. Every day since my awakening, I spent it at Rome's bedside. My eyes studied the way his chest rose and fell with every breath he took. The reminder that he lived filled me with some semblance of peace. His wounds healed slowly. The cuts faded, barely.

The only thing he didn't do was wake up.

On the night before we headed out here, Hail joined me in the clinic to see how I faired. He seemed smaller to me than he was before, as if all the problems had taken the very soul of him and crushed it. His blond hair had shortened. The tattoo of the raindrop on the back of his neck a lot more visible. I remembered our conversation about it.

"What does the tattoo mean?"

He grinned, the very picture of ease. "It was something I had done for you around the first year you disappeared. Raindrop. Rayne..." He winked.

I blushed. "Yeah, I get it."

He took a deeper look at Rome. "I'm thankful for that asshole," he pointed to Rome with his chin. "He's really in love with you, and I know you feel the same

about him." Hail put his hand up to stop me from say-
ing a word. "I know he's your brother and all, but he
wasn't before, and in that time, you guys built some-
thing."

I nodded, grasping at his words with all my heart. "I
do feel something for him, but maybe it's because we
are brother and sister."

Hail shook his head. "Yeah, I don't think so. It's like
the way I feel for Seaa. Misplaced feelings."

My body jolted. Alert, I watched Hail's every move.
"You're in love with Seaa."

He grinned. "I kinda am. Always have been, actually.
Since you disappeared, Seaa became my best friend.
I didn't realize it until you disappeared again that it
was always her. Our little romance ended when we es-
caped. I just couldn't see clearly until it was too late."

I pondered it for a minute, asking, "Why is it too
late?"

He got up from his chair, pulling the shirt over his
head. "I got this done recently."

On his entire back was a beautiful silhouette of a
mermaid. The scenery behind her mimicked a cor-
al bed with various sea life, all watching the woman
in rapt attention. The artist had painted the woman
in all the colors found in Seaa's scales. The mermaid
painted into a perpetual spin. Her hair floated around
her in the exact same colors as my sister. The water
blended perfectly with the raindrop as if encompass-
ing that it took rain to create the sea. The tattoo was
beyond words. It took my breath away.

I studied Hail. "Did she see this?"

Hail shook his head. "The day I wanted to show her,

I got caught up in the way she moved and all those feelings and practically attacked her, you know?"

I nodded, caught up in the story.

"She didn't even get it, Rayne. It's like Seaa can't see how beautiful she is and how much I care about her. Then the alarm went off, and we left it at that. She had no damn clue that I wanted her as a woman." He leaned down with his elbows resting on his knees. "I get a distinct feeling that she thought I wanted to wrestle."

I burst out laughing. Hail's face contorted in confusion. Thinking of Hail trying to seduce Seaa and her utterly oblivious to it made me giggle to no end. My insides tickled until it went numb. I wiped the tears from my eyes.

"Oh, goodness. I'm sorry, Hail."

He sighed, wrinkling his nose. We sat in the clinic together for another hour, talking about everything I had missed during my compulsion. I hadn't had time to speak with Seaa. She had barricaded herself in her room after hearing of Zane's death. Hail tried to talk to her, but he said she had ignored him. He didn't push, and neither did any of us.

I blinked the memory away.

When the time for the fight came, Seaa had readied herself with the rest of us as if nothing happened. She fought in front of me now as a woman possessed. She kicked a soldier, then flipped him over her shoulder. The man landed in a pile on the floor. I saw her turn to the right. She spoke in her earpiece that she would take the right side of the wing. Thunder acknowledged, and I called that I'd follow.

I worked behind her. When a soldier threw open a door, I punched him back inside and closed the door. Seaa turned in time to see. She nodded and kept moving. The inside increased with movement from every angle. We only used our weapons if the threat was too high but kept to physical combat otherwise. Seaa turned left. I followed. My gun aimed at a soldier down the other hall. He dropped to the floor. Seaa dropped another, grabbing his weapon and putting it on her hip.

We ran down a long hall where emergency lights blinked in a pattern. Doctors ran between the intersections into rooms, barricading themselves inside. We saw a large metal door at the end with a red light over it. We made it down the path when another doctor burst from behind us. He screamed and ran away. Seaa and I paid him no attention. She pushed at the door, but it wouldn't budge. She slammed into it and nothing.

I helped. Neither one of us could get the door to move even a little. Dents appeared on the metal, but nothing busted it open. I turned on my earpiece to speak to Gavin.

"Gavin, it's Rayne. Are you in the system yet?"

We heard the sounds of fighting come through the line. "I'm working on it, Rayne. Almost in. Silk and I got ambushed by some operatives. She's—" The line cut.

Before I could say something, Thunder had already yelled into the comm. "Come back, Gavin. You there?"

"Yeah, sorry. Silk threw one of those beast-men off the roof. Shit! I almost got shot."

We waited for him to come back on the line. "You're

clear. You're clear. I'm watching the surveillance feed now. I see you girls. Okay," he cussed again. We heard him tell Silk to watch behind her. We listened to our sister grunt, and then a few punches told us that she hit back whoever sucker-punched her. "Ladies, you're clear to go in."

The line went dead, and the door buzzed. The red light went green. The sirens in the facility died. Seaa and I nodded at one another and opened the door. We took two steps and stopped. Seaa gasped. The door behind us clicked closed. I watched, trying to grasp the room we entered. My sister shuffled to the side, emptying the contents of her stomach all over the crisp tiles. The room looked like a galley with tables in the middle and large tanks full of embalming liquid against the walls. Inside of the tanks and jars were different body parts and humans in mid-transformations. The room used a blue light, so our eyes adjusted to the differences. The problem with the light meant that we could see everything that much clearer.

"Seaa, you alright?"

She nodded, wiping at her bottom lip. "What is this?"

One tank had a human female with the bones of her ribcage in full view. They had burst from her chest, opening wide. A slit down the center of her stomach showed a child with different fish traits hanging from an umbilical cord. Both the mother and child were dead. The doctors hadn't even removed the baby from the mother. They'd left it in the same position to float around in the water to their scientific enjoyment.

It disgusted me.

Seaa focused on the mer-baby. "They were trying to create mermaids with human hosts."

Hail told me all about Seaa's transformation. I grabbed her cold, clammy hand. "Seaa, what they did here is unforgivable. We'll end this place so that these people can finally be at peace."

She shot blood-rimmed eyes at me. "I'm just like them."

I shook my head, squeezing her fingers together. "Seaa, you are not like them. You aren't like anyone I've ever met. You are Seaa. You are my sister. You are a beautiful mermaid-goddess that deserves to be worshipped, not caged."

My shaking finger wiped a tear from her eye. I pulled her away from the tank with the mer-baby and down the room. We saw limbs in mid-transformation suspended in water for the world to see. Notes on everything they studied littered the tables. I noticed a gas line running through one side of the room. I walked over and ripped a pipe out. The smell of gas fumes hit me immediately. Seaa covered her nose. We walked back out the door. I grabbed a long butane lighter from the table on my way out.

"Wanna do the honors?"

Seaa sniffled. She grabbed the butane lighter and clicked it. A bright flame shot from the lighter, swaying in the open. Seaa threw the lighter inside the room. We closed the door, hiding behind it for impact. The room burst into a massive explosion. The door blasted from the hinges. Seaa and I flew back, pushed by the large metal door. We landed on the floor. The air in our lungs escaped—the heavy door over us.

Seaa and I pushed the door off us. I coughed against the smoke. The entire room was ablaze. Seaa got off the floor first, helping me up. We rushed down another hall, not seeing any soldiers anymore on this floor. We climbed down a set of stairs at the end, alerting our group of where we were. The team, too, had made it a level deeper. They had cleared the floor.

Gavin came back on the line. "Seaa and Rayne. The group is ahead of you to the right. You're clear to move. No one is roaming the halls."

I came back on the line to thank him. "Gavin, did you see that room?"

He cleared his throat. "Yes, I did. I'm making copies of this surveillance footage."

We turned the corner like he said and watched as Snow shuffled out of the room paler than usual. "What's inside," I asked.

Snow shook his head. He didn't say a word, only gestured to the room. We walked inside and saw rows and rows of dead patients. The room was blistering cold as if I had walked into a freezer. Each patient was in some sort of physical transformation. Some had the face of a wolf or the body of a fish or bird. The bodies died in the position they had screamed in. I felt the bile rise. My stomach tied itself in knots. Seaa ran out of the room with a fresh set of tears. This mission had troubled her greatly.

I searched for Rock. He, too, seemed more disturbed than usual. He stared intently at a patient that seemed very similar to him. Rock was one of Pops' first creations, so his genome cocktail had physical abnormalities. If Braggart had taken that first cocktail

and had Plumboy imitate it, then this would probably be the result. Pops had hidden the real perfected
cocktail within his journals. There was no way that Dr.
Plumboy could've known how to recreate batch 001's
abilities with batch 002's more human traits.

Batch 002 seemed more normal than we did. Dr.
Plumboy had taken Dr. Lester's recipe and imitated it
the best he could. He made the soldiers more human
and less animal, but he couldn't get them to share
the same powers that we had. Their greed for science
created and destroyed the people in here. Against
the wall, another set of tanks lined up the wall. These
were empty of water but not of creatures. The beast-
men that had died were displayed against the wall like
stuffed animals.

Viktor reached up to caress the glass of one beast-
man. I walked over to him. "Mr. Veracruz," I called out.

He jumped but didn't move away. "Hello, Rayne."

"Do you know him?"

Viktor Veracruz nodded. "Yes, he's my older brother."

I couldn't say more to him. When Gavin came on
the line to tell us that we had company, we moved out
into the hallway. Soldiers came around the corners,
but we were ready for them. Gavin called out how
many were in each hallway and which way to take until we got to the central part of the floor Viktor had
told us about. We made it to the door. The sounds
coming from inside made goosebumps rise from my
skin. I shook my arms, hoping to dispel the sensation.

Inside the room were rows of cages against the
walls. The entire center of the room had computers

and monitors set up and one chair with silver clamps. We saw some doctors and scientists cowering in one corner. A few operatives clamped these controls on their wrists and gunned it to the beasts' cages with collars in their hand. We wouldn't make it in time.

"Gavin!" I heard Hail and Thunder yell at the same time.

He came on the line. "No worries, I've got this."

The two operatives slammed the buttons on the cages, but nothing happened. They hit them again, hoping to get a different response, but frustrated, they screamed instead.

"I've disabled the silver mist they used to make the animals complacent until their collars were on. Get ready to fight, team."

The cage doors opened. The two beast-men walked out to the surprise of the operatives. They eliminated the two men in one blow. We readied ourselves. The moment the animals came near, the howls echoed around the interior. We rushed in to subdue them. The animals cried out, swiping at us with long arms that swung around. They had claws so sharp they would cut through anything they touched that wasn't silver.

Bird-like humans and varying animals screeched and hollered from their cages. The sound grained on my ears so loudly I wouldn't have been surprised if my ears bled. One of the doctors covered his ears. He ran over to the center console, barely avoiding a swipe from the beast. We all avoided a swipe from the crea-ture. He punched in a few buttons, and a mist covered the entire facility from above. I rushed to the other end when I saw him try to escape through the other side. He dropped to the ground, busting his lip open. The mist descended over everything. We covered our noses and mouths. The entire group of us dropped to the ground as the mist-like fog slowly made its descent.

"Get out now!" Gavin yelled in our ears, and at that moment, we didn't argue.

I grabbed the doctor who had busted his lip open. I dragged him through the doors. Snow and Hail followed me out. "Snow, Hail, Rayne!" we heard Thunder yell through the comm.

Hail came on the line. "Don't worry, we're fine."

"You guys have got to see this," Gavin uttered. "Give me a minute to flush the room.

After a few minutes, Gavin told us to walk back in. I had the one doctor in my grip. I saw Guy walking in with the other two who had cowered in the corner. No human had died inside of the monster room, but the monsters had. I watched as Viktor took in the entire room. The creatures in the rooms were all dead. Thunder moved the beast-man on the floor. It didn't budge.

"What did you do?" he asked the doctor in my grip.

The doctor sniffled; blood also gushed from his nose. "I didn't want to die. We have procedures in place to kill these creatures should they become a liability."

Viktor rushed forward and punched him in the face. The doctor flew back, but because my grip was secure, he didn't go far. Thunder held Viktor back.

"Don't worry, Viktor. They'll pay for all this," Thunder promised.

We dragged the humans, taking them with us for questioning. Gavin alerted us that we weren't safe going through the same door we had walked into, so he recommended the same exit Viktor had taken years back. We ran down the hallways, some of us shot back at operatives that got too close. We made it inside the doctors' labs and through the back door where Gavin and Silk waited.

Gavin held up his KeViewer like a camera. We turned in time as the facility burst into flames. The sound of crumbling metal and stone thundered all around us. Flashes of light and implosions drew our faces to the collapsing facility. I noticed the flashing lights and a new group of operatives. We had made it out of there in time. Tears ran down every eye out here.

We'd accomplished something we never thought possible.

We'd ended their growth.

Now to end Project Hercules at the root.

CHAPTER THIRTY-FOUR

Open Waters
World Defense Assembly Battleship
General Brockton Braggart

PANDEMONIUM ERUPTED IN the command center as every monitor in the room lit up with New States live feed. The network engineers we hired to keep our system running moved around the interior in a flurry. Fingers moved over holographic keyboards. Hands ran through sweat-covered hair.

"I can't break through," one called out.

The other yelled back from his spot by the end of the table. "This hacker created so many VPN tunnels."

While another yelled, "I cracked the password for

this one, but it took me to another goddamn country!"

I gritted my teeth in hopes it would keep me from shooting these incompetent fools. Instead, I diverted my attention to the screen where images ran in full color. The first was of our building in Foxtrot and the second of the one in Alpha. The photos were bits seen on the news hours ago. But the other images were fed from the surveillance cameras of both facilities—one hand fisted on the hilt of the gun and the other at my side. The voice speaking belonged to Gavin Foxhand—Son of Foxhand Sr., the first person to pull funding from Project Hercules.

I quieted the room as I leaned in to listen to the live broadcast.

"All these images were brought to you with the sole purpose of educating you on the comings and goings of Unit 13."

The images showed glimpses of the beast soldiers, the science lab full of oddities, torture chambers, and the way we handled matters in the privacy of our facilities. I could sense the eyes of everyone in this room as Foxhand continued.

"They've experimented for far too long, picking off the people standing in their way. The rich have over-indulged, and the poor live in the subway tunnels. It is time to clean up New States. It is time we work together to rid ourselves of the soldiers that forget to put the people first, and the Ground Force officers who have lost their humanity."

The next showed images of my soldiers instilling peace using harsh methods and male Ground Force officers abusing their authority to rape the women they've chosen. I felt the migraine form. I rubbed my temple with the hand that rested on the gun. I could only stand here demanding that they hurry to cut the broadcast.

The men rushed around like chickens with their heads cut off. They knew that in only so much time, I'd end up shooting them all. I hated incompetence. The soldiers had all failed me. My funders had all failed me. I could not go down like this. I slammed my fist on the table. The W.D.A. would stop at nothing to take my head, especially if I failed the goals I had set in motion.

The next scene showed three personnel from my Alpha facility. One doctor had a busted nose and lip. The other two seemed relatively unharmed. I squeezed my fist together so hard I could feel nails break the skin.

"Explain your purpose in Project Hercules." The voice came from one of the eldest in the group—the boy, now a man, who led those children in everything they did.

The man with the busted nose spoke. "I am a doctor there. My job was to monitor the health and vitals of the experiments."

I gritted my teeth harder, almost enough to wear the enamel.

"By experiments, you meant those vile creations on the screen and the super soldiers?"

The man visibly shook, swallowing he replied, "Y-yes, the creatures mainly. Doctors in Foxtrot took care of the super soldiers. We mainly dealt with experimental species."

"You mean such as this?"

The camera panned to a cell behind them. Inside of it was a man I had not seen in a long time and one Dr. Plumboy might regret knowing still lived. Viktor Veracruz, Dr. Plumboy's nephew, roared in the cage and shifted into a beast-man.

Through gritted teeth, I had a soldier call for Robert Plumboy.

The camera came back to the doctor, who visibly paled. "Y-yes," he answered truthfully.

"What about the other two," Thunder demanded.

The doctor paled some more and turned to stare at the other two shaken men—both scientists. "Were scientists. Our role in Project Hercules was to create different species."

Thunder's voice replied, "You played God then?"

The men flinched. The camera turned from them to Thunder himself.

"General Brockton Braggart, we can see how hard your men are working to shut this broadcast down, but you're too late. New States already knows of all your treacherousness. You see, we were Braggart's first creations—the first of his super-soldiers. Although we are not all human, we are not all animals either. And we have grown tired of slinking away in the dark like discarded abominations. It's time for you to pay the price, Braggart."

The camera zoomed in closer to the man's handsome face. I bared my teeth.

"We're coming for you."

The transmission ended, and the regular news broadcasters stared at their blank screens with identical shocked looks. I watched as they blinked, seeking guidance from their staff. I yelled at the soldiers in the room to turn off the monitors. The anger inside of me boiled over. Trevor came in the command center, scarred from his last battle with Mueller and Rayne. He didn't seem at all happy about the situation either.

"Yes, I know," I yelled out.

Trevor stopped. He stared at the blank screen and then again at me. "Sir, we've received word from the finance department of the W.D.A. All of our funders have pulled out."

"What? Every single one?"

He nodded. "Yes, sir. All of them."

A scream of pure madness cascaded from my lips. "Sir," another soldier called. Pure anger radiated from my eyes. The soldier flinched but not as bad as Robert Plumboy standing beside him. The old doctor stared at me with pure, genuine fear.

That's right. Fear me, son of a bitch.

I gave the boys at the command desk some orders. They immediately moved to comply. Within minutes they turned the monitor up behind me. I watched Plumboy as he watched the screen, trepidation in every second that passed. Behind me, the screen showed Viktor Veracruz from the last broadcast. It went from his face and into his beast form. Robert Plumboy's eyes grew wide.

One of my soldiers came into the room at that moment. Plumboy watched the screen as I turned to the soldier who had probably borne terrible news. "What now?"

The man didn't flinch, maintaining complete professionalism. "Sir, we've received word from Ground Force Headquarters. The sectors are in disarray. The slums are rising from the sewers and heading straight into the populated areas. They're demanding retribution, sir."

My nose flared. One hand curled the tip of my mustache. The move relaxed me. "The lawlessness shall not be tolerated. Eliminate those in our way."

The soldier saluted and walked away, but not before questioning my authority with his eyes. That infuriated me further. I turned my attention back to the fat, slime-ball.

"Did you not tell me that all your nephews were dead?"

The doctor squirmed. "I-I'm not sure how..."

I pulled my gun out. The man put his hands up, pleading. My finger squeezed the trigger, and the bullet went right through the man's skull. He didn't even have time to scream as blood splattered the doorway behind him and the soldier at his side. The man blinked once but didn't bother to move. He didn't wipe the blood, and he didn't watch the dead body at his feet.

I do not tolerate insubordination.

Sector Bravo
Safe Haven Headquarters
Roman Braggart – ID: MIL116.002

THERE WAS A heavy weight on my chest, and another almost numbed the sensation in my hand. I blinked the sleep from my eyes. I only felt exhausted as if a tank had hit me, backed up, and rolled over me again. I groaned. The thought made the pain radiate throughout my limbs. Damn, but I felt like hell. I inhaled her before I saw her. My head turned to the side as my hand throbbed.

"Hey, gorgeous."

Rayne's eyes widened. She squeezed my hand tighter. "Rome, oh my goodness."

I flinched. She jumped up and called for Dr. Ferdinand.

"Rayne, could you lighten the hand hug you got going on?"

She squinted and then realized I spoke of her hands squeezing the life out of mine.

"Oh, I'm so sorry, Rome."

I smiled. That woman could let go of me physically, and it would feel as if she hadn't let go. I felt her hands on mine. Rayne was permanently engrained on my heart. In every fiber of my being.

Dr. Ferdinand came around to check on me. I let him as I watched Rayne, watching me. I felt like hell, but I sucked it up. Instead of focusing on the pain I felt every time the older man touched a wound that hadn't healed, I decided to ask Rayne questions. Nothing would be better than finding out how the hell I ended up in this place when the last thing I remembered was getting dragged toward the chamber.

"How'd we get here," I asked Rayne.

She blinked a few times, tears forming in her eyes. The beautiful woman always had this increased amount of moisture she couldn't help but contain. Word around the bunkers was it was because she could dematerialize into liquid. I hadn't personally seen the act, but I was sure it was an incredible ability she possessed—like the rest of this exceptional group. "Zane and I brought you to safety." She seemed sad.

I stared at the door, expecting my best friend to rush in, but the look on Rayne's face again in my mind made me turn back to her. "Zee's dead, isn't he." It wasn't a question. I could tell from the drawn brows and pouting lips.

"I'm sorry, Rome. He died protecting us."

I bent at the waist, feeling the pain in my entire body burst through my bones. "What else did I miss, and for how long was I gone?"

She sat there in the chair by the hovering table. Her body had drawn into itself as she explained what happened since my capture. Every time she spoke, I could only nod and listen. I was afraid if I spoke out loud, then I'd cuss up a storm. The group had made significant changes while I was out, and I hadn't helped at all by letting myself get captured. She scolded me for doing just that, I heard the door open, and Silk walked in.

"I knew I smelled a disgusting cat."

I heard the teasing tone, so I smiled. "Yeah, Rayne told me she met my alter ego."

The panther in me didn't get along well with any-one else. I couldn't control him when he was out, and I only let him out when my life well and truly depend-ed on it. I sure as hell didn't want anyone in this place to deal with him. If someone got hurt by him when I could've prevented it, I didn't know what I'd do—es-pecially if that someone was Rayne.

"You know that you giving yourself up made this entire thing more complicated than it needed to be, right?"

I sighed. "Yeah, Rayne filled me in on that too."

She crossed her strong arms over ample breasts. Damn, the women in this group were beautiful but none more bewitching than Rayne. I watched her bite her lower lip. Silk cleared her throat.

"Geez, you two need to really get a room."

Rayne's face turned varying shades of red. I'd love to spend every moment I could with that woman, but the idea in her head that we're related made things plenty tricky. I felt deep down in my gut that this woman and I didn't share a sibling kind of love. I didn't trust my old man. She shouldn't either. I made sure to make it clear to her that my feelings were pure—plain and simple.

I shifted on the hovering cot, pulling my legs over to the side. Rayne gasped from behind me, and I felt her blush deepen. I was butt-ass naked under this simple sheet. The woman had gotten an eyeful of my backside. Silk laughed out loud. In the time I was gone, the black widow had changed drastically. It suited her. The woman pointed at some clothes on a chair in the corner. I got up and felt my knees buckle. My weight felt heavy as it sent me straight to the floor.

Rayne came around the corner fast enough to grab my arm. Silk came forward too, lifting me from my armpit. The sheet fell to the floor. Rayne made some kind of throat gurgle, while Silk seemed non-plussed. She didn't take a look at the goods, nor did she seem to care about my nudity whatsoever. Instead, she leaned over and grabbed the black cargos that appeared to be essential gear around here.

She shoved them into my bare chest. I wheezed out a thank you. She turned around out of courtesy for Rayne because it sure as hell wasn't about modesty. That woman didn't give a shit about other's feelings. I got my pants on with little assistance. The door opened again, and Gavin Foxhand poked his head inside. I watched as he stared at the black widow with a severe case of the lovey-dovey's. The woman turned to him, and I expected her to sneer or outright reject him. Instead, Silk turned a cute shade of pink.

Holy fucks!

I pointed at both of them. "You two a thing?"

Silk growled, but it sounded more like a purr. She would've throttled me if I wasn't already beat up. Gavin smiled at me. I grabbed the white shirt and pulled it over my top half, hiding the panther tattoo and tribal artwork. Rayne bit her bottom lip again.

"Damn it, girl, if you keep doing that, I'm going to kiss you." Rayne's head shot up.

Gavin chortled, and Silk grinned.

Rayne gave me what could probably pass off for a glare but seemed more like a bewildered stare. "I'm serious, gorgeous. I told you that you and I are the real thing. Like it or not."

I tried like all hell to get on one knee like those gallant knights in the books in her bedroom when we first met, but the wounds in my body screamed in rebuttal. I almost toppled over to the side. Silk and Gavin righted me. Rayne had her hands over her mouth. I didn't have a ring for her, but she didn't seem like the type to hold a grudge against me. I did, after all, almost die for her.

"Marry me, Rayne. Ever since the first moment we met, I couldn't get you out of my head. Marry me, please."

Gavin and Silk watched in apt rapture. Rayne dropped her hands from her full mouth. The old doctor pretended not to hear in the corner, but he, too, watched and waited for her answer.

Rayne visibly swallowed. "I can't marry you, Rome." There were tears in her eyes again. I didn't understand why she couldn't give in to her feelings.

"Is this distance thing because of the sibling fiasco? Or maybe it's because of Hail?"

The woman went from hot to cold in what they called a "New York Minute." Her arm shot back, and before I knew it, she knocked me on my ass. She huffed. Gavin and Silk parted like the Red Sea as she walked out of the clinic. I rubbed my jaw. Silk leaned down to face me.

"Real subtle, dumbass."

Silk turned to leave. She put a hand on Gavin's shoulder, and he almost melted. Those two were way into one another. Gavin watched her go. Once gone, he turned to me. "So you know, I still don't trust you, but Rayne's my friend, and whatever makes her happy makes me happy." He ran a hand through his hair. "She loves you. That's plain as day. Heck, everyone around here knows that—even Hail. But so you know, she's struggling a lot with your familial bonds. So, next time keep your petty jealousy in check and deal with the real issue, and that's the fact that you and Rayne share the same bloodline."

Ah, fuck.

CHAPTER THIRTY-FIVE

Switzerland
World Defense Assembly Command Post
W.D.A. Co-Founder & Head Director Alexandra Gibbons

THE LARGE, GLASS office had more foot traffic today than ever before. We handled the world's cases from the very beginning of the war—the W.D.A came together when the nations fought a losing battle. To keep humanity alive, all the nations had come together to create the World Defense Assembly. The presidents, prime ministers, and royals of each country survivable resided in Switzerland—the only land untouched by war's filthy hands. I watched from my spot in the back of the large meeting room as the President of New States argued with the other leaders.

They spoke about General Brockton Braggart's abuse of the military. He'd taken New States, in other words, America, also known as Unit 13, into a state of totalitarianism. He'd fed the president lie after lie, all the while hiding his true intentions. Now the General was on the run, having taken one of our vessels into waters controlled by another unit. He argued with the leader, wanting the authority to send his military in to retrieve the fugitive.

Behind the leaders, a screen played in the background. A new leader should be placed to run Unit 13, but Braggart's influence in that place ran deep as of right now. It was best to bring in someone new. Others thought it best to find someone worthy who had already learned of the sectors, the people, and its military. The screen took the majority of the front wall. There we saw the faces of Braggart's batch 001. Each one came on the screen with their information beside their photo.

After the photos passed through, videos of their behavior around the sectors leading up to Alpha's destruction highlighted their patience with humanity. It was clear as rain that they wanted New States to grow the fuck up. I couldn't disagree. I've been in deep with the military for a long time. I had initially been a lieutenant in the United States military. Now I served as one of the leaders of the W.D.A.

One of our secretaries ran into the meeting room; she looked wild-eyed about the open space. When she finally settled on me, she visibly relaxed and ran toward me. She had a file in her shaking hands.

"Ma'am," she rushed out. "You need to see this."

I opened the file, ignoring the heads arguing up-front. The face that greeted me immediately made my heart pound feverishly. His bright green eyes were more vibrant than mine, but his overall appearance matched my late husband's. The same skin color and hair. The same bone structure and smile. I saw this boy, and I saw my husband's image. I saw a grown man take the place of my late son.

Roman Braggart

I felt the blood rush to my head. My jaw clenched as anger extended to every part of my body. Instead of letting the righteous anger consume me, I read the contents of the file. They had here that he belonged to Braggart, that he betrayed the military by aiding batch 001, and had been arrested and disciplined. I skimmed through all of the notes until I got to the one I wanted to see.

"Roman Braggart fled Foxtrot with the assistance of operative Rayne Braggart and operative Zane Mueller."

Ah, yes. So it seems from the files we collected from New States that Rayne shares Braggart's blood. But there is no way this boy does. He couldn't share blood with that god-awful man because he shares blood with me. Roman Braggart is my son. His real surname matches mine.

Roman Alexander Gibbons

He was the son of a leader from the World Defense Assembly. I squeezed the file folder in my hand. The heads of the nations had ended their arguments over territory and now discussed the matter of a new commander for Unit 13. I studied the file in my hand as I walked forward.

"If I may interject."

The men and women of the group turned to me. All of them quieted out of respect. There was a lot I've done for this world. They recognized that if words came from my lips, it was best to listen.

"Madam Gibbons," the French president greeted. "To what do we owe this honor?" he said in his deep French.

I knew several languages. Deciphering his was a cinch. "I have a recommendation as to how to move forward, and I'd love to be the one to lead."

They all studied me. "I want to personally reach out to batch 001 after monitoring them to see what their end-game is. I also want to see exactly the type of man my son has turned out to be."

At that bit of remarkable news, the entire room erupted. All political figures turned to one another to see if any of them knew what I meant. I clicked the control a few times, and Roman's face lit up the screen.

"I received word that Roman Braggart looked like my deceased husband. I'm sure after a DNA test; you'd see what I already know. That man there is indeed my son. However, I will monitor them for now. I want to study their tactics and get a feel for their ultimate goals with the sectors. Roman Braggart is a dedicated military soldier with high honors who left Braggart's army, which tells me that he didn't like what he saw."

My voice dropped. "We need a commanding officer with morals and humanity. Not someone who is in it for political gain."

The Russian president walked forward. She had long blonde hair and a piercing stare. "I know I speak for everyone here when I say that you might be giving this team preferential treatment because your long-lost son is with them. None of our countries have super soldiers but for Unit 13. I find the power to be slightly more on your side," she uttered in her native tongue.

I smirked at her. "I don't mean to be rude, but Unit 13's power advantage has nothing to do with this situation. But I will say that if we pushed to control them, that group *will* push back. Do you all want a repeat of the last war?"

The group blustered but didn't argue. "Give me a few months. When the time comes, I'll make the first move. Until then, President Connor—" Unit 13's president stared at me "—I suggest you place a temporary rank on one of the remaining military personnel. Remove all rank from General Braggart and those still under his direction. Let the military and Ground Force know that he and all his men are fugitives of the law."

The President didn't argue. He spoke to his chief adviser, and the man moved quickly out the door. I watched as the faces of batch 001 transitioned on the screen above again. I won't make a move for now. No matter how hard the maternal strings that lay dormant pulled me toward confronting my son, the world needed to stay on track.

I'll watch you for now.

The photos of the young adults transitioned again.

I'll watch all of you for now.

Acknowledgments

I can't believe we are here. I'm so grateful to my readers. The Black Widow probably wouldn't have seen the light of day if it weren't for all the encouragement I received from my avid readers. When The Rayne Project was released, it happened during a horrible time in our country. Promotional events scheduled for the book release had been canceled, and it was devastating for a first-time writer. Although I couldn't get a market out for many readers to learn of the Project Hercules series, I was more than excited that a select few readers couldn't put the book down.

You made it happen.

My family shares the spotlight again because they have been super influential in my life. Their support has also been crazy incredible. The most significant part is how well they tolerate my moments. When mom is in 'The Zone,' they know not to bother me unless the world has ended and there are zombies at our doors. Luckily, nothing *that* crazy has happened. For the most part, my husband knows that when the door is closed, the kids aren't allowed to bypass him to get to me. My family's the best.

Working with a writer isn't easy, so I'd like to share this page with my longtime editor, Martha, at MK Editing Services LLC. She's always super busy but always makes time for my work. She's a talented editor and also one of my greatest fans. Thank you, Martha. You've been a blessing and one of the reasons the sequels happen. She always reminds me she's waiting for the next book, so I can't slack. Another notable person I will continue to work with is the wicked amazing Andrea. Known as CReya-tive, this book designer takes mere words and translates them into artwork. I love the work she's done for others and me. Thank you for being so wonderful! Lastly, the head at Websterland Books deserves the credit for keeping me on my toes and for providing me an outlet to share my work. I couldn't be more thankful.

Finally, for all my online friends and family, I want to scream a huge thank you. I may not have met all of you, but I consider some irreplaceable and others the icing on the cake. Your support is fantastic. I love when writers help writers. Support in the writing community is essential.

Thank you, Everyone!

Lyna

Don't forget to sign up on my website www.lynalopez.com. You can also find me on social media with the handle @lynalopezauthor.

Just when Batch 001 thought the end of Project Hercules was within reach, they learn that Braggart has taken refuge on international waters where New States can't tread. Seaa and the rest of her siblings know something sinister is cooking up within the remaining countries, and before history repeats itself, they'll do everything in their power to end it.

But, Seaa can't seem to get her abilities and act together. Between losing Zane and Cameron and not quite understanding where she stood with Hail, she's had more on her mind than usual. Her sisters Rayne and Silk have their own problems, so how will she be able to pull herself from the ever encompassing darkness alone?

The team needs to work together to end Project Hercules for good. Seaa knows she can't do it solo. Can she pull together in time for the final showdown?

Find out in **Project Hercules's**
final installment...

THE SEAA FINALE
CHAPTER PREVIEW

CHAPTER ONE

Sector Bravo
Safe Haven Headquarters
Six Months Later

THE SOUNDS OF explosions threw the tranquility and serenity of *Tutus Portus* into complete anarchy. The high-pitched wails of the residents running from danger propelled me into action. My legs felt filled with lead. I tried to get them to move, but they'd barely budge more than a couple of feet at a time. Another explosion, this one closer than before, rang in the interior. The blast threw me against the wall. Pain spread from my back to my chest and down to my toes.

I blinked back the confusion. Snow came around

the corner. His white-blue eyes took me in. The white strands of his hair now covered in soot. He seemed like an entirely different person. I reached for him as he ran. A blast from our left shot him forward. The burns on his body disfiguring his pale skin.

Pushing through the pain, I went to grab Snow when Rock appeared out of nowhere. He had Beatrice in one hand. He grabbed me with the other.

"You can't save him," he yelled as bullets ran through the interior.

We ran down the main hall, farther away from the entrance. He dragged me behind him. I didn't know what happened or how we came to run, but one thing was clear to me—we were in danger. Beatrice screamed. The sound dropped me to the floor. Rock lost his balance. Shots pinged against the wall.

The sound of Rock's agonized howl drew tears from my eyes. I watched as he wrapped his long Popeye arms around the woman in his arms, rocking back and forth with his body. Rock never cried. But I watched as his large, doe eyes dripped salty tears over her, the eye patch on her face. He engulfed her petite body tighter to his, screaming at me to move on without him.

I shook from head to toe. Rattled, I got up from the floor. My legs couldn't move straight. I fell into another wall as a man with a cowboy hat and scarred face came from the area I had escaped. He put a gun to Rock's forehead and shot.

The sound made me cover my ears. I slipped on my tears, dropping hard to the floor. Hail came from within the smoke. One strong arm covered his mouth and nose. His brownish-blond, cropped hair came into view first. He sought my eyes—his blue to my lavender.

"Get up, Seaa," he cried over the battle within the walls of Safe Haven.

I nodded but made no effort to move. He lifted me off the ground and into his arms. The crook of my arm came around his neck, right where I knew a tattoo of a raindrop fell into a puddle that spanned his shoulder blades. We pushed through the smoke. Thunder hollered from within it, calling for all of us to escape. I could barely see him through the smoke, but I knew his blond hair slightly swept the top of his shoulder blades. His golden honey eyes would be crackling with energy.

Beside him, Rome and Rayne ran for cover. Blood poured from cuts and bullet wounds. I tried to pull from Hail's arms, but he held me firmly. Rayne shouted at Thunder, but it was too late. A bullet pierced the back of his head, leaving a clean circle where it exited his forehead. He dropped where he stood. Rayne screamed, but I couldn't get my throat to work. Rome pulled her as far as the final tunnels, where we stopped to see General Brockton Braggart moving closer with three other residents of our bunker.

A heavily pregnant redhead cried from green eyes—a lean man with long blond hair and glasses—lastly, Guy, with his All-American good looks. Rome and Rayne seemed worse for the wear. Hail held me in his arms, refusing to let go. From the ceiling, Silk dropped on top of the soldier holding Gavin.

Gunfire broke out in the small tunnel. Rome dropped to the ground. Blood pooled around his dark, black hair. Rayne called for him, but he wouldn't rise. She screamed at her father. He merely smiled and shot her too. I hyper-ventilated. The soldiers with Braggart aimed at Silk and Gavin. She tried to encase her body in her web-like armor, but it was too late. Both of them dropped to the ground, unconscious. Suzanne got pulled away from the group kicking and screaming. Braggart didn't shoot her, which meant he wanted the baby she carried. The baby Cameron had left behind when he died.

General Braggart twisted his handlebar mustache at the tips. I hurled over Hail's firm arms. He only stared at the man murdering our family one by one. We both knew we were next. Hail stared at me in his arms. He pulled my long multi-colored strands from my face, exposing the part where scales met skin.

"You'll always be my best friend," he whispered.

The sound of gunshots echoed out as bullets dropped him to his knees. Hail gave me a crooked smile before blood dripped all over my body. I fell hard to the floor. Braggart and Trevor Dallas walked closer. Their evil smiles were pushing my heart to its limits. My skin crawled. The men laughed. I couldn't move one bit. They pointed, calling me names. I turned to see that I no longer had legs but a mermaid's tail in purple and blues.

The tail slapped the dusty ground. Trevor Dallas leaned into me, sneering the entire time. He yanked the choker that gave me sustenance from my neck. I felt blood dripping from where it cut. I coughed, immediately feeling the effects of the air. I didn't breathe like ordinary people. The choker injected oxygen from water directly into my vein. I gasped like a fish out of water because that's exactly what I was—a mermaid.

Their laughs morphed into one giant mouth with a handle-bar mustache. I flinched, squeezing my eyes shut from the nightmare. The sounds of laughter came again from hundreds of mouths. I again opened my eyes to see my ombré of teal into purple hair wavering weightlessly around me. People were surrounding me. I pushed myself to the surface but slammed into a lid. Glass encased me in a box. People pointed and laughed. I screamed, but only bubbles came out of my mouth. General Braggart wore a blood-red jacket like the ones worn by circus ringmasters. Gold buttons went down both sides of the lapels, and another set down his arms. His pants were black like his soul. The vest had intricate weaves of gold thread.

He laughed, exposing the gap between his two front teeth. I banged on the solid glass, but it didn't crack. Everyone merely pointed and laughed. The sound echoed in my ears until I couldn't hear anything else. My throat went raw from my screams. No one came to help me. After I could no longer scream, a weight fell to my shoulder. When I turned around, Trevor's disfigured face stepped closer to mine. I gasped, almost as if choking on the water.

Squeezing my eyes shut, I thrashed wildly, swinging my arms around to push him away. Screams erupted from my mouth as I yelled for him to leave me alone. My entire body was covered in a cold sweat. I kept swinging, but the hands continued reaching out to me. It became harder to breath. I fully expected to smell his rotting flesh, but instead the scent that engulfed me was comforting and sweet. I opened my eyes to the morning light.

I sucked in more air, jolting from my bed. Rayne brushed back the sweaty strands from my face, then wiped the tears from my cheeks. I took deep breaths as the nightmare washed over me. She ran her hand soothingly in circles on my back. I took a look around the interior, lit only from the few small rays of the morning sun. The white walls covered the interior that consisted of a full-size bed in the center of one wall, a chest dresser on another, and a desk on the last. Beside the desk was a slide-out with space inside for our clothes to hang. The only one upfront had the door to exit the room and a small thin table with my neon-colored fishes swimming around in a tank inside.

You're living my nightmare.

At the foot of my bed, Silk only watched. She always watched. Everyone formerly knew her as the black widow spider because of her spider characteristics created by Pops when he worked for Project Hercules. One foot skimmed the floor as the other curled on top of my sheets. She tipped her head to the side. Her long obsidian curls shifted. Pops made her absolutely perfect. Silk didn't have scales on parts of her skin or webbing between her fingers and toes like me. The only thing that gave color to her even tone was the tiny beauty mark right below her right eye.

I sniffed, inhaling a shaky breath. Rayne, too, was beautiful in her homey girl-next-door looks. Her recently cut brown hair with natural highlights kissed by the sun at some point in her life came up to her dainty chin. Her hazel eyes, lined in long dark lashes, shifting in their intensity depending on the lighting. Both of my sisters stared intently at me. They didn't push me, but I could tell that they both wanted to know what happened.

I can never say the words out loud.

The nightmare had been re-occurring for quite some time since we destroyed the old Alpha facility for Project Hercules. Six months later, in its place, stood an architectural masterpiece with only five floors on the surface and one floor beneath. We lived on the top floor of this building. I sighed. It gave me the creeps to live here, knowing full well what Braggart and his scientists did underneath me.

But the order came from Thunder, who had listened intently to the person in the temporary position of commander. He wasn't like Braggart and held no fear or hatred of our kind. He wanted to change New States for the better, but he knew he could only do so much. With the help and assistance of the World Defense Assembly, the former military fixed the mess Braggart and his men left behind. Today would be a different day. Today, we would meet with the woman in charge of W.D.A.

Rayne cleared her throat. I changed the subject, knowing full well that they wanted answers. "Don't you ever get this disturbing feeling living here?"

Silk and Rayne shook their heads. Rayne said, "I don't feel weird at all. We did what we had to here, Seaa. Those creatures weren't killed by us and weren't going to live a normal life either."

Silk adjusted herself on the foot of the bed. "Seaa,

is that what you dream about? Are you having nightmares about what we saw in the old facility?" she asked in a breathy voice—almost raspy. It suited her.

I nodded, even though I knew they could tell that I lied. Neither one of them called me on it. "I feel like the people that died here are angry or something."

Rayne took a deep breath. "Seaa, when this place was gutted, anything that had a body was buried and prayed over." She shrugged. "I mean, I'm not a big religious person, but I feel comforted somehow knowing that they were taken care of in that way."

I understood her reasoning. Being here didn't bother me that much because I did see the former military and facility personnel hired by the W.D.A. do anything in their power to give the group that died here some peace of mind in the afterlife. Brockton Braggart couldn't have cared less. He escaped with a few men on a stolen vessel that belonged to the W.D.A. The last we heard, he coasted on foreign waters away from our reach. The foreign dignitaries didn't feel threatened by him, feeling more threatened by the remaining super soldiers. The temporary commander of Unit 13 said they preferred we stayed on our side of the world.

The woman in charge of today's meeting would explain in further detail.

Sliding my legs to the cold gray tiles, I noticed my sister's shift their positions. Each one gave the other a look, and before I knew it, they had thrown themselves over me. My body slammed back on the mattress. The corners of my lips shot up. The two giggled as they wrapped their arms around me in an embrace meant to remind me of their unconditional love. I knew they only had my safety in mind. My nightmares must've really done a number on them, especially since they shared rooms on either side of me.

A knock on my door quieted our little pile-up. I took stock of what I wore: a long-sleeved t-shirt and some boxer shorts. Trotting from my bed to the dresser, I shuffled around for some long pants and rushed into them as I opened the door. The soldier on the other side didn't look at me distastefully. He didn't even bother to see if I was dressed. He merely looked into my face and then beyond me to see my two other sisters standing behind me.

He cleared his throat. "Good morning," he saluted. "I have been sent by Dr. Marcos to retrieve the three of you. He asked me to let you know that the young woman is in labor."

The three of us didn't wait for him to finish. Barefoot, I ran past him down the long corridor with doors on either side. Each entry went into a bedroom similar to mine. The interior had recessed lights down the entire hallway. It was also bright enough to see any flaws in the building, although none appeared. I heard my sister's right behind me. We turned the corner at the same time, neither one of us losing our footing. Instead of jumping into a Gidget that would take us to each floor, we rushed past them into the emergency stairwell with its winding stairs and platforms separating each floor.

Silk threw herself over the railing, hanging from the banister that led to the second floor. She pulled herself over the side. We heard her feet step on the landing. Rayne lovingly cussed her out but followed.

Both were at the door of the second level by the time I reached them. We all studied the hallways filled with doctors and nurses. They smiled at us but kept to themselves. Unlike in the other facilities, the doctors and nurses here were brought to take care of us and nothing else. No experiments were conducted. No orders superseded Dr. Ferdinand Marco's.

We shot into the maternity wing at the same time. Thunder beat us to it. He sat on a chair in the waiting area. As the leader of our group, he pretty much knew everything. His hair was a little longer than usual, and he had run his hands through it a few too many times. Rome always compared him to Thor, the god of thunder and lightning. It was a pretty adequate description. Thunder did resemble the god. Both had long blond hair and a massive body. But although Thunder didn't run around with a hammer, they both could command lightning.

"How is she," Rayne asked.

He smiled at us. "The nurse came out here a minute ago to tell me that she is doing fine, and the baby is indeed coming."

Suzanne Benedict was the only person left of the Benedict line. Her mother had died during a shoot-out between the former general, us, and his goons. She used to fund Project Hercules. Suzanne and her mother never had a relationship, which led Sue to pursue her own life. Although she resembled more of a mobster with a network of people telling her the comings and goings of New States, she was anything but that. Sue didn't have the ability to see like we did. She treated those around her with kindness and respect. In return, they'd figure things out for her when she couldn't for herself.

Somehow, she had met and fallen in love with our brother Cameron, otherwise known as "the chameleon." He stayed with her to get away from Silk for reasons only them two knew. We never asked her, and she seemed to be in harmony with him. I stared at my sister with her dark curls bouncing around her head as she flittered from glass to glass, gawking at the babies behind it.

The new Alpha facility had its own medical wing for employees and soldiers that lived and worked here. There were only three new babies, one set being twins from one soldier. All of them were normal babies. None of the former operatives that survived could reproduce. Batch 002 had been created without the ability to foster children. Pops' journals claimed we couldn't either, but there we were, waiting for a baby who came from a normal human woman and a genetically-engineered one to come into the world.

Rayne paced the small waiting room, wearing a line on the clean tiles. A nurse ran to the door. We watched as she scanned her badge. The door clicked, and she pushed through it. I wanted to burst right on in there behind her. From my sister's faces, they wanted to as well. Thunder stared at us three with equal intensity. Either he was running a scenario in his head on how he'd subdue us at the same time or figuring out how he'd survive if he intervened.

Silk gently tapped on the glass, goo'ing over a baby who had stuck his thumb into his mouth. She may have been the tougher one of us three, but she melted when it came to children. A nurse walked into the baby room with a bottle. She wore a medical suit over her clothes. Silk and I watched as she lightly walked over to one of the twins. The nurse lifted the baby girl into her arms, cradling her into a position where she could be fed.

The nipple of the bottle came toward her pert little mouth. Her mouth moved, seeking it out. When she finally felt the nipple in her mouth, she latched over it, intent on drinking her fill. The woman found a rocking chair, sitting back and resting as she fed the baby. The chair rocked back and forth. Noticing our stares, the woman looked up at us. She smiled. We were already smiling back.

The door of the waiting room opened again. Dr. Ferdinand walked out. He was a small older man with a bald head and thick glasses. If it weren't for him and the help the doctor showed us in Safe Haven, most of us wouldn't be alive now—super-soldier notwithstanding. He didn't wear a smock like the woman. He had on his usual lab coat with a stethoscope hanging around his neck.

"Hello, girls."

Thunder got up from the chair. Silk pushed between him and Rayne. Thunder had way more muscle than we did. He barely budged, but I felt us all toppling toward the other end of our line ending with me. I kept my ground, keeping us upright.

"How is she?" Rayne asked.

Silk asked at the same time. "Did the baby come?"

I bit my lip. If I asked a question, too, Dr. Ferdinand would hush us all and probably walk back into the wing just to spite us. We eagerly waited for him to speak.

At long last, after what seemed like an eternity, Dr. Ferdinand smiled and said, "Mother and baby are doing great. It's a girl."

We cheered excitedly at the excellent news. Even my stone-faced brother smiled warmly, knowing that our line would continue as an homage to Pops.

"Can we see Sue?" I asked.

Dr. Ferdinand shook his head. "Sue is exhausted and did lose a lot of blood. Let her rest, but the baby is right there." He pointed to the side where we watched another nurse walk in with a pink bundle in her arms. The woman feeding the baby greeted the other. We watched as the little girl got closer to the window. The woman nurse lifted her so we could see her pretty little face and pink button nose.

I could feel the tears roll down my face. Rayne was already a blubbering mess. Silk caressed the glass as if touching the baby's face. The woman placed the baby in an open bassinette. She grabbed a card and marker from her pocket, scribbling unto the little card. Like the other bassinets, the babies had their names displayed for all to see. We felt the emotions bubble through us in kaleidoscope glittering bursts. Sue picked a perfect name. The card read:

Welcome to the world, Camilla Sebastian Benedict.

PROJECT HERCULES TRILOGY

THE RAYNE PROJECT

THE BLACK WIDOW

THE SERR FINALE

L Y N A   L O P E Z

has an obsession with reading stories that separate her from the real world, especially those geared toward strong women. After a hurricane ripped through her neighborhood, it left behind so much devastation that it got her to imagine a world in chaos, which is how The Rayne Project was born. Now, Lyna spends as much time as she can writing books that can transport her (and her) readers to whole new worlds. She lives on a mini-farm in Florida with her four crazy kids, rascal-of-a-husband, four wacky dogs, one prissy cat, and all the chickens and ducks—cows coming soon.

Follow on Social Media

@lynalopezsauthor

&

www.lynalopez.com

www.ingramcontent.com/pod-product-compliance
Lightning Source LLC
Chambersburg PA
CBHW011126100726
47898CB00009B/2874